A FINAL REMINDER

Buzz McCord

Oztruck Productions

Hi Robin and Carl,
I think there may be a
little something for each of
you in here. Hope you enjoy!
Thanks for your supportive
input!

Buzz McCord

16 August 2021

Dr. Dirk Samuelson, uber-capitalist, philanthropist, second wealthiest human, describes his Golden Rule in *The Final Reminder*. "Do unto others what they cannot do for themselves." This book is dedicated to friends who live Dr. Samuelson's ethic. Emblematic, Patricia McCully, founder of Circulo de Amigas, Jinotega, Nicaragua and Jean Forbath, founder, Save Our Youth (SOY), Costa Mesa, California. And Carol Burke, Emily Bush, Flossie and Paul Horgan, Kirby McCord, Nora Pedersen, Jenny Pridham, John Scott, Connie Sutton, Pam Tonge, Dawn Usher. In their honor, the profits from *A Final Reminder* will go to Save Our Youth, Costa Mesa, California. http://save-our-youth.org/about-us/

All paths in spacetime are curved.
Imagination is our ticket to ride.

BUZZ MCCORD

PREFACE

Ethical clouds threaten Arctan International and Dr. Dirk Samuelson's newest achievement, an invention that can stop pandemics by tracking every person, every move, every breath. Under pressure from a new, more deadly virus, a team of Arctan elites is at work to create the ultimate Augmented Human. Implanted in young scientist, Matt County, the Intelligence quickly grows a personality, Soh. The team discovers an Arctan insider has started a criminal enterprise centered in Vietnam. Matt and his boss Souchi are sent to investigate. In richly sensuous Ho Chi Minh City, they fall in love. But the romance suddenly becomes an uneasy triangle. With a ragtag team of locals, Matt, Soh and Souchi discover that the crime is more sinister than they imagined: a diabolical foe and a malignant foreign power look to take over Arctan itself. They race against time and the spreading virus. Blackmail, sex-slavery, abduction, murder. Will the power of Arctan be turned to evil? How far will either side go to win? Will the pandemic make it pointless? A Final Reminder describes a fantastic future coming soon to a reality near you.

THE NEAR FUTURE

"We can beat this." Glacial eyes blue-radiant in the 3D holo-screen.

"The last virus was bad enough. It should have been a wake-up call. Turns out, you and me, we slept through it. Instead, we volunteered pools of human biology.

"Now. It's mutated. Out of thousands of new strains, two were sufficiently vicious to earn names. It first took the old, then the weak. Now it's taking anyone. Anyone." He looked away. Clumsy, had he been an actor.

"Everything has changed. There is no going back. No hiding. Pharma moves too slowly.

"There is one salvation. One. Exoculation.

"I'm Dr. Dirk Samuelson. I invented Exoculation. I want to share it with you."

A FINAL REMINDER

Buzz McCord

PART ONE:

MONEY.

BIG MONEY

CHAPTER 1
ARTIFICIAL INTELLIGENCE, PAT'S GYM

He never saw it coming. Her punch landed undeflected, left jaw. His lights went dim. With nobody home, she aimed low, unleashing a gut rattling uppercut to his belly. He folded up, sat down, flattened into a Da Vinci snow angel, sucking wind. Upright and fierce, she wondered. Was it her Germanic gene or his gender-condescension that brought on that little extra coup de grâce?

Either way, un-lady-like.

"Yo, guys, guys! Alicia just decked Matt, git over here quick!" Devon, story-teller extraordinaire, was less concerned for his best friend than on missing this epic bar-story. A boisterous crowd gathered in the center ring at Pat's Gym.

Epic-decked-Matt wasn't unhappy. He was simply looking up at a star-burst pattern of voyeurs looking down, a dreamy Sistine Chapel ceiling of celestials. Getting chin-tagged had not been unpleasant, more like just being suddenly sleepy. He felt so cozy having friends watch over his nap.

Pat's Gym didn't have a nurse. Emergency care con-

sisted of whatever the bossiest person had last seen on
ER. One dude grabbed Matt's belt and started jerking it
up and down. Matt hadn't taken a shot to the testicles,
for which belt-jerking was an old, frustrated-wife's tale.
Deciding that it would be better to stir than be cured
like this, Matt struggled to sit up under a chorus of lame
encouragements. The sportsman's "Shit, he'll be fine,"
and "Walk it off," failed to rouse his team spirit.

Alicia pushed through the crowd, bent close over his
face and gave her pre-mortem, "Damn Matt, why'dja
have to patronize me?" He had to laugh as she struggled
to stand him up, but her barely five feet and his over six
made Alicia more trip-hazard than support.

Devon was eager to flesh out the bar-epic. "'Nuff for tonight. Let's hit Zig's for a cool one."

"OK, sure, but we gotta agree, no more head shots." Alicia's punch had wiped clean some details from Matt's
afternoon. Being world elites in techno-centric Silicon
Valley, head shots were evermore verboten. Given that
Alica was a smallish fem with a biggish attitude, the
new boxing rules worked for her.

Heading to Zig's Bar for a beer, there was something
Pat's three gym rats didn't yet know. Dr. Dirk Samuelson was about to help them finish their dream, connecting a computer directly to the human brain. Theirs
would be the first.

CHAPTER 2
MUCH EARLIER. EDWARDS AIR BASE. THE STRIKE

His thoughts tumbled down from the desert stars one by one to the wasteland below.

"Sir? Seven minutes." His engineer whispered lightly.

"Of course. Thank you, Samantha," he glanced at her over his shoulder. "Is everything set?"

"Yes sir! This will be a beautiful Strike tonight!"

"Then let's do it."

She spun away to break the seven-minute set-hold. The countdown was on.

Desert life flourishes at night. It's safer at 15 Celsius than 45. So, Dr. Dirk Samuelson's Arctan International team got busiest at midnight. Besides, the night's black dome would make for stunning visuals at Strike time.

His privately held corporation had sixteen billion dollars invested just above and deeply below ground and two and a half billion more invested in this last quarter's activity. Tonight's Strike would dwarf Hiroshima as the specie's most impactful single moment. This place, ten klicks north and east of Edwards AFB, would become a historic temple.

Dr. Samuelson started down the unlit path toward the launch silo. It was a simple path, crushed white quartz glittered by starlight. He had told his team, no lighting. Decades into the Twenty-first Century, it was primitive to waste light. Anyway, he had five-and-a-half minutes.

Anne was already there, at the end of the path, waiting. She had been with him from the start of the odyssey. She was facing away, toward the launch silo, as he approached. He spooned her affectionally, then more intimately.

"Ummmm." It was her purr, but they shared the privacy. "You brought me back, babe. I was fluttering toward Ulondra." Their secret, a sensual place of ecstasies and deep calm.

"I know. They betrayed you." She elbowed him in the gut. "Mister Romance."

"You hate it." He smiled, the mischievous schoolboy.

"And you know too much. I love it. I love you Doctor Samuelson."

The embrace was short. The countdown was grinding forward with the momentum of a gigantic warship. In just minutes the earth would open and a rage would spiral skyward.

They were as close to the launch aperture as Arctan's investors would permit. If there were to be a big failure - there wasn't going to be - he and Anne told the press that they wanted to go out with it. Oddly, their presence here wasn't required but the drama was. It meant a lot to the Team.

A simple wooden pedestal had been set up for them at the end of the path in the desert. Two buttons were wired back to a console somewhere. For the launch to go, both buttons were to be held down simultaneously. A loudspeaker was counting down.

"Three."

"Two."

They held hands and pushed the buttons.

"One."

"Zero."

A shaft of violet black-light shot into the sky. The beam sprang straight upward out of the center of the silo's aperture. At first just an inch around but glowing sharply, it grew in size and brightness. A tang of ozone drifted in the air. And a crackling sound. The beam connected ground and sky with a brilliant slash.

Within seconds a throb began at the aperture. A meter round disk of fire appeared. It moved up a bit with each pulse, six times, then hovered, testing itself two meters above the glowing hole. It crackled, snapping synchronously with whipping tendrils of light. It looked electric. It acted electric. A disk of air had been ignited by an invisible light, the Thermal Beam.

The disk hovered, stabilizing, testing, then in consonance with a visceral sound rising in pitch and volume, flew up away from the aperture, following the path pioneered by the ultraviolet beam. As it rose it left behind a sharply glowing tube of crackling atmosphere, straight into space. Its razor light was visible for twenty miles.

Arctan International had just bored a vacuum hole into the Void. The Thermal Beam had burned through and was holding off eight point three tons of California desert atmosphere. It was intended to be there a while.

A loudspeaker intoned, dull, as if announcing bus arrivals. "Satellite reporting Thermal Beam contact. Oscillations rms 28%, 0.2 Hertz. Dropping. 8%. 5%. Oscillations stable under 0.5%, 0.2 Hertz. Thermal beam locked." Anne and Dirk could hear a muffled cheer from inside the facility. The Team couldn't help themselves.

Loudspeaker. "Ready for launch, at your signal." A dramatic way to give Dr. Samuelson some initiative in the show. He obliged, into the mike. "Launch."

The interior of the glimmering, crackling tube lit up, a spectrum of blazing colors, laser beams twinkling off remnant molecules of vaporized air. Each beam could carry thousands of billions of digital bits per second. Too many colors to count, half a billion billion bits of data flowed inside the motherly vacuum tube. Overhead, a fleet of Arctan satellites was poised to receive and redistribute the river of data.

Anne and Dirk gasped at their creation. The electrical crackling and base-audio throbbing was loud, almost symphonic. The conduit could carry all the data that humans would need in this their, perhaps, final era of existence. They had gasped fearing they couldn't guarantee it's use would be pure.

Within seconds, the effect of the launch was felt as a sudden surge wherever in the world data was being used big. Samuelson had prepared cadres at selected sites for the surge and they exploited the preparation.

It had been artfully sculpted to avoid any implication of insider manipulation. But a thousand people each made a million plus at the moment of the surge. Dr. Dirk Samuelson believed in instant rewards for inspired hard work.

It's one thing to laser-weld steel and another to bore a hole into space through 25 miles of atmosphere and almost ten tons of air. Subject of 27 international patents, the Arctan laser-powered Tera-Tower vacuum tunnel had to sense and correct for every wrinkle along the path of the one hundred twenty-five-thousand-watt energy beam. The costs had been staggering. But Dr. Dirk Samuelson had, again, managed the funding and now looked forward to reaping the profits. Data had made him San Francisco's richest person, third in the world. By tomorrow morning, his fortune will have multiplied once and a half, shuffling the order.

The Strike became top news, coming up a month later in congressional hearings on the threat of Big Data. "Dr. Samuelson, ah hope you do unnerstand that mah voters back home are worried about all that info-mation you are collectin'. And they sure are worried that your laser beam inta space seems mighty powerful. Why, a hundred thousand watts sure woulda dimmed the lights on Friday nights in mah 'lil ole hometown football stadium." The Senate committee hearing audience tittered. "But cain't that be dangerous. Ah mean, like what if an airaplane flew through that? Wouldn't it just go poof?"

Samuelson shuddered, but beneath the level the jackal-cameras could detect. He answered disingenuously. "The plane would notice nothing, Senator." He didn't add that the brief stutter effect on the world's data flow would be profound. It's why he had used his influence to bury this prize within the confines of the country's most secure military compound. His sacred river of zeroes and ones was safe.

CHAPTER 3
EVEN EARLIER.
ANTIONETTE
CÉSAIRE

It hurt, a lot. Henri didn't notice, or care, or maybe worse, enjoyed it. When he was finished, he gave her a harder than playful slap, as if to get her attention. "*Vous dites à quelqu'un* You tell someone, you be daid."

Fourteen seemed too young to die, so Antoinette Césaire nodded. Besides, there was work to do, cleaning up. Henri turned away, fixed up his trousers, looked back, faked a menacing charge, and disappeared into the night. One rapist guy in a world full of rapist guys. Just another violation. Could have been anyone, anywhere but it was her, here, Cite Soliel, Haiti.

One thought lingered. She would make him pay.

The opportunity came, or more accurately, she created his opportunity a week later. Henri spotted Antoinette, as she had arranged, momentarily alone on the side of the broken road near one of the now sleeping convenience stores stocked with one bare lightbulb, some bags of greased salted potato junk and a variety of unrelated soft drinks and beer.

Tending to the shadows, he stalked her. She feigned not

knowing he was coming across the street and jumped dramatically as he grabbed her shoulder and push-pulled her into the grimy space between two grimier shack walls. Urine smell dominated the fetid air. "A thousand arrogant dicks," she thought absently, putting up a faux struggle, careful not to anger Henri. He leered, half lit by the streetlight, and pulled it out, growing with primitive purpose. "Little girl gonna learn to like Big Jacques, huh? That first time last time wuz a good time, huh, wasn'it?" Leaning toward her he thought he'd snatch an appetizer.

Her left hand flipped the lid off a small jar and with a short step backward she flicked the battery acid into his eyes. Coolly, she recalled how easy it had been to get it from the oily motor shop in the marketplace. Screeching, his hands flew up to his face. Frantic rubbing made the corneal burns worse. She dropped the bottle. Sidestepping, Antionette pulled out a pair of eight-inch scissors, borrow-stolen from one of her seamstress street sisters. Agile, young, knowledgeable, she dodged Henri's blind thrashing. She had practiced secretly with rope behind her wretched hutch. This would be easier than stealing mangoes. She got hold of Big Jacques and took off a fistful, leaving him a demi-Jacques.

Learning to deal with blindness, screaming-Henri grabbed for his victims but came up short. Antionette waltzed in behind him and thrust the scissor points viciously, hard up into his buttocks, then, ducking, twisted the blades out and made off down the road. At the bridge, she washed her hands and tossed some warm bait into the river. She wouldn't stop walking until four hours of darkness and two *arrondissements* of Port-au-Prince were behind her. No big deal. She left behind only misery in Cite Soliel.

Having raised herself on the streets, as sharp as anyone in the quarter, she had learned to stick with what you're good at. That night she made it a goal to teach bad guys good lessons. She earned a public nickname, Virgin Vigilante. Antionette smartly ended the fish-feeding habit at three and moved, within the anonymity of poverty, eight slums south.

After she was gone, ghetto sisters adopted the meme of pointing scissor fingers at pushy men. Stats showed a 37% decline in street attacks. The nuns in various Catholic girl's schools were puzzled by the sudden popularity of Blind Man's Bluff on the playground. The reggae tune "Cut You Papa Short" hit the pop charts within the year. Antionette shunned the curtain calls.

At fifteen, scrawny, dirty, hard as nails, instincts of a feral cat, she spotted a long line leading up to the one building in the arrondissement with solid walls and an intact roof. A sign marked it as a French NGO, *Cercle des Amies*, CdA. Girls and women only. She scouted the front of the line and picked out a lone girl, younger than she, and grabbed her in a slightly painful neck hug. Between exclamations of "Sister" and "Finally!" she whispered in the girl's ear that she best play along. Antionette's aggressive posturing quieted objections from the line behind them. She was nineteenth among the 25 who got admitted inside that week.

CdA's French matron, Cloe de Rochechouart, a fierce feminist, had invested her all in Haiti, specifically in the girls and women of Arrondisement Bois Caradeux.

She spotted Antionette's quickness on first introduction. Antionette had made sure of it. With blazing native intelligence and a fire in the belly, she exploited every available resource in the club. Occasionally, she exploited more than what was allowed but her intensity and fast thinking got her out of jams and deeper into the heart of Mdme. de Rochechouart.

Antionette hungered to learn from the foreign patrons who passed through CdA. Women from Paris and Lyon and Marseilles polished her French. Antionette suspected secretly that they, too, had suffered a Henri. She picked up functional English and everything else taught at the local schools and non-profits. In time, Mdme. de Rochechouart placed her into the rigorous Lycée Alexandre Dumas. Unlike her peers, she avoided men and pregnancy.

Under the sponsorship of Mdme. de Rochechouart, she finished a degree in law from the Université d'État d'Haïti. Antionette quickly earned Port-au-Prince fame for prosecuting domestic abuse cases pro bono. She made enemies easily, eventually powerful ones.

Aware of talk about an ominous *situation négative* that involved Antionette, a prosperous businessman, graduate of INSEAD-France,[1] referred her to Dr. Dirk Samuelson, who sent an emissary to pull her out. Antionette worked herself up to Third Personal Assistant within the year. No one would ever know about Big Jacques. Or his brothers.

CHAPTER 4
ESSENTIALS.
ZIG'S BAR

San Francisco has its highs and its lows. Zig's Bar has both. It's hidden on the southern edge of the city's skanky Mission district, as the 'hood decays into "charming." It's named after Zbigniew Brzezinski, a Polish-American hero from the Johnson-Carter era. Zbig, advisor to two US presidents, talked tough and thought fast; Poles hate Russians, love Zbig. Zig's owner, Stefan Krzyzanowski tends bar, cooks and cleans. He bounces ad lib every Saturday night.

Alicia, Devon and Matt made Zig's their second home based on beer, privacy, and tasty-cheap food. They had pendled the five blocks between Zig's Bar and Pat's Gym for three years and a piece. They liked its simplicity. One fixed menu prepped in the morning. No choosing. Just signal and when he could get to it Stefan would put his unctuous dishes hot on the bar. Obey the rules: bus your own plates or don't come back. And don't ever call out "waiter." Or Stefan's name, if you knew it. Ever.

The three were headed to a back table. Devon zinged Stefan. "Yo! Old man, they still let you work here." Behind the bar, Stefan flipped him a silent growl and loud bird.

"Hey! That dinner you made last week was super. This

time didn't almost kill me. Getting fresher roadkill, what?"

Stefan liked Devon so he threw an ice cube spewing gin in his direction. The three other regulars didn't look up.

Stefan held fast to the Boy Scouts Ten Essentials.[2] Top of the list, a sawed-off, 32-ounce, fat-handled Jimmie Foxx Louisville Slugger,[3] kept just under the counter to his right of the taps. Sawed-off because, as an ex-professional boxer, Stefan was comfortable in close quarters. And as proprietor he wanted to keep collateral glass and liquor losses to a minimum when he had to use Jimmie.

The Second of Stefan's Ten Essentials: an obscure rear exit into an alleyway fenced off from street access. He didn't use it much. He owned the building and lived upstairs. Stefan kept his outings to a minimum. He expected his suppliers to know about the locked gate and concertinaed fence and to notify him if the delivery man changed on any given day. Stefan didn't tolerate surprises and valued privacy. He had stirred up some trouble among Russians on Long Island a few years back. It would be nice to stay anonymous for a while before once again augmenting his American dream.

The middle part of the list of Ten were carefully designed interior features. A long, narrow room with two tables to the right and left of the bar. Drink and food slapped on the bar, self-service. Stefan never turned his back to the front door. He hadn't consulted Feng Shui to lay out Zig's. But then, Mr. Shui didn't have Stefan's problems.

Stefan kept Essentials Nine and Ten in case the first eight didn't secure his privacy. Under the bar, a compact SIG Sauer 9 mm P365 with a 12-round clip, top loaded blank, 11 live cartridges under. And a second, prints-clean full clip with 115 grain hollow points hidden within what looked like an unsafe electrical wiring box next to the back door. Made it easy to grab on the way out in the unlikely event that Round One was a draw. He kept SIG hidden but easily reachable on a sous-shelf to his left of the taps. He checked the clip and action every night after closing and every morning before opening. That habit, and the blank-topped 11-round load, were acquired in a prior life.

One last Essential didn't count for Stefan. It had been forced on him. Like all interior public spaces, he had the government-mandated Instant Pathogen Detectors in his entryway. Every patron was required to insert their official ID card then blow two times into the obscene looking port. If you weren't carrying your own mouthpiece, there were sterile disposables for sale in the box. The IPD would detect pathogens from your breath-aerosols in thirty seconds.[4] Fail, it keeps the card and notifies local health authorities. Truth? Stefan had hacked the IPD. No one in his bar was ever denied entry. Either way, Stefan believed in Ten Essentials.

Stefan's low profile in Zig's had one possible hang-up. He had learned to cook from his mom. When she went off on sex-and-booze-benders during his childhood in Warsaw, he would use her recipes to feed his two, then three, then four Catholic siblings. So now, unknown to the city, he served San Francisco's best *gulasz*, meat and vegetable stew seasoned with paprika. He made his own *kapusta kiszona* sauerkraut. Most delicious at Zig's were the simple *kartofle gotowane* dilled potatoes slow cooked in week-old *kielbasa* sausage water with fermented butter.

Stefan's pub hideaway had some risks. He worried that "socialist media," posed the danger of discovery and that the day would come when some urban yuppie dropped in and praised the virtues of his kitchen and its wiry chef to the wired world. So, Stefan screened patrons carefully. Anyone trying to take pictures of his food or place was sent packing. Anyone fussy was addressed rudely in Polish to encourage their departure.

Stefan didn't have the luxury to like people, but he looked forward to Matt, Devon and Alicia visiting. They were secretive and he liked people with secrets. Besides, these three used big words and talked ideas, not gossip. It resurrected memories about Poland's glory days and heroic Lech Wałęsa.[5]

Stefan watched the three digiteers huddled over a sticky table shrouded in shadows. Alicia had resparked a discussion. "Augmentation, guys. Screw robotics. It's about humans. Every Josephine's got unused superpowers, just augment us."

Devon, fresh off the joust with Stefan, slanted feisty. "Sure, Leash. Average human. Just jack-in a computer. Neuromancer-it.[6] All good. But what if you need something a little more...practical?"

"*Sheisse* crap Devon. You all lathered up 'bout sex robots again? If you'd clean up that hovel of yours, maybe you could find some warm, human companionship, *eine freundin*. Enough bleach, your place could be really *gemütlich.*"[7] Alicia felt everyone should know the ninety-seven German words she found irreplaceable.

Pointedly talking toward Matt, "Think about the human eye." Devon mouthed "that again" behind her back. Without looking, "Yes, THAT again, Devon." Back to Matt. "Sure, robot's eyes have all kinds of power[8] but they're still no match for our retina. And even now the hardware is plenty expensive."

"I mean, I get it." Matt held eye contact with Alicia so the 12-year-old Devon behind her couldn't make him laugh, "and the software driving robot eyes is really nasty. But I gotta think the biggest plus is that we've all been bombarded with doomsday anxieties about robots. Augmented intelligence isn't just smarter, it's less threatening."

Devon. "No way. People are just fear-machines waiting to be lit up. Think: politicians. Adding computer power to the brain will freak the masses. My opinion."

"Yea but dream a minute." Alicia's nerve-energized, luminescent dyed hair roots glowed faintly.[9] "No clumsy web searches, keyboards. No peck peck peck. Just think it and your computer loads you up. Somebody tells a fact-lie, pfoosh. Gotcha." And so it went, Zig's night.

Alicia was way out there, a PhD in neurophysiology, specialty: opto-genetics. She had been born in East Berlin, her procreation inspired by the resistance crooning of East German singer Bettina Wegner[10] who, like Alicia's parents, had stayed one step ahead of the Stasi[11], until one night they didn't. So, orphan Alicia was abruptly weaned by friends off mother's milk onto black bread, brats, and beer. A few decades on, she became a world authority on electric signals in the human eye with a cult-following among young academics for her bilingual techno-blog and her idiosyncratic, changing appearances topped by psychedelic hair color.

Matt was born to privilege. His parents commuted as professors to Vanderbilt University in Nashville Tennessee where they were super-academics in medicine and engineering. Matt was smarter than both of his parents but, unlike them, easy to be with. He was finishing a doctorate in computer science, already famous for his Big Data analytics. Might say he knew how to snoop data.

Devon didn't need a PhD. He was gifted with a one-in-seventeen-point-five-million mind (he knew the statistics). He had been born with an over-active happy gene, $1p33$ for the protein FAAH, which he vitally needed since just about any family calamity that could befall a child had visited him. He had made a name for himself winning at international e-sports. He translated that to inventing organic electro-optic visualization devices,[12] which had nothing to do with clean agriculture.

Eventually food and beer numbed the Augmented Intelligence bluster. The three devolved to a reenactment of Alicia's knockout punch to Matt's chin. Stefan couldn't stand to watch their amateur hour and glided in from behind the bar.

"Never mind chin. Liver, left hook, liver, right ribs low." He pulled Devon to his feet, momentarily stunned since he had only ever heard Stefan speak in Polish expletives or the imperative, second person present.

No one had ever heard Stefan attempt a multi-word English phrase, never mind two. Stefan pantomimed Devon into a boxer's stance; the resulting lanky, half-hearted nerd looked like he was about to fail the audition for Scarecrow in Wizard of Oz.

Stefan threw a fast jab, short of Devon's unwilling face by a centimeter, feinted a right cross, reflexively bringing up Devon's hands, and then swung a sharp left, pulling up just short below the right ribcage, firm but gentle. Devon sagged to his seat, eyes like salsa saucers.

Matt and Alicia were delighted. Devon, unhurt but schooled, not so much. Punching surgery! Where did that come from? Is it legal? Stefan, upset for revealing so much of himself, retreated to the bar, having spent all his words for the week.

Zig-veterans, they asked no questions.

CHAPTER 5
SAMUELSON
HITS PAT'S GYM

Some gyms are populated by narcissist gym rats. Buns and breasts covered by two wrinkle-resistant epidermae, the outer one sexy, transparency-adjustable Spun-dex.[13]

Other gyms fill with striver gym rats. Holding back time. Fighting decades of indulgence, too misshapen to wear Spun-dex. Bubbly cheerleader-trainers tease them to a numbing beat with quick flashes of see-through-and-peek.

And then there are gyms with rats thriving on self-inflicted pain. Musty, dimly lit places that smell like cast iron and old sweat. With a ring for combat. Such was Pat's Gym. Pat's rats wear tatters and scraps of whatever was least smelly on the bedroom floor. Matt, Alicia and Devon like Pat's.

All gyms fall in the government Infection Potential category IP-2, likely to spread contagion. One step safer than the ICU, one step worse than dive bars. Pat's had the mandatory sanitizing vestibule and three Instant Pathogen Detectors. Pat's clientele knew the IPDs worked. Regardless of how thick-skulled anyone in Pat's might be, they followed contagion protocol. Oxygenated nostril filter and mouth dam. Implanted thread-biosensor[14] and paid subscription to tracing software. To not follow infection rules in Pat's was to invite disdain, maybe abuse.

"Uhhhh, seven. Hunnn, eight." Matt pumped for alone-time. Three hundred and twenty-five pounds of cast iron is a latch key to privacy. Nobody interrupts a dead-lift set. "Huuuunnn. Fiiiiff. TEEN." He drops the bar, the end of another session aerating brain cells.

Authorized to invade sacred space, Matt's girl-bud, Leash, *née* Alicia, signals him to pop off the phones. "Matt. You gotta see this. Like, it's written for you." Yanked back to reality. If someone should have that privilege, then Alicia was Matt's someone, cropped fluorescent color-of-the-week hair (about which she was very sensitive,) banger T shirt and private piercings.

Alicia, extending her cell, "Seriously, Matt, this is written 'zactly at you."

"Wup, let's have a look, dude." Devon snatched Alicia's cell. "Check it OOOUT!" Reading loudly to the air: "Arctan International, world leader in Enterprise Data is now opening a Special Projects position. For Computer Science professionals with super-outstanding tech ability. Candidates must have demonstrated Imagination. Project reports directly to CEO Dirk Samuelson." Devon whistling, "Samuelson. Woah, Matt, Da Dada Man hisself."

"Read the end, you *putz*. That's all about Matt." Alicia indulged Devon; nobody was as likely to get you in and then back out of big trouble and have so damn much fun at it. Devon was the human embodiment of good drugs.

Devon laughs bigly and drags in the nearby gym rats. "Hey guys, Leash thinks this is 'all about Matt.' Listen up, this is some weird stuff." Devon's greatest strength, just ask him, was ensuring that no peer ever felt too special about themselves.

"Specialist will be an integral part of Arctan's corporate image-building campaign." Raising his voice, "Therefore, personal presence, in particular, *YOUTH-FUL PHOTOGENICITY* will be an important part of any candidate's evaluation."

The buddy group, but for Alicia, broke into an uncoordinated campaign of derision. Their howling traced back to primeval tribal rituals meant to subdue undeserving challengers.

"Damn, Matt, Leash's got a hardon for you or what?"

"Hey, look o-vah. Competition! Devon's got one, too. Swinger!"

The sharks fed on their frenzy. The jabs were humorous and hurtful, personal insight added pain. As the torrent peaked, it was hard to tell which part of each author's brain was aroused. Or if any brain was involved at all.

"Don't look now but there goes Matt," as the renowned blush began fulminating on Matt's checks.

To an outsider, this frenzy could have seemed punitive, even cruel. But Matt wasn't a needy feeder fish. He pumped weights for solitude, but the physical consequences were real. Lifting made his martial arts fearsome, though with reticence. In spite of his Iberian blood, Douglas Matthew County III was painfully shy and loathed conflict.

When the sassy verbal gang bang lost its momentum, Alicia finished it off. "Come on, you dweebs. Computer science, Big Data, Imagination but also Photogenicity, that's our boy, no?"

Matt weighed in, "Heck no. But Devon's right. Isn't it, like, just a bit weird to job-troll for age and appearance? I mean, in this century?"

Devon. "Maybe, but what's gonna happen? You go to an interview and get, what, laid against your will?" Matt blushed.

"Right, so you go. Blow 'em away." Alicia's unfortunate word choice elicited guffaws. The intellectual level plummeted once again.

"Maybe you even get to eyeball Samuelson himself. What could go wrong, dude!"

The discussion went downhill from there, but the decision was nearly unanimous. The gym rats' destiny, and maybe even Matt's, rest in answering the Arctan International invite.

CHAPTER 6
INSIDE ARCTAN
INTERNATIONAL

Kings, Gallic and Baltic, Han and Hanseatic, build their castles to impress: "I am rich, and this is mine." Dirk Samuelson became King of Big Data by amassing the code and hardware that allows business large and small to access, refine, confirm, and process humanity's numbers. His genius started with means to let everybody massage medical megadata seamlessly, unseemly fast, securely. His most recent genius, the San Francisco Datafile Exchange, controlled commodification of Big Data and therefore Big Money.

Samuelson protected his data business with technical moats.[15] Twelve 64 Qubit computers connected via a network of laser data-to-space-and-back transmission Tera-Towers and satellites. No one would come up with the funding to match his investment. The world's data (and money) flowed through his software and hardware siphons. On this fortune, King Dirk had built his castle in San Francisco.

Today was Matt's day at the castle. As an Arctan interview finalist, Matt spent the night all-expenses-paid in the toney Mark Hopkins Hotel. He felt misplaced among the pretensions of wealth and near-wealth that roamed the saccharine *riche* lobby and halls. Headed out the door, he nodded sympathetically to the bell-man about his Halloween costume of blue and red over-trimmed with silly faux gold. The Kardashians used to love this place. Tourist Matt went straight for the cable car.

"Hop on, boy, and hold on. That'll be ten bucks for me and a ticket to ride for the mayor. Costs extra to hang off the brass rail. Double if you want me in the photo. Autographs free." The operator casually threw himself into the handbrake to keep the near-empty Van Ness & Market Car from plunging downhill into the Bay.

"I love this bell, don'chew?" rendering his "Flight of the Bumblebee" at an antiquated, non-EV Chevy with Indiana plates that strayed inside his comfort zone. "Whatsa sweet healthy boy like you doin' up so early? Stock market ain't open for an hour. You dressed all wrong anyway." Matt didn't try to answer. "Down where you headed, muscles or no, those ladies not gonna give you a second look wearing those shoes." He laughed at life and Matt.

Second stop, "Fella, here you are. Arctan-land." Matt looked surprised. "C'mon man! You, all nerves, and thoughts, you gotta be headed to The Tower. Don't mess'er up, hear?" Matt hopped off, the Van Ness car pulled away, ringing, with laughter.

Arctan's edifice of mill-turned stainless steel and filtered copper glass towered but it didn't dominate. There were too many kings in SF for that. Its pyramid shape narrowed to a dark, sharp peak, a metaphor of the slogan behind Dirk Samuelson's data wealth: "Harvest widely. Exploit wisely."

Matt approached the tower from the south on Front Street. A breeze and the tower's warm, reflected morning light hit him as he rounded the diminutive HSBC Bank building. Matt's soul was data held together by the laws of nature, still, this burst of air and sun stirred him. He was grateful that the pre-demic alert had just yesterday been officially lifted. The ominous 24-7 ultraviolet sterilization lamps lining the walls in every building were finally off again. No more misdemeanor tickets for exposed skin. He felt liberated. Like Pat's gym rats had speculated, perhaps this would be a great day.

Virtually any metropolis opens the day with a rush. But San Francisco is the heart of a manic, driven, powerful, modern economy-beast. People here don't just succeed, they shred the past and sculpt the future out of molecules, digits and money. Matt was accelerated through the automatic revolving doors and deposited like a bewildered child on the mirror-shined, cold marble floor, a waif lost on his way to school.

"Good morning, you must be Douglas Matthew County. The Third?" This, maybe Korean, maybe young, woman appeared before him in a trim body with trim makeup and a trim St. John's grey business suit, that he could have recognized from page seventeen of Saturday's slip-in Wall Street Journal magazine. It was trite for Matt to think she was perfect. But think it he did. She was the only stationary point in the swirl of humanity rushing around him toward its day sculpting the future.

"Uh huh, Third. Right." It was trite for Matt to be flustered, but he was.

"Welcome to Arctan International, my name is Souchi Kim, Dr. Samuelson's Second Personal Assistant. I am here to guide you through the interviews. Do you have your ID?"

"Right, the passport." He fumbled momentarily but delivered without more embarrassment. Souchi inspected it, turned with ballerina precision to walk flawlessly on black business spikes in the direction of the isolated, stainless-steel executive elevator at the far end of the crystalline interior hall. Matt was expected to follow, implicitly accepting his subordination.

Souchi approached the elevator and, as Matt arrived at her side, turned away toward a subtle security camera lens-port in the mirrored wall. A quick, vaguely flirtatious widening of her eyes elicited a click of approval from the iris scanner. She flashed it Matt's passport. A clean health report had been e-transferred down from the Mark Hopkins, so the doors glided open. Inside the chill-edged car, Souchi selected the "25" button.

The most self-controlled and, perhaps, most intelligent woman Matt had ever been alone with turned to brief him. "Dr. Samuelson has asked me to convey his personal regards." The possible accuracy of her words constricted Matt's respiration. Dr. S. had been a very, very serious entity throughout Matt's computer-linked life. "Your portfolio impressed us. You are one of three finalists out of one thousand eight hundred and fifty-five applicants."

"Dr. Samuelson is pleased that we have given him such a special cohort. We would like to see you succeed. To ensure this, please follow exactly the instructions you were given."

"Advantage, County" Matt mused to himself, sure of his self-discipline and attention to details.

"Perhaps some of your exercises today may seem unusual. Rest assured that we at Arctan value time above all else. Excel and enjoy." As if choreographed, the door slid open and Souchi suggested with a lean that Matt disembark into Arctan International time.

CHAPTER 7
INTERVIEWS

Matt's interviews were structured, customary: Human Resources, Marketing, IP-Legal each explained their role. They questioned Matt about this and that, good-cop, bad-cop moving from relaxed to serious to probe his intellect and personality. Smart, impressive professionals. It looked like Arctan had spent a lot on people. He felt special. After each interview, Souchi arrived to convey Matt to his next meeting.

The unique feature of the first ninety-five minutes was time-efficiency. Every moment was cordial, nothing wasted, as Arctan staff moved from one "experience" to the next. Time was of the essence. Matt hew strictly to the instructions and completed his contribution at deadline.

Souchi led Matt to a conference room outfitted with advanced AV gear for his next-to-last experience. Several large hi-def monitors were auto-running graphical stats around the perimeter. A beautifully crafted three-inch thick walnut table crowned the center of the room. Matt was introduced to a panel of four engineers about his age. Matt had sent forward a presentation deck, queued up on the main screen, to explain a part of his research. He deftly dismissed the technology of the three leading purveyors of enterprise blockchain and wrapped it up, at twenty-nine minutes fifty-five seconds, with his algorithms to improve on integrating blockchain into multi-tier corporations. The panel closed with four, five sharp questions. With compliments on his work, the computer tech guys departed. Matt felt real good.

Souchi reappeared exactly as the session closed. She gave no hint of his progress thus far.

"Thank you for your patience and punctuality, Matt. We have one experience left for you. As you recall, the Request for Applications mentioned that Arctan International intends for this position to do more than just add creative stimulus to our technology. Marketing has identified a need to freshen our public image. We want a genuinely technical person with appeal to youth. We need to assess each candidate's ability to impress the camera. The surest way to do well is to be yourself and follow the photographer's instructions."

As Souchi was speaking, two AV techies were delivering Photoflex light boxes, a Nikon and Red Vee Six cameras. Matt and Souchi, like the conference furniture, were respectfully moved to one end of the room and a bar-stoolish chair placed in among the three-point photoshoot that was evolving. The peripheral monitors and general room lighting dimmed to off. A woman in attire more New York SoHo than SF business entered the room. She began directing adjustments. After the gear was arranged to her satisfaction, she cast an eye on Matt, from a distance. Holding a camera, she prowled around outside the shoot volume, eyeing him, cat-like.

Souchi interrupted to obtain his signature on a photography Release. "I'll be leaving you with Svetlana, who will be doing your photo audition." And she left.

Svetlana moved in. Her accent was just enough to make it necessary for Matt to listen carefully, even watch her lips move, with its own benefits. "'Ello Matt, I am Svetlana. I am to make some photos of you. Please to sit on the stool, zer." Before he got completely situated, Svetlana abruptly started shooting, the Photoflex lamps flashing. Snap-pop, snap-pop, studio-miniaturized blitz and thunder, Svetlana moving confidently.

"Matt! Here! Give me your math look. I need some-sing serious, you inventing big sings. C'mon. Show me the curious problem solver, you Matt."

Matt began to flourish. His boxing experience, recovering from nose-cracking left jabs, served him. Focus, get your bearings, remember Corner's instructions. Defend. Act. Matt scrunched up a "is-that-all-you-got" face.

Low and deep, "Yaaaa. Zat is the Matt I vaunted." Svetlana had always had wants and she was accustomed to fulfilling them. Maybe a decade older than Matt, she had filled an ocean of wants, but for Matt her throaty purr was the first encouragement today. He liked it.

"Matt, give me some happiness, do me something for kiddies out here." Matt had enjoyed teaching school kids about coding, so why not. He put on a happy face. Snap-pop. Then a welcoming teacher face. Snap-pop.

"Oooooh." Snap-pop. "Uh-huh, sveetly." Svetlana was a professional. Snap-pop. Matt was spinning down her rabbit hole.

Svetlana backed off. Looking at the camera, making as if to play with an aperture or an f/stop, she began to setup Act Two. "Matt, zat is all good, thank you. But let's change us up a little bit now, OK? All good?" She left Matt no time to blunt her wants. Svetlana glided ahead.

Leaning in to get a little closer, with eye contact, "Let us make some strong guy, hmmm?" She backed off and gave a direct command, "Move for me manly, Matt."

This catches Matt way off guard. Kiddies to manly? Moves? Manly moves? This is new territory and not a street Matt, or any computer science student before him, had walked down. He searches Svetlana for clues and is surprised by what he finds. Her face transformed. A twisting elevation of her eyebrow and a tightening of her mouth short of a thrown kiss melted into a simple inviting smile. Matt is being worked by another consummate Arctan International pro. He likes it.

Svetlana's wants became his wants. He ventured an uncomfortable gesture, trying to accommodate her but he is far outside his lane. The two technicians, waiting alongside the shoot volume, suddenly feel invasive. Reading Matt's furtive glance, she dismisses them with a flick of her hand.

"Matt, let's work some for the ladies, warm up the ladies, huh?" She starts playing Matt with professional enjoyment. "For Svetlana please, Matt, turn up the temperature. Work with me."

Matt, erstwhile but deflated, "I'm sorry ma'am, I just never...."

Svetlana, backing off, "Shhhsh! Not talk. We just do some nice pictures, so Matt." She takes one shot, snap-pop, but it's not working. She shifts the camera deliberately to off-duty and pushes a stool over to sit close to

Matt. She eases into sexy, reassuring. "Matt." eyes painting over his face, "Where you from?"

Matt, still nervous but happy for the break, "Tennessee. Murfreesboro, ma'am."

Svetlana, getting closer, slinkier, "Svetlana, Matt. Svetlana."

Matt, "Yes ma'am. Sorry. Svetlana."

"Matt, do you have a girlfriend in, where is it, Murphy's Burrow?"

"Yes I do. I mean, no I don't right now that is ma'am. Svetlana."

"So you like girls?

"Yes I do Svetlana."

"A lot? Or a little?"

Matt, losing signal from his GPS, "Well yes, a lot I guess."

Svetlana, moving close, treating the camera like a delicate erotica. "Matt. You can tell, can you feel that I like you, yes?"

Matt, nervous but attentive, with no idea of the right answer, "I suppose, yes, that I do, Svetlana."

"Could you make believe, like, you like me ... a lot?"

"Why, I think, I guess I think, yes. Yes, I could."

"Can I ask you to do something for us then. Hmmm?"

Matt, sold, "Uh huh."

"Slip out of your shirt real slow so I take some photos of you showing me you really-really do like me Matt." She stands, pulls him up by the hand.

Matt complies with her wanting him shirtless. He's an amateur but Matt's heart is in the right place and he improves, following her instructions, working it. Barely aware of his physical accomplishments at Pat's Gym, he puts on a great performance.

Svetlana shoots, moving to catch all the angles, an occasional purr of approval. Abruptly, she stands up, thanks Matt, and brisks away to study the monitor, now image-boarding the shoot, verifying she got good stuff.

The lights pop up, converting the studio back to a re-purposed corporate conference room. Svetlana walks across the room to Matt, without guile, "Sank you Matt. Zis was very nice for me." The second technician, in the background, is reviewing images on the monitor. He and Svetlana exchange glances. They think Matt is good. Svetlana goes to a dedicated comm line in the corner and places a call, a couple of words, and leaves without looking back.

The room clears. Matt, pumped up then cold-showered, pulls together his clothes and dignity, thinking that he liked it, maybe.

CHAPTER 8
MATT'S NEWS

For the first downtime of the entire experience, making a half minute seem like five, Matt waited. Then Souchi came part-way through a doorway not yet used by anyone and stood uncharacteristically stiffly, holding the door open. A step behind her and moving briskly, a vibrant soul buzzed into the room, male, slightly above-average height, slim, average good looking. Dr. Dirk Samuelson.

With Tralfamadorian[16] vision, Matt would have seen the four-dimensional trail of a fine-tuned, twenty-first century corporate adult. Nutrition, from mother's milk to Konbu kelp, ideal. Sports, from badminton to rugby, school from La Cañada Palm Crest to Langford Day. Then Stanford, then med school and internship before diverting to a stint in Artificial Intelligence at MIT Lincoln Lab to MBA at INSEAD Fontainebleau France, bits and bytes of OTJ at Watson Labs, all challenging, augmenting, building the man. The whole while meeting, greeting and impressing eminent people and imminent peers in the sciences, arts, industry with his quick wit, ability to assimilate knowledge and decisiveness.

Matt was mesmerized. The singular living legend of the Twenty-First Century was walking toward him. This man had amassed a fortune in reputation and dollars by funding patient data bases that led to transcriptome diagnostics that had led to genomic therapeutics which he mortgaged to fund the first fully operational 64-qubit quantum computer which funded a fleet of Q-64s that he then leveraged into the famous Tera-tower network of laser beam, space-based communication conduits. And the San Francisco Datafile Exchange.

He got rich, but he had made his inside investors, several dozen of them, richer too. His ability to forecast technology, find talent, fend off anti-trust, and create products, prosperity and investor wealth was unrivaled in history. He walked up to Matt.

"Hello, Matt, I'm Dirk Samuelson." Bumping knuckles. "Please call me Dirk. Like time, its brief." One particular feature stood out, ice-blue eyes; Samuelson had blood relatives on the Kamchatka Peninsula.

"Matt, I have selected you for my Project." Matt would have had a thought or two and composed a shortened version of the usual gratitudes but Dr. Samuelson was a whirlwind.

"You were the best in a great field. I'm not sure I agree with your use of the non-linear part of a Wiesenblatt Tensor, but it could work." Smiling, "I hope we'll soon see." At Arctan International that fleeting Samuelson smile was a resounding compliment. Matt had received his start-up loyalty booster.

"Matt." Samuelson shifted, a subtle major-minor drop in his voice, his blue eyes drilled into Matt's.

"Success depends on finding and developing the best, very best humans. Arctan expects a lot from its people. I expect a lot from you. In return, we'll reward you with opportunity through resources. Wealth flows from success. You could eventually have a great deal of both. This Special Project is just an initial test."

"Thank you, sir."

Easing into adieu, Samuelson relaxed. "Souchi and her staff will brief you on your day-to-day. Please understand, when you are not given specific instructions, I expect you to make bold, independent decisions. Your ability to succeed individually within our team is paramount." He was taking leave.

"Oh, by the way, I noticed you might be over-developing your deltoids." With that, Dr. Dirk Samuelson was gone.

CHAPTER 9 MAKING A NEW FRIEND

Souchi closed the door behind Samuelson, or perhaps his vortex pulled it shut. Without a hint of how, or even if, her boss had affected her, Souchi walked gracefully, eyes averted, up to Matt, put one hand softly on his now-clothed chest and kissed him languorously on the cheek just to the south of his mouth. The effect of a few hundred drifting molecules of her delicate Chanel Five coursed through his nerves and crushed his id. Matt felt dizzy.

Stepping back a bit, with a pause, she reported, "Dr. Samuelson wanted me to be sure to welcome you warmly into Arctan International. Like you, I have been instructed to make bold, independent decisions."

No ring experience had prepared Matt for his confusing shift of blood flow. She handed him the kerchief from her breast pocket so he could wipe off the Dior 999 lipstick and asked, "Shall we discuss what you are to do now?"

Out of perhaps a dozen possible responses, the majority of which would have shortened his future at Arctan, Matt answered well, without thinking about it, "I'm ready to go."

Looking momentarily away, "Excellent. Are you ... sufficiently composed?" Matt's nod contradicted his pupil dilation. She waited.

"The main direction of your work will be 'Optimizing the Human-Machine Interface to Enable Scalable Exploitation of MegaData for Any Data Space with an Emphasis on Algorithms to Make All Information Fluidly Quantifiable.'" Matt realized this was basically an impossible carte blanche "assignment," even for a lifetime.

Souchi anticipated. "This is an independent project, directly under Dr. Samuelson. Feel free to explore any means within our realm of interest, which is by its nature almost everything. Dr. Samuelson wants to find and move Arctan to the next level of how humans shape the world based in real, quantifiable data. There is no failure mode in your work, only levels of achievement. Indulge yourself.

"You will not be required to report anywhere or anytime. Dr. Samuelson doesn't believe in work hours. He believes that paradigm shifts come from prepared minds. Dr. Samuelson thinks you might be inspired by Alan Guth's long struggle to define the Inflationary Universe." Note to Matt, check out Guth.

"Every computer station at Arctan, via your iris and facial scans, will be your window to all our resources. I am sure that you already know that encrypted security is not an issue for us. Should you require additional resources, hardware, software, personnel, consulting, I will arrange it for you; I will be accessible twenty-four eight." A slip, a jest, or a suggestive innuendo? At this pace, no way to know.

"About your project. When you're ready, say six months, please give me one-week notice to set up the first reporting, a seminar with Dr. Samuelson and department heads who may have interest in your work. You tell us how little time, up to forty minutes, you'll require.

"Of course, should you have any needs, I am at your disposal." Innuendo-exhaustion was allowing Matt to settle down to Twenty-first century gender ethics. He was striving to see Souchi as the Second Assistant working extension of Dirk Samuelson.

"Questions?"

Matt suspected that he might not get another moment like this, so he let fly, "The photography?"

Souchi figured that the photoshoot had an impact on Matt. "Yes, Svetlana Vlasenko. You recognize the name?" The full name half rang a bell for Matt. "She was one of Dr. Samuelson's early discoveries. She had been a budding *ingenue* model. Fifteen, in a Ukrainian bushtown, she was on the way to becoming an ugly victim. A contact in Kiev recommended her intelligence to Dr. Samuelson; He salvaged her out of a suspected criminal enterprise. She had spent some time being groomed by unsavory people. Dr. Samuelson supported Svetlana's schooling, put her through Ecole de Beaux Arts in Paris. She built her own practice, photographer to the stars in New York. Dr. Samuelson asked her to become the image maker at Arctan. Her assignment is to define our future public persona.

"Svetlana will be feeding web, print and display media with powerful artistic imagery. You might become part of that effort."

Matt appreciated Souchi's discretion in describing Svetlana's early life, but he speculated. Child pornography, prostitution? His encounter with Svetlana made the possibilities wretched.

CHAPTER 10
INTIMACY IN
PAT'S GYM

"She did whaaaat?!" Under his personal credo, "Do (first) or Die," Devon didn't believe that other people experienced improbables that they did not initiate. Matt's nod confirmed his original account of the kiss. "OK. So, Sushi walks up and gives you a hot, sweet, wet one, with feeling." Devon sometimes embellished reality to meet his expectations.

"Sou-Chi," interjects Alicia, a bit gen-dignantly. "Like 'sue' your ass in court and 'Chi' rhymes with tree. *Mein Gott.*"

"Sure, whatev. And you wrestle her, or she wrestles you to that walnut conference table and you guys do it. Bareback, right?" Matt down-shrugs, basically acknowledging that, no, there was no steamy intercourse. Devon is baffled, an outsider in a foreign, parallel universe. "Maaan...." drifting off into a salacious dreamworld. "Me, I know how I like my sushi."

Just too much for Alicia, "*Supergeil verdammt Tierschwanz!* Horny damn dick. Get your mind out of the sewer. Matt had just met Dr. Dirk Samuelson, one-on-one. And this Souchi is a real, classy adult person, you know."

"Woah, Leasha. Matt described something more than just a 'claaaaasy, Adult Person.' And what ta hell did Sush' mean with '...discuss what you are to do now'? Huh, Leash." Devon was right; Matt had spun a distinctly male slant on his description of Arctan's Second Personal Assistant, a prejudice Alicia had also noted.

The other gym rats began to take sides across the human-animal boundary line, Alicia refereeing but also advocating on behalf of an optimistic future beyond testosterone poisoning. This mosh pit with no defined intellectual level was, like all politics in Pat's, bound to end in a worthless split decision, everyone declaring victory.

Matt, elbowed to the sidelines, regretted the intimacy of Pat's gym-rats. But as the war for civilization soared and sank around him, Matt began to bubble with inventions. He began to look forward to going 24/8.

CHAPTER 11
NUMBERS. BIG DATA ONE

Numbers can express beauty, like Mandlebrot spirals,[17] or awe, the distance between galaxies. But numbers are mostly carnal because humans like to own stuff. Commerce flourished when humans found a way to quantify ownership. Pelts, shiny stones, amphorae of olive oil, barrels of oil, explosive power, pounds, yen, dollars, cents, and time. Humans want to own and control quantities and for that humans need numbers.

Matt loved numbers. It was hard for him to understand why human love and even sexuality was subordinate to number-love. How could anyone be happy with "love you bunches?" Not that Matt couldn't appreciate human emotions; on the contrary, Matt envied contact. It was just that it didn't work for him. He perceived things in a glance, a shrug, a shoulder, that others didn't notice. But he also didn't see the meaning in a wince, a wink, a nod, that others did. The intricacies left him confused, the worst state of being.

Matt loved numbers and they loved him back. All he had to do was respect the rules. In school, he felt warm when he mastered addition and subtraction; his teacher's adulations were a minor sideshow. Mastering a new set of rules made him hungrier. He learned that the numbers transcend boundaries. In university, he met like-numbered people with whom language was merely a useful nicety. Numbers let them all work easily together. And feel powerful.

Perhaps the greatest magic of all, Matt learned that numbers made it possible to predict the future. When and where will two spacecraft rendezvous? It wasn't unimportant to Matt that the spacecraft were carrying real people, the pride of families and nations, it's just that being able to make their rendezvous happen in a predictable way to a predictable likelihood thrilled Matt deeply.

Over time, he'd developed skills to dig under reality's surface. Matt could pull valuable data from the tracks that humans leave behind when shopping, Googling, texting and sexting. He could teach a machine to know stuff about anyone.

Technology and society had moved a long way in the short time since Matt started doing his numbers. Cashless shopping, social media and implanted personal sensors had pried open everyone's life and behaviors. People were delivering their numbers to the internet data siphons. And to Arctan International.

This data was not just deep - shoe size, birthday, languages spoken, mistakes made - but four dimensional. Immense value lay in the exact time a morsel was created. And while humans might take an occasional day off, time ticked on. Impossibly large rivers flowed into data banks in polar regions[18] to save power and stay cool. Arctan had even put data banks in orbit, beyond the reach of mortals and laws.

Matt had started his doctorate knowing that gathering facts about a person's personal lubricants or streaming or clicking events is simple. Verifying, tracking, retrieving, protecting, and interpreting was tougher and more valuable, not to peep on your neighbor's wife but an entire continent. His three years of effort had paid off. He had created and was ready to test the fastest, most accurate tools to wring out crazy-big data.

But he didn't have Big Data. Arctan did.

"Matt, there's a real risk in taking this path. Most people, lured off to business, never finish their degree." The Dean sat thoughtful, surrounded by the trappings of an accomplished academic: books, piles of print yet unread, mismatched furnishings.

"Ma'am, I'm not putting my PhD on hold. This Arctan project is just what the doctor ordered. I'm hoping you can let me just refocus my work using the data bases over there at Arctan."

"You're not asking for a stay of execution," the Dean paused to enjoy her joke, "just a change of venue?"

"Right. I won't need the stipend, and I'll miss the teaching moments. But I promise, this will let me wrap up a year faster than otherwise."

Putting on her serious parent face, she let Matt hang a moment. "Do it, Matt. I'll work out the administrative details."

"Thank you, Dean. I know this'll lead to some surprising discoveries. I'm truly grateful." All understatements.

"Oh, one thing, Matt. Can I have your student football

ticket allocation?" They laughed. Neither had been to a game in years.

CHAPTER 12
SAMUELSON.
LIFE IN THE
FAST BRAIN

"Babe, you were magnificent last night." It wasn't the first time he'd slept with her, an influential member of his corporate Board of Directors.

"Umm, you've always said that was the move you like the most." Anne, his wife-soul-mate-inspiration of 18 years in rough and tumble-in-the-hay California, hadn't yet opened her eyes.

"Right, sure, but I mean the way you handled that speech. You had them mesmerized."

Anne one-eyed him. "Wow. Cold. Here I am luxuriating in our Ulondra[19] and you talk speeches. No more Paris Croissant for you, buddy."

She laughed. "But true enough. I was damn compelling. You like the Nasty Nancy joke?"

"I had to laugh, they loved it. Hey, enough sweet nothings. I'm off, someone has to earn a living." Most days, Anne was twenty minutes ahead of him. But then, fundraising dinners for the Governor and a thousand supporters tend to run overtime. She relaxed an extra moment as Dirk hustled away.

He headed for his privy, built around a personal invention inspired by conversations with Bill Gates.[20] It compacted each movement by a factor of four[21]. When done, it yielded briquettes with a range of uses, from construction to energy to farming. The relieved user provided manual energy with an integrated high-pressure hand pump. This and other devices Dirk had invented was earning seven figures annually for its non-profit. But like Bell Lab's first efficient solar cells[22] made from sand and Impossible's first meaty hamburger[23] made from vegetables, Dirk's invention was intended to help rescue humankind from its eight point something billion selves.

Dirk Samuelson moved briskly to breakfast. A projection on each wall presented information for the day; Dirk relied on Third Personal Assistant Antoinette Césaire to anticipate his needs. Updated by cameras that monitored Samuelson's eyes, Antoinette distilled out seven words for each of ten topics. Antoinette provided a first and then two subsequent morning bursts. Thirty daily pieces of time-compressing data.

Germany sues Mediatech for repeat data breach. Afghan oil discovery estimated at 12.5B barrels. Scanadium futures jump threatens battery development …

Dr. Samuelson's news was shared throughout the Arctan domain. Fondly called the "A'Nette," these info-screens were located just outside every elevator and staircase. A glimpse of what affected the boss's thinking. Most everyone was grateful for their presence.

Antionette was waiting for him as he finished breakfast. "Joaquin Hernandez from EIT will be in half-day today. His wife and new son, Adrien, are home. He wanted to see his team before taking two weeks with family." Antoinette had arranged for Dirk to personally drop off a generous spiff to the new parents. "Right after your meeting with Senator Oakley. He's back from DC for a day." Dr. Samuelson was as certain to remember Joaquin by first name as Senator Oakley. It was a talent.

Unlike some of his billionaire cohort, Dr. Dirk Samuelson was not searching for the Fountain of Youth. He had not contracted to freeze his body infused with a dimethyl sulfoxide liquor in a perpetual bath of liquid nitrogen. Instead, convinced that this was his one and only life, he focused his resources on making the most of every moment. Criticized as rigid, he was living approximately two point three times as much as his less thoughtful critics.

Anne and Dr. Samuelson lived on the top three floors of Arctan headquarters. It had nice views. Three hundred sixty degrees. Their home was subtle. Driven by time-compression, everything lie conveniently within the 35,000 square feet of apartments, gym, pools, entertainment rooms, kitchens, wet lab and Anne's art production studios.

Both Dirk and Anne collected art. They were as likely to own a student sketch as a Basquiat, of which there were two. Anne's work, selling well at various Gagosian galleries including Hong Kong, London, Geneva and down the street in San Francisco, was displayed strategically.

The founder and CEO of Arctan International was not a bizarre hermit like Howard Hughes[24] in the past century. Arctan needed an explicit mission to preserve Samuelson privacy. Few photos were available and Antionette was responsible for purging online images as fast as they appeared. Still, Dirk and Anne did not live as prisoners of wealth. A personal elevator could deliver them to a basement passage that connected to an underground garage with two obscure, secure exits one and two blocks away.

Ex- Kenyan Special Forces soldier Rehema Njoroge, Dr. Samuelson's First Personal Assistant, a highly trained security agent, was on call to watch over private outings. She knew how to track the Samuelsons unseen by them or potential threats. Rehema had a valid firearms license, but not for the caliber of the weapons she carried; if something went down, financial and political influences would make her mess disappear.

For getaway trips, Arctan maintained an extended range, all-electric AgustaWestland AW229-M4 helicopter on the roof.

Antionette had three Samuelson minutes remaining. "The Wall Street Journal interview, it's coming up in two days."

"They have the whole press package, right?"

"Of course, but they want some personal touches, insight into The Man."

"The Journal does? Holman suddenly getting touchy-feely? He sure is ageing gracefully."

"Sells news. Here's what he wants. I'm quoting, 'People and events that inspired you.'"

"People and events? Easy. Work up something from

this: Admire the scientists who built the Worldwide Protein Data Bank. Early 1970's.[25] Set up their own network back before social media. Volunteers. Gave us exact pictures of the hundred thousand molecules life's made of."

"Can you add a business angle for the Journal?"

"Put in something about the hundreds of billions in pharma money that the data base spawned."

"A single person? Patrick Brown at Stanford. He invented how to parse out DNA and he gave the secret away. Free to anyone. Slamming the door on racial supremacists and opening the door to the backbone of all biology, all of it Antionette. Inspiring."

"Perfect. Financial angle?"

"Easier yet. Arctan's billions in transcriptomic diagnostics and epigenetic therapies.[26] That's a start. Personalized medicine tuned by genetic makeup. The Journal will love that one. Maybe add something about vaccine discovery based on viral RNA analysis."

"On it. I'll have the CDC contract revisions from Legal by then. *OK. On se voit après le déjeuner.* See you after lunch."

"Très bien. Bonne chance avec Jenkins au Journal. Il peut être aggressif. Great. Good luck with Jenkins at the Journal. He can be aggressive."

Dirk Samuelson had Tech Vision and off-the-charts numbers for eleven of the one dozen measurements of IQ. To test drive his brain would be like driving a Ferrari full speed along the serpentine Pacific Coast Highway below Carmel. The landscape would fly by, but life's intricate details would flow like graceful poetry - golden blades drying in the sun, butterflies on flowers, brambles. Fast, complete, relaxed, unhurried.

There is a limited reservoir of such intelligence on Earth. Unfortunately, not all such brains have an ethical core. The Joker haunts Batman. Dirk Samuelson would discover his Joker, too.

CHAPTER 13 GROWING UP FAST. REHEMA NJOROGE

"I see you Wild Beast.

You have eaten well today, and my Family has not.

For them, I must be The Taker of Life.

Respectfully I share this last breath with you."

"Well done, Rehema. Now I will teach you to shoot."

Simbatu taught his daughter, Rehema, The Hunter's Oath when she turned ten. She memorized The Oath because it was one of her passports to spend time together. He fabricated The Oath so he could teach her about an earlier time, when the Cape buffalo, Thompson's Gazelle and Wildbeest flourished in Africa and her people hunted to eat. They were both entranced by his stories.

He was a good teacher; he energized his sole student, Rehema, with his fabrications. "And then I can go with you to hunt, Papa?"

Simbatu laughed heartily, "In due time, you will earn that right."

Thinking to himself, "But only for rodents and varmints." After a century of animal butchery inspired by the Great White Bwana, Teddy Roosevelt,[27] it was illegal to hunt big game in modern Kenya.

"Your mother would have taught you to sew and thatch. But with her gone, I will teach you to hunt. I can't be your mother and you can't be my son but we can be us." As they walked on the fertile eastern plains of Kenya, he longed for the wife and son lost in childbirth. Simbatu's stride slowed thinking of how their children had inherited her smooth complexion, broad face and broader smile. He loved how his genes from the Mount Kenya highlands Kikuyu tribes and her genes from the lowland Mbeere tribes had produced beautiful coffee-toned kids. It pleased him immensely when he learned at University that they were living only a few hundred kilometers from the seed source of all mankind, The Oldupai Gorge. But the loss of his wife and son weighed heavily on his soul.

"Hey child. The long-legged ones there are free of ticks today." Rehema knew this game well, "Oh my, but the momma has a burr on her belly." His laughter caused long ears to flicker in the spindly-legged impala herd grazing on abundant Spring savannah grass a half kilometer away toward the brightening eastern horizon. "Yes, indeed, but the burr looks quite dry and will surely fall off on its own." Baritone and soprano laughter lilted onto the grazing plains. He was teaching Rehema to see.

Simbatu had been the first Njoroge to attend college, good move as the family shifted from survival to prosperity. Unlike his peers, he didn't disdain dirt farming.

At breaks, he returned home to test his book-learning with a shovel or tractor or plow. Njoroge lore included speared uprisings, droughts, neighborly feuds and even a fratricide but the fact remained that luck, work, DNA and adequately rich soil left each generation better off. "Look there, daughter. How far is that *quinche* plant?" Rehema squinted to where he looked. "Hmmm. I say 125 meters, Papa. Maybe a bit more, because the rise makes us think it is closer than it is." To hunt well and mercifully, she would need to gauge distance. She was an apt student.

"Perhaps. Let's see." They paced off the distance, counting his measured strides out loud together, through the nettles, deviating neither left or right. As they walked hand-in-hand, he hid his sorrow knowing that the intimate closeness of this morning on the veldt was short-lived; he would miss these fleeting moments of instruction once womanhood called her to a husband's lodging.

Rehema was good to within two meters. "You have learned well, child. How about that distant *Mbuyu* tree?" Simbatu, ever the teacher, used the Swahili name to point out the giant baobab. Stretching her neck, "I believe that is 310 meters, Papa. Will I shoot that far! Would be a great joy for me."

"The rifle will shoot that far, but you must make it true. And that starts with knowing distance. Let's go. Count." And so these two lives passed, intertwined on the dusty productive farmland of eastern Kenya, step by counted step. The morning sun warmed Simbatu and Rehema.

When farm chores allowed, he took her out on the range to continue lessons. Over the course of her thirteenth year, she mastered windage, tracking, the tricks of shifting shadows, how to move silently or wait patiently. In her fourteenth year, she handled weapons, starting with a .22 rifle, then moving to the local favorite, a relic of British colonial rule, the Enfield .30-06. Stripping, cleaning, and reassembling its parts displaced girlie play. Shooting, she cherished the buck of each recoil and the smell of cordite. Above all, she loved Papa-time, full of patience and devotion.

He taught her the positions and grips that give the steadiest bead. He taught her to aim small, to align molecules in the sights with molecules on her targets. He insisted that she respectfully recite The Hunter's Oath for each purposeful shot. Most importantly, she learned how to draw and hold that "last breath" before caressing the trigger to unleash a round. She became quite a good range marksman; earning his pride pleased her very much.

In her fifteenth year, after all the preliminary steps had been fulfilled, it was time to hunt. Africa is still home to magnificent creatures, but in shamefully dwindling numbers. Kenya experimented with laws trying to stem the hemorrhage of species by foreign trophyists.[28] So Simbatu treated varmint hunting as though they were bringing down a Thompson's Gazelle or an Eland or a lion. The diminutive size of their prey didn't diminish the dignity with which they killed but it did sharpen Rehema's aim. Their croplands became re-markably clean of critters.

Once per year they journeyed to Nairobi to shop, see the tall buildings, and reinvigorate their love of the plains homestead. This year was special, **21 September 2013**, the International Day of Peace so Simbatu headed straight to the Westgate Shopping Mall know-ing it would be busy. The mirror and glass and chrome and marble artifacts didn't impress Rehema. The trap-pings of urban civilization were trivial compared to her profound role as "The Taker of Life" and apple of Simbatu's eye. She had grown to be an exceptionally at-tractive young woman.

Simbatu and Rehema walked in a bubble-wrap of se-renity among the dozens of early visitors. Colors and adornments and laughter and smiles enveloped them in the grand hallways where modern mall vendors en-courage customers to unhand their hard-earned cash. They paused at the intersection of two wide, polished mallways. Suddenly a disturbance came to the perfect Day of Peace. Pop-pop. Pop. While some people looked at each other in puzzlement, this father and daughter of the veldt immediately identified the sound. Gunfire. Powerful gunfire. They even recognized the close bim-bam of shot followed by impact. The shooter wasn't close or far. But he was here.[29]

Without hesitation, Simbatu grabbed his daughter and dragged her to the nearest doorway, a clothing store. Another series of pops exploded a luxurious crystal chandelier above and behind them. Shoppers screamed and ran. Some fell. Forced under a rack of long, elegant formal wear, Rehema saw her dad slink over to the door and look away from the direction of the sound, studying the reflecting glass at the end of the long hallway. He flashed her a one finger and scurried back to the rack. She saw two people were now down in the mallway, one still, one trying to crawl. There was blood.

"Rehema. Look at me." She had no trouble focusing. "There is a man, fifty meters to the right. He is coming this way. He's a bad shooter. Listen." They listened. Bam. Bam. "Wasted shots." She could tell this was not a hunting rifle. It was too sharp and too fast. She saw that the damage outside was mostly random. "Shooter's a fool." Simbatu touched her chin and pulled her eyes to meet his, "You know how the *firigogo* bird fakes illness to distract us from her nest?" She nodded, calm. "I am going to distract him. Do you understand?" Again, she nodded. "You must stay under here like the nestling. Don't move, don't make a sound. I love you deeply my little hunter." And with that he crept to the entryway, waited for the shooting to pause and bolted toward the open mallway twenty meters straight ahead.

Simbatu ran with the speed of a gazelle. He never looked back. He shouted insulting Swahili phrases about the shooter's mother and god. He ran with the speed of a gazelle.

Shots rang out but the gunman hadn't been schooled nor had he learned anything in these last minutes. Simbatu made it to the cover of the opposite perpendicular mallway and continued running, shouting insults over his shoulder. And then evil came from the right into Rehema's view. It glanced into the clothing store. Rehema, stone-still, felt cold and hot as their eyes met. His head scarf, shouted Swahili devotions to his god, and his young face dug into her spirit. Then, realizing with urgency that his running prey might elude him, he turned, took aim, and fired at the running Simbatu. He missed. And the fleeing *firigogo* bird drew the religious fanatic down the mallway and around the corner until Rehema could no longer see either one. She obeyed her father's command to stay hidden as two gunmen jogged past looking to kill.

Next day, after a night of silent hiding confined by explosions, smoke, screams and gunfire, Kenyan Defence Forces soldiers found her and took her to safety. She caused some trouble for the soldiers trying to remove her from the mall without Simbatu.

A controversial official investigation followed. It identified four attackers and confirmed that Rehema had seen the final moments of the first Al Shabaab terrorist to die. He and his accomplices killed 51 civilians and 5 KDF during a three-day siege in a fit of retribution for KDF actions in Somalia.[30] Contrary to rumor, no American or British or Norwegian agents or the Israeli mall owners were involved in the attack. The report indicated that "a heroic citizen" had ambushed Attacker One at a corner of the mallways and strangled him. Even though he had been shot, Simbatu's farm-strong hands clenched and clenched until he had crushed the terrorist's larynx. Simbatu bled out from a single AK47 belly wound and died entangled with blood-wet Attacker One in the mallway intersection, fifty meters from his daughter.

It's not impossible, just not easy for any woman to join an army. Even more so in Africa. But Rehema Njoroge wouldn't hear of that. On 21 September 2013 she acquired an interest to be a Ranger in the Kenyan Defence Forces, an intense, personal interest. So, after her father's funeral and after finishing her school year like he had desired, she applied, cajoled and otherwise pestered her under-age way into the Kenyan army. Simbatu's little hunter had a mission. She thought of it as her Fifty and Six.

CHAPTER 14
YOU'RE IN THE ARMY NOW AND THEN YOU'RE NOT

Fifteen scruffy, uniformed Kenyan Defence Forces recruits standing at attention in the hot dusty sun. One had been singled out for a lesson in humility by Range Director, Big Sarge, wearing sharp, clean but sweaty camos and holding a KDF standard-issue Heckler & Koch G3 assault rifle.

"What did ah do wrong, bushmeat?" Aussie-trained, outback roughened Big Sarge screamed, standing over Rehema Njoroge, at least a foot taller and 30 kilos bigger. "Ah ain't done nuttin' to the Captain. Not ta hiz wife. Not ta hiz brats! Not ta hiz caa! Why me?" This was old school, last-century boot camp and Rehema was getting fed rations. "Wha' make me git you, you piece of shitpie here in da middle of shit-where, huh?"

"Sir, I do not know, sir." Rehema stood perfectly erect, unafraid, taking it. That made Big Sarge even madder.

Whiny voice, "You 'do not know, sir'? You don' know shit. You just a shit. Why you here. Woman-shit?"

"Sir, I am here to learn to shoot bad guys, sir." Serious

truth.

"You! Shoot fuggin' bad guys! You! What wit'? We use real guns, dull-shit. You gonna get scared when it make some noise huh?" The recruits stifled a giggle, glad to be off Big Sarge's radar but one Big Sarge glance shut that down, real quick. Back on Rehema, "You don' even know where the bullet comin' out. Sheeet."

"Sir, I am here to learn to shoot bad guys, sir."

Sarge, really mad now, shrieks at Rehema, "I fuggin already heard dat shit. An' I wanna jez send you home sistah!"

"Sir, glad to go home if Sergeant pleases, sir," a lie.

"Nuttin would make me happier Maaaam. But den Sarge is stuck wit' dat pile a shit." Big Sarge sweeps his arm at the recruits who recoil as if he was swinging a loaded gun, which he is.

"Sir permission to speak, sir?"

"What ta fugg you gotta say, so's I can send you home?"

"Sir, you teach me right now to shoot, sir." Rehema was rigid as a dead stick, chin on her camo blouse. "If I ain't no good right now, I go home right now, sir." She pops up on her toes emulating a bit of British colonial impudence for the closing "sir."

Big Sarge has been in and gotten out of a number of traps and ambushes in his life, most of it in this Army. He'll never forget **Somalia** two years ago, in an incident that earned him this easier assignment and some wounds and medals. He walks around Rehema looking her up and down, dust rising around his boots, buying time to figure out her trick.

"Sir, permission, sir." Big Sarge gets in her face, and growls, "Talk. Fast. Freak." She feels the spray, smells the stench.

"Sir, you teach me how, now, I stay and clean your boots evr'y day, sir." Big Sarge dreams, a bit salaciously. It's sad that a man who could keep himself safe on the racially unfriendly back streets of Moscow, Charlottesville or Milan, would stoop to that.

"And if you don't learn how, now, you asks the brass to leave? You tell'em you chickenshit and even I can't fix you."

"Sir, yes, sir." Sounds good to Big Sarge. "You gottit, bushmeat," and he turns to walk to the range, ten meters behind the now alert recruits. The whole scene - golden savannah, distant mountains, crackling brush - shimmers in the sun.

"Sir, permission, sir."

He stops and his shoulders stoop, really trying not to get old or have an infarct. A shrapnel wound aches. He doesn't turn to face her. "Whaaat ta fug now, shitturd?"

"Sir, if I shoot bettr'n Sergeant, you sign me up for Rangers, sir."

Mount Kenya is one of the world's premier volcanos. It has been dormant for over two and a half million years. But right now, it was about to erupt. Except, that can't happen. Abusing recruits to teach them humility is Big Sarge's job description. But abusing a recruit who's upped him, he'd lose all credibility. Big Sarge seethed inside. At himself. He'd been snookered.

He stood collecting himself, shaking in anger. "What'd she know?" Then he got it. One bushmeat recruit before her had learned to shoot at home. And he was damned good. Plus, the kid proved out to be one hellava asset in a fire fight. But then there's this challenge in front of the troops. By a female. Big Sarge had to face it. Snookered. His day was going downhill.

Silent, his most threatening state, he glared at the line of helpless recruits as he trudged menacingly through their panicked scurrying file toward the firing range. To the closest recruit, "Fetch da shitpile a weapon, dickhead." Recruit scurries off. Rehema is marching behind him overly full of obedience and respect. Big Sarge walks heavily over to the range line and waits for the recruit to hand Rehema an H&K. He toes the firing line and begins to sight up on the standard 50-meter target.

"Sir. Permission please, sir." Big Sarge screams, "Whatta-fuggin-hell-is-your-dickless-fuggin-problem, dickless?"

"Sir, Can I pick da target, sir." He's insanely tempted to resort to his standard line about using the recruit's tiny balls for a target, but Corps has put him through gender sensitivity training[31] so he bites his tongue. Quivering with rage, "Pick. Pick!" his voice rising two octaves from base to mezzosoprano, "Pick da fuggin' target!"

Looking calmly downrange to the slight rise about 150 meters out, she points to a *beru beru* tree. "Sir. See da tiny branch sir. Looks like a *danga* tail. Sir." Rehema had learned the flora and fauna of East Africa from her dad.

She'd harvested her first grasscutter at this distance with a .22 rifle at the age of fifteen. "Sir. You 'n me, sir. Who take her down first, sir."

Most of Big Sarge's shooting has been on the run, falling, bleeding, rolling and ducking. Resigned, very tired, he kneels in the dust, looks downrange and starts to line up his shot. Rehema plays the student and moves up to stand not-so-innocently on the wrong, ejector side of his H&K. She's had enough of men to know their weaknesses, so she starts twitching her pretty camo-covered butt ever so slightly. Un-lady-like.

Against such insurmountable odds, Sarge, a good shot but known more for his bullying, bellowing and cool under hot fire, managed to kick up a sand fountain about a quarter meter to the left and low. The proximity of the 7.62-millimeter bullet would have scared the living shit out of its intended victim, but close is otherwise disappointing with ballistic rounds.

"Sir, good shot, sir. I try to be so good, sir."

Now, proudly all alone on the grand stage of life, H&K slung across her body, she caresses her bullet with one finger, whispers to the little Belgian-made phallus and kisses its full metal jacket.

Big Sarge is about to literally pop a blood vessel, two of which are clearly pulsing in his neck.

With a clean sweep, she chambers the 7.62 X 51 mm NATO round. The prior confrontation with Big Sarge has stirred up some sexual tension but holding an assault rifle with one live round made Rehema especially self-assured in front of the Greek choir and its leader. She looks at her fellow recruits and, unseen by Big

Sarge, smiles ever so slightly.

She kneels into the dirt, and like Simbatu taught her, she wraps the one-inch wide shoulder strap around her left forearm, tightens down a triangle of webbing between the stock, her elbow and the rifle butt. Sarge's deep brown face, it seems impossible, darkens, his cohort of trainees is fixated. Rehema cheeks the rifle butt and becomes ferociously oblivious to the audience, all but one of whom is irrelevant to her long-term goals.

With nothing but silence and the Westfield Mall in her head, she begins to narrow her vision to the iron molecules of her sights and the cellulous molecules at the top of the narrowing end of the *dango* branch. She recites The Oath and finishes with the last, long, hunter's breath, then fondle-squeezes off one round at the little doggie tail. It bends, swings and drops. Rehema yelps like a child before catching herself. No need to dilute the respect that shot deserved. She mutters to herself, "Thank you, papa," and jumps bolt upright to a parade attention that would have made any of the Queen's Royal Fusiliers, Seventh Regiment proud.

"Sir, you make me a Ranger, sir. Send me to Al Shabaab and let me be me. Sir."

Big Sarge did just that and, a year later, received the last of his commendation medals, this one for Excellence in Recruit Development.

Rehema completed all the training Kenya could muster including an undocumented special ops anti-terrorist session with Eric Prince's hired Blackwater professionals (later changed to Xe Services then Academi.[32]) Detailed to Somalia, where Kenya, as part of AMISOM[33]

Operation Shortcut, was systematically working to eradicate Al Shabaab. She became a legend. The stories of her hundreds of sniper kills were grossly exaggerated, especially because her unstated personal goal was fifty and six. But the story of her MO was accurate: If she returned to camp wearing lipstick, she had offed a bad guy and left an empty cartridge at the site with a red ring around it. And she had recited The Hunter's Oath for each.

"I see you Wild Beast.

You have eaten well today, and my Family has not.

For them, I must be The Taker of Life.

Respectfully I share this last breath with you."

All good things must come to an end. The KDF with AMISOM had nearly rid southern Somalia of terrorists and a strategic withdrawl was made. Faced with budget cuts, downsizing was ordered and Rehema was returned to civilian life. Living on the outside with an Al Shabaab bounty on her famous head, she was an endangered species. A Samuelson INSEAD colleague, high-ranking deputy in the Kenyan Department of Defence, heard about her decommissioning in the regimental newsletter and passed Rehema's name to Dr. S. Within a week, she was flown to England under the tutelage of a Samuelson INSEAD colleague who situated her in a private college in Oxfordshire. After three years, she was sent to the US, fast-tracked through Immigration, interviewed, and hired as First Special Assistant at Arctan International.

CHAPTER 15
HOME SWEET ARCTAN HOME

"'Lo Matt. I'm Dr. Eldbjørg Tollaas, Senior Medical Officer, I'll be your guide through The Pasture."

Matt met her elbow tap awkwardly. Eldbjørg seemed too young to be wearing a "Dr. T." medical smock. But her youth was overshadowed by the solid Nordic physique that for centuries had made Vikings weak in the knees.

"My apologies for greeting you in the foyer, but the Pasture starts here, yes." She looked past him to a bank of the most modern Instant Pathogen Detectors[34] in the city.

"Arctan wants everyone to know we are serious about health. I choose to meet all newcomers so I can reinforce that idea from Day One.

"I and my staff feel great pride in keeping all of you in peak form. You are my personal responsibility. Your health is top priority, working or playing. I expect that you will do your part. You are to please sign up with our nutritional and fitness programs as soon as you can." Her no-nonsense affect left no doubt "soon" meant today.

"For sure, ma'am."

Her gaze measured his sincerity. "Um. Fine."

Dr. Tollaas pointed Matt to the IPDs. "Test. Now." He approached a device. The woman inside the machine greeted him. "Hello ... Douglas Matthew County. Please inhale deeply then blow into the illuminated port." He felt a light vacuum as his breath triggered a crisscross field of multicolored laser beams within.

"Thank you." A ping. A second. "Congratulations. You are clear. The current RamanTec pathogen list has been downloaded to your cell. Have a fine day." Traces of sanitizing UVC lamps glowed in the port as Matt pulled back.

They moved through the auto-opening door. Unlike Dr. T, everyone Matt saw looked rather ordinary, nerdy. But there was an energy. Bright eyes and friendly nods welcomed.

"You will no doubt learn about the sexual vitality in the Pasture. While I know that you will make out just fine on your own, should you have any difficulties do not hesitate to consult me." Matt wondered what kind of difficulties she handled. Her Nordic kept him from asking.

As they walked, Dr. Tollaas explained. "Arctan has over a thousand apartments in this complex. Residents enjoy the sweetest Bay views in town. Top assignments are between the 10th and 30th floors in the Pyramid HQ. Rookies like you Matt, start off with spots in the upper 30 floors of the Terra-Tower, next building over."

Eldbjørg stopped at an A'Nette display.

"Today's Resources."

An illustrated list popped up. Gyms. Lifestyle and health consultants. Clubs. Coffee houses. "We keep something going on almost round the clock. Everyone can link anyone electronically, anytime. Still, you're within minutes of a physical assignment or meeting, if there's a need."

"Matt, Arctan's Pasture mixes together hip, critical, informed minds, what Dr. Samuelson calls 'the international currency of the Twenty-first Century.'"

Matt knew about the jokes, that residents were Pasture-ized and cult-ivated. But the economics, ergonomics and egonomics were irresistible. He wondered if Karl Marx would be proud.

"Dr. Samuelson believes that daily chores drag people onto 'the misty flats'[35] where it's easy to get bogged down in the mundane. Here, you can reduce your mundane to near zero. Or not."

With that, she opened a door. Matt peered in and saw a mix of amateurs and flirts making lunch for themselves in what could have been a five-star hotel kitchen. A number of worried or happy pro-chefs busied about, keeping people from harming themselves.

"In The Pasture you have access to world class kitchens, theaters, seminar rooms, meditation, maker-spaces. Weekly chats with Noble laureates, political candidates, Death Row inmates. Take it or leave it. Stimulation, relaxation. Simplifies my job keeping people healthy.

"Celebrities, authors drop in to test their intellect. I hear that Arctanners like to say it's the only pasture with no herds and therefore no bullshit." Her Nordic dignity made the profanity vegan.

Dr. Tollaas had been explaining their way past various attractions. On the third floor, Dr. T. stopped to open the "Auditorium" door. Intimate, maybe 200 plush seats and a half tennis court sized open floor.

"We don't need to pay artists to perform here. Hottest gig in town. Press reviews swayed by the guaranteed rowdy, informed audience. Health screening means you're safe from the virus.

"After work, hang out in one of Arctan's restaurants." She ordered the nearby A'Nette to display menus. "The city's best chefs drop in to test their new recipes. We provide discerning influencers and the best kitchens in town. Our places for brainstorming, relaxation. Tracing, laminar flow ventilation, UV sterilization. Again, safe from virus. Dine in confidence."

Halting in a quiet space on the edge of the social zone, Dr. Tollaas turned matter of fact.

"Matt, there's a dark reason to live in the Pasture." An inch shorter than Matt, she held his gaze. "While you creators have been busy, the outside world has become restless. Leaders are encouraging animosity toward intellect, achievement. You attract abuse and scorn, maybe worse. The Pasture is a haven.

"Arctan takes no chances. We spread a safety net outside the building. Our head of security runs the most ... respected ... private force in San Francisco.[36] The area surrounding HQ, even down in the BART, is under twenty-four seven surveillance. Not a being passes through our perimeter that isn't immediately ID'd by our AI engine."

Matt couldn't hide his shock.

"Don't worry. You or casual visitors won't feel oppressed. Our "street sweepers" make malicious lingering in the HQ volume ... discreetly unpleasant."

Looking over Matt's shoulder. "*Oopla!* Here comes our head of security, Rehema Njoroge, Dr. Samuelson's First Personal Assistant."

Salt and pepper, Tollaas' Viking *skjaldmær* warrior maiden to Njoroge's *malkia wa afrika* African queen.

"I have been looking forward to meeting you, Doctor County." Oxford colored her English and manners.

Matt flushed. "Sorry, not a doctor yet, still working on it."

"Oh, yes, but your reputation anticipates the achievement."

"Thank you, ma'am, just Matt is fine."

"So it is, Matt. Dr. Samuelson explained to me your hyperfast data analytics. I have several applications for what it can do. But we can talk technical later. My friend, Dr. Tollaas," they exchanged warm glances, "wanted me to greet you. In case you have questions about my safety measures?"

"The surveillance. Is it all really necessary?" Versed in data, he didn't like the idea.

Rehema's face clouded. She reflected, briefly. "Matt, a short while ago three undesirables got one of my Arctan boys cornered in the BART, three stops out on his way home. My surveillance was minimal back then. They beat him up quite badly. Lost vision in one eye." She searched Matt's face.

"They didn't steal his computer. Seems they took exception to his eyeglasses and using a laptop on the train, Matt."

Matt remembered the news story. The coding community had been devastated. And fearful.

"His face will never be the same. We're not sure his coding will either. It was his passion, his life desire to make good code. Ironically, he was working on an algorithm to limit pandemic spread in prison populations.

"It took an hour for my AI to track down the three young men. Once we had positive ID, DNA and all, my professionals invested twenty minutes in attitude adjustment lessons. In fact, to this day we randomly, maybe every couple of months, we do a reinforcement."

She laughed at Matt's reaction. "No, Matt, not that. No kneecap vengeance. We find a personal place to leave each a dead rat with a piglet eyeball in its mouth. My touch. I have always like to leave a calling card. So they know we've got an eye on them. One spooked and left the country. We found him in Cambodia. He didn't know it's cheaper to complete our 'deliveries' there. He's saving us some money."

"Matt. I will not call off the lessons until my coder is healed. May take a while, but I have patience Matt." She stopped for him to balance the ledger.

"Is the surveillance necessary? No. It's just me Matt. Just me. You see, I once lost someone to bad guys. I shall never fill that void. But I can limit it happening to anyone else. I worry so you can relax. Trust me."

Dirk Samuelson, Arctan, invested sixty-seven million

US annually to keep The Pasture stimulating but safe. Comfort, food, stimulation, safety. Productivity for Arctan. Win-win. What's not to like?

Matt wondered.

CHAPTER 16
ARCTAN DAY ONE, NEW FRIENDS

"Welcome back, Matthew. The Pasture OK for you?" Souchi greeted him with a breath of warmth. He smiled, warmed.

"Today, you'll need to do the customary security checks, scans and so on. I'll leave you with Personnel to complete the list."

Fingerprints, probably unenforceable Non-Competes, etcetera ate up half a day among the gatekeepers of ownership in Twenty First Century tech.

Souchi returned, apologetic. "I found that your Biometric Signature is outdated. No problem, universities usually don't keep up. We need to get you a Gen Three Bio Sig." Joking, Matt asked if it would hurt. "Not too much," opening the desk drawer to flourish a syringe sized for a stallion. She laughed as he jerked back. "Just kidding," as she pulled out a sterile sample kit, still grinning. "Let's have three cheek swabs, one in each tube." Below the radar, she enjoyed how easily he let her jibe roll off, no insecure defensiveness.

"Your bio-file, appropriately compressed, will be attached as metadata to all your work product. Prevents counterfeiting. Ensures authenticity. Enhances data value. By the way, Arctan pays an annual commission to everyone who maintains Gen Three data authorship verification."

"There's one more item. Wear this pin. It's an encryption transponder and will attach your Signature to transcribed discussions as well. Your contributions will be tagged. It's a compliment. I've been told that you will be a Level Four author in Gen Three." Noting his puzzled look, "Right, all data authors are rated. Level Four means your data will have a top rating for reliability, accuracy, all the good stuff. Tough to get. It's important. Watch what you say." Her smile, humor?

Souchi toured Matt through Arctan. Communal and private work areas, phone cabins, dining and winddown recreation spaces, all on the principle that a happy employee is a profitable employee. Each A'Nette screen monitored his approach and switched briefly from Samuelson's news bites to a cheery "Welcome Matt!" One display even popped up a winking meme adding "That's a good one!"

None of it mattered much to Matt. Not planning a pregnancy, not liking a desk, not eating on a schedule, not needing caffeine to get inspired, not looking for companionship except to test ideas, Matt was a self-contained creation machine. He strove to be cordial but his demeanor, under autonomy promised by Dr. S. himself was, "Let me alone without leaders."

As they ended the tour, Souchi led him up to a dignified-looking man. "Matt, Dr. James Brogan."

"Hi, you're the young prodigy, Douglas County." Brogan

came off surprisingly informal for his C-seat and forty-eight years. He liked clothes but a button-down no-tie Michael Kors shirt, casual hand-crafted Berluti Scritto shoes and fashionably tapered trousers were standard amidst Bay area money. "My engineers told me about your presentation. They were impressed. Pleased to have you join Arctan."

Matt, who had been raised Old South offered the New Reality hygienic fist bump and "Yes sir, pleased to meet you sir."

Dr. Brogan was recognized in the Valley for his entrepreneurial adventures and big bucks earned before Arctan. He could have felt and displayed some animosity, given that Matt had not been placed under him as Arctan's CTO for R&D. Matt had heard that territory and authority is lustily, even maliciously, defended in the corporation but Brogan radiated a welcoming vibe.

"I'll be looking forward to your progress report. I've been informed Souchi will be available to fill your resource requests but let me know if I can personally help in any way." A parting dap and Dr. B. strode off. Matt figured this was a man with bigger stuff on his plate.

"Dr. Brogan?" Souchi looked at Matt, her eyes suggesting friendship. And that he should be curious. "Dr. Samuelson started planning your project two years ago, about the same time I joined Arctan. As the project heated up, he hired Brogan to take over day-to-day Technology. He's done a great job of freeing up the Doc."

"Is he OK with me, I mean not reporting to him and all?"

"Matt. Your project is huge." She glowed, "and you have been chosen by Dr. Samuelson to consummate it.

That's what we're going to do."

CHAPTER 17
REPORTING
BACK. ZIG'S BAR

Matt was pumped as he headed into Zig's, moving through Stefan's Third Essential: one public entrance, three meters off centerline from where Stefan presided over business. That offset gave Stefan a chance to size folks up seconds before they came through his Fourth Essential, the cramped, harshly lit vestibule, and adjusted to the dank interior.

Matt squinted as he pierced the obscenely bright lights going in. His Arctan-ID scan let him skip the contagion blow tube. He hadn't yet had enough traumatic life experiences to comprehend that the glare gave Stefan time to check him out and leave SIG and Jimmie at rest under the bar. Devon and Alicia began calling to Matt even before his eyes adapted to the bar-dinge.

"Math-Yew! First day! How'd it go?" Alicia was electric with curiosity. "Did you have any deep tech talk with Samuelson? Did he explain what it feels like to be worth billions? Give us the whole report."

"Dude, I wanna know about Sushi, man! Second at-bats with the walnut table, huh?" Alicia glared at Devon who "woah" backed off, intimidated by her intensity. "Shut up Dev." Long stare.

"Matt, what's it like in the den of data, did they like ya?"

"Guys, amazing. Souchi, cool lady, met me in the lobby and escorted me to the top floor onto an elevated stage in a corporate-wide meeting in a huge conference hall with maybe five hundred people and everyone popped champagne corks when I walked in and then Beyoncé broke into "Here Comes the Bride" and Taylor Swift came out to give me a kiss then..." Up to the champagne corks, Devon and Alicia were sucked in, willingly duped. At that point they started flicking beer suds at Matt. They would have drowned him had he continued.

"OK OK. So I filled out legal papers, surrendered all the usual rights and privileges. They gave me a crazy generous cut on IP though. And instead of Samuelson, Souchi introduced me to a Dr. Brogan who's apparently Chief Tech Officer. Guy's a typical engineer-made-money. Fancy pants and shoes. Smelled awfully sweet, too. He rubbed me the wrong way talking about how 'his engineers' liked my interview." Alicia and Devon knew the type. They had also done some homework.

Devon started "Yea, me and Leash have been digging up background on people you might work with in there. He's at the top of the list." Smiling like the Cheshire cat, Devon paused. "Wanna know about Brogan or Sushi?" Matt hesitated. The ultimate cock-tease, Devon dove in with a shrug. "OK, Brogan."

"Net worth, over two hundred mill. Made the first tranche himself based on his PhD in AI. Then he went hippie off the grid, an early midlife crisis. After a year, came down outa the woods, promptly hired by VCs to put a grownup face on a promising biotech startup, which went great, particularly for Number One. Appears he left some bad feelings by manipulating his ownership share, slippery deed shaped by his wife, Carlotta, a corporate attorney in a family law firm with history and connections downtown. Her grandpappy and father were thick with the likes of the San Francisco Browns, Pat and Willie and Jerry."

Devon loved sleuthing. Digging up personal dirt on people was second only to making dirt himself. "Then Samuelson picked him up. Hired on for mid-seven-figs of salary and a nice chunk of Arctan A stock. He's done a lot to stabilize daily technical operations and strengthen the company. Reassures the Board when Samuelson goes off the reservation on Special Projects. Then with a smirk, "Like the one you, my friend, are now on."

Devon added, "Brogan's pretty square, not into dreams and far-out R and D. Likes money. His. Maybe a guy to watch out for?"

Devon was bursting to flesh out Souchi for Matt but Alicia glare-stared him when he tried to scoop the story. "Zip it." Stare. "Stop. Can it."

Devon was frothing to spin his dirty version of The Souchi Story but knew better than to man-splain over Alicia, whose vengeful memory and right-cross in "friendly sparring" was legendary, Matt recent witness thereto. Devon zipped it, stopped, canned it.

Alicia gathered herself and began to recount with dignity. "Samuelson has a history of finding young talent. He has a considerable number of scouts all over the globe, mostly INSEAD friends he rewards for their personnel discoveries. He gathers youthful raw intelligence with demonstrated drive. Samuelson prefers kids from adversity. Turns out, most of his rescues give him deep loyalty." Alicia choked up. Rescue was personal.

"Souchi's grandmother was a Korean *wianbu*, a 'comfort woman' abducted to Japan during WWII to service Imperial warriors.[37] Repatriated to South Korea after the war, her grandma suffered under the stain of her abuse in Japan. Eight years later, the Chinese-American war in Korea reduced the entire country to a decade of starvation.[38] Late in life, Grandma Souchi found a little tenderness, call it love, and Mama Souchi was conceived, a late Boomer in Busan."

Devon wasn't making eye contact. Alicia looked over, thinking and hoping *Lernfähigkeit ist ein Zeichen von Intelligenz* Ability to learn is a sign of intelligence. "Turns out the non-sins of her grandmother were visited upon the child so Souchi's mom, Kimiko, had a tough time in a tough Korea. Massacres,[39] political revolutions, religious persecutions." Alicia stopped for a moment, brooding and muttered, "*Verdammte Mann Scheiße.* Damned man-crap."

Devon glanced up and added his fav word spice "fuuuugg."

"Souchi's mom, Kimiko, grew up right when a military dictator dictated prosperity for his people. Park Chung-hee invented the South Korean dynasties we know and love: Samsung, Hyundai, LG.[40] Just in time for Kimiko to take on the man-project who created Souchi. The man-project went AWOL around the time the girl-child got her name." Alicia looked hard at both Devon, a convicted man-project, and Matt, still merely an accomplice.

"The facts get a bit vague, but here's my take. Little Souchi was a survivor from the beginning. Anybody who knew something, she hung around. Learned whatever she could. Turning tin cans into kitchen utensils. Mending shoes. Writing, reading, 'rithmetic. At the local sports club, badminton, martial arts."

Devon, tentatively, added in two cents. "About that. You don't want to try any walnut table action without the express written consent of the management. She's apparently got some kind of Taekwando quals, including international full-contact competition victories. Age 16, she got rough with one Japanese girl. Busted her up real good to the edge of the rules. Rabble press made her a one-day Korean national hero."

Alicia continued, "A Samuelson INSEAD bird dog in Busan spotted Souchi's off-the-charts results on her *Suneung* CSAT, national college entrance exams, and put that together with the news story of her Taekwando victory. He checked up and connected the two. Intelligence, drive, resilience. Presto. Skipping the details, Samuelson settled financially with mama Kimiko and put Souchi through Cal Berkeley."

Devon shares, "We don't have to tell you her GPA as an international biz major or math minor, right?" Matt guessed she did pretty well.

Alicia wouldn't hide her gender pride. "That's how Souchi gets pulled off the streets of Busan and into Arctan International. One tough kid."

CHAPTER 18
ARCTAN DAY TWO,
A DREAMY STORY

Day Two. After lunch, Souchi met Matt and explained that the rest of his day would be in the Arctan Story Room. "There's too much inaccurate street mythology about Dr. Samuelson and Arctan. So, he wants new associates to hear the real story. He invented Arctan speed learning." They had taken the elevator to the 38th floor and were walking in a particularly quiet, plush-carpeted hallway. An engraved brass sign suggested this was the "The Schoolhouse." Rounding the corner, they came upon Svetlana.

"No intro needed. You've met. Svetlana asked to take it from here. Matt, let's you and I meet tomorrow in the lobby, eight AM. Good Luck and enjoy." She glided off.

"Hello, Matthew." Svetlana's patois was memorable. "Zank you again for the photo shooting, surely was good fun for me and vebpage vill be zensational. Promise, I do." He enjoyed the audio cocktail, neat.

"This time here, is internal PR. Is not my job, but I saw you on list and asked to do the guiding. Dr. Samuelson story video for news-bees." Matt enjoyed the mangled vernacular. "A good way to get everybody going." She was walking him further into the School.

"So let me explain today. We have a funny immersion experience for you." Svetlana turned to look at him, "OK with virtual reality type things, yes?" Matt nodded. He had some hours of Blizzard combat under his belt. That probably qualified.

"This will be, let me call it, impressing you. We want everyone to be on same one page with Arctan history. Dr. Dirk knows it helps making big ideas, thinking bigger." Matt appreciated the thought. "So, we give you Virtual Reality surround show." She pointed him toward a wall of windowless doors. "Over there is Story Room. We go together." They posed for iris scans, and with a click of acknowledgement, the door opened into a compact room with a comfortable-looking recliner and a single business-like chair next to a small desk. Matt was "Welcome" by name on the computer monitor there. It was playing the exact soothing music he favored.

Svetlana motioned him to sit in the recliner. He sank in. "Comfie, a lot, no?" She sat down across from him, knees almost touching. Matt's id slid.

Following Matt's eyes, she twisted to look down at her feet. "Yes. Very lovely, my ankles. Sad. My sister got athlete feets. Mine, legs and ankles, like ibex, no?" Matt blushed.

"Now, super glass for you." She handed him a set of virtual reality goggles slicker than any he had seen out in the open market.

"Wow. Really light, nice. Where'd you get 'em?"

She pointed out the Arctan logo on the sides. "Exclusive

in-house. Not affordable. Super high rez. Great sounds too.

"When we start, you hold onto these, one in each hand, OK?" She showed him a pleasantly pliable half-ball at the end of the arm of the recliner. "It will help you to move inside the glasses world."

Svetlana stopped him from trying on the VRs. "One moment only please. First to prep up. Here is for you." She extended her palm, where a white pill rolled in a disposable 30ml plastic cup. "Dr. Samuelson's recipe for better focus and to learning. Celaquinab." He eyed it, not happy. "Yes, yes, is OK. Arctan did long private contract, full research, safe for you. You will feel relaxed but very smart, video goes in easily and you will keep all you see.

"Matt. It is routine. Trust me, everyone does it. We also cross check your medical chart, surely no problem. No problem, Matt." Matt held back. "Of course, like signing-papers say, totally voluntary." Svetlana pulled back her hand a bit but left her wants in clear view. She wanted Matt to take the tablet. Matt tentatively picked up the med and tossed it down with water from the cup she pointed out on the desk.

"So, waiting, let me explain. You will relax in the glasses, watch VR all around you. There will be much detail, but don't worry, no notes, you will capture and keep in your head. That's what the medicine is doing. Then in three hours..."

Matt felt taken, "Three hours! For a corporate PR video? Seriously?"

Svetlana squelched her Russian temper. "That is all, only three hours. OK? Not PR, not You Tube. When done you will be all smart about history and details of how Arctan gets us here. Three hours. Are you ready? I am here to catching you at end."

Touching the goggles, "Try it on, go ahead, yes?" Matt pulled it on. There was none of the usual claustrophobic mass. The preview loop playing before him was mind-blowing. He was flying around, over and through rocky geologies and rain forests. Smooth, sharp, bright. And maybe the med was kicking in because he was feeling very, very perceptive. Svetlana was gone, out of mind. He was hyper-aware of the geo-texture, trees, waterfalls and his motion above it all. He couldn't know that the glasses measured his feel-good and then fed him more. His subconscious directed the VR into a deep, breezy forest.

He heard a voice, gentle, sounding like Dirk Samuelson but more... polished, reassuring. "Hello Matt. Oh, sorry, didn't mean to startle you. I've arranged for this walk-about so we could talk."

Although Matt didn't think it, he had never felt so sharp and yet so at ease. He had transported himself to a familiar forest, like home in Tennessee. The voice came again, from his right. He turned to see Dr. Samuelson, a few meters away.

"Matt, I've enjoyed learning a bit about you. I'd like to tell you more about myself and Arctan." Felt like friendship. "Let's start. If you have a question just ask. I'll be listening."

Dr. Samuelson started walking down a path Matt hadn't

noticed. The VR smoothly swept Matt along. The virtually real Tennessee forest felt moist. A warm breeze fluttered leaves. Time didn't have dimension as the two made easy small talk, something that Matt had never enjoyed before. The older man reminded Matt to call him Dirk.

They shared stories about growing up, Matt in Tennessee, Dirk in California. Matt was surprised by how much they had in common, boy style. Sports victories and defeats. Teacher-moments. Parent-flaws. Pet-loyalties. Dirk opened up, ashamed about a girl he'd jilted, indelicately. Matt told about his college girlfriend, Caroline, and the careless trouble he got her in. Dirk's sad empathy gave Matt a tinge of pain and Caroline dignity. As they moved through the sunlit-dappled ash and oak, Matt felt good with Dr. Samuelson's VR persona.

"Matt, healing patients wasn't enough for me. In the best of lives, I might have helped not even a hundred thousand patients. I wanted to be bigger. I hit on the idea of a scientific Universal Patient Data Registry. Private for patient and doctor but open for research. I pulled a team together and we worked out a foolproof way to protect privacy. Then we figured out how to rate every data point. Strong data had a high rating, weak data had a low rating. And we permanently attached a rated authorship before it got published. The combination of rating, authorship, privacy, and accuracy was compelling. We tested it in one midwestern town that needed the extra health care we offered in exchange for our data experiment. It worked. I pitched the system to investors."

Dirk stopped to look up. Rays of sunlight streamed

through the canopy and turned the floor ferns into every green that ever was or would be. "Great place you've brought us to, Matt."

Walking again, he laughed, "In the movies, this would be where Dr. Samuelson collects a billion bucks and Arctan is born. But noooo. Investor after investor didn't believe our algorithms could be secure enough. Back to the drawing board. We recruited some infamous hackers in Russia and Vietnam and India to break us. Scary. Tested our confidence. But our Timeless Evolving Dodge algorithm held off every attempt."

Dirk started chuckling. "Better than that, some young friends invented a hackback. Any unkeyed attempt to access our data got sent back an encrypted self-learning, vanishing virus. Offense defense. First time, we made like we 'forgot' to tell the hacker. Man, was he mad. Cost us a bundle to fix his network. But word spread fast. The respect we got from his shady friends was worth it."

Matt's subconscious had guided the VR to a gentle stream. Dirk halted and turned to Matt. "The investors loved it." Dirk and Matt jumped the freshet, VR style. It just happened, over they went. It felt good.

On the far side of the stream, Dr. Samuelson stood close, looking into Matt with blue crystal eyes. "The last, most important element. Trust. People trusted me. I promised them their dreams, both riches and Big Things, and they gave me their money. And then I made their dreams come true, plus a lot. That's when I knew I had a special skill."

Stepping over a water-slick, moss-covered log, a spider

web snagged Matt's face. Sickened, he jerked back. He hated spiders. To the core of his soul. From the depths of his childhood. Silken strands stuck, stretched, and then snapped in a subtle staccato cascade. He thrashed at the net entangling his hair, across his ear, clutching his cheek. More snapping. More trapping. He saw the spider angrily running toward him. Pincers and poison. Hairy. Bigger than a bird. The size of a dog. He choked a scream and slipped. Contorted in anguish, inhaling moist forest musk, he felt a hand press gently-firm on his shoulder. A voice penetrated his nightmare, starting with an accent of Russian, then becoming Dirk's voice. It eased his revulsion. "Whoa, that was an ugly one! But you scared it off. You OK Matt?" Matt turned and saw Dirk Samuelson looking down at him, concerned but calm. "You're lucky. It's just a tarantula, *Theraphosa andrewsii*. Gives a nasty bite, hurts but doesn't last. C'mon. You'll feel better away from here, they like the dark." Matt felt warmly reassured. The adrenaline rush started to burn off.

Matt's wishes headed them toward a brightening in the forest, up a steep rise. Dirk stayed in the lead. At the crest, they stopped. Dirk searched Matt's face. "Your color's coming back. That gave you a nasty start. Sorry, those things've been showing up here, moving north from Costa Rica with the warming climate. Let's get back on the brighter paths."

With Matt recovering, Dirk picked up where he left off. "Capital, contracts, sex. Before getting down to it, you have got to have trust. And that explains all that has happened for me, Matt." He stopped.

"I, and Arctan, we've never broken the trust."

Dirk started to walk again. "Of course, making people filthy rich helps." He laughed and continued along the path. "Arctan pulled in a couple billion bucks investment in three phases over two years. Our data-heads grew the database and solidified our numbers even more. And we nailed the most basic part. We incentivized patients and docs to tell us their outcomes. We knew how and when patients got better, or worse. Big Pharma couldn't buy our data fast enough, to the tune of seven, eight billion per year. And we built a billion-dollar income stream by getting patients involved in controlling their care and costs. Plus, all kinds of marketeers paid for data access. Arctan started making quite a bit of data-money." He looked over with a grin, "We were having a lot of fun." They walked on.

Matt's feelings guided them toward a waterfall. Silver water tumbled five meters down a black granite precipice making a foam sheath at the top end of a small grey-blue pool. A rough wood bench perched next to it. They sat down.

"Matt, I could have stopped there but the next step jumped out." Dirk's eyes shrouded for a moment. "Think about it, all that patient data. Age, location, treatment history for every ailment. Meds, doctor visits, outcomes. We had all that. But how to link start to finish? And there it was, mRNA transcriptomics. It had a rudimentary start just before the Roaring Twenty-Twenties.[41] Using Big Data to read blood chemistry."

"Your body reacts to everyday life and disease by minting messenger-molecules. mRNA. Arctan set out to fund a mRNA technology that could tell you what's happening in your body based on a simple cheek swab. And we did it Matt. We did it." Dirk stopped. Emotion swept over his face. It looked like he needed to compose himself.

"First money, then science, then product. The money wasn't so hard. My trust factor was at a peak and Arctan value-to-earnings was out of sight. Happy investors. We pulled in five billion to start. We bought two start-up tech companies and put some Arctan digital talents on the job. My favorite part was enrolling famous health centers like Mayo Clinic and Cleveland, MD Andersen, Peking Union." The persona of one of the richest people in the world looked at Matt sheepishly. "1 invoked FOMO, Matt. The Fear Of Missing Out. Join or be left out in the cold. Shameless. But not ashamed." Samuelson sales smile, famous for its warmth.

"To start, I had to get over the data security problem. I convinced the top medical people, one by one, of how tight our security was." Dirk shook his head, ruefully. "Tough job. The key was coercion. Misbehave, misuse our data and you got the worst imaginable pain, The Machine would ban you from our network. That put some fear in the users. My pitch led to mass collection of patient swabs to feed the mRNA disease data base. Then we put our deep learning and AI bots to work on a growing base of over ten thousand patients, two thousand data points each. Chemistry, clinicals, doctors, everything including the wash basin." Dirk chuckled, enjoying his humor.

"The richness of our database fed the riches of our investors, who lined up to fund 'swab, mail, result' medical diagnosis." Dirk looked at Mat. "Unlike some famous boondoggles of the past,[42] it worked. A year and a half, two years later, our clinical partners were happy. They all got a piece of the funding and a piece of the fame. Arctan got data.

"As obvious as it sounds, it still was a fight. Doctors, AMA, mad as hell. Health insurers were buying guns, or I should say, Congress. Then we lost a research center. Someone was taking shortcuts and The Machine had to cut out over a year's data. The project was running short of money." Dirk explained how much money they had spent. Matt winced.

"Then, I got lucky. We cured a California senator's husband. He was looking like a goner. Somewhere buried in our databases, Arctan's deep learning algorithm discovered a transcriptome match for him. He survived. The senator became our best advocate and recruited some heavy artillery, influential names, Matt. Recognizable celebrities. The second wave of funding rolled in."

Dirk started moving to a close. "There's a lot more I'd like to share. Our success in genomic therapeutics. And how we'll use the brain-machine interface to access the connectome[43] and attack mental illness." Perking up with energy, "And all our Big Technology, Big Buck moats, like the Q64 Quantum computers and Tera-Towers." Dirk quenched his excitement and surveyed the forest and fading light.

"But we're almost back. I'll just tell you about the San Francisco Datafile Exchange before we head in. I'm gonna talk fast but that Celaquinab will help you absorb it."

His speaking rate picked up. "Arctan. Big Data moving through our tills. Each customer with their rivers and lakes. So much data, so little time, Matt. Or better, so many restrictions. Arctan had AVA, Arctan Validations Algorithm, our way to sanctify data, give it quality ratings and even help customers improve their own stuff.[44] But there were tough walls around most of the data. Understandable. Proprietary sales, expenses, customer counts, hospital ICU failures, on and on. Proprietary. Our value was in keeping impenetrable walls. Trust. Still, I wanted to commodify data generally, to benefit everybody. It hit me, the rough and tumble Chicago Mercantile Exchange. Instead of pork belly futures, Big Data futures."

Dirk looked at Matt and saw comprehension. He charged on. "We had the most important asset. Trust, Matt. We had built the company on trust. No government snoops. Not selling someone's data without telling them, sometimes compensating them. We had a track record. People knew we would and could protect data.

I had access to people, Matt so we roped in important people. Companies and governments and civil rights people. ACLU. Arctan proposed a manifesto for data sharing. They refined it. Arctan adopted it. The San Francisco Datafile Exchange was born under the World Data Access Constitution. The first group signing on had revenues bigger than most countries' GDP.

AVA was already adding value to data lakes. Cross-checking reliability. Ascribing authorship, and the rest. AVA was telling our data-cloud-and-flow customers how to improve data, add value. The Exchange allowed companies to offer data lakes up for bid, with some obvious monetized shrouds to protect anonymity. Clients could bid against each other and the source. A source can get value from selling internal data or gathered data or processed data. Provisions to bid against others for first but limited timed access."

Matt, on Dirk's pause. "How did you keep track of compliance?"

"We invented Clockchain, a time-sampled, cross-correlated blockchain-like check on all transactions. Followed encrypted sampling theory to lower the data processing overhead but still have a log 7 interception rate.[45]

"Arctan was making money as brokerage, custodian. And as defacto police. Carrot and stick. The stick, you violate the rules, screw with data, Clockchain will find out. Worst punishment, you lose your access rights for a defined time. The equivalent of the French Revolution. Quillotine, off with your data head. Remember, when I started this, we were the major purveyor of data. Punishment time offline determined by The Machine. Automatic. Got to do the WDA Constitutional Process to be allowed back in, time-consuming. Plus, you get bad-branded, drop to the bottom of the ratings heap. Carrots. Be good, just keep playing by the rules. Good guys get reputation, benefits, privileges.

"Damn, Matt. The Exchange was the hardest thing we ever did. Down your way in Tennessee, I think they like to say, 'He's a hard dog to keep under the porch.' Well, that's our experience with data. But it's working. Too much benefit for all the large and small players so they won't let one jerk wreck it. All that growing consortium of data keeps going based on Arctan's trust quotient. And cost-effectiveness, our fees are...worth it."

They had been walking on the widening path toward the thinner part of the forest above the waterfall, and Dirk stooped down. "Hey, Matt, take a look at this." He pointed to a flame of color on the ground. "There's one of your favorite flowers." Matt's vision followed the point. He'd never seen such a striking flower before, but now, it was his favorite. "Look closely Matt. Look into the details." Taking the cue, without effort, Matt's VR view zoomed in on the delicate flower. An orchid, it didn't belong in his Tennessee forest but no matter, in this world, it was stunning. Flowing colors and textures and botanical details. A dew drop. Matt felt like he was a living part of the moist cells of the leaves. He inspected it all over, feeling completely normal.

"Matt, I believe that's what you can achieve with data. I think you can make it possible for anybody to live and move within any data and feel its meanings, make profound discoveries. I think you can do that Matt." Dr. Samuelson's words had crystalline edges; his voice carried the feelings of a music. Matt believed.

"I've got to go now Matt. You'll find the rest of the way. Souchi will set you up for another session. We can do some tech. I promise." Dr. Dirk Samuelson nodded adieu and set off down the path. He disappeared in the dusk.

Matt was inspired by the avatar, but he was drained. Svetlana's voice interrupted. "Matt. Story done. Time to coming back."

Removing the VR set, Svetlana suggested he recline,

close his eyes and rest. She chatted with him about his technology and the Team then let him go for the evening.

CHAPTER 19 EXOCULATION. GETTING TO KNOW YOU

Day Three, eight sharp, Souchi was lobby-waiting for Matt. They both liked punctuality.

"Sleep OK?" Souchi, filling Matt's vision, seemed to know his answer.

"Like a baby. That was quite a VR ride yesterday." Souchi beamed at him, like she had taken him out for his first beer.

"Funny, Svelana said something about being able to remember it all. I do."

Souchi had taken more than one cowboy and cowgirl to the Story Room. "Dr. Samuelson spent quite a bit of his own time and then invested heavily in research for Celaquinab and virtual reality-based Psycho-Dynamic Learning Experiences. It saves time. People get both the intellectual and the emotional side of Arctan in one go."

They were headed to the special elevators, walking crossways to the heavy traffic. She asked, "Have any surprises?"

Matt stopped in his tracks and blurted, "A spider, I got attacked by a spider! Biggest damn monster ever. Dr. Samuelson said it wasn't poisonous but seemed life-threatening to me."

Souchi stifled a laugh, careful to respect his honesty, "Yea. Mine was cockroaches. Everyone is different."

"Wait. You mean you did the Story room and got attacked too?"

"Matt, that's the point. PDLE and Celaquinab remove the inhibiting distractions of daily life. Relaxing on the couch, the VR cameras, temple band and hand-trodes read your subconscious so you take yourself to a place where you feel good. But it also sharpens your senses. Works on synapses in the corpus collosum for receiving and retaining information. The shocks help cement the lessons you were learning."

Matt was, well, dumbfounded at his innocence.

"Ever had a packed three-hour lecture and come away remembering 95%, no notes?"

Matt got it.

"And your mission. Clear how you fit in now?"

Matt described the flower and the vision-mission.

"So there you have it Matt. The Arctan story and your role. In three hours. What did Dr. Samuelson want you to come back for?" Matt rattled off Arctan's fingers in genomics and connectomics and quantum computing and the Tera-Towers.

"Ok. After a couple days, we'll fit in another session for all of that." They walked along quietly. "There is one topic he skips with all newbie's."

"What's that?" She explained that Dr. Samuelson always skipped "exoculation" on a first walkabout.

"Exoculation?"

"Exoculation. Digital tracking of everyone during an epidemic. Software, cell phone and implant to help catch contagion."

Matt was stunned, cold. "What! No way. Arctan sponsoring surveillance? On how many people?"

"Well, its contagion so you need to follow everyone."

"The whole country? Maybe the whole world?" Souchi let Matt go off on the idea a bit. Reinforcing what he already knew, she launched.

Plagues make people into walking petri dishes, talking or singing executioners.[46] Bees and ants can sacrifice individual interest to greater good but people, not so much.

People with a high SQ[47] thrashed about. There were stupidities.[48]

RNA fragments stayed ahead of the scientists impeded by bumbling politicians driven by anxious constituencies. Even with wholehearted support, a new cure for each virus required months, inoculations, a year. Minimum.

The twenty, or maybe thirty, million dead in the 1918 flu were long forgotten. Pandemics had never been a surprise but who believes epidemiologists? Each new contagion caught humanity with their brains down and superstitions up.

Then the virus picked up a fresh RNA strand. Viable for days outside the body. Transmissible even if you didn't have symptoms. High mortality even in the young and healthy. Unique twist, young women succumbed at a 5% higher rate than men. People got nasty. Victimization, buying guns, and using them.

Bodies. Images of piles in first-world cities popped up weekly. Cremations and composting[49] became tech rituals with tight controls to contain the RNA bloom within its cadaver. Caskets were replaced with HyperCons, hyper-containment bags.

Governments, corporations, states, cities, families, individuals were forced to change, not a human strong suit. Job stability is job one among elected officials, so governments became desperate. Notions about security, privacy and personal freedom died with the sick millions.

As another Big Die Off began, Dr. Samuelson directed Arctan to help engineer the recovery. Not a new one. Shin Bet in Israel had used it.[50] Even MIT worked closely with the convicted data bankers[51] to further develop it: IS, Interventionary Surveillance.

Matt was still struggling to reconcile surveillance with Dr. Samuelson's avatar. "But Souchi, spying is malignant. Even Arctan's brand for it is ugly."

"The name? Look, inoculation protects a person from bugs on the inside. Exoculation protects people from bugs on the outside. Arctan's X-Oc software tracks a person's cell phone and—" Matt interrupted, "X-Oc? And Arctan shares this with customers?"

"Yes, health care agents, law enforcement—".

Matt, still pissed, rolling his eyes, "Great. Just them."

Souchi plowed on, "—but only after stripping off personal information. Data all stays local, no central data bank. And it's only turned on when a pandemic warning is issued. That has to come from the Pandemic Security Council, Washington. X-Oc is launched solely if contagion is official. Every cell gets a notice every hour if it's on. No secret tracking."

"How thoughtful. So what if I want out."

Souchi looked at him sorrowfully. "Not an option, Matt. The idea is control. Sending everybody, willing or not, into isolation, social-distancing, or home stay or whatever, is a brute force, medieval[52] way to block the spread of bugs. X-Oc targets isolation precisely, person by person."

"Great theory, so what if I conveniently leave my phone off or maybe just 'forget it at home'. You can't track people who don't want to be tracked."

"Matt, do you remember how many people died in the last contagion?" She had him. So many dead. No psyche had survived unscathed. "Laws had to be written for X-Oc, Matt."

She outlined the plan. By law, everyone had to get the iChip implant, a sensor-thread. Made available at work sites, schools, pharmacies. Like polio vaccine in the 1950s.[53] It would store 6 hours of data, transmit two meters. Powered by bio-thermo-electricity. Sending critical personal data, like body temp, respiration, to the mobile where it linked with location and time. Detects breathing, talking, violent exhalations like coughing. The Law specified penalties if someone dodged data, like leaving the phone more than 2 meters from the implant for over 6 hours. Initial penalty lose cell phone privileges for a day. Second penalty, one month. Third penalty warrant for arrest. Souchi looked at him with some regret. "Discipline, Matt."

"So what good's all that data? You think surveillance stops disease?"

Souchi brightened. That was the genius part. "X-Oc kept track of touches and respiration. You get the virus by touching contaminated surfaces or by breathing someone's exhaled bug. Molecules, Matt. A few thousand atoms, nucleic acid bits. And not just from coughs and sneezes. The worst threat are the microscopic aerosols. Airborne, floating, not living but toxic. Inhaled, they go to the bottom of your lungs. Bam. And they come from everyone. Just breathing[54] and talking[55] and singing[56] and worst of all, laughing." She saddened at the malicious irony. "With the new bugs, you could die from someone's laughter, Matt, from laughter." He began to feel her grief. The heartache in his belly rivaled the headache in his brain.

Souchi pulled herself together. She wanted, needed Matt to hear the story. "The sensor data can keep track of the changing aura of aerosol you make and remember your pawprints, wherever you've been. Think about it, Matt, a four-dimensional contrail of everyone's potential to infect. Potential, calculated, numbered, less over time as the aerosol spreads and the pawprint germs die off.[57] Factors in the effects of local temperature, humidity, winds.[58] So X-Oc could track people, calculate the strength of giving or getting the germ, map risk. Pulled together with Arctan's Personal Exposure Algorithm based off the famous Ferretti-Wymant equation.[59] It highlights danger spots and alerts sterilization and testing teams. Most important, as soon as a person showed symptoms or tested positive, X-Oc tracks that backward to connect all their risk-contrail crossings. External inoculation, lets you know who's been exposed, how badly, when."

"So how come I didn't ever hear about this?"

"Dr. Samuelson had to shut it down. The local outrage – it only rolled out in one town—was so intense, it cast a shadow on all of Arctan's work. The mayor made Dr. Samuelson pull it. He said, "Let the curse run its course." Over time, his town took a beating, he died from pneumonia."

Death by viral drowning versus privacy. Pandemic. Big Brother. Matt was torn-up. "Souchi, I don't know. I still can't accept invading everybody's life."

Souchi demurred. "I can schedule you for a walkabout tomorrow with Dr. Samuelson. Ask him." Somehow, Matt didn't relish the thought.

CHAPTER 20 EXOCULATION. GETTING TO KNOW YOURSELF

A frigid gale, terrifying gusts. Scattered raindrops, painful as buckshot. Cutting ice crystals. Rivers of cream-thick fog. The drum of pounding surf up through his boots. Matt had been thrust in the path of a late-afternoon storm a hundred meters from the edge of a cliff overlooking a wind-tortured ocean. And he couldn't change the channel.

He had followed Souchi's suggestion to do an exoculation walkabout. On the couch, he even prompted Svetlana for the pill cup. But when he landed in VR-landia, he got hit with the old joke, "It was a dark and stormy night…"

Barely visible, across a stretch of tundra grass, close to the edge of the cliff, he could see a man, arms spread wide, defying the wind, pea-coat open, flapping violently. The man turned; it was Samuelson. He cupped his hands to his mouth and shouted at Matt to no avail. The wind overwhelmed everything except the pounding surf thirty meters below.

Matt fought his way toward the cliff. Samuelson was

afire. He was shouting, hardly audible, "Matt, *dobro pozhalovat*. Welcome to Kamchatka, man! This is fantastic! What a storm! What a life!" The ferocity of the wind and the rumble of the surf kept Matt from seeing Dirk as deranged.

Matt leaned in close. Dirk hollered, "I've got to show you something." Dirk grabbed Matt's shoulders. "Something, from my great grandparent's time here on the peninsula, Matt. Ritual sport. Helped steel kids to be fishermen in that." Dirk looked over his shoulder at the ocean, whitecaps on dead grey. Turning back, face close to Matt's, blue eyes ablaze. "Watch." He stepped back, looked Matt full in the eyes, turned, skipped once, then sprinted like a crazed vaulter toward the cliff edge. Matt couldn't help himself, "Dirk! Stop! Dammit, nooo." But Samuelson plunged ahead full blast. At the edge of the cliff, he leapt up into the air. Matt's stomach clenched. He gasped.

The updraft off the cliff blasted Dirk up and then back. Like a rag doll. He fell rolling into a heap, laughing on the turf.

Popping up, the gale drove him to Matt in leap-steps still laughing and yelling. "I can't let you try that. Takes some mentoring. And you're too important to our work." Looking over Matt's shoulder, shouting, "My cabin's over there. Let's go." He started off, dodging rugged tufts in a wind-pushed jog, looking more nine than CEO. Matt kept up, like a younger playmate, toward the rustic wood and wattle piece a quarter mile downwind.

Up close, Matt guessed it had been a shepherd's refuge. Not old, not new, not charming. Useful. The thick walls were made of opportunity stuff, driftwood, meadow sticks, mud sod. Low to buck the wind. On the lee side, a pile of firewood. Stubby, smoking chimney. Small windows up high made of the kind of wrinkled antique glass worth a fortune back in The Bay, shutters already secured open.

On the wooden step, Dirk pulled the cross-stick out of a rudimentary latch and the door popped inward. Leather hinges. Ducking to get in, Matt saw a roughhewn floor and table. One wood-and-rope bed frame, three rustic chairs and a field-stone hearth, fire crackling.

Closing the door, fighting the wind, "My blue eyes come from here, Matt. Russian, Petropavlovsk. Mutation of the HERC2 gene[60]. In a while, way south down the coast we might see some lights off the port." A sudden gust rattled the whole shed. Dirk smirked, "Then again, maybe we won't. C'mon, let's slide the table over near the fire and siddown." Matt felt oddly homey arranging a heavy wood table and chairs for a fireside chat with one of humankind's most productive intellects.

Settling down, leaning in, elbows on the table, focused one hundred percent on Matt, Samuelson asked, "Souchi said you had some questions about X-Oc and exoculation."

Matt had spent countless tormented hours thinking about surveillance. Now, he was speechless.

Dirk waited then let him off. "You know Matt, mass surveillance is a shit business." He let Matt digest the profane condemnation. "Can't we all just get along? Sadly, no. That's not how we're built. A threat comes up, too many folks go it alone. Take care of Number One, maybe close family. Even when taking care of others is in your own self-interest, like quarantine."

He stopped. The gale outside had risen. Dirk tilted his head to appreciate the straining of wood and mortar against the storm. It subsided and his mind came back. "Pandemic scofflaws. Gorged on the bounty of science, but not believing scientists when their message is inconvenient. So, without enforcement, self-quarantine doesn't work."

"Your parents probably told you about, protected you from the virus. Too many non-believers and there you go, explosive, exponential, runaway train. Even Tennessee, as I recall. Completely predictable. Whadaya think?" Dirk radiated sincerity.

Matt had gathered his wits. "Dr. Samuelson." But his boss stopped him with a smile. "Remember? Dirk, It's brief."

"Sorry. Surveillance flat-out bothers me. Big Brother, looking at everyone, all the time. Collecting personal data. Maybe you want to use the data for tracking and stopping epidemics, but who else gets access, and who controls the controllers?"

"So, your question has to be, can people trust data gatherers? The answer is no. Any more than you can trust bankers, stockbrokers, newscasters, doctors, plumbers. Where there's a buck to be made, there's always going to be exploitation. In this case, X-Oc and Arctan, we offer our corporate, my personal pledge to guard people's privacy. To not use data illicitly. Since Arctan and I began to get rich, I have always told people how much we're worth. It's a perennial PR message. Arctan and I got plenty. We have principles. And then we back up the pledge with performance. Immeasurable lakes of data have stayed safe with us for a decade. Our clients know that. Our PR sends that message to the public. Trust based on performance, Matt."

"What if someone breaks in, mines the mines."

"Understand. Matt, Arctan has managed billions, trillions of gigabits for over ten years. Hacks, sure. We slammed the door on innumerable invasions. Still going on. And we publicize our every failure immediately, keeping everyone informed. Transparency. Didn't sit on our failures like some of the famous cases a while ago.[61] We had to make some restitutions, which helped signal our sincerity." Celaquinab kept Matt right up with Samuelson's thinking.

"Best part. We aren't passive. We treat hackers badly. Our hackback security has injured some data thugs big-time. We spend a lot on punishing thieves. We make sure there's PR for that. People like to hear the bad guys get burnt. Can we guarantee perfect security? No. But we ensure that everyone knows when we have a problem and how we fixed it and how we hunted and punished the evildoers. Always about keeping the trust."

Matt. "Sure, OK. But people get creeped out by just thinking there's someone watching. Surveillance messes with their mind.[62] We start to doubt our freedom to be, what, unique, to think our own thoughts."

"That's why I insisted that Arctan tell everyone every time we pick off some data. A bigger danger, Matt, is most people start to not care. There's so much surveillance out there, not just the humiliating Facebook and

Google dustups in the 'teens, that people just give up. Sad, but as the world's biggest purveyor of data, we make a point of trying to inform everyone. Our teaching programs are famous."

Samuelson perked up to the sounds of the storm. "Matt. I lost track. People here call this part of the storm *napominaniye* The Reminder, like reminding us we're mortal." He stands up, "Just in time. Want some adventure?" Matt nods, curious.

"OK. We're out of firewood. If you're up to it, head out around back to the pile. At the front corner of the cabin, you'll see a heavy rope lashed to the wall. Hold onto it. Here. I'll help with the door."

Matt could barely get out as Dirk braced the door open. Dirk shouted something to him but it was lost in the roar. *Napominaniye* punished him. The wind hit in bursts; icy shrapnel stung his face. He slid along the front wall, pressed against it by the tempest, unable to look toward the cliff. Approaching the corner, he grabbed Dirk's rope. Just in time. The wind picked up speed as it screamed around the corner of the cabin, whipping him along the wall. He held on with two hands, driven down along the weathered wall.

At the back of the shed, he fell. The wind rolled him against a hummock. Staying low, he crawled into the wind shadow next to the wood pile. His heart raced. Then he saw Dirk's hand appear, opening a foot-square latch-door at the base of the cabin wall. Catching on, he passed one, two, three logs in through the portal. Dirk waved, enough.

Bracing along the back wall in a wind-beaten old man's

stagger, he pushed around the corner, into the strongest wind. He pulled himself painfully along the rope, hoping not to be blown loose from his mooring by an unpredictable gust. The sound, a shrieking, overwhelmed his hearing. He almost lost hold at the corner. Just in time, Dirk reached out, grabbed his wrist and half-dragged him to the door.

Tumbling over each other, Dirk struggled up and forced the door shut. "Thought the wind had you there."

Matt had been tested. "Dammit. Me too. That was treacherous."

They shook off the wet and stoked the fire. Settling back down at the table, they let the heat penetrate their clothes. Dirk asked, "You OK?" Matt nodded, feeling something close to elation at having survived a close one. "Wow. Memorable."

Dirk laughed.

Matt laughed with. "Some serious helpless floundering out there."

They fell into a clumsy pantomime of crawling and flailing. Dirk would have poured some vodka if the VR had any.

The tension and spoofing wound down. Dirk looked at the younger man. "Makes you think. *Napominaniye*, Matt. Mortality. Precious stuff."

They sat silently for a bit. Dirk let Matt bring them back to their discussion. "Can we go on?"

"Sure. Let's."

"You said X-Oc is on only for emergencies. Who gets to say?"

"As far as X-Oc, we helped write the law requiring an official declaration of pandemic emergency to throw the switch. At the Pandemic Security Council. Elected officials. And your objection should be, 'how can we trust people whose major concern is their own political neck?' Tough one there. I try to keep Arctan important enough so we can keep the politicians honest."

Matt was skeptical. "That means controlling political decisions. Ouch. Is Arctan trustable forever?"

Dirk shrugged. Not a good sign.

Matt pressed on. "Look at how dictators use data against enemies. I mean, like Putin years ago. Starts in the KGB, makes himself boss, rewrites the Constitution, stays boss for decades. And gets fabulously wealthy. He loved surveillance.

"Before him. Enver Hoxha in Albania. He had surveillance on the surveillance. The joke in Tirana, you would only see cars in twos: state security, and their security tail. A country of a couple million ended up with tens of thousands killed for violations of whatever self-serving law Enver invented.

"Alicia. Our own Alicia, her parents dealt with the Stasi. Communist paranoia polished by German thoroughness. They used surveillance to track and arrest her mom and dad. Killed 'em both. Who you gonna trust? Once the file collection starts, are your teachers or your minister giving data?"

Samuelson had not lived as a hermit. "I heard about Alicia's parents. I'm sorry. And Matt, I had family disappear in postwar Berlin. Russian blood wasn't all that welcome there. Like you said, surveillance on the surveillance. Problem. How to let Jeannie out of the bottle but not her demons. All I can say, the upsides have got to powerfully outweigh the downsides. For Arctan, pandemic death and suffering made the upsides urgent."

Samuelson leaned in close to Matt to be heard over the wind, rain and sleet pounding outside. "Matt, you might remember. Governments ignored the warnings about pandemics. So, the world had no vaccines ready. Only cure was to keep everybody apart. That saved lives but created havoc. Economies were devastated. Then, the word on the street said that another virus was just around the corner.

"That's about the time the fastest mobile makers developed the iChip to implant cellular behind the ear. Communicate without the handheld chunk. Personal assistant software, improved voice recognition. Walk-around talk-around, hands-free. The chips, micro-scopic, fit inside a needle, created such a sensation that the companies bought laws allowing even tattoo-ists and hairdressers to implant them. Loaded with all the biosensors people loved for their competitions, and then some. Social media flourished with people comparing their biometrics. 'Privacy? Who cares? I got more steps with fewer heartbeats than you.'

"Then the epidemiologists started talking again. Bigger trouble coming. Pandemics were no longer once a century. Vaccines still took a year to invent and deliver. Quarantines had squashed the world economy, which hadn't recovered. Lockdowns were a sledgehammer. We needed a surgically precise means to rapidly find people who were sick and limit who they infected.

"There was plenty of accumulated data from the pandemics. That data and the iChip, Matt. Together that goes straight to exoculation. Biometric chips measuring respiration, heartbeat, body temperature. Senses when you touch something. When you talk to someone. How loud you talk. How much you laugh."

Matt felt his stomach churn. Souchi. Laughter spreading the bug.

"All of that produces aerosols Matt. Most of them hang in the air for hours. If you got a respiratory virus, you launch it in the aerosols. But scientists had already measured how much aerosol we make moment by moment, breath by breath, laugh by laugh. Why? Because in the pandemic, with people dying like so many poisoned locusts, details like that fucking mattered, Matt."

Samuelson's F-bomb jolted Matt.[63]

"The chip measures how much bug you leave around moment by moment. Picture this. We all have a respiratory aura and a contrail as we go. If we're sick, the contrail has bugs in it. X-Oc calculates how many bugs we shed into the contrail. And its trackable with the iChip implant and your cell. A cough, fever, odd heartbeat. Better check, you could be a bug shedder.

"When someone registers high enough numbers, find and inform. Follow their contrail back in time. If their contrail envelopes someone else, better contact them too. Instead of shutting down a whole city, you focus on individuals, clusters.[64] Good for them, good for everybody."

"Souchi said you ran a test of X-Oc but shut it down."

"We had a deal with a city in the Midwest. Can't say who but sizeable, prosperous enough to have some IT. Almost half the town had already gotten their iChip, in fact some even had the stereo implants. Arctan funded the university to run the X-Oc in a part of their town. We involved their IT people and lawyers from the start. Notified decision makers, they contacted their constituencies. Everyone in town seemed on board. Before the launch, everyone got a series of short messages on their cell phone, explaining what was coming, how it would help protect people, minimize lockdowns, keep life as normal as possible. Etcetera. Even a form to be excluded. Content all worked out by our people with their people. We verified that our messages were being read by over 87% of the inhabitants. We launched with anybody who consented."

Samuelson paused for effect. "Third day, X-Oc was building a web of contrails, we got a hit. One of our subjects pops up abnormal. We call her to our doctor, tests positive with the virus. X-Oc shows she had crossed paths with three people at a church choir rehearsal. Two-point eight times threshold exposure. They got notified. All asymptomatic. Health department got notified. The mayor got notified. Then hell broke loose. I won't go into detail, but civil liberties people got involved, church attorneys. University tried to re-explain the technology but to no use. Even when that one contrail-crossing discovery led to 14 additional infected people.

"I had a choice. Fight the mayor, who was afraid he would be blamed. Or bail out, pay the price. But if we fought it, I would bring Arctan out from under cover of the local university medical center which was running the whole show.

"Our crisis management team said that any attempt to stay the course, explain the risk benefit, would lead to a monumental PR hit. We had fought and won many of those battles. But this time our trust quotient was at risk. That intangible asset is our business, Matt. If we lose trust, our data business collapses. Our competitors, always less than seventeen percent of market share, would have a PR field day. The SF Datafile Exchange, house of cards." Samuelson shook his head.

"I shut it down.

"As it played out, within ten days the town had a major outbreak, numbers shot up. Another two weeks, deaths. With that, the mayor and the rest all just wanted to ignore X-Oc. Our team, they'd worked with people in the town, was devasted. They knew some of the dead. Did Souchi tell you the mayor died too? The rest, dumb thought, is history. Like I said, Matt, a shit business."

A powerful gust smacked a window shutter closed. They both startled.

Samuelson, "Matt, with your permission, I want you on the team writing Arctan's pandemic strategy. When the time comes, you can help decide, to launch or to stifle X-Oc.

"Take a day. Consider it. Our technology is in the vault." Without pride or persuasion, "It's ready."

Thinking out loud. "But I'm not sure we are."

Dirk Samuelson stood up. "There's a lull outside. I've

got a four-hour drive over some rugged terrain to meet family down in Petropavlovsk. You'll be getting back the usual way. Svetlana will ease your reentry. Matt, I hope you can figure this out. I haven't." In a moment, Dr. Samuelson was gone.

Matt sat and waited for Svetlana to coax him home. He was relieved to relax for a half hour and chat with her about ARz.

And forget pandemic surveillance.

CHAPTER 21
TEAM BUILDING

Matt's request for funding had gone straight through. Devon and Alicia were in. Not the usual corporate reaction when someone tries to hire friends. Screw loyalty, he needed their expertise. At the customary couple grand plus per day, Matt was bringing on capable techies. And some loyal support.

Matt's friendship with Devon and Alicia wasn't just 20-pound Eleikos plates and punches. Their friendship started up over lifestyles built on bleeding-edge tech. Visually they were the most unlikely Three Mouseketeers anyone ever insulted. Devon's lanky, loose, almost two-meter, rock climbing frame and devil-may-care lifestyle alongside Alicia's diminutive but solid meter-and-one-half body and resolute, in-your-face gaze were odd cufflinks to Matt's Greek stature and dark Mediterranean Adonis.

Devon had been a talented grad student in optics at the prestigious University of Rochester, specialized in visualization for virtual and augmented reality. His primary support came from DARPA. Though he couldn't talk about it, he knew a lot about the heads-ups displays that give "situational awareness to the soldier on tomorrow's battlefield." Through DOD, he spent plenty. On a secretive arrangement, he had left the doctoral program and was given lab space at Berkeley's Helen Wills Neuroscience Institute.[65] Rumor suggested that the Army had paid handsomely to corral his publishing. Still, he had become a world-recognized, unorthodox innovator.

Alicia, was from the branch of the pre-WWII Hoescht AG family that was trapped in East Berlin at the end of the War. Her parents got in "some terminal trouble" with the Stasi, *Ministerium für Staatsicherheit* Ministry of State Security in the late '80s. Born before The Wall came down, she and her adoptive parents escaped via Tunnel 57 and fled to Frankfurt am Main's tough *Hauptbahnhof* neighborhood. After one too many uncomfortable late-night encounters, they moved south into Munich's bohemian Swabing. Alicia studied biology at Ludwig-Maximilians-Universität and collaborated at the Fraunhofer Gesellshaft. She left Prof. Prof. Dr. Mueller von Minden's neurophysiology *Arbeitsgruppe* to pursue her research in the States. The Work Group had become too regimented after von Minden passed on at eighty-eight. His replacement didn't like Alicia's fluorescent hair color, so he cut her funding for retinal neurophotonics, the leading-edge tech to use light pulses to probe nerve cells. Kooky sounding but it worked. She chose the best of four offers for its climate and open-minded community.

In her new home at Stanford University's Musk Laboratory for Advanced Biomathematics, Alicia was a major contributor to the growing brain-computer interface science. While Big Names like Elon and Hawking had warned that artificial intelligence threatened humanity,[66] Alicia pushed fearlessly on its envelope.

Matt had invented technologies that would allow any

user, with modest training, to get inside of a massive data base and "feel" its shape and flow and impact and to draw conclusions from the experience. His system could decipher a million data points as intuitively as finding a wine opener buried in a cluttered kitchen drawer. And it could learn and grow with its user. His ambition exceeded that of most corporate R & D departments, but then naivete is how youth chases startling discoveries.

Fortunately, these three geeky stars were about to do Big Data a Big Favor. They just didn't see the dark clouds in that direction.

CHAPTER 22
HARDER THAN IT LOOKS. THE PITCH

Matt's problem was to inform his buddies that they were hired. Devon and Alicia had a volatility that kept Matt from telling them right away about the Arctan consultancy. All three shared ethical concerns about Big Data and Arctan.

To lure them in, Matt aimed at their bellies. He invited them to Kim a Jumma Ne, the Korean mom-and-mom restaurant where they had celebrated occasional victories. At their first visit two years before, maternal Ma Minjung sat them at the best smoking BBQ pit and handed them the customary 25-gallon plastic bag.

"Dude!" Devon was delighted. "Doggie bag for a Great Bernard. This lady knows how to feed." Minjung laughed salacious Korean and stuffed his jacket in it.

"Yo, even bedda! Splash bag!"

In the beginning, Minjung practically hand-fed Devon. She relished his foodie-joy. They learned dining protocol by watching: wait for the marinated pork or chicken or beef or squid or shrimp or intestines, nibble on the *banchan* side dishes, *ko choo* spicy seaweed salad, then the *kuk* rich salty broth and maybe some *kongnam-jul* seasoned soybean sprouts. Lubricate with *soju* rice liquor, green cap is safer, and Hite beer.

Tonight, these seasoned veterans laughed their way through a kilogram of various animal parts, four spices and deciliters of *kimchi* and *banchan*. They eventually hit an intermission. The grill bore no further scrap, and the glasses were nearing empty. Alicia asked, "So, whazzup, Matt." The two recruits with piercing gazes, wanted an explanation.

"I've hired you two at Arctan." Audacious and happy-dull in soju and beer, Alicia and Devon piled on.

"Fugginhell."

"Cool, uhhh, exactly when did I send in that application?"

"Ooooo. I just can't wait to get my first retirement check!"

"Do we get maternity leave?"

"Tell me it was my Gucci tie and Armani suit that clinched it."

Matt let the abuse roll on. He knew it would ebb and when it did, their curiosity would get the better of them.

"We have been BS-ing forever, about the Brain-Machine interface. Well, I proposed and Arctan has agreed to make you consultants in that project. I need you two to make it work."

"Oooo-Kay. Soooo..." not that Matt could read humans, especially women, but Alicia was already turned on, though camouflaging her arousal, "Details?"

"There are three major blocks to computer-power a

human. What are they?" Matt was not a salesman; he couldn't tell a lie. But he could tee-up an argument based on honest passion.

Alicia, trained in Germany to not let guys give a stupid-answer first, shot back, "Information in, Information out. Promptly. Computers can manage vast amounts of data super-quick, but how do you get that to the Human, in real-time? Not solved."

He'd laid a good trap. "And second?"

Eyes on Devon. He had never before seen a grandiose idea (or potential mate) he didn't immediately and energetically love. So Matt was surprised when Devon answered tentatively, "What channel to use? What sense organ to move the slave-computer's information to the master-human's brain? People don't like holes in their skull, not yet anyway."

"And the third hurdle?"

In a mumbling between Devon and Alicia it was agreed that the data would have to be streamlined so the Boss and slave could adjust on a whim, intuitively. To function fast, the computer needed to anticipate the boss's needs.

Matt, brilliant grad student, clumsy salesman, knew it was time to kill it. Young, naïve and grand, choking-up he said, "Human and machine. The Big Opportunity in Artificial Intell. And who, what three people do we know, are best positioned to attack the three hurdles?"

CHAPTER 23
DEVON'S LAB

Matt had been "down to Devon's lab" any number of times before. Devon had sent a specific time to Matt's e-planner. The request was for lunch the next day right after their Korean barbeque at Ma Minjung's.

Berkeley's "B101 - Information Sciences" building was the usual university techie structure. Undistinguished exterior and, behind swinging wood frame doors, an echoing, linoleumed entryway featuring a bulletin board plastered with daily-life posters like, "Sofa to give away, no big stains" and "O-Chem 112A Notes for sale."

Matt took the stairs to the basement, a narrow corridor with cinderblock walls painted in undefinable bland colors so often that all sharp edges had been rounded over. The leisurely visitation changed as Matt approached the metal door four steps to the left from the stair well, featuring an officious sign, "Authorized Personnel Only," and "All Visitors Check In." Through the Serious Door, he encountered a scholarship student putting in time behind a chest-high counter.

Matt wrote his name and then Devon's name on an old-school clip board, surrendered a photo ID, scanned his fingerprints and waited, standing of course. The student watchpuppy tapped four numbers on the telephone and announced, "Male named County here to see you."

In a minute, Devon popped through the door next to the desk with a lot less than his usual enthusiasm. "C'mon dude, filet mignon or Souffle de Canard?" his sarcasm, though repeated, was original each time. They made their way to the nearby restricted-access dining room down the hall. After sorting through the non-decisions of one tasteless versus another tasteless lunch option, time-efficiency and ketchup being the only reasons to dine in the cafe, Devon observed, "Man, not like Minjung's, huh?" and stared pointedly at Matt. "Hey, Matt, I apologize for being so cool toward the conversation last night. I think you've got something big, really big, and I want in. But there's a problem."

The reason for the lunch date became suddenly apparent. Devon looked across the room and Matt's eyes followed. Lunching at one of the tables were two US Marshalls, serious, square guys replete with badges and web gear. Their message was clear. What happened here, in this basement, stayed here.

Matt had dealt with the weight of intellectual property most of his adult life. Wielding IP was one arrogance of being a part of the world's Geek Squad. But Devon was sending a wordless alert that he had to deal with a different kind of IP burden. It came under various labels, including National Security, but in the end it always meant the same thing; unlike patenting to protect commercial IP, these secrets were not to be shared, ever, for any reason and woe to they who should violate that creed.

"I see. Right. So... how about those Giants. Great game yesterday, huh?" Matt didn't realize it wasn't baseball season.

"Thanks, Matt. I'm glad you get it. Those dudes are just the bottom feeders, enforcers. Up above them, serious shit. I don't want to spend several years holed up in a Danish embassy somewhere."

"Nice people, the Danes, Devon. But you'd gain weight dude. Besides, we need you. There are no replacements. You're the Man."

"Yea, that's what she said too. Just, we gotta be smart."

"Got it. Think on it. We've got your back. You need to be safe."

Devon was crucial. The one scientist Matt or Alicia could name who might get signals into the brain harmlessly, no holes. Matt left deflated but not defeated.

Over the next days, at places checked by Devon to be certifiably private, the three of them discussed the depth of Devon's knowledge. These places tended to be beer dives, like Zig's, non-corporate, serving local brews. A single security camera would have driven off the clientele like the emergency claxon horn on a coastal freighter.

Devon clearly felt the weight of his security status at the first sharing. Hunched over suds around a small, sticky corner table, Devon went back several years. "Then I got an inspiration. The stars."

"How cool," he recalled. "When we look at a star, any star, we see a point. While each one is huge, most bigger than the sun, by the time the light crosses space they're only the tiniest point the eye can manage." He broke off his flight to check that Matt and Alicia were with him.

"You think you see a everything out there like a movie screen. But you only use a fraction of your megapixels on a tiny spot known as the macula."

Alicia held her tongue. Devon was wandering where she had done real science. She didn't interrupt. "The starlight we see is stimulating, maybe, a dozen pixels. Out of all those megapixels, we only use a few to see a star."

"But then I got curious, 'How much light is a star?' and I found something amazing. The dimmest stars we can see sends around a billionth of a billionth of a watt into your eye. Like nothing, dude. Attowatts. The eye is the most amazing light detector there is. We can see as little as one photon of light at a time. Damn." An optical scientist with a top-security military clearance was starstruck. "Damn. Eyes are amazing." His pals were riveted. Devon was talking to himself.

He snapped out of his dream. "Miraculous, I guess, but then, to hell with miracles, I wanna make stuff. So I figured out how to inject targeted star-points of pulsed light into human eyes. Took me three years on top of decades of all those other people's work. Oh, and thirty-eight million dollars."

"Micro-lasers, molded in a contact lens, shooting messages into the eye, thought-by-thought."

Devon shrugged. He had wrapped up his briefing. They knew that they had gone into territory where the cafeteria-Marshalls' boss had a legal interest. And yet they continued, their curiosity overruling caution. Devon obliged them, his own imagination more vivid and compelling than that of a feverish suitor on the way to a stupid infidelity.

CHAPTER 24 MARITAL FIDELITY. PACIFIC HEIGHTS

Carlotta eased her car, assembled *con amore* in Sant'Agata Bolognese, up to the garage door and waited. In a scant 850 milliseconds, the home security system would authenticate the plates, the car's e-ID, her facial profile and, finally, that there were no unusual features in the surrounding landscape. When all the survey parameters fit the trained profile, the door began to slide open. Ms. Cabrini was home.

Dr. James Brogan's second wife had chosen to drive the Lamborghini because it was all hers: color, model, suspension, engine options, country of origin, cash payment. Unlike some trophy wives on this hillside neighborhood, Carlotta gave no reason to be viewed as kept. She was fully capable of and was affording herself every material pleasure. Her family, atop San Francisco's power elite, her education, corporate attorney, her savvy and guts had allowed her to accrue a fortune that was purely hers, at least in a legal sense. It's hard to get Carlotta-rich and not have bent a few rules or rulers.

This had not been a day filled with gym work, hot-yoga, mud facial, Gucci, stone massage or love tryst(s). Carlotta had overseen a staff of two attorneys and four paralegals complete the paperwork on another patent-loaded start-up for one of her venture capital clients. The terms would please them, eventually confound their supplicants and, of course, further enrich Clayborne, Hamilton and Cabrini. Climbing out of the nereid blue car, she was done-in. Minus the physical bruises, she was much like a successful NBA or NHL star, right down to her juicy CHC hourly compensation.

Carlotta was grateful to expect that her husband, soothed like she with a glass of chilled D'Alic, would not be frisky this evening. For both of them, this was a time to enjoy the acquisition of assets and triumphs at the expense of less regular conjugal moments. In any event, Carlotta had exercised her libido while studying at, serially, Vassar, Smith then Wellesley (family connections greased the transfers) and later Harvard. Banned in Boston was a challenge she had accepted and nearly achieved, although the two years of her JD education were far more settled, focused on loving just one professor, to mutual benefit. No, tonight would be wine, conversation and counting, not courting.

She was also expecting Dr. James to bring home special good news, and that he would attempt to suppress it until dinner time; Carlotta would play along, there were two hours to fill. She enjoyed what she could of her husband's style. The awkward, boyish streak with which he approached marriage was cute, balanced against his occasional moodiness when corrected or when he perceived she had had a better idea. She and he were equals in many things, providing stability: comparably wealthy, good looking, healthy, lovers of agile cars by the half-dozen, socially adept. This union could endure; besides, she was the Italian.

Carlotta knew plenty about Dr. James Brogan before she agreed to marry. He had moved his PhD dissertation into the traditional Palo Alto garage. Three and a half years later he cashed out with 125 million, shortsticked at least another hundred mill by smart investors, divorced his grad school sweetheart, and went off to try a variety of New Age enticements. Although he had been a sufficiently bright engineer, he was not good at life-style experiments. He returned to the Bay VC scene after a year, not for the money, since he was Scot-frugal, but to prove to himself that the first success was not a fluke. He applied his technical skills and entrepreneurial reputation to help two Valley-tech-youth skyrocket a biotech company, while cashiering another eight figures in stock options, ultimately fulfilled by the IPO. The venture culture gossip around Brogan attracted Carlotta. She guided him into a beautiful wedding and sumptuous reception. Their lives were going very well and getting better, but she became aware that his achievements were, unlike the father she so admired, based more on technology and careful planning than on a dominating, powerful personality. Still, Carlotta had few complaints.

She gave domestic staff advisories about the scheduled dinner, including the night off after serving. She would wait for James to come home from what might be seen as a relatively easy job as Chief Tech Officer at Arctan International. James had been hired to supplant day-to-day for Dr. Samuelson who needed time away from operations to pursue "visionary" projects on behalf of Arctan. James Brogan was selected for his successes, technical acumen, and cool, well-met personality. Arctan's founder was aware of James' connections, a significant number of which derived from Carlotta's family and law firm; he was not yet aware of how such connections could irrationally skew the future.

As smoothly quiet and as visually loud as Carlotta's coupe was, so Dr. James Brogan drove big. He eschewed Italian automobiles, even with German components and funding, in favor of British tradition. In his Bentley Continental GT, he faced-off, like Carlotta had, the same security confrontation at the garage door, he passed the same smart test but once admitted, Dr. James dismounted in a fever, not from shepherding six hundred horses to stable but from the day's victory. He hadn't ever earned hourly. Entrepreneurially speaking, he earned in bursts of equity harvested through patient years of persistent grooming, falling, re-saddling. And today he had seen the table set for a coming harvest festival. He was enjoying an unaccustomed heaviness in his trousers.

"Whoa, Big Boy!" managed Carlotta in the warm rarewood and brass vestibule, after James lingered on her lips beyond the usual perfunctory welcome-home peck. "Someone had a good day, or just happy to see me?" She knew she had to shift gears from the planned sweet relaxation to mission orientation, if not position. Vassar-Carlotta began to follow a sustaining trajectory that prevented James' unexpected ardor from becoming a two-minute stand. (She had tried that modality and enjoyed the amusing before and after more than the fitful during.) So, she aggressed. Athletically wrapping one leg behind him, she returned the kiss, raising it one point five. This surprised and slowed James; she followed up promptly with a firm hand on his buttock, just enough to kindle his carnal without deflating his man-plan. No sense wasting pent-up testosterone. Following Carlotta's plan was going to be good for him and decidedly improve her prospects.

And the evening developed. She'd let him get somewhere, and then parry, enjoying his attentions and her own successes. Grabbing became touching, groping became caresses, speed begat shyness-arousal. James could hardly realize how well he was lovemaking and certainly was too distracted to question the source of her leadership authority. They proceeded through the manual of arms, nape, legs and so on. She, wistfully, never needed to resort to something unusual or exotic. She simply kept James on an upward roll. With delaying tactics that would have made Sun Tzu[67] proud, Carlotta continued to heighten their arousal until they finished, each with their own marvelous climaxes, reward of the love gods for what was originally intended to lead to two, usually miserable, decades of rearing offspring.

Dinner followed the acts, languorously; Lupita had discretely withdrawn to her quarters at sounds of the early *consejos* flirtings. Resembling kids who had just completed their third or fourth experience together, Carlotta and James recollected and blushed and giggled. Finally curled up in bed, (they had pursued their satisfactions on various furnitures in the vestibule) they slept without reflection or awakening, the second reward of the love gods. Along-the-way, Dr. James Brogan had forgotten to announce his day's business victory. Not surprising, given the spontaneous, carefully orchestrated sex that interfered. It was better that way. Carlotta Cabrini Esq., the consummate attorney, would never ask an unnecessary question, but there were aspects of Dr. James Brogan's current venture that could have dampened the night's passions.

CHAPTER 25
DEVON LIGHTS
UP ZIG'S BAR

Greasy light bulbs gave Zig's the shadows thinking people who shun social media crave. It also featured a thick red ale, heightening each night's creativity.

Devon burst in. Five minutes late, he didn't mind that his fav beer was ordered and waiting. Zigs' red was better a little soft with the chill knocked off. Matt and Alicia owed him a good ration of shit which they delivered with enthusiasm; they weren't parents so they could teach by pillory. Didn't matter, since their last meeting Devon had ascended to pig heaven and was loving it.

Without coming up for air he live-streamed, "So guys, I'm all in and it ain't 'cause it's honorable or that I'm looking for trouble or cheap thrills or even that I wanna screw The Man or be hero or heel. Matt's idea and our humble part in it is too important to bury in a muddy political foxhole."

"Let's do this. Let's build the brain computer interface."[68]

Matt and Alicia had already concluded that Devon couldn't say no. The story about stars had betrayed him. He needed time, they had given it, and now, time to rock.

"So, here's some details. My contact lens lasers can shoot near-HD video real time onto the wearer's macula." He cast a brief glance at Matt to see if was up on the macula.

"It can be tuned to control how much video you get. If you don't need to watch the real scene, then add VR and you get more video. If you want a subtle overlay, like just object outlines or labels, then turn down VR and you get AR, 'augmented reality.'"

"No head set."

Matt and Alicia shared a WTF glance. They understood.

Matt looked skeptical. "Wait. Where's all this data coming from?" Moving data was Matt's thing.

"Right, thought of that. Warning, the following may upset some viewers."

"Try us." Alicia, as resident biology expert, was stoked.

"The power– remember all this has to be connected to the outside world – goes through capsules implanted in the user's eyebrows."

"What!" Matt had been seduced by every detail so far but now he felt like, not puking, but a bit sick. "Devon! you need surgically stuffed eyebrows to use this thing? I'm thinking the slogan will be, like, 'Neanderthal-me.' You gonna get Stallone to do the advertisements? Slug line: 'you too can look like Luca Brazie'? Sheesh man!" Devon glared. Matt was sounding like a Baptist minister confused that his unwed teen daughter was pregnant.

Alicia was thoughtful, in a thinking kind of way. "How small have you made these implants, Dev?"

Grateful to be dealing with an open mind he explained, "Gracias to DOD, I can pack the rechargeable battery, and electronics, including comm channels, into a flexible, rod-shaped device about two-point five millimeters diameter and 38 mm length. Will run indefinitely by being self-winding, by the way, acquired for a tidy licensing fee from Tissot watches."

"So it can be inserted with a, say, 8 gauge canula?"

"Thank you, Alicia, yes. Hey, that was good. Thank you," looking reproachfully back at Matt.

"But I was still talking about the full range of capabilities. That video part was easy, conventional." Devon treated "conventional" like it was a four-letter word. "Importantly, I found how to make this device inject ideas to the user at supra-normal data rates.

Normally humans allow themselves to be satisfied with conversational speed." Imitating an exaggerated speech pattern, "Hi Maud, good...to...see..you...today. How..are...Billie Joe...an'...Bubba?" Shaking his head, "I mean, gawd, let's move along. Which isn't so hard. Have you ever discovered a tool or beer can in a messy place, flashing across the corner of your eye, a sliver of the 'Budweiser' showing? I have. So, I got to thinking, 'Dev, how do we build that into the contact lens so it can transmit data and the human can take it in but at pumped up, higher rates?' Well, I done it."

Matt and Alicia were hooked, but skeptical.

"First, cut loose the Western, letter-built word model. Think Confucius, think Asian. Concentrate on digesting shapes. Consider how dogs can spot another dog amid a sea of legs at a hundred, maybe a hundred and fifty meters. Or how man-dogs can spot a specially shaped calf amid a sea of calves. No words, no letters, no diction, no vocab, just pure pattern recognition. Based on what? Interest and training. And those messages can be picked up even somewhere out of the corner of your eye, right?" Matt got it. Alicia got it, too, but at a somewhat higher level; she had neurosensory vocabulary for it, though she took exception to Devon's sexualized calves.

"I speculated. Might it be possible, for sake of argument, to train selected rods or cones to tell the brain it had received a signal and that signal meant....whatever?" Devon was re-living the moment of discovery.

Devon became temptress. "Sooooo...?" letting the next thought roll.

Alicia, feeling an almost conjugal moment with Devon, "...you could map a few thousand-word vocabulary onto peripheral rods and send in word patterns as fast as video. Non-invasive brain machine conversation through the eyeball."

Devon. "How fast? A human can take computer data in directly to the brain through retinal neurons, dozens of words per second. Ten times people-talk rates." He took a breath.

"With proper training and an interest."

"If that were true...," Matt began to imagine the impact of Devon's computer-to-human port.

"Not if, Matt, not if." Devon leaned back into a proud look that said he had already delivered for the DOD.

Alicia leaned on the sticky table. "So, Dev, these contact lenses can be imprinted front to back with molecular lasers and still be contact lenses?"

"Yup." Devon practically vibrated, trying to stay patient.

"And that includes steerable organic micro-laser diodes, that can be scanned around on the retina?"

"Yup again. I can flash and sweep 'em like laser spotlights." Devon was funning, but Alicia and Matt sensed he could back up braggadocio with solid reality.

"Wait, power! How to get power to the lasers?" Alicia was sure that power would be the demise of Devon's devices.

"The lasers and detectors are molecular-level picowatt devices. Power comes from integrated photovoltaics. Like solar cells. As long as the wearer isn't in the dark for too long, room light will keep everything running. Peak power in the near-IR so even with eyes closed there's still enough light through the eyelids to run 'em."

Devon reached into his backpack. He tossed an inch-thick tome on the table. "Merry Christmas. Be careful with this. Don't want an electronic version out there so here's a print copy. It's all in there, description, photos, test results. But guys. Lose track of that and its goodbye Devon, hello San Quentin."

A quiet came over the table. Unveiling discoveries had happened many times before in bars and *bierstube* and pubs and *izakaya*. Was this equal to Einstein's General Relativity or Lemaitre's "a day without a yesterday"[69] or Planck's quantum? Probably not. But the three were struck silent by this peek into the future.

Matt was satisfied that Devon had mastered a way to send computer data into a human brain via the eyeball. They still needed a way for a human to communicate back without the archaic keyboard or clumsy speech recognition. Did Devon have a solution?

"Getting a human signal back to the slave-computer is, I gotta admit, a tough problem. That's where I think Alicia can help."

A normal person would have felt intimidated, but Alicia was already preoccupied. "You can use your organic semiconductor structure-building to make detectors, right?"

"Right."

"Can you match your injector lasers with detectors, same technology?"

"Uh-huh. Just tested the third generation, seven prototype devices, it's essentially the same."

"I gotta sleep on it." Alicia got up and drifted out of Zig's.

CHAPTER 26 READING YOUR MIND. THE BRAIN-MACHINE INTERFACE

After the red ale-fueled night at Zig's, Alicia went AWOL. She didn't show up for the usual workouts at Pat's Gym nor was she spotted at her scheduled sparrings.

Some gym rats began to wonder and when humans lack data, they turn prurient. New love interest? Guy? Gurl? Freaky? Guy-gurl and freaky? Alicia had appetites and imagination to spare but not enough to deserve the soaring gym-rat stories her absence inspired. Of course, neither Devon nor Matt could defend her with facts but they were convinced she had gone off on a creative bender, in search of a way to let humans talk back to computers without the silly little fingerings or that spelling- or speech-impaired Siri in the way. They were confident that she would come up for air, hopefully sooner rather than later. And with some answers.

Four days and nights of silence and wonder later, during customary after-dinner math vespers, Alicia roared into Zig's. Stefan reached for Jimmie but then recognized Alicia. No Jimmie, no SIG tonight.

Pulling up aggressively, arms spread, faux-pissed, "Dev shows up late, he gets a Red, ready and waiting. Me, I get this? Two long-faces, like as if you expected me to never show again." Matt jumped up, all too happy to fetch a beverage for the prodigal daughter. Stefan had already placed one, light on foam, on their end of the bar.

Sliding into an assembly of sticks that passes for a chair at Zig's, looking ragged but bright and relieved. "I almost gave up on it many times. Due diligence, I dumped every version of the EEG-style skin patch electrode, way too noisy; every movement throws out confusion. The user would have to lie still as death, not even sleeping is still enough. And the info there is a jumble, all you can sort out is this or that muscle twitch. Good for prosthetics,[70] not thoughts.

"Then there were some dumb possibilities I had to check, like a videocam reading eye and facial movements, that were reliable but primitively slow. Something like 'one twitch if by sea, two if by land'" She mimicked blinking and twitching and laughed.

Then a cloud came over her. "Implanted brain electrodes? In the deep-military literature, we're not supposed to see I found that some of Devon's predecessors," she glanced at him, "favored inserting wires into the brain. If you're desperate, even threading a chain of hair-like electrodes into someone's brain seemed reasonable, like back in the day according to Elon and Neuralink.[71]

And then one night it hit me. You know how a bio-molecule can change color dramatically after a small, physiological event? Like how hemoglobin, and therefore blood, changes to bright red when it's oxygenated? At your last physical, the nurse clamped a red-glowing doojey to your fingertip. That red color wasn't chosen to be Christmas-cute. That red is the color where oxygen changes the hemoglobin molecule the most. Redder, more oxygen, in a measurable way. Just numbers, no magic. And guess what. Every human's the same. The same. Every human. Bad news for the bigots, good news for the guys who build the machine. And good news too for the healthy, or the anemic depending on how your blood oxygen is doing." She poised a moment.

"Well, the photosensitive molecule in cones and rods, rhodopsin, changes molecular configuration, and color, quickly, briefly, when stimulated." Alicia waited for her students to catch up.

No need. Devon had run ahead to the rest of her explanation, "You're thinking that a rod or cone color change might be used to read the retina."

Alicia, "*Jawohl!* Yes!"

Devon let out a low whistle.

"But now the sweet part. Conjure up a dream. I bet you've done some of your best work in a dream state, no? 'Lucid dreaming.' You 'picture' stuff, right? Dreams are like movies, just in your head, right?" Matt and Devon sensed her urgency. "Turns out, dreams start in your head and those pictures, they run back up the nerves and smack up electrochemically in the rods and cones." Alicia stopped abruptly.

Devon in awe, subdued. "Wooooooaah. Cool. Dream pictures pop up in your head and go out to your eyeball."

Matt in awe, agitated. "Seriously, Alicia, there's a brain signal accessible in your retina?" He looked stunned. "But...can we read 'em?"

Alicia could only nod. Their lights went on. The noninvasive brain-machine connection. She had found the Shangri-La of computer science.

"Alicia." Devon, hoarsely, "Alicia, I think you better take a sip of Red." He leaned toward her and summarized, his voice solemn and intimate.

"You figured out a way to read a person's thoughts in their retina."

Behind the bar, Stefan had been enviously monitoring the table. A regular customer leaning on the bar asked for another drink and Stefan growled back, "Zhuddup." Stefan knew something big was happening for his barchildren and he didn't want to miss the moment.

A poet once said that eyes are windows to the soul. Alicia, Devon and Matt were on their way to looking through that window into a person's brain.

CHAPTER 27
STEFAN'S BROOD

Early, real early every Sunday, Stefan peeked out his second-floor window. The old, red neon sign missing one "S" was blinking "Ma sages." It threw a glare off his window and a shadow on the wall so he could see up and down Loomis Street without being seen. Stefan was careful with this one indulgence. He was preparing to leave his monastery for a luxury excursion, figuring that the guys who might be looking for him were sleeping-in.

Every Sunday, Stefan headed to church.

At Saint Basil's High Orthodox Church of the Redeemer, fifteen blocks uphill in and out of alleys, he could nail confession by prior arrangement and catch early mass in Russian. Then he headed to the kitchen where he prepared an authentic old country feast for the dozen or so ragamuffin urchins he had attracted to the Church under his stewardship.

Stefan, a mysterious, generous donor, viewed as a shady saint by some parishioners, had convinced the Church to allocate a space for his kids to learn about computers. No computer-illiterate old Ivan or Olga could resist. So, on the day of rest, he cooked *borscht* and baked bread and then spent a couple hours preaching coding to teen-ish girls and boys. After the basics, they mostly played violent video games. And developed a loyalty to Stefan who fed and piqued them. But like all kids and any man without female supervision, they got into mischief. Stefan taught them to hack.

CHAPTER 28
THERE'S A NEW MARSHALL IN TOWN

Devon was abuzz in his basement lab, hair and arms competing for most askew as he made adjustments to the busy diagram on the whiteboard. The two young engineers with him were jazzed to watch him invent.

A uniformed security guard, late-twenties, close cropped hair, a clutch of black-cloaked martial tools strapped on left, right and center, stagger-walked among benches cluttered with circuit boards, soldering irons, prototyping circuit boards and electronic wizardry. Over in the discussion corner, a massive Newport Corporation optical isolation table, hulking in at twelve feet by four feet by two feet thick, stood on foot-and-a-half diameter pneumatic shock absorbers, looking technical and expensive; the replacement value of this two tons, including labor, was just over half a million bucks. A couple of monochrome laser spots were visible on the hundreds of intricate glass and metal Tinker toys attached to the magnetic stainless-steel tabletop. Occasionally something clicked.

The guard stopped a polite five or six meters short of

the group, clearly not intending to observe or listen in. He caught Devon's eye, signaling that the time for his requested meeting was now. Devon sort of acknowledged, loathe to interrupt a productive session. The guard's stoic demeanor and additional nod prompted Devon to pull the plug. "Hey guys, I told the officer I would meet with him, so let's pick up wavelength multiplexing later today."

Devon walked over toward the guard. "Hey, how are ya? I'm Devon."

Completing the offered dap, "Morning, I'm Slade. Officer Robert Slade. I'm with DOD Security Police."

"Right. I've seen you guys in the lunch room." Lying, "Pleased to meecha."

Slade flashed his picture badge. Devon bristled; he had had a mixed relationship with the law through his teen years. And now, two abuses in one day: interrupted tech talk, oppressive Authority. "Nice photo Bob, makes you look older."

Unsmiling, Officer Slade continued, "If you don't mind, sir, could we talk in private?" The jaw, southern drawl and the request for privacy caught the engineers' interest as they dispersed.

Slipping into a side office dedicated to desktops, Devon couldn't, as usual, contain his wit. "I bet you guys found out about my chucking dihydrogen oxide down the lab sink, or was it my unpaid parking ticket?" If Devon wanted to push buttons, he had succeeded.

"Sir, I got this assignment because I earned a master's degree in forensic chemistry from the University of Arkansas."

"Razorbacks!" piped up Devon, unable to control himself and failing to recognize Officer Slade's intent.

"I recommend that you hear me out before attempting any more jokes." Slade was miffed. Devon needed to re-adjust his game.

"Sir, in reviewing your visitation records, I have seen an increasing frequency on the part of two individuals who are not members of the SPRC community." Devon couldn't help but choke on the "community" part. "Do you happen to know who I'm talking about?"

Play-Dumb-Devon not yet fully grasping that this is not the Principal's Office and not about smoking in the lav, "I get lotsa guests, I gotta think about it."

"May I help you recall?" Slade shows Devon two lo-res photos, both from the high surveillance camera angle one sees on the late-night news channel right after a liquor store robbery. "Are these two people acquaintances of yours?" Amateur bad guy, Devon makes a clumsy and doomed effort to obfuscate, "Right, sure. Yup." Slade leans in, his body suggests he is waiting for Devon to volunteer some names. Devon had spent teen-time on a curb after midnight with police flashlights in his face. He wasn't easily intimidated.

"Sir, might the initials A H and D C help you recall?" Slade was patiently working through the Academy playbook, Devon realizing smartass-time was over. "Hey, right, Alicia and Douglas Matthew." Slade smirks and looks away. He had grown tired of dealing with the superiority of these tech types, especially those who look so skinny-frail. "Thank you, sir. Are you aware that one of these people was born in Communist East Berlin." Slade radiated the smug feeling that he had tried and convicted someone of espionage, case closed.

Lacking Slade's trained posturing, and with a deep hurt in his heart, Devon leaned in and growled, "And you Slade, are you aware that the Stasi killed both her parents? After torturing them. If you think she's a turncoat, you and me, we got a problem." Stalemate. Officer Slade was no dummy. He'd grown up respecting righteous. Momentary standoff.

Cold stare softening, "Sir, I'm sorry to hear that, I know she and you are friends. My apologies." Something about Southern guy manners can be disarming and Devon was vulnerable to charm.

Slade, "I understand that you might not hold me in the highest regard," Devon mused that Slade sounded like a character from *Gone With the Wind*, "but you need to understand the current situation."

"Dude, sorry. I got outta line. I've had a couple run-ins with badges and sticks and so on. I'll keep a lid on it."

"Got it. Thanks. Listen, I needed to talk to you *mano-a-mano*. I haven't passed on my observations to anyone yet. But you need to know that your visitation records, personnel history, some of the movements and time spent in our Lab here fit a Reportable Profile." Slade looked at Devon with a tinge of collegiality; deep down he admired egg-heads. "Sir, you don't want to be in a Report. That's all I have to say."

All this took the edge off the afternoon's redo of wavelength multiplexing. Devon needed to talk with Matt and Alicia. It was Zig's Time.

CHAPTER 29
FRIENDS IN
HIGH PLACES

"Lets step into a Cat Room." Silicon Valley privacy included carpet-lined, soundproof phone stalls. Millennials had given them a cute branding.

"Well, Dr. Samuelson, one of my colleagues on the Project got nervous yesterday. He was approached by a DOD Marshall on post at the SPRC."

"You mean Devon McBain?"

Not surprised by Samuelson's instant name recall, Matt nodded. "Seems an Officer Slade noticed how 'two outsiders' have been coming and going."

Samuelson raised an eyebrow, "You and Alicia Hoescht."

"Right. And the officer wanted Devon to know that he hadn't made any security notes on the Record. Yet."

Samuelson paused, "Everything OK there, work progressing, and so on?"

"Much as we hoped. Just did our first test run, wrote up some engineering change orders, waiting for sub-projects to deliver."

As Matt was wrapping up his sentence, Samuelson turned to Souchi, "Can you get General Frank Patterson on the line for me?" Souchi turned away to launch the call.

"Let me understand, you need freedom to operate down there at SPRC. The place's gotten tighter over the years. Seems like détente didn't last as long as we all hoped. Let's see if we can get you some relief."

Souchi stretches her cell out to Samuelson, "General Patterson."

Taking the phone, "Hey, Frank, how are you doing?" Samuelson lights up to the cell phone voice. "Right, right, well at least I'm at work, Frank. What hole you guys on?" Listening and laughing. "Well, maybe, but my drone up over your head says different." The voice gets loud enough for Matt to almost hear. Samuelson laughs until he can't breath. "Frank, you shoot down my drone and you or DEVCOM West will pay for it." They're enjoying a break from the day's heavy lifting.

Samuelson's cradling the phone gently. "Uh-huh, she's doing great. I don't see her much. Painting morning noon and night. Working on a Siqueiros-inspired mural. Your kid back from the Middle East yet?" Serious face. "Right, right. Of course, he'll take care, but he's feeling his T. Like his dad did."

"What's that?" Starts laughing. "That's just age Frank. There's still plenty else to look forward to, old dog." Voice on the other end barks and laughs too.

"Hey Frank, got a situation for you. Small but it's an 8 out of 10. Need to keep it small. Seems one of my guys down in SPRC, yeah, right, down in the basement at Berkeley, has attracted attention to himself and two more of my folks." Listening. "Name's Devon McBain, smart guy but irreverent." Listening. "Right, McBain. The visitors are Douglas County and Alicia Hoescht." Matt could tell that Patterson, like Samuelson, didn't need to take notes. "Right, same family, uh huh. East Berlin." "We did a full security work up, she's clean. Bright girl, just as, ummm, irritating as McBain but my kids are onto something."

Laughing again. "No, I don't think they play golf," then the serious face, listening.

"Got it. OK. Right. And watch out for that sand trap on 15." Samuelson handed the cell to Souchi and took a moment to savor thoughts of an old relationship before coming home. "Great plan. Frank will tell the CO to commend Officer Slade. You three will take a two-hour security briefing from Slade. Then get on with it. I think you'll find the going clear."

CHAPTER 30
ALICIA'S WRAP UP

The watchpuppy at Devon's Berkeley lab had become noticeably respectful following General Patterson's intervention. In fact, Matt and Alicia could walk in like royalty.

Early morning, Matt cruised in. He found Devon and Alicia tête-à-tête. An average human or a less dedicated computer scientist would have smelled gender-stress. Not Matt, he dove straight in. "Funding secured. What's the plan?"

Alicia, shape-shifted to casual, "Got it mapped out. Most of the laser optical problems have been solved by Devon's team over the last three years. Catching the reflected signal is a bit tricky. Good news is, we found that we can catch enough to read the retina."

Devon saw confusion in Matt. "Lemme back up a bit. Remember the overall scheme calls for scanning the lasers over the whole area of almost ten thousand points." Matt nodded, recalling the first tech meeting.

Devon pushed ahead. "We can have any one laser fire at low level for reading a spot or we fire in it at a higher level to send a signal into the spot."

"Won't the flickering signal lights be distracting? Remember Google Glass One back in '12 or '13? Zombie-people walking around reading their email like they're looking for Pickachoo." Matt's face scrunched recalling the car accidents and cliff walkers.[72]

Devon remembered better than anyone. "The pulses look like a twinkling. Thoughts will pop into your head. Four to five times faster than conversation."

Alicia, "Each spot has a meaning. The trick, training the retina."

Matt, still puzzled, "How do you get the owner to 'know' what each spot means?"

"You tie the guy down, flash the laser on the spot for <send mail> until he gets it right. Something like that."

"That's where I come in." Alicia's specialty. "REM sleep. A person goes into REM sleep, the brain becomes vulnerable. That's when we send in laser pulses on assigned retinal spots. At the same time, pump in words, reinforce by repetition. At first, I estimated we could get two, maybe three hundred words per hour or in one night. But then Samuelson threw Celaquinab at our feet."

"It turns out that it lets me speed up training by a factor of seven or eight, punch in maybe two thousand input units in a night."

"We can give the wearer an eight-thousand-word vocabulary in one week."

Matt. "What's magical about eight thou?"

"That's what you need to communicate in a foreign language. With eight thousand words, our user could talk silently with her computer."[73]

CHAPTER 31
PROTOTYPE ONE

They hadn't been to Zig's for two weeks. It wasn't a good night.

"Dammit. Stop bitchin' at Devon, Matt." Alicia, carrying two beers, got up in Matt's face. "The only reason you can gripe is 'cause his work is easiest to track."

Eight months of late nights, weekends, pushing hard on each other and everyone they worked with, patience was wearing thin.

"But I was told over and over the work was almost done. 'Just a tweak here and there.' Now two months late and I'm getting the same story. 'I need another week.' Maybe Dev needs to buckle down a bit."

"Screw you, man, you and your tight-ass, nose-in-a computer-middle-class-nerd-ethic. Sit at a console. Don't talk to nobody and tip tap code. You just gotta download most of it anyway. Producin' stuff man, hardware. That's what's tough. I got seventeen freakin' suppliers strung out there. Excuses. Pre-demic alerts. Polymer shortages. Truck strike. 3D printer goin' futch. Fuggit dude." Devon stood up. Matt matched him.

Stefan was enjoying the distraction. He knew when two guys were going to go. Wasn't happening here tonight.

"That's it? That's what's buggin' you! 'Middle class nerd ethic?' Where's that come from, huh? You wanna play some kind of ...of...Army-man card?"

Alicia'd had enough. Her emo-luminescent hair roots were on fire. Her voice was low and awful as she stepped between the two. In German, the world's default authority language.

"*Ach du lieberzeit! Das ist aber a scheisse. Jetzt bin ich kindergarten mutti. Zwei kinder. Zwie* fucking babies?[74] One more gripin' word, you're both goin' down."

The "army-man card" slur and Alicia's vibrating pixie crouch and hair-on-fire was too ridiculous. Devon and Matt cracked up.

"Funny! Huh? Funny? You want some of this? C'mon. Let's go." She started to boxer-stalk Matt, when Devon smothered her from behind, lifting her feet off the ground. Her two-sentences-in-one-word German curse made them all laugh.

Stefan, grinning salaciously, brought the third beer to their table. A first. Temperature dropped. They muttered, embarrassed, and cooled off.

After eyes-on-the-ground apologies and some rehash laughs about Alicia's pugnacity, all's good.

"So, Matt, you said you had something to tell us."

"Guys, I got it. Immersive data animation."

"Huh?"

"OK. Imagine a grocery store, modest size. You've got maybe thirty-six thousand individual products, scattered over 30 isles. Potato chips, Family and Regular and Snack size, crisp and jalapeno and seasalt. Each package with ship dates, trucks, shelf life, handlers, on and on."

"Say, a half million pieces in your store, mega bucks. Now, peak, you're moving fifty items per minute, 30,000 per day. A thousand customers. And each of them has their own data history, age, pay date, children."

Alicia: "OK. Big Data."

"Lotsa numbers. You would like to milk it. Pump up sales for, say, Thanksgiving. Could do it old-school, spreadsheet. Line by line, cell by cell. Makes ... your ... mind ...go dead. Or maybe the company purchased a data base software, corporate-wide, half a million bucks."

"But you have a brainstorm like 'Did that sales promotion work better for Halloween candy or organic blueberries?' So you need a coder. Who comes with acne, junk food, attitude, Red Bull and bull."

Devon rolls his eyes, "Coders should do more acid."[75]

"But then we come along and give you a tool to let you just talk, walk, even fly your way through your data. Dev, like your gaming days."

"You glide among the products with animated, color-coded overlays to answer your queries. 'What's December's turn over for that Cocoa powder over there?'

"Your glance is all it takes. No keyboard. No monitor. It's all in your head. Look at an item, think what you want for data, and bam, you get it.

"The software learns with you. The software writes the software. It gets better and faster as you use it. You forget there's a boundary between you and your machine."

Then Matt hit a snag. He started to describe how the

human-master could experience the numbers as feelings. He was flashing back to Samuelson's lesson with the flower in the forest.

"Feelings? Like, person-feelings? Wooaaah?" Devon was not on board. Alicia was, very. "Yes, Devon," condescending, "like feeeelings, like what you could have had for some of those young women who passed through your life recently."

"Leash. That's not cool. That's punching below the belt."

"Ex-act-tally Devon. You nailed it." Pause to glare. "Right." Glare. "Yessss, that is the geography."

"C'mon, man. Who? Who? Name one?"

"Jannette"

"Well..."

"Or Felice. Except in that case she ended up playing you like a worn-out fiddle. Good for her."

Matt, tried to re-track. "OK, OK. Remember Devon when you explained to us that you had solved how to steer the laser beams? You were in love."

"You explained that it 'hit you,' that you just 'felt it'" Matt was shamelessly making this quote up. "Remember?"

Devon, "Yeaaa, that was great."

"Dev, that was 'feelings.' That was your brain intuiting the next steps. It wasn't magic, you had a prepared brain. You had the right stuff in there and it gelled. It was your intuition, a feeling. That's what I think we can do."

"Huh, yea, wow. Cool. Computer back-up in the brain. How fast can we make it go?" which is why friends don't let Devon drive a car.

"Real fast. It'll outrun even your thinking. But look, let's keep the prototype basic. I'll get the code ready for a limited volume of data. Alicia finishes up on reading the retina. You gotta wrap up the hardware end, including implants and comm channels."

Devon. "Maybe you can swing some bucks our way, hire some help, write some code in Sumatra to keep under the radar, buy some beers for the geniuses? Huh, maybe, Boss?"

"Sure, budget no problem, but for the moment, let's get a road test running with just what we have."

Devon, inspired. "We gotta brand this, give it a catchy name!" Alicia sent him a skeptical side-eye.

Undeterred, Devon forged on, "Something twenty-first century, like 'Victoria's Secret' or 'Hooters.'"

Alicia, suspecting she was being pinged, shot back, "How 'bout 'Ball Busters.' That'd be great Dev. Sad 'Crotch Rocket' is taken but we could go with 'Prick Trick!' How's that Dev?" He didn't like those ideas. Alicia continued, "C'mon Dev, branding, that's so proletariat. Besides, ours is a high-tech thing."

Devon: "Oh great, 'Hey folks come check out The Thing.' Lord. Someone would think you were a furriner."

Alicia, in German, superior conjunctive, "*Du bist eigentlich einen sussen unmittlebaren Ami Banauzer.* You are truly a sweet American primitive."

"Love you too, Leash."

Matt felt like he was taking a fifth-grade class to an Adults Only Novelty store. Everyone's agitated but they don't know why. He stepped in, having given it some thought. "Augmented Reality, so how about 'ARs?' like in AR-plural, you know like glass-es and contact-s?"

Devon, still in combat mode, "Great, 'til someone says, 'piece of ARs,' or 'your ARs sure is looking good, babe'?'" which was excellent branding insight for an amateur.

Alicia's pissed. "One person. One out of eight point two billion, Dev, that's who says something like that."

"Like you didn't think the same thing there, right?"

Matt is helpless to abort the food fight. With some cajoling, the three got around to calling their technology "ARz."

Devon wanted to move ahead. "OK. So we got a rodeo, we need a rider." Devon and Alicia simultaneously looked at Matt.

Matt's eyes widened. "What. What?!" He squirmed, "Whao, no way! Me? Why me? I hate medical stuff. My dad always came home smelling like antiseptic. I'll get sick, I'll pass out, I'll..." His team stared, pitiless. Two versus one, on early vote-by-mail.

Devon, "Look, you're the full-time employee, and Alicia has to do the ophthalmic side and I've got to maintain the lens optics and you've got your coders down in Singapore working for you on software. Someone has to try this out first, right Cap'n?"

Matt was outgunned. Alicia would do the implants. Devon would jeer her on.

A week later, they scheduled to meet, off the record, at Alicia's Stanford University lab. Devon was Best Man, ensuring that the groom didn't have a change of heart. He and Matt stopped for a beer, then a second. Devon, insensitive as ever, toasted to the pre-surgical anesthesia.

Nighttime parking was easy. Devon led the way to Alicia's lab, the one lit space in the cavernous Biomed Building. For Matt, ominous, and he said so. Alicia greeted them at her office. She caught on quickly, disgusted with Devon. "Boys been to the waterhole, huh? A little liquid courage?"

She led the way into a lab space near her office and locked the door behind them. A layback chair next to a stainless-steel rolling tray-table. She gestured Matt to the chair as she pulled on a mask and lab coat. Seeing Matt's queasy look, she reassured him. "Sterile, Matt, no problem." With flawless technique, she extracted gloves from their sterile zip-pack and donned them. Matt flinched when she snapped them in place. "Sorry. We learned to do that in Munich. Gets patient respect." She covered the table with a sterile drape. Matt started to sweat. "Patient" had been a bad word choice.

Matt flinched again when the steam sterilizer in the corner popped off. She used tongs to pull out the sterilizing canister and transferred it onto the tray table. One by one she extracted surgical tools, forceps, scalpel, needles, and a metal sample dish. Matt watched, wretched. He feared for his blood pressure. But he forgot all that when Alicia pulled out two syringe-and-needle packs for the implant. She was going to use an 8-gauge canula, about a third bigger than an eighth of an inch. To Matt, these needles looked like the railroad spike from Promontory Point.

"Alicia? Stop joking around! You're not serious, right?" He tried to sit up. Devon coaxed him, with some physicality, to relax back down, which is by definition not relaxing. "Matt, this is for the team. Easy does it, big guy. Only gonna take a moment. Alicia is good at this. She's done it plenty before." They were telling Matt a lot of lies this evening.

Matt sat back. Bending close, Devon asked him, "Is your estate in order." But for the sterile gloves, Alicia would have smacked him.

Alicia looked to Devon. "You got them?"

The Best Man stood in shock. "Got what?" Then fumbled in his pockets. Best man forgot the ring? After a bit, laughing, he pulled a black box out of his inner jacket pocket. "Kidding. Here they are." The ARz implants, an eighth inch in diameter and three-quarters of an inch long, nestled inside a radiation sterilized pouch.

Alicia slid them into the sample pan. Suddenly Devon became the nervous soul. "Easy there, Alicia, that's a shade short of a hundred large there. Totally custom one-offs."

Alicia made as though she dropped the rods and laughed at Devon's gasp. "Give, but can't take, what?"

She pulled sterile solution into a syringe and filled the implant dish. She pulled one implant up into a canula, then a second, placed each aside. In classic movie style, she held an anesthetic bottle and syringe up to the light and withdrew a dose, then bubbled out the excess air.

"OK, Matt, lets numb you up a little more." She wiped his brows, far to the outside left and right, with alcohol swabs. Then, positioning the light carefully, moving close, told Matt, "This will pinch," and gave him two slow, methodical, almost painless shots, one in each brow. "That'll take a minute to work."

Twenty minutes after entering the lab, Alicia was done with Matt. The insertion had gone smoothly, but he had fainted twice. "The butterfly band aids come off tomorrow. Should be no problem with infection."

While she was finishing, Devon had opened his laptop. "Helloooo. Baby brow-worms are talking to daddy. Both channels taking a charge. Tomorrow the moon!"

Matt loved his buddies, sort of, but yearned for the steadiness of Souchi.

CHAPTER 32
TEST RUN

"Test ruuuun!" For Devon life was an ongoing test run. He was all in to take ARz-Matt out for a look at the world through organo-integrated-circuit glasses.

"Matt, remember. You're limited to have augmented and virtual reality. No data in or out."

"Better that way. Thanks. I'd like to keep the stress manageable. Less failure, more observation." After a brief conference, the three foolishly chose a real-life situation, Zig's bar.

Back at The Pasture, Matt popped in the ARz contact lenses. Much the same as his usual daily-wear lens. Devon and Alicia called him from their ride-share downstairs. They planned to hop out three blocks from Zig's and walk in to test the augmented reality on a real street.

The test walk revealed some glitches with the ARz. "Devon, there's fluttering when I move in and out of streetlights."

"Right boss. Software tweek needed. But if I add in damping, you'll have slower adjustment to light changes. Give it some time. Your call."

Speculating how the ARz would handle a dank interior, they popped into Zig's. Stefan, accustomed to sizing up customers with a glance, took note that Matt was acting weird, occasionally staring into nowhere, walking stiffly, talking to himself, but then, college kids on drugs popped in from time to time. He passed it off as all in a day's youth.

As analytically as the beering would allow, Matt reported on idiosyncrasies of the ARz. The instruction set would have to be short; it was hard to stay "in the scene" while absorbing input. "The user will need some training to watch overlay without eye movement."

"We noticed."

An hour later, an unwise two beers smarter, they headed out of Zig's. Unfortunately, a local drunk returning from a vomit-run to the parking lot was headed back in at the same time. Devon, maternally guarding his $100,000-dollar protégé, or at least the ARz contacts, tried unsuccessfully to avoid bumping into the guy, big, round and lurching.

"Wasch wear yousch-goin. Damn freakin nerds fuggin ev'r'ware."

Devon returned a profane suggestion. Alicia bristled at the anti-techie bigotry.

"Washchew do about it, hippie," un-tetherable, Devon started lining up the possibilities, but Alicia could see the trial run needed to stay on mission, piping in, "Let's just go home, guys."

"Ya teensy mama here 'stew pur-tect you egg 'eads?" Noticing her fluorescent green hair, the drunk made a mistake. "Whadda hell happened to 'er 'ead? Growin-weed?"

Belying her stature and pixie-ish face, Alicia let

loose with a torrent of unprintable bilingual invectives, printed here, "fuckyouaschlochmotherbumsenpricknosedickhead."

Not appreciating that his sloppy 6 foot 2, 265-pound anatomy left him badly positioned relative to her five feet, Soft Serve put his hand on top of Alicia's head and pulled fruitlessly at the tightly cropped stubble. Bad move, grabbing at her head. She crouched into a low boxer stance and left-righted his sensitalia. When Alicia thus rang Soft Serve's bells (excuse the misspelling) he blew like a lunch whistle, and sagged.

Every competitive athlete has seen the world slow down at the moment of peak performance. Time flows like warm honey when the sweet spot of the bat hits the centerline of the ball. In slow motion, Alicia watched Soft Serve fold up, sustained by mass and inebriation. As his face, crumpled into a gym-sock-bear, slid into Alicia's range, she, with the accumulated rage of generations of misused women, tattooed his nose with the heel of her right hand. Straight arm, full shoulder turn, legs and body giving power, she rearranged substantial nasal cartilage. Gravity finished the job. It was over in a fraction of a second.

Silent for a moment, Devon looked at the form on the ground and back at Alicia. "Hay-zeus shit alive! What was THAT?"

Meanwhile, the excitement had caused Matt to lose control of ARz. He was swaying lightly, displaying blindisms,[76] trapped and confused behind somewhat psychedelic random digital patterns playing out before his eyes. Excitedly, "Whuzzup! Can't see! What happened? You guys alright?"

Devon caught Matt and shut off the ARz. Looking down, Matt caught up, "Wow. That's a lot of blood. He might have trouble breathing?"

Alicia was massaging her hand. Unsympathetically, with misplaced medical and ethical judgement, she growled, "He's got a mouth, don't he?" They shuffled about, discharging adrenaline.

Stefan came out the door, looked down at the prostrate jerk from whom he always expected trouble and then straight-faced Alicia, "Missed his liver," and walked back into the bar.

Matt suppressed a helium-giggle, "Devon, can you tag the GPS coordinates so I can wipe the security cameras over there?" Devon looked across the street and pulled out his cell. "OK. Let's git."

No persuasion necessary, they walked briskly away. What they didn't know is that Stefan would take care of the messy aftermath. From earlier days as under-class immigrants, Poles shared cultural bloodlines with Irish in the SFPD. Plus, Stefan had made a long-term investment in schmoozing Mission cops with free food and a warm hide-away from reformist, politically-correct lieutenants and blustery Bay breezes in winter; Soft Serve would not appear in a precinct blotter report nor would he be back at Zig's.

Devon, hoodie up and slumped to disguise his height, walked into the Seven Eleven a quarter mile away to buy a Super Slurpee bucket to stop the swelling on Alicia's hand. They chalked up Test Run One as a valuable learning experience.

CHAPTER 33
MATT FEELS GOOD ABOUT EDUCATION

Matt moaned. "Uhhhmmm." Low, pleased.

Souchi lay next to him, naked, caressing him intimately. Soft. Slow. She cooed and purred in his ear, repeating his name, breathy. Her touch, her voice spread though his body, curling his toes. He was soooo taut.

Matt moaned. Lying on his back, he heard Alicia whisper into his other ear. "Matt, are you ready?" He moaned again. "Ooooh yeaa. Please." He could feel the wet warmth of her breath on his ear, raising the hairs, each one itself alert to her voice and the closeness of her lips.

Alicia persisted. He liked that. "Matt, it's time. Wake up. Matt, I know you're in there. Wake up dude."

Unwillingly, Matt opened his eyes. To his right, Alicia. To his left, Souchi. Clothed and looking concerned. He looked down the sheets. Mr. Happy had made the Great Rock Candy Mountain. He groaned and rolled on his side toward where Souchi wasn't naked. Standing behind her, Devon, grinning.

"Awww, sheesh. You here too?"

"You got it man. You forget? We launched your ARz experiment with Celaquinab last night. They wanted me here to help push back the foreskin of science.[77] Looks like they didn't need my help." Souchi laughed. Alicia wanted to punch him. She made a mental note that this punch-urge was happening too regularly.

Groggy, Matt remembered. The team had put him to bed for advanced ARz training. Unlike his training for the prototype runs, based only on REM sleep, this time they experimented with the white pill Samuelson had developed for Arctan's Psycho-Dynamic Learning Experiences. Celaquinab hypothetically should enhance ARz learning much like it accelerated learning in the walkabout sessions.

Matt. "You think it worked?"

Devon, pleased for Matt, "Are you kidding! That looked like a single-handed success to me!" Alicia threw up her arms, ready to send Devon packing. Her inner clinical supervisor stayed on task. "Matt, We don't know. We'll have to run the planned tests. As soon as we get some coffee and you're back to normal. One thing for sure, the nighttime dose should be less than the daytime dose. Looks like maybe we overdosed you."

Souchi followed Devon downhill, "I don't know, looks like it worked fine."

Alicia shot her the mother look. "Oh come on! You too! Next thing I gotta deal with is you guys going to Samuelson with this as a pharmaceutical business offshoot. The Learning Person's Viagra. I am not, no way onboard with that." Devon and Souchi looked at each other, eyebrows up, lights going on.

"*Ach sheisse.*" Turning back to Matt. "Get up and get a shower. You'll need some coffee in ya."

"You two. Go to your room. Whatever. See you downstairs." Ten years older, team intellectual leader, Alicia was feeling their youthful spirit. She headed to the breakfast room to wait for the damn puppies to settle down.

In two hours, after morning revivals, Matt inserted ARz and synched to the Arctan Cloud. He and Alicia and Souchi headed down to a testing room on the fourth floor. They found Devon there with his laptop. He was sitting next to a modified peripheral vision tester. [78] It looked like a tabletop version of the Hollywood Bowl, one half of a two-foot diameter spherical shell. The chin strap was modified so the user could talk while using it.

Alicia and Souchi looked on. "First we're gonna do vocabulary, accuracy and speed check." Devon could be all business when the mood took him. "Matt, put your cheeks against the fork assembly, that's it, there, and press your forehead against the headrest. There will be a video playing in the dome. Simulation of real world. Watch it. The computer will be randomly pump words into your brain. When the display blinks green, say the first words that come to mind."

"Three, two, one, start."

Matt began to recite words. Alicia and Souchi could see the 1903 silent film *The Great Train Robbery*[79] playing in the dome.

His recital ran through a random selection of words.

Numbers, colors, verbs and adjectives. After maybe thirty words, the pace picked up. And again, after one minute, after ninety seconds and two minutes. After two and half minutes, Matt was blubbering like a meth freak. At three minutes, the tirade stopped.

Devon. "Relax, lean back Matt."

Devon waited, watched, then whistled. "Good boy! Ladies, let's have a biscuit for Rover. Hit 98% accuracy all the way up to 132 words per minute. The speed could improve with practice. Based on this random sample, the patient has acquired the 2,067 word vocabulary we fed him last night."

"However...." Devon concentrated on the monitor. His audience of three leaned in. "I believe that the training may have caused some permanent sexual inadequacy."

Matt grinned, weakly. Alicia refused to take the bait.

Matt had been registering mental input from the Cloud through ARz while watching "the world" in the display. Not huge (the movie was silent and simple), just earthshattering. He was halfway to being able to conduct a lucid thought conversation with his computer. Through his eyes.

Devon worked the keyboard. "OK, Matt. Next test. Similar routine. Slide back inta the tester. You'll see photos. Ask ARz to Google search something about the photo. Like, 'Who is that?' or 'What is their birthday?' Your vocabulary is still limited so stick to specifics. ARz will give you a search result. After a short pause, the screen will test if you got the result. Think your answer back to ARz. Questions?"

For the next fifteen minutes, Matt watched pictures.

Some were simple, a single face. Occasionally, complex images, a group of costumed people displayed. Matt sat, silently staring into the dome. The link was completely private, between Matt and The Cloud. Alicia and Souchi waited, peeked in, wandered out, came back. Devon daydreamed. This was between Matt and ARz.

At the end of the fifteen minutes, Matt had responded to sixty-five photos. He hadn't noticed that the allowed response time got shorter as the test proceeded. Toward the end, he was reduced to one point seven seconds to think his answer.

Matt leaned back. A "Complete" prompt showed in the dome. Alicia and Souchi had returned to hear the results. Devon was mentally absent, off thinking about what it was like to be starving, elder-sex and his favorite fruits. Matt kicked his chair and Devon jumped. It was an awfully long journey, coming back from Devonlandia. "Hey! You're done. Let's see how we did."

Devon searched the already processed on-screen summary. "Hooo-kay. Bright boy." Looking up, "You too, Matt."

"The subject has some political leanings. And the data says...." He looked at the team. "Matt is able to do a thought-driven cloud data search and integrate the results at..." he looked back to the monitor, "...two point four times normal conversational rates. Depending on ambiguities in the question, corrected for his limited ARz vocabulary, looks like the accuracy is around 89%. I'd say we have a winnah."

The results had been far better than expected. Devon,

"Time for lunch, I'm buying. And then, howzabout a street run?" Some people never learn.

An hour after lunch, Matt and Souchi were walking together up Market Street. ARz was in full facial recognition mode. The plan was to test if ARz could help Matt identify a random passerby and then obtain query data back. Some steps and eleven candidates past Grant Street, ARz put a name-halo "Alex" around an approaching pedestrian. Matt walked over to him.

"Hey! How are ya? It's...Alex, right?" The pedestrian stopped, puzzled, trying to recall this friend. "Right, yea, and you... are..?" Matt had queried ARz for Alex's family data and most recent large purchases. "Matt, you know, from the furniture place. Is Mary enjoying the Tesla as much as you?" ARz had found Alex in a Bay-area online chatroom.

"Well, not really," floundering to be polite, "we've been separated for a month." Matt flustered. Lacking leadership, ARz flustered. Souchi amused herself, covered a grin.

"Oh, oops. Sorry. One hundred eighty-five. January 27, 1995." AR was feeding Matt random data and birthdates. Alex, city-cool, looked at Matt like he was a real SF Downtowner. "Right, great, Matt. Happy Cinco de Mayo to you too buddy. Have a nice landing. Gotta run." Souchi started to laugh enough that Alex wanted to ask what brand they were smoking but decided it was simply better to get separation.

Matt and Souchi laughed at Matt's ARz-up to the point of tears. A moment after their hug they digested what had just happened. Matt's brain was computerized. Not well, but computerized.

The Team had a lot to do. One thing for sure, they needed another Celaquinab night to get Matt's vocabulary up to eight thousand units. Second, figure out how to make sure Matt didn't get too much data too fast. Then, practice. Matt needed to simply get used to the parallel channel coming from the outside.

But for sure. Matt was merging with a machine.

CHAPTER 34
GENESIS. IN THE BEGINNING

1 In the beginning God created the heaven and the earth. 2 And the earth was without form, and void; and darkness [was] upon the face of the deep. And the Spirit of God moved upon the face of the waters.[80]

Matt had grown up in Tennessee surrounded by lyrical Old Testament poetry. Owing more to youthful friendships than to his parents, whose Vanderbilt University credentials did not include active roles in the football booster club, he acquired swatches of Bible and wiffs of Gospel song on occasional Sundays and sleepovers. There's nothing quite like the rhythmic soft voices, humid lassitude and perfume smells of living privileged on a Tennessee summer night to reinforce spiritualism and young lust. That, and the resulting mistake he and Caroline Fortaine made, led Matt to contemplate creation.

Fortunately, Matt's and Caroline's parents sat down to talk. The families helped to smooth over their children's problem, putting them back on track to finish their studies; the contrast of Caroline's peaches-and-cream to Matt's swarthy Mediterranean may have played a role in the decision making. Caroline ultimately joined a legal practice in Chattanooga and

Matt discovered his calling as an introverted Computer Science genius. But his brush with creation left Matt curious, so he was fertile ground for the suggestion made by his hero, Dirk Samuelson, to look into Guth's cosmological discoveries.

Matt liked what he found.[81] As much as he was moved by Southern roots in the Bible, Matt worshiped mathematics and the power it gives to predict the future, accurately and reproducibly. He learned that at an early point in the twentieth century, based on protocols evolving only since the seventeenth century, a German-Swiss semi-believing Jew proposed a mathematical formulism to describe Everything. An instant pop sensation,[82] Einstein's General Relativity hit some early speed bumps. Less than a dozen people could understand it, but it was soon measured to be accurate,[83] since then oft-confirmed.[84] What a thought, the whole universe in one equation. Moses would have been proud of Albert for such concise verse.

Matt read about the Jesuit priest, Georges Henri Joseph Édouard Lemaître. On assignment from the Vatican, Georges was sent off to learn the arcane mathematics so the Church could deal with GR. Father Georges solved the math and discovered that The Equation said, "The Universe is expanding." Space and time are getting bigger. His results were securely buried in an obscure Belgian science journal.[85]

Next, Lemaître calculated that The Equation also said that the Universe began at one indescribable moment. Shortly after, Edward Hubble measured the expansion, and made an estimate of The When; several dozen folks honed the estimate to 13.7 billion years ago plus or minus a percent.

In 1945, Gamow predicted the exact color of light at the beginning of observable time. Twenty years later, two capitalist scientists working to improve long-distance profitability for American Telephone & Telegraph Company[86] actually "saw" the first light. They won the 1978 Noble Prize[87] "for their discovery of cosmic microwave background radiation" confirming Lemaitre's prediction. As Devon would say, "Damn."

3 And God said: 'Let there be light.' And there was light. 4 And God saw the light, that it was good; and God divided the light from the darkness. 5 And God called the light Day, and the darkness He called Night. And there was evening and there was morning, one day.[88]

But all was not fine with this model of Everything. Some issues remained. And that's where Alan Guth stepped up. With years invested in his research, he was on his final temporary professorship running out of time and money, struggling to find a new job, a new place to live, and listening to his baby's nightly crying. He was hit with a brainstorm. He could mathematically smooth out the rough spots if the universe had a "phase change" right after birth. Like water on a stove suddenly boiling, he envisioned the young Universe going "pop." Problem solved, August 1981.[89]

Matt understood Samuelson's message, inherited from Thomas Edison: Persistence. Sweat. Doggedness. That's how The Big Ones are made.

CHAPTER 35
DEFLATIONARY
UNIVERSE

"Alicia Hoescht!" Matt was scared. "Let Devon drive!"

"What're you, nutz? He'll get us killed," swerving to avoid her third collision on College Avenue. To show how in control she was, Alicia lingered on a look-over at Matt. Her silent, "See?" screamed malevolent-innocence. "Besides," right-thumbing over her shoulder at Devon with laptop in the back seat, "he's busy trying to debug ARz."

Another violent swerve to skirt intersection traffic brought out a one finger salute. Alicia's narrow-minded Bavarian-born prejudice against Austrians as the world's worst drivers was directed at anyone who had the audacity to share her road. *"Verdammten Österreichischer! Verrücktes kleines Bergvolk!* Damn Austrians! Crazy little mountain people!" as she bounced over the curb with a violent snatch and jerk inside the car. Devon in the back had long ago assumed a three-point brace so he could keep the laptop stable under his pecking finger. It wasn't enough for this last 2.5 g bump. "Leash, waddufug. People'r coding back here!" Matt, concerned about mortal life pleaded, "Please, Alicia, please watch the road. People are packin' out there."

Chin down, eyes narrowed, hands locked, "Fine, bring

it!" Having learned driving as a blood-sport in Bavaria, Alicia was writing her own rules of the road for each vehicle she approached and passed. "And Matt, you said we were late for the demo."

Matt gave up and held on. He had called this management review meeting one week ago for four PM at Arctan and just as they were packing up ARz and the presentation software, it crashed. Rather than call off the meeting, Devon assured them that he could solve the problem in the car on the way over. That was forty minutes ago. It was now bad juju to call off the meeting with just 18 minutes to start time.

"Matt, it was the DDL to the image fit subroutine. It got corrupted. I almost have it patched. LEASH! Take it easy willya!"

With a simple finger tap, Devon rejoiced, "Got the mo fo! Got it got it!" Devon was your ten-year-old neighbor who had trapped a rat in the kitchen sink. "All we gotta do now..." Matt didn't like "all we gotta do" statements, "...is let'er reload and we are...live!"

Matt's neck stiffened. He sat upright. He had ARz real-time in his eyes. Each building they passed now had a color-coded box around it with address and dollar sales volume for the day attached.

He speechlessly requested data with thought-projection. <Arctan> <ETA> and the system responded in the Request-Data Field with [9:52PST]. As Alicia almost sideswiped another errant Austrian, Matt lost his focus and mentally crossed up the ARz inputs, causing wild static on his retina.

"Great stress-test, Leash driving," Matt muttered as he

concentrated fiercely to regain ARz connectivity with Devon's laptop.

Devon, fixated on the monitor, rattled off what he was seeing, "Passing Red Hill Ace Hardware on the right. They've done three hundred fifty-eight dollars thirty-nine cents on two cash registers today." ARz had been pre-programmed to check retail sales. Matt confirmed that was what he had in his vision.

Matt projected thoughts into ARz. <Arctan> <25th floor> <conference room> <status> After a four second delay which Matt blamed on Alicia's unpredictable driving, Matt saw in his display [2 techs 0 attendees. WiFi on. Maxell 5503 connected] and knew they were expected. Seconds later, the video feed showed that the room was ready.

Matt thought-projected into ARz, <Send> <ETA> <to Souchi> and the Connect Confirmation Icon blinked green-positive as Matt welcomed the projected-answer [4.7 min].

Alicia pulled up to the signaling guard at the private Arctan back entrance with a triumphant smile and pulled off her Czech Engelmüller driving gloves. "Grüß Gott! Bergauf zum Spaß!! Hello! Let's go!" she declared, without looking for anyone's affirmation of her performance. Devon beamed in approval. "Alive, wired and pumped," handing Matt the laptop. Matt loved his two homies like never before. No time for niceties, fist bumps all around and he was off at a brisk clip. Eight minutes to get upstairs for his presentation, scheduled to start promptly at four PM straight up Arctan time.

He left the laptop node live while walking through the

back lobby. ARz accessed the room camera. Floating text labels identified that Dr. Brogan was in close conversation with Lydia Merati, CMO. Matt was puzzled. Top-level marketing at a prototype demonstration? Souchi had sent back an SMS wishing him "Good luck, better skill." Nice touch.

Devon and Alicia weren't allowed to attend the demo. They knew the stakes and constraints Arctan put on their edifice. Even the windows were tricked out with random audio frequency vibrators to prevent sound detectors picking up remote oscillations from internal voices. They also knew that ultimately, per Arctan protocol, the whole meeting would be recorded and available in the archive at a security level they could afford.

Channeling his show-nerves and recent near-death experience, Matt closed his eyes and breathed deeply as the elevator crept up to "25," thankfully with no added guests and their pleasantries.

The doors snapped open and Matt felt a fine, warm sensation overwhelm him. Souchi. Calm but concerned, red lipstick, jet black hair, a faint anticipation hovering over her composure. To message confidence, she stiffened and looked him square in the eyes, "Room's all set, Matt." She squared her shoulders and body to block his way.

"Some plan changes you should know about." Maintaining eye contact in silence a moment over-long, she turned to lead him down the corridor, walking deliberately, aware that each step was three fourths of a second of the 227 seconds until the meeting started. "Dr. Brogan has asked to bring in Ms. Lydia Merati..." Matt whispered back, "I saw. ARz picked it up. She's talking with Brogan right now in the power-seats corner by the window." Souchi was cool but impressed, "Oooo. I like ARz more and more."

Approaching the open conference room door, she continued with lowered voice, "Brogan brought her on board about a month ago. They Boarded together at Visitech. Brogan also asked to invite Ari Arinpinder, newest Board member, another friend from a prior venture." She turned again to face him, out of line-of-sight into the conference room and he felt her support. *Sotto voce*, intimately, leaning in, Souchi made a calibrated step out of her space and whispered, "Go get 'em Tiger." At that moment, without knowing it, Matt began to fall in love.

As he entered the room, he turned off the ARz and camouflaged his inappropriate lingering erection with a firm smile and business-like aggression. That was the last of Matt's fuzzy warm feelings on Tuesday.

Starting pleasantly enough, three execs, one Board member, and a high-level engineer, eager to impress, tossed about the customary mix of "morning," hygienic fist bumps and "glad to." Souchi guided Matt through the greetings and left him at the head of the walnut conference table where, against his will, Devon's fantasies flicked through his consciousness scrambling the boundary between lust and love. He refocused, linked in his laptop and cued up his deck. He glanced around the room recalling the interview and photoshoot, so long ago. People took their places in pecking order precision.

Two breaths before four, Dr. Samuelson, again preceded

by an attentively polished Souchi, strode into and lit up the conference room with a blazing smile. "Let's go," and the lights dimmed, as Matt launched into his Power Point presentation. Last week's nineteen-word memo announcing the event was sufficient to skip the usual introductory platitudes. Thirty minutes. Never waste Samuelson time, the clock was running.

"We have succeeded at developing prototype hardware and software solving IT's two biggest barriers." Matt didn't need notes, this demo was engraved on his soul. "Our prototype gives Arctan the ability to make any and all Big Data intuitively useful to any user and creates a seamless interface uniting a human brain to computer resources indistinguishably as one."

Matt paused, stunned at his own audacity, as Samuelson, Brogan, Kavalkovsky, Merati, Arinpinder, among the most accomplished people in Big Data on the planet, sat weighing the hefty claims of a thirty-something university grad student. Matt knew that Dr. Dirk Samuelson had already figured out all of the next twenty-nine-and-one-half minute presentation. He was simply waiting to see if Matt had realities to sell. The others were intrigued.

Matt reviewed the optical, ocular and data principles. Eager Engineer took notes, asked a couple of answerable questions. Matt delineated each specification with graphics, including data fields, infrared sensing, the 8000-word vocabulary, user training. The most difficult concept to convey was intuitive flying through data, the ability to wear data clouds like a warm coat.

With seven minutes to go, he dropped his bombshell. "I am currently wearing ARz." A side glance was cast between Brogan and Samuelson, then Brogan and Arinpinder. Merati had been muted through the presentation, as Marketing is wont to do, but now her face lit up: product demo! No one in this town had forgotten Steve Jobs' insights, product-reveals and billions.

"I can let you into my head," he had chosen that phrase carefully, "via the laptop link." Putting on eyeglasses, Matt pointed to a small lens centered in the large-ish bridge. "This CCD camera, will duplicate on the big-screen what I see with my eyes. The display will mimic the heads-up augmented reality that is laid over my natural vision." With a minor theatrical flourish inconsistent with his personality, Matt tapped the keyboard to open the live show and...nothing happened. The concluding slide, a close-up of his eye with the ARz contact lens clearly visible lingered on the screen, mocking his discomfort.

Anyone who has had to rely on technology to perform in front of an audience knows the heart-rending jolt of failure-adrenaline. Some spectators enjoy the *shadenfreude* smell of blood in the water, and some start clucking with motherly empathy. At least one wants to get his, it's always a male, knowing hands on the keyboard. But nothing can relieve the sinking feeling. No matter how often you have stumbled before, the endocrines dissipate slowly.

"Let's see. This could be a driver issue." He worked frantically at the keyboard. "Wait, maybe...no. OK, let me try this." He was losing his audience.

Nine, ten, eleven seconds. Intellectually, Matt was bleeding out in public. Type, type. Bam! Trivial. The app had locked out the video by not closing properly. The screen lit up with a stomach-churning live view that faithfully followed Matt's jerking camera. It jumped from the keyboard, to the laptop monitor, to the projector screen, to the faces of Brogan then Samuelson. The CCD that imitated his vision was fine but the data prototype was running slow, so the effect was nauseating. Composing himself, Matt steadied and looked at Brogan. An uncomplimentary version of the frowning CTO settled down in center screen.

Matt thought-projected a request to display <name age>, and [James Brogan 43] appeared near Brogan's head. He then spoke "Age," to let the room know, after its appearance on screen, the meaning. Without thinking, he looked to Lydia Merati and her name and [47] showed up on the screen next to her head. At least one person sucked wind. Before he could thought-project <age off> he had also revealed how old the newest Board member was.

Matt walked to the window, looked out. The Staples store below showed on the projector screen. He thought-projected <retail> then <today> <cash registers> and then <revenues>. The projector screen lit up with a colored overlay framework around the nearby store. The numbers for cash registers [3] and revenues [$492.57] appeared. Matt repeated the commands aloud so the audience could interpret the numbers. The sales number jumped $85.76. When his sight drifted toward the marketplace on the distant Embarcadero, the screen got crowded with color and frames. He thought-projected <filter> <top five revenues> <this month> and the screen highlighted just five stores. He repeated his commands aloud, but always after the data had displayed. Matt was confident that the top intellects in Big Data were appreciating his voiceless command of the computer.

"Let's get practical." He thought-projected <data display off> <Arctan> <parking> <personal vehicles> and looked at Merati, whose fascinated face appeared on the screen. Listening to the data coming into his head, he repeated, "Ms. Merati, you're parked on the executive first floor E-4, blue zone." He looks straight at the engineer, "Helmut, you got a top spot today, 4th floor, D7." The screen, featuring Helmut's nod, doesn't show any text data. The screen shifts with Matt's attention to Brogan. "Dr. Brogan, you also are on the executive floor E-1, yellow zone, slot 5." Brogan looked surprised, "Huh!"

Matt thought-projected <number of visitors today> and looked back at the Staples below and stated, "Staples has had 79 visitors today," while no data appeared on the screen. Brogan asked, "We haven't been seeing the data. You see the data in your vision?"

Matt responded, "No I hear it in my head." Provocative choice of words. Except for Samuelson, a discernible shudder ran through the room. "I have trained my retina-cerebral cortex connection to accept input intuitively. My brain can receive data subconsciously. The laptop, or link, can send me newfound data and I then "know stuff."

"What you have been seeing thus far," Matt started at a deliberate pace, "has been quasi-static human access to computer resources. Nice enough. But you and I, the human species in general, are designed to hunt and kill tigers, not arrange flowers." Aware of the room for debate, Matt forged ahead. "Our brains and our eyes are capable of dynamic data magic."

Matt tosses a dry erase marker to Dr. Brogan. He catches it, partly puzzled, miffed at the insolence. "Doctor Brogan, you were just then and continue now to process visual information at around 10 megabytes per second." He cued up a slide of today's Wall Street Journal daily Major U.S. Stock-Market Indexes table.[90] A blaze of numbers. Matt continued, "Inspecting that page, we are, by the nature of the data there, rigidly limited to processing, one item at a time, around a tenth of a megabyte per second, one hundred times slower than our potential."

"Hundreds of numbers, numerous colors! But what truly interests you in the table? Certainly, the numbers themselves, the bottom line. Like the Latest Close, Nasdaq Composite, this morning down 0.7%. But what really want is to compare that to its past value. At opening. Or yesterday or when you bought in. Oh, and tomorrow. Right? Buy low, sell high. But now the rate has now dropped to one thousandth your brain's capacity.

"Your brain is a Ferrari. Your reading is a flat tire.

"So now watch this. I am going to demonstrate two tricks with ARz. I will reformat the data dynamically through thought-projection. Remember, what you see on the screen is the same as what I see in my head through ARz.

"First, I switch to 90% VR mode leaving just a faint background from this room."

The screen changes to show Director Merati, at whom

Matt is looking, visible through an utterly baffling array of Wall Street Journal numbers, lots of color. Matt thought-projects <rotate> <values axis> <rate slow> <isomorphic> and the bar graph begins to rotate, rotating toward the back and around to the front. Matt repeats the thought commands out loud, after the animation has started. "You can also do that in Excel, but it'll take minutes in the hands of a sharp data-ist." He stopped the graphics on the screen.

"Now, I am going to request to inspect specific company stock data, look at changes over the the most recent 30 days and then search for correlates. Ready?"

Wordlessly, Matt thought-projects commands to compare hourly securities of Advanced Micro Devices to Arcelormittal to Niocorp for the last month.

"We're going to see if the stocks of a major semiconductor business and a manufacturer of stainless steel relates to niobium processing. Hourly." He tells the display to add a calculation of how much the hourly price movements of AMD and MT are related to Niocorp.

Matt then projects <VR 90%> <display trailers> <time cycle> < 30 days> <1 hour per 0.5 second> <cycle>. The screen lights up with a graph of five lines, three for the hourly daily stock price of AMD, MT and NIOBF, two for the time relation between the two manufacturers compared to NIOBF.

"Let's see what we find." Dramatically, he snaps his fingers while thought-projecting <animate>.

The dynamic display jumps. What appear to be luminescent liquid surfaces grow out of the screen, trailing the hourly course of the three stocks plus the two correlates. The five surfaces undulate like horizontal flags in a breeze. Striking, colorful.

Wrinkled brows signal that Matt's audience is struggling.

Matt tries to explain. The motions in the graph reveal a subtle correlation in stock prices. But if you must explain the joke, you've lost. What he demonstrated was too much, too fast. Except for Samuelson.

Matt thought projected <VR 5%> to bring the room back into the foreground. He looked to his audience for questions.

Brogan spoke first. "Impressive Matt. I'm just not sure it convinced me to jump into rare-metals futures." He got agreement nods from Ari, Lydia and Engineer.

"But lots of potential. Nice." He was looking to the ceiling, thinking. "I would like to go back to a practical, human-factors aspect that worries me. Would you stand over at the far end of the conference table." Matt, eager to comply, walked to the suggested spot. "Right here OK?"

"Close enough. Now would you repeat that last demo?" Matt thought projected <repeat><last process> which snapped it to the data graphics. The big-screen animated as before, same stunning effects.

"Matt, would you please walk toward Dr. Samuelson, slow and easy like, please."

Matt turned and started to walk. The screen graphics stuttered a bit. On his second step Matt staggered into the chair of Eager Engineer. Lydia squeaked, leaning forward to catch him before he fell onto her. He steadied himself, in an athletic crouch. The display continued to roll but with jerks and pixilation.

Brogan jumped up from his chair, alarmed. "Matt! Jeez, you OK?" There was a collective gasp. Matt had come close to collapsing.

"I am so sorry Matt. I was expecting there might be a baud rate limitation, but I didn't think it would be that bad. Lydia, let him sit down there for a second." Matt was nowhere near needing a seat. The display and his ARz had settled down as soon as he steadied his head.

Matt had been careless. He hadn't reduced the video show. With all that data running and so much VR, his visual balance was lost. It made prototype ARz look hazardous.

Matt bumbled around trying to explain but the damage of his stumble-fall was done. He finished his planned wrap-up and directed his attention to Samuelson who sat frozen, intensely still. A therapist would have suspected anger, sexual arousal, or an absence seizure.[91] Dr. Samuelson was envisioning the future at warp speed, all three diagnoses at work.

The presentation was over.

Everyone stood up and gave the usual, obligatory compliments, wishes for future success and pledges of personal support. Brogan came over, leading his two guests. "Great work. Ambitious project. I know you have a bright future. I'm glad Ari and Lydia had an opportunity to see you in action and understand more about your ... prototyping. Keep it up, let me know if I can help." Marketing, Engineering and The Board drifted out, casting a reminder toward Dirk that they would be seeing him at this or that meeting in so and so many days. Their voices trailed off toward the elevator.

Samuelson strode directly to Matt, one, two, three giant steps and looked straight at him. Souchi, sensing that the Second Assistant was needed, followed behind. His blazing, glacier blue eyes dug deeply into Matt. "I want you out of Arctan, now."

Stefan's liver punch. Matt froze, he couldn't breathe. He had not imagined that the Master of Innovation would have been put off by a few, well, OK, five glitches. He wanted to protest but had neither breath nor heartbeat to succeed.

"Effective immediately, I am moving you off Arctan's official books to work solely under me. Souchi," he looked her way, "let's call it 'Insights'. You'll have a separate budget, which I'd like you to increase dramatically, please." Sending an unmistakable reinforcing glance over his shoulder, he continued, "Souchi manages all Secret Ops for me, she knows the protocols and the means to ramp up without leaving a record in Arctan financials. All your work will be covered under my personal double-ended encryption account. You, I want you to know this, and your team are onto something big. Let's all of us not blow it.

"You'll recall that your Confidentiality and IP Agreements assigned invention rights in my name, with generous benefits for you. If this goes as I intend, we stand to make quite a bit of money. And you, I believe, will be rich and famous."

Dirk Samuelson softened. "Matt. Human affections, ambitions are complex. Moving forward, I don't want you to miss out on anything. I've invented means to enjoy emotions and successes. I'll tell you more in time if you wish." Although his ice-blues were focused on Matt, Samuelson was talking to two people in the room. Matt and Souchi wondered what the master of Big Data might know about their "Tiger" encounter outside the conference door.

"After today's events, I think you'll need all the support you can muster."

CHAPTER 36
MUSTER SUPPORT

Dr. Samuelson swept from the room leaving Matt and Souchi to figure out what needed to be done. increase the budget. Leave no trace. Above all, make bold decisions.

For most people, the meeting would have been a resounding success, but Matt was down. The technical glitches had ruined his day.

Souchi broke his funk. "I've got oversight of Arctan Secret Ops. ARz is not the first top secret project here. And not the last. But it might be the greatest."

Souchi could smell gender skepticism. "As your friend Devon might say, 'I get shit done.'"

"Money's not a problem. Arctan's floating on a bundle of cash. Almost a hundred billion. The Board would love to dole that out, but Samuelson has and will hold off any attempt to dilute his devotion to new product development. Given his track record for making R&D profitable, the Board is stuck.

"Matt, Our 'Insight' expenses will be a needle in the cash haystack.

"Ramping up a couple million dollars a month needs professional management; I've set up help from two Stanford and Berkeley MBAs. Tough part is to keep them from feuding about football. Let's start by outlining the work to complete.

"Matt, think big, make a full-on wish list. Don't worry about budget."

This was new ground for Matt but he got into it. "We gotta improve how the computer sends in data audio in case the user gets busy with things happening in the real world."

"Slows things down, Matt."

"Sure, but otherwise I get caught off-guard, like what happened when it hit the fan during my demo to the Board."

"Right. Maybe we need a routine to measure how much you're paying attention?"

When done, they had a wish list and tech specs for twenty-one ARz features, many already being developed. "Our MBAs will estimate the resources needed and by week's end identify where to get them. Software development will be sub-contracted to our people in India. By the way, Dr. Samuelson has positioned Arctan to partner with ESRI down south in Redlands and to buy GeoSpatial Immersion GmbH Munich by the end of the month. He knew you'd need their mapping technology. Now that you know, don't tell anyone. Insider trading allegations get sloppy."

They kept pounding on it. Someone at the security cameras noticed their dedication. Around 7:30, a meal was delivered to the walnut conference table. The flower arrangement, silverware and cloth napkins suggested that Dr. Samuelson's Third Personal Assistant was offering encouragement. Souchi guided the dinner break toward personal. "I could have said that Arctan

HR informants knew you like salmon and veggie ravi-olis but I just guessed."

Matt laughed, "Honestly," not realizing that truth wasn't the point, "we grow up on meat and pota-toes in Tennessee..." Sensing a misstep, "...but seafood's cool." Souchi smiled lightly but enjoyed his blush. She used the slip-up as an entrée. "Tennessee. Do you miss home?"

"My parents were dedicated scientists, so I had plenty of alone time. Learned how to be independent and cook for myself." Back-peddling unnecessarily, "but we had salmon, too." She smiled. "Miss home? Sure, a bit. Cer-tainly grateful for the freedom they gave me as a kid."

Matt gathered some courage. "Dr. Samuelson brought you here from Korea?" Souchi chose to send a mes-sage. "Devon got that right." Matt showed surprise that she could finger Devon. "Matt! We're Arctan In-ternational. Antoinette updates us immediately when we get searched. It's OK. That data was restricted but Devon's resourceful." Matt wondered. How deep could Arctan dig?

"You probably know about the Japanese girl?"

Matt nodded. "Sounds like you were tough at Taekwando."

"Was and am, but the papers blew that incident way out of proportion. Older Koreans handed their War down to me. I brought hatred to the match. My emo-tions ran away but the Japanese girl and I, we were all good afterwards. I apologized, Asian style. She hadn't heard about the *waisan*. Still, I can't let go of my grandma and mom's stories. What happened, the soldiers...." Souchi stopped to regain her composure. "I am proud that my moms persisted but I'm ashamed that I can't let go of hating what those men did." Matt could have said something dumb, but instead reached out to touch her hand.

"I'm sorry, I really am," and he gave her a hug.

Dr. Samuelson and capitalism motivates. There are always one or two Arctan offices and conference rooms lit up into the wee hours. But the great majority of the three thousand plus people who worked in Arctan headquarters filed out in time to fill pubs, local and Pasture, before happy hour ended. Not Matt and Souchi. They worked halfway to midnight. Finally, Matt declared that he was done in.

"Yessss, work's over!" Souchi walked to the control desk next to the main door. She pulled out the drawer where white board markers and notepads were kept and removed a roll of tape. She pushed a chair into the far corner of the room and climbed up to put a piece of tape over the surveillance camera lens, blinding it. She jumped off nimbly and walked over to Matt.

"I had the impression you were going to ask me if we could make love right now. And I had the idea that I would agree." With no further prompting, or any thoughts about Dr. S, MBAs, the ARz team, they tangled beautifully, satisfying desires that had been mounting for weeks; Devon would have been disappointed, but the walnut conference table never came into play.

CHAPTER 37
DISCOVERY OF
THE OCCULT

Mid-morning, Matt gave Alicia and Devon a quick de-brief by phone and arranged for a sausage and beer meeting at Zig's. He forgot, maybe, to mention the tryst with Souchi, though it preoccupied his amygdala.

Having been transported from Earth to Ecstasy the night before, Matt was private-shy entering Zig's; Alicia side-eyed him closely.

Devon had been working, "I sent Sush a few items for the wish list."

That "Sush" again. Alicia's head dropped, chin to chest. She hadn't given up trying to fix Devon but he was a hard case. Oblivious, Devon explained, "There's loose ends to clean up with my laser contacts and implants. She passed it on to the little biz geniuses." Devon held MBAs in low esteem.

"But I'm beginning to like that girl." Alicia glared at to-tally-out-of-touch Devon. "Whaa. Whaat? What'd I say, Leash?" Her silent look of, "Seriously?" caused Devon to pause, then look at Matt. The blush he found there lit him up. "Noooo. Really?" Looking back at Alicia, he met a toxic, icy stare, the eyes of an executioner. Devon clamped up so suddenly he choked. Alicia was in no mood to offer a Heimlich, even out of national pride.

Matt replied weakly, "Yea, me too," prompting Alicia to crab sideways. "Let's schedule Souchi for an in-depth show and tell. How soon?" Since the latest ARz software updates were already installed, they agreed to meet the next day at Devon's Berkeley lab. They would get there early to setup the demo for Souchi.

Next day, Souchi arrived exactly on schedule at DOD SPRC. Looking at her sign-in, the student watchpuppy asked, "Are you the replacement for Mr. Souchi?" Accustomed to western ignorance of Korean naming, she smiled broadly, "Oh, no. He's irreplaceable. I'm his daughter." Still puzzled by her US Passport the student was relieved when the newly empowered Devon popped through the door. "C'mon Sush," Souchi enjoyed Devon's breezy casual, "let's rock and roll." Guessing deliciously about her involvement with Matt, he worked to cover his suspicions. Waving ahead, "We're all set up down the hall," he followed while trying not to enjoy her walk. Souchi played the role, letting him man-flounder behind her.

He clumsily opened the conference room door for Souchi, who greeted everyone with a pleasant, businesslike demeanor. Alicia watched her like a hawk. Was there a slight wink at Matt? who was limiting eye contact all round. Devon luxuriated in profane confusion.

They were in a twelve-by-twelve government issue room with a grey, bent-sheet-metal, faux-wood, government issue conference table in the center. Walls matched the halls, cinderblock under uncountable coats of beige-grey paint. No Naugas[92] had been injured in the making of the seat-sprung chairs around the table where a laptop and old-school projector were running. In contrast to the furniture, several fourth-generation AR goggles were scattered on the table. Souchi noted, "I didn't think those were available yet." Devon, sarcastically proud, "DOD Sush baby. DOD." She liked how his informality kept everyone loose. But why did Alicia wince?

This was Matt's show. He opened, "Basically, let's start where the Arctan meeting ended." Oops. He stammered a bit, embarrassed by the blush he had given himself. His distraction was made worse when Souchi agreed, "Excellent idea." Alicia wanted to hug Souchi. Devon simply glowed and looked away, revisiting the walnut table.

"Um. So. We. Uh. We were. I was talking about ... being able to move through data fields." Recovering, he put on his camera glasses, "like at Arctan, my contact lens ARz view will be mimicked on the screen and in your VR headsets by these." The three put on their head mounted displays. A 3D view of the room filled their vision. "Now you see what I see." He looked around the room, sweeping deliberately toward them. They wriggled at seeing themselves. Devon, of course, flipped two birds at the camera.

"I will be sending thought-projection instructions to ARz. I might sometimes narrate verbally but otherwise any changes in your display are the result of my thought-commands."

Four people in a nondescript basement room thought they were the only humans on the planet who could experience such a show. Unless Devon's deep DOD search was wrong, their pride was justified.

"Now, I am going to slide from reality to augmented reality." He thought-projected <augment> <80 percent> <birthdays> Matt threw in facial recognition <facial R>. An overlay of birth dates appeared on top of Devon, Alica and Souchi.

"We're going to inspect Arctan's international business data. I'll change to full VR and the room will disappear. <clear> <virtual> <globe> <whole> <England> <London> and Matt's eyes and their displays gently shifted (they had added that software fix yesterday) to the familiar Google Earth-like view, centered on London from a simulated altitude of 1250 miles, 1000 miles higher than spy satellites.

"Everybody OK?" With no objections, Matt continued. "I'm now going to add in dynamic flying so I can use my thoughts and gaze to steer our view." <flight> <gaze> <rate> <20 percent> and everyone began to see their view of the planet move toward Paris, where Matt was taking them with his eyes.

Matt mentally actuated an overlay of Arctan's current business data. A swarm of lights in multiple colors at various intensities lit up all over the hemisphere. The lights blinked.

"There we see individual Arctan sources of revenue in real time. Brightness is proportional to projected daily total sales, color is type, like corporate customer versus retail trade. Blinking represents momentary rate of cash flow."

He paused to let them inspect the densely colored globe. "Next, I'll filter it.[93] Many lights vanished, leaving maybe several hundred red and green dots blinking at various speeds. "I averaged, in 10-kilometer squares, Arctan customers who are using more or less than $10,000 per hour of our streaming and analytics services for consumer-products manufacturing business data."

Devon gave out a low whistle. Gamer skills let him quickly adapt to virtual worlds. Even as a creator of ARz, he was still as impressable as a child. "Guys. That's cool. Real cool."

"You like that? Watch this." Matt wanted to demonstrate time compression. "How about we look at Arctan revenue generation in Southeast Asia?" <clear> <back> <boundaries> The display jumped back to the globe centered on London with international boundaries overlaid in yellow. Following Matt's gaze, the scene began to move toward the east, in ten seconds passing over Ukraine and then Turkmenistan, Myanmar, gradually stopping over Vietnam. Matt's thought-injections <view> <500 kilometer> made the scene zoom to spy-satellite altitude of 240 miles, encompassing an area from Phnom Penh to Phu Quy Island in the South China Sea. His gaze centered the map on Ho Chi Minh City. The geo detail was so sharp that it was easy for the three viewers to imagine that they were spying from space.

"Now, let's look at how Arctan made money down there today.[94] The display flickered.

"There's Arctan revenue sources in two-kilometer squares, over $1000 per hour in green, between $1000 and $100 is red. Blinking is proportional to dollar rate."

Souchi knew the geography, "All kinds of green around

cities. See, HCMC[95] looks like it has at least a hundred greens. And similar activity in Long Hau and Ba Ria." Alicia and Devon liked seeing the money flow and loved Matt's massaged data, graphical, understandable, at the flick of ... a thought?

"OK. Now I want to see the last week of income by the hour in those two-kilometer squares starting at midnight Thursday to right now. Ten days will go by in two minutes. Oh, and I'll leave it in night-and-day mode so you won't need to look at the map-clock to know what time it is." Matt thought-projected commands into ARz but didn't start the animation. In the high-res, AR glasses, the Earth below was midnight-dark except for some dozen clots of city lights. Strings of pearls radiated out of cities. A Space Shuttle awe hung over the room. Matt sent a thought to ARz to turn on the static display of colored revenue dots. He got the same "ahhhh" effect as plugging in the family Christmas tree. "Ready, let's roll." He launched the animation.

The show started at midnight, so some of the city lights and many red, high dollar, lights flickered out right away. After three seconds, the scene began to lighten for dawn and all but two revenue lights had gone out. Devon guessed ahead, "C'mon Vietnam. Back to work!" The edge of dawn lit up the coast and proceeded west over the Mekong Delta. "Sunrise and look at the light show! Makin' money!"

The show continued for ten night and day cycles. It was like watching the economy breathe. On the first weekend there were almost no reds and some greens. Nighttime stirred with minimal lights. Alicia and Devon and Matt had built this monster but were still learning its capabilities and enjoying every minute. Souchi was speechless but tearful within her goggles. She had an emotional attachment with the people below and understood how far their lives were from this basement room.

As it ended, the team bubbled with ideas, some for improvements, some for sales and marketing, some just simple awe. Alicia requested another look so Matt teed it up, same commands, and put it on continuous autorun so everyone could get their fill.

As the animations flew by, hours reduced to seconds, the team blurted out observations. In the fourth cycle Alicia interrupted. "Stop there Matt." Alicia stayed quiet and introspective. Everyone took off their HMDs. Devon and Souchi compared notes.

Then Alicia spoke heavily, "Something's funny there." Devon thought she meant funny-ha-ha. "Right, we just watched Arctan bank a trillion Vietnamese dong."[96] Alicia ignored the lousy joke.

"Matt, can you run just Thursday noon to Monday midnight. And half as fast." Matt nodded as Alicia explained. "The revenue pace picked up in the morning, peaked mid-morning, slowed mid-day and then surged at the end of the day. Almost died off completely by six or seven. But then something odd happens, slightly overlapping the end of the day's burst. Watch." Matt said, "HMDs." He sent thought-injections and launched the run.

Just as the slower-paced Earth animation entered darkness on Thursday, and most of the blinking lights had expired, Alicia blurted, "There, there, in Ho Chi Minh

City!" but the moment passed too quickly; some red lights had momentarily flickered in and out for maybe four seconds, two real hours on the ground. Everyone was ready for it to reoccur as Friday night lights flickered again. There it was. Saturday and Sunday, when there were fewer revenue dots during the daytime, the short, low-revenue nighttime bursts reappeared, like the daytime dots, but less frequent. Monday, the daytime red and green revenue dots popped up and intensified, dropping rapidly with sunset. But the brief red bursts consistently lit the City, starting around six or seven PM and continuing to midnight-ish. Devon offered a profound analysis, "WTF?"

Alicia commented, "Red. Small potatoes revenue at night just after business hours." Matt, can you color code for type of income, whatever you got?" Matt nodded, "I have thought-vocab for 'cloud software' versus 'cloud data' versus 'manufacturing data.' Those numbers we saw are oddly small so I could throw in 'retail sales' a catch-all which includes Arctan OTC analytics products." Matt looked blank for a moment as he thought-projected to ARz. "Ready," They watched, alert to a new replay of four days of dancing dots.

As it finished, Alicia summed up, "Somebody's running an Arctan consumer business late every night of the week in downtown Ho Chi Minh City. Retail?" They agreed, odd.

Souchi looked puzzled; she knew all about Arctan's businesses, "That's off the wall, no way."

As Devon had said, "WTF."

CHAPTER 38
DOWN IN THE WEEDS

"Drugs! Gotta be the TMC Cartel."[97] Devon's imagination had run wild, but no one had a better suggestion, "Need more data."

Matt wanted to continue geo-flying ARz. "I can fly us over some other cities." Alicia and Souchi wanted to look back at how long it had been going on. Devon, reluctant to give up on his drug mafia, "How about just getting down low for a closer look? I bet there's some meth moving around."

Matt started flying ARz through the team's list. Filtered for <retail> he searched ARz all over South East Asia. Even a random sample in Honolulu, Sofia, Milan, Kuala Lumpur and Sydney didn't turn up any pulses of nighttime income. The business showed up solely in Ho Chi Minh City.

Continuing back through time, five, six, seven weeks, they found that the first burst of income was sometime about six weeks before, starting small, maybe a dozen transactions a night for the first week but ramping up over twenty or thirty days. Again, nowhere other than HCMC.

Matt thought-projected for type of payment, limited

to <cash> <credit card> <bank draft> and <other>. The result was bizarre. The remittances were all classified as "other." No credit cards, no cash, no bank transfers. Souchi guessed: "Some kind of membership or club with automatic debiting?"

Removing the HMD's, Devon insisted on moving down for a closer look. He wouldn't be put off any longer. "Focus on a spot with the most activity. Zoom in close enough to look at about 10 meters resolution, far enough to capture a good-sized sample, like from an altitude of one kilometer. Use the same time-lapse speed."

"Woah. Gimme a moment." Matt was still learning to pilot ARz. The jumping display mocked his learning curve.

In about a minute, with two false starts, he had the display set up. "Headsets everyone." Before launching he explained, "The hot spot was north and west of the chi-chi downtown around Đồng Khởi street and Nguyễn Huệ avenue. I set up for around thirty blocks east to west and about fifty blocks north to south just off the Sông Sài Gòn river." Matt thought projected <business> <sector> <colors> <top five> <revenue> <last month>, "Looks like the neighborhood is mostly finance and import-export management. That's the blue and green outlines."

"This time-run we'll look at individual sources of "other" income and ignore all the conventional revenues. I'll add a comet function, so the spending stays visible longer. Ready?" He launched the time-lapse, again, starting at noon on Thursday ten days earlier. This time, one then two afternoon dots blinked on then faded off. Like before, activity picked up as the sun set.

Alicia counted dots. "One... Two... Three, four... Five, six, seven...." and stopped as the dots diminished after midnight. The pattern continued through the ten-day run.

Devon quantified, "Maybe thirty-five, forty pops any given night?"

"Maybe a hundred bucks each," suggested Matt.

Alicia added, "It seems like a random distribution around the area. Weekends were a bit slower." They were narrowing the puzzle.

Souchi knew the most about Arctan businesses. She shook her head. "Can we dig deeper? Matt, can you color tag the revenue sources so we can see if someone collects more than once."

Matt thought-projected the specs through ARz.

"Heads-up," Matt waited for everyone to put on their displays and then launched the ten-day run looking at unusual income sources in downtown Ho Chi Minh City. Alicia named the colors as they popped up. "Mister Scarlet. Gotcha. There's Frau Red and Miss Candy Apple." Devon looked blankly at her.[98] How many could she name? She kept it up for three new reds. Her entertaining ability to name reds made it easy to forget the puzzle. And then came a surprise. "Woah, Mr. Scarlet is double dipping." Then Candy Apple showed up for Round Two. The color palette of income never got past six reds! The result stunned them all. One more cycle and the headsets came off.

"What was that? There's only six?" Devon believed

Alicia but wasn't so sure he could make one red from another, so he asked Matt to simplify the palette. "How about a rerun with six primary colors. Can you add map trails, so we see where each dot goes?" Matt thought-projected in the specs. "Headsets on?" This time the run would show red, orange, yellow, green, blue and indigo dots popping up. If a color dot repeated, a line connected it to the prior dot. It looked like the revenue makers were moving around the downtown. Yellow and blue disappeared off the map area once each.

Alicia wondered, "Does Arctan have a Lyft or Uber affiliation in Vietnam?" Souchi was certain, "Not a legitimate one, not possible. Too far off mission. Besides, those dots almost all stayed within a four-block area. Green actually did three loops." She turned to her cell to initiate a scan of Arctan business centers, wishing she could thought-project the request.

Devon waxed analytical. "Drugs. I mean, maybe you guys don't have much experience, but I tell you that reminds me of a drug ring. Why else anonymous collection, no credit card, no banks involved? No traceability. Moving around looking for customers. The neighborhood knows how to spot the dealer's car, after hours, connecting with the well-heeled office worker. Better yet, based on some software, cell phone connection. You know, Grubbyhub for coke. DoorHash for the dreamy."

The discussion that followed couldn't improve on Devon's hypothesis. Then Matt offered an alternate option. "I could try to find a link between the start of this business and expenses nearby. If it's a new thing, there should be prior start-up expenses and they might have been paid with Arctan funds."

He thought-projected a cross-correlation function to look for coincidence between these weird income events and Arctan expenses in the general geographical area starting three months ago.

"This might take a while. It has to go back and forth looking at strength of combinations and permutations for expense events and income events across 90 days," but as he was explaining, the projector screen popped up with a find.

"Hey. Ninety-eight percent of the dots' business correlated to funding based out of 17 Front Street, San Francisco. Arctan headquarters." Someone was launching an Arctan startup business in Vietnam. Off the books.

Normally an illicit seed business of a couple million annual US would have gone straight to corporate Ethics and Accountability. Pin down the perp. Investigate. Punish or reward depending on the story, after all, Dr. Samuelson encouraged intrapreneurs to be bold. The fact that it was under the table, offshore and firewalled weighed heavily against reward.

Souchi voiced their mutual conviction, "We've got to tell Dirk."

CHAPTER 39
TELLING THE BOSS

"So what've you got?" he charged into the twenty-fifth-floor conference room, no niceties. The founder of Arctan knew Souchi wouldn't summon him unless it was real. Samuelson read the four glum faces around the walnut conference table, "That bad?"

"Sir," Matt was Tennessee-programmed for good manners, "we believe," he looked at the team for support, "that someone at Arctan has started a business in Ho Chi Minh City on Arctan funds with proceeds accruing to Arctan." Samuelson was never over-reactive when thinking. At this point he looked underwhelmed.

"And we think it may be illegal, perhaps involving drug trade."

Dirk Samuelson hated deceit, disloyalty and crime; top of the list, hurtful crime driven by greed. He leaned back, thought a moment, then leaned in. "Evidence?"

"Using ARz, we have discovered that, starting three months ago, someone funded a start-up with about three, three and a half million in Arctan funds. It looks like there are six mobile units generating income independently in downtown HCMC. We think they are subscriber driven, cell phone summoned."

Samuelson interjected, "Uber?"

"Sort of. The business revenues are now over $10000

per night growing steadily for the last month."

"Take a look." Matt reran the time-lapse dot-show. Samuelson watched, "Impressive," then asked sharp questions. Devon and Alicia addressed tech issues, Souchi reported, "Looked through our branches. No solid leads."

Matt speculated. "Whoever started the business knows how to protect it. We could hack in but then the operators might find out. We figured, we had better move carefully."

"Right, right. So, the revenues come to Arctan. Model looks profitable. Scalable, works in HCMC, could work in...any town? Drugs? Small quantities, high price, thinly spread. Vendors keep moving, online site buried in an encrypted VPN. Records expunged within thirty-six hours. Police would likely have a tough job stopping more than one vendor-operator at a time. Never mind getting convictions, even without corruption. But why through Arctan? Could just as easily been private." Samuelson looked around the table for answers.

"Maybe the brains couldn't or wouldn't risk raising the startup capital given the illegality, number one, and number two they figured it was easier and safer to hide under an Arctan umbrella."

"After proof of principle on Arctan money, take it private?" volunteered Alicia.

"Income to cover unit losses of a boss here?" Souchi asked.

"All of those are good ideas. He looked pointedly at Souchi and then Matt, "but be careful about jumping to conclusions about who. The sums and timing narrow the possibility down to a dozen candidates. No matter what or who, you guys need more data, meaning boots on the ground." He looked at his watch.

"Souchi, would you and Matt please get on the Emirates plane at four forty-five tonight. Arctan planes're in Europe, NATO business. There's the dateline day to lose. You can be in HCMC in two days. It looks like ARz is travelable. Get IT to set up secure links for you."

"Devon, I'll have General Patterson deliver some Geode-P and Geode-T devices[99] to your lab. Program them for ARz. Get them on that plane." This was Devon's kind of fun. He ran out like he was headed to an Irish party.

Matt, not used to Arctan travel, stammered, "Packing? ..."

"Antoinette will have all your needs TSA-compliant and on the plane in...three hours. We know your sizes. There will be a few extra conveniences and passports too." Seeing Matt's confusion, "Arctan has all your personal data. You'll need to take the 'copter from the roof. It will be flight-ready before you. Let's nail this bastard."

A FINAL
REMINDER

PART TWO:

THE DARK SIDE

CHAPTER 40
FORTY THOUSAND FOOT CLUB

Antoinette greeted them at the Emirates gate. She and Souchi hugged and kissed in a mosh of Caribbean emotion and Korean dignity. Antoinette had a lilting French accent to her island English but everyone at Arctan knew that her tongue and wit were venomous. Loyal to Samuelson and Arctan, never missing an assignment, not a girl to cross.

"*Bonjour* guys, I have all you need, *J'espère!*" Her lingering, mischievous gaze made Matt wonder whether the tape over the conference room camera had been effective. Or were Souchi and Antionette much better friends than he knew?

"Let's go, we get you on the *aeroplane*." As they ran-walked past security, another privilege of Arctan connections, Antoinette handed over their carry-on bags, passports and an envelope, explaining, "From zis flight, you must send nice thank-you note to the Emir. The Doctor set up a hospital for him a long time ago in Abu Dhabi. So, The Doctor fly free Emirates Air." Laughing Caribbean-style, "Ohh my, you be friends of The Doctor, you lucky people!" She gave them a folder with a print copy of their Emirates First Class ticket, which looks like an invite to Buckingham Palace.

"Geodes?" Matt wondered, approaching the gangway.

"Ahh, soon. Mr. Devon is already out from le BART but he is making way *à toute vitesse* quickly. Go in, go in, not to worry. You just have a *bon nuit!*" as she hustled them into the rampway.

"Not to worry" sums up the Emirates First Class experience. In Saint Laurent-inspired uniforms, attendants greeted and accompanied them every step of the way. Their seats were private compartments plush in leather and hush. Slippers and champagne. No opening up pesky, pedestrian swag bags. Needs were in place; requests were delivered in a moment. Attendants moved gracefully among the eight seats, as though with ballet credentials. Matt heard at least five languages in use with passengers. He was addressed in charmingly accented English. Dignity without deference, an atmosphere of complete indulgence.

The second-in-charge attendant apologized in three languages to passengers, "We shall be underway shortly. We are awaiting an important courier delivery." Matt shared with Souchi his humorous vision of Devon as courier-in-bell-boy-cap.

Standing in the isle, privacy-seeking passengers preparing comforts or headed to the open bar, Souchi dropped her business-persona and pressed close to Matt. Pulling him in she said, "Matt, let's go to Vietnam. Just you and me. A little holiday, hmmm?"

Looking at the "S-Class Mercedes seating"[100] in the Emirates Airbus 380, Matt was inspired, "Wanna play tiger?" Souchi smiled, happy with this boy.

In the last century, the Boeing 707 started people

dreaming about the Thirty Thousand Foot Club. Musk and Branson raised people's horizons to the One Hundred Thousand Foot Club. The Space Station created a special membership, the Five Hundred Thousand Foot Club. Today, there are day and night dreams of the Moon and Mars Clubs. Humans are fond of intercourse and altitude is an aphrodisiac.

Under the pressure of twenty-four hours of international intrigue, Souchi and Matt had almost forgotten the Night Under the Walnut Conference Table. First-time sex can be exhilarating, or it can go sour. Souchi and Matt had hit pure gold. Satisfied, in several goes, they had luxuriated, two idyllic bodies in the prime of life, tuned by sport and nutrition, a trifecta of love, sight and senses. The helicopter ride was behind them. Their travel needs had magically appeared at the airport. Devon had delivered programmed Geodes. Matt and Souchi were on their way to Round Two, the Forty Thousand Foot Club.

CHAPTER 41
BOOTS ON THE GROUND

The Emirates flights connecting Souchi and Matt through Dubai were uneventful, at least as far as the flight crew were concerned. EA 392 vectored into Ho Chi Minh City airport at 21:30 local. First Class service included a limo to the five-star Sofitel. Conscious of their rumpled state, the chauffeur escorted Matt and Souchi into the sumptuous lobby and handed them over to hotel staff. "On behalf of Emirates Air, I hope you have a wonderful evening." Souchi beamed and Matt blushed. Exhausted, he was looking forward to sleeping, just sleeping.

One day later, Souchi and Matt were stunned when they popped out, middle of the night, onto the vibrant, crazy-crowded Lê Duẩn, in Ho Chi Minh City's chi-chi Bến Nghé neighborhood. Over a half century before, this same street was just as crazy, but from confusion and fear. In April 1975, you needed to look haggard but joyful, wear a red head scarf and carry a well-worn AK47. Folks who couldn't muster that look were hiding or had fled the city. By the thousands they were boarding or swimming to shaky boats in the South China Sea[101] with gold sewn into their clothing.

Seventy percent of the survivors would end up living in

Orange County, California. There, in two decades, Little Saigon[102] became one of the most industrious communities in the USA.

Disproportionately, the children of the survivors would go on to attend university and become prosperous professionals. Arctan employed several hundred accomplished descendants of the Debacle of '75.[103] But tonight's optimistic energy in Bến Nghé didn't wash away the stories for Souchi.

"Matt, wait." She clutched his arm. "Can you feel it?" Matt looked around, lost. Her darkened eyes searched his. "The tormented souls, Matt, the wars." She released his arm and gave him a soft push. "Go ahead a bit. I'll catch up to you at that Starbucks on the corner." He looked at her, worried. "I'll be fine, just need a moment."

She stood alone letting the crowd flow around her. Survivors. Her mom's stories of wartime in Korea flooded her memory. Thoughts of the ensuing wars in Cambodia, Laos and Vietnam swept over her. She wept at the tragedy of it all and her own good fortune. Souchi made a silent offering of *gip-eun seulpeum,* deep sadness, to her kin.

Matt waited anxiously inside the generic international Starbucks, Seattle-in-Saigon. He melted with relief when Souchi shot through the door with, "Let's eat!" He held back, "You OK?" With a nod, avoiding talk, she dragged him out to the street, waving to fetch two green-vested Grab drivers from a clutch reclining precariously on their scooters nearby. The lead driver, mid-60s, pulled up close and handed her the helmet. Souchi signaled universal sign language for "eat" and tried her best online-Vietnamese for street food. "*Thức ăn đường phố. Thức ăn đường phố*" which he repeated to his partner driver. Both burst with laughter. She had expressed an interest in eating street signs. More hand waving and maybe communication, and off they went. Matt perched precariously, more astride his driver than the Honda. Joining the never-ending river of mopeds and chaos, they set out on a mission.

Driver One pulled up at an artfully illuminated garden restaurant three blocks from Sofitel. Lots of palm architecture. Up lighting. Menu on a pedestal. Maître de at the entry. It exuded French colonialism and pricey cuisine. Matt was raring to go. Souchi made it clear this wasn't what she had in mind. The pantomime with her driver started again. She Asia-squatted on the sidewalk and made air shovels from an imaginary bowl to her mouth. The driver and his partner got it, "*Thức ăn đường phố! Thức ăn đường phố!* Street food." Enthusiastically, he got her saddled up, a soul sister discovered.

Back past Sofitel, left down Hai Bà Trưng avenue in a river of scooters jockeying for ten extra centimeters at the red light. Matt imagined and rejected a Great Escape from the compacting horde. He tried to share his anxiety with Souchi but she's having too much fun. Light changes, their drivers forge right, diagonally across three lanes in twenty meters. Why not plan ahead?

Driving over the curb, they wiggle the 200-pound bikes in amongst seated sidewalk diners who pay no heed. The restaurant, on broken concrete and dust, is forty-three fully occupied nine-inch-tall blue and red and yellow plastic seats, rejects from one of Vietnam's kindergarten seat manufactories. And three open fires heating three steaming pots.

For two hours of pointings, Matt eats better than ever before in his life. He wonders why his culture had cheated him of these pleasures. Something to sleep on.

The next morning they began work on the plan to pinpoint a physical source of revenue, at least one cash register. Matt's algorithms had not yet cracked the money flow; the colored dots were only dots. They needed to connect one dot to something real.

They hadn't thought about the detective stuff. How to blend in was a problem. They dressed like the tourists, but Matt's height stood out. When he suggested that Souchi would blend, she bristled. "Matt! Every local will see I'm a foreigner, even before I open my mouth. My skin, hair, face. Like you, I'm a tourist. We'll just be who we are."

Matt tried to patch it up, "Just two hot young lovers on holiday fighting an international drug ring looking for simple eternal happiness under the auspices of a powerful multi-national corporation." She poked him and they wrestled onto the mattress.

The match ended in a draw. Matt recalled the old Tennessee saying, "It's not the size of the dog in the fight but the size of the fight in the dog," but didn't use it. Too risky. They got back to business. Matt saddled up in his ARz contacts. Souchi pulled out a backpack stuffed with a DOD laptop and a handful of Geodes.

The uneasy wedding of Vietnam's last-century communism and this-century capitalism had drifted away from Marx. Infrastructure had improved during the infamous pre-'20s trade-war that spawned the China Plus

One[104] policy, so Ho Hi Minh City was blessed with enviable high speed connectivity. They could conserve Devon's Geodes as they prowled the city.

Matt had mapped a month of illicit transactions. He brought the map up in VR. Souchi shared on the laptop screen. For the past thirty days, money flow centered around the neighborhood southwest of the hotel. The two blocks both sides of the Vuitton and Gucci lined Đường Đồng Khởi avenue were thick with deals. It wasn't going to be difficult for a buff semi-white guy with a slim, uber-attractive Asian chick to blend among well-heeled shoppers, but this intersection didn't have a harbor in which to loiter. They searched on.

Eventually, they settled on a fourth choice. The Cà phê Hương Chiều sat on a side street two storefronts upstream from a bustling intersection which had averaged two illicit red dot transactions per night for the last month. The Café preserved French colonialism; patrons lingered in the sidewalk boutique behind low planters containing fragrant jasmine, sitting around wrought iron tables with flower centerpieces. Clients smoked and sipped *cà phê sữa đá* iced espresso with sweetened condensed milk to pass lazy hours in the dying day's heat. Occasionally gringos dropped in to avoid corporate coffee, providing cover for Matt and Souchi. The genre was good for sleuthing, somewhat hidden among the tropical foliage but with sightlines down two streets. Matt surveyed the action in augmented reality. Souchi, acting social-media-distracted, followed his view in her iPhone.

Matt worked to act normal. The old head mounted

displays never got better than just OK. There was the irritating mass-on-the-head. The outside world was always through a half mirror. Devon had solved that. His integrated organic lasers beamed augmentation from within the contacts, no mirrors. Matt enjoyed high-contrast vision. Still, he struggled. He was learning On The Job how to appreciate graphical pop-ups without being obvious.

Detective novels in the last century taught a devouring public that Sam Spade or George Smiley's greatest stake-out skill was to avoid drowning in coffee or bourbon. As rank amateurs, Matt and Souchi made frequent trips to the Asian style bathroom, nerves jangled by *cà phê sữa đá*, Vietnam's legal equivalent of meth. Matt learned that caffeine upset the clarity of his thought-projections to ARz. He needed to consciously corral his thinking to avoid having names or ages or statistics pop up on random Café customers. Pumped on coffee, he even let his focus wander into questionably intrusive inquiries revealing employment and personal histories. Souchi had to scowl at him once when he whispered to her that a fat guy in the far corner was a two-time felon in Holland.

Since the illicit Arctan transactions register so briefly, Matt would have to actually see one in ARz. On average, there had been about a hundred hits spread over six-hours in eighty square blocks, so they would also need to be lucky. The Café stake out was a grind.

Starting at dusk, they sat and tried to appear casual, sipping, reading and shifting. All around them customers smoked cigarettes, the Gudang Garam as acrid as smoldering clove rope. The street was perpetually crowded with traffic, motor scooters competed with delivery trucks to see who could create the most noxious fumes. The air irritated Matt's ARz; the job was not glamorous. Unknowingly, Matt missed his first transaction while on a coffee repurposing trip to the men's room.

It wasn't until the third night, when their continued presence had begun to feel odd, that they got a hit. A compact commercial van splashed with colorful ads for Japanese whisky, typical in the city, pulled up to the stop light on their side of the intersection. Matt watched as a passenger hopped out and threw the door closed as the light changed. Pressured by the traffic, the van revved into the intersection. Its passenger hurried off down the smaller cross street to the right. Just as the van reached the far side of the crossing, ARz pinged a transaction. Matt jumped noticeably, poking Souchi subtly as the van disappeared into traffic.

They had made first sight.

Matt and Souchi hid their excitement. They smartly surveyed the patio and surrounding street. It didn't look like anyone noticed how closely they observed the van. They had had two nights to plan for this event so they settled back into their seats, electrified but protecting their stakeout. After a few minutes, ARz-Matt still focused on the intersection, they rose as casually as possible and left the Hương Chiều.

Matt and Souchi walked arm-in-arm a block along the same direction the van had followed. They found a place to stand where Matt could still watch the road. They speculated: with a slim sample of one, they had a place to start, commercial vans with a passenger climbing out leaving behind an ARz transaction. They decided to find a place where they could watch a van after money changed hands. They needed to change hotels.

Sen Vàng Spa Hotel was a giant step down from their first digs, but it loomed over a T-bone corner with great sight lines. The upper floors had small, wrought iron trimmed balconies allowing visibility up and down both streets. The façade was worn and lush with humidity-inspired biology.

Pushing through an inadequately polished brass door, they entered a dim and musty lobby. Seven heads turned. At the front desk, the aging staff acted as if Communism had erased their personality. Souchi didn't need Vietnamese to recognize snarky when the check-in clerk snicker-commented to his partners, surely about the different surnames in their passports.

Greasy cracks and chips in the faux-marble floor complimented the worn fabric on five edge-browned couches, two occupied by old men with cigarette stained fingers. They had run out of conversation topics long ago and now sat waiting, in sight of the dark at the end of the tunnel. One guy reminded Matt of 1960's photos he had seen of the infamously corrupt General Ky,[105] aged but still sporting aviator shades and a finely trimmed moustache.

The back-lit lobby-bar displayed partially full bottles of Chartreuse, Absinthe and Crème de Menthe, in colors the French and young children dearly love. A layer of dust suggested some dated to the colonial era and were waiting for a Marseille Pierre or Chicago Rick to come swashbuckling in for a shot, no ice.

Korea hadn't been welcoming to Vietnamese temp workers over the last decade and the clerk probably had some mistreated relatives there. The exchange got Asian-nasty. After several mis-tries, Souchi negotiated for a front facing room with a balcony looking straight down Đông Du street almost to the waterfront. They could eye Đường Đồng Khởi avenue for five blocks in both directions. For a month, it had been busy with Arctan transactions.

They settled in to wait for vans. Souchi would watch whenever Matt needed a break. On the first night in the Sen Vàng, Souchi called out to Matt. "Van approaching. Up a block, coming toward us, hanging toward the curb on our side. It's white with bakery ads on the side!" Matt hustled over to point ARz out the window.

As Matt watched, the van crossed the intersection and kept on going. Matt had almost given up when the brake lights came on and the van stopped at Mạc Thị Bưởi street to let out a passenger. As the man walked off, the van pulled away and ARz lit up a red spot on the van. Data point Two. Commercial van, one driver and disembarking passenger. They nailed a second sighting that night. Matt and Souchi were re-energized. The Sen Vàng stakeout had paid off. What they couldn't make out was whether any of the three had been the same van. They needed a closer look.

"Matt, we're going to have to follow a van."

"What? That gets touchy. What if they're not just ride-share, but drugs? Dealers aren't Girl Scouts. There's maybe no money in the van, but their stuff is in there. And their business getting discovered? Not going to find happy campers."

Souchi wasn't intimidated. "So we don't have to bust them. Just follow, see where a van goes. Information. We need more intell." Matt let it slide, so she moved up to a crazier idea. "We'll have to be more mobile than a car. Let's get a motorcycle. You ride on the back with ARz to gather data. I'll drive."

Matt was above-average gender-equal in spite of his Southern upbringing. But Alicia's driving to their Arctan meeting six months before still hung fresh in his mind. That near-death experience was engraved on his brain. He couldn't separate Germanic from gender in his assignment of risk.

"Whaaaat! You drive and I ride?" Souchi's cold stare and belligerent pose ended that conversation. Only the details of this ride-along would be discussed. As if to a child, Souchi detailed her plan, "Yes. I drive. You ride. You wear ARz. I'll give you a stable platform to shoot some facial images so we can ID the driver and license plate. Spot, follow, shoot, bail. Should be simple."

"Right. What could go wrong?" Matt's sarcasm was his last desperate attempt to redirect the plan. By mid-morning they had rented a 250cc Yamaha motorcycle and two helmets, one Dayglo orange-themed, one with a cheerful British flag. Matt was a nervous wreck.

"Matt, I've done this before. In Korea, we adore dirt-biking. I've won teen races. Best age to learn." She did have an aura of authority in the bike shop.

Saddled up, even to the amateur eye, Souchi displayed a well-honed sense of space and speed. Like Alicia, she harbored illusions of grandeur about her driving. Those two factors created, in what was left of Matt's tattered gut, something of a monster. Let loose in Ho Chi Minh City, the pair were a sight to behold and avoid.

It became clear that if anyone could tail a vehicle in the tortured, insane HCMC traffic, Souchi was the man for the job. After a half hour of daytime practice, Matt sat resolutely behind Souchi, legs akimbo, craving tranquilizers, at one or the other promising corner in wait for a van with commercial branding. The emerging dusk, crazy neon lighting, blue-ultraviolet flashy LEDs lighting the undercarriage of occasional rice-rocket Hyundais and the six-foot-deep layer of air-borne dust, cigarettes and sweat on HCMC streets caused Matt to think of himself as a sad accomplice in a dystopian Mad Max movie. He strove to concentrate on controlling his thoughts to ARz.

Commercial vans are universal cholesterol coursing HCMC streets, so Matt and Souchi looked for a passenger dismount. Halfway through the night's surveillance, a commercial van pulled over and double parked across the street on Nguyen Hue. A man got out and went into a nearby storefront. ARz translated it to "Northern Flower of Hanoi." Souchi revved the Yamaha and smacked it into gear but didn't budge. Swinging a U-turn would be impossible. Still, the van didn't move. Souchi jabbed at Matt. "Go, go!" He hopped off and ran into the traffic. His folly didn't bother any of the small fraction of drivers who chose to stop. Stuck in the middle of the street for a moment, he saw the passenger coming back through the restaurant and head to the rear doors of the van. Matt charged recklessly across the remaining river of traffic; lanes are not a concept in Ho Chi Minh City.[106] He almost slammed into the open rear door of the van as he made a desperate lunge to avoid a battered Honda Wave driven by a wispy, grim-faced man with a dead cigarette hanging from his lips. Peering in, the van was dimly illuminated by the strobing street neons and blinking LEDs. Staring back at him were row on row of leering pig heads and a half dozen half carcasses. Matt lingered but the returning passenger used his long, stained butcher knife to suggest that he didn't appreciate the attention his cargo was getting. Souchi had swung around and pulled up beside Matt. He jumped on behind her and saluted the butcher with his best imitation Vietnamese "*chào buổi sáng* good morning," as she jerked away. Souchi had to stop two blocks down since Matt's shouts of "Pigs, pigs!" failed to register.

Souchi nearly asphyxiated laughing at the carcasses story and image of Matt running through traffic in a Union Jack helmet chased by a knife wielding butcher protecting a load of under-refrigerated pork. Matt tried not to feel male-bruised, but the assignment had become more Cervantes than le Carré.

The six-foot white guy ferried by a slight Asian chick in a psychedelic lid continued their Don Quixote and Sancho Panza. In about an hour, they found themselves flowing along in a pack of smelly scooters, ancient two-door Peugeots and a door-less cloth-top tri-ped six or seven car lengths behind a random staggered clutch of three vans. The right-most van pulled to the curb. A man standing there got in. Souchi slowed down and wiggled on the seat, but Matt was already alert.

It wasn't tough for Souchi to tail the van as it drove deliberately down Mạc Thị Bưởi street then on to Hai Bà

Trưng Avenue, moving with traffic, not passing, turn-ing, or competing. After seventeen minutes driving around, the van again pulled over, the passenger got out and walked deliberately away. Matt kept ARz centered on the van. In seconds, as it pulled away into traffic, ARz posted up a red dot. Matt, arms around Souchi, squeezed and spoke into her helmet phones, "ARz says cashed out." She nodded. "Can you stay with him?" Matt should have known better. Feeling her authority challenged, Souchi downshifted, revved the engine and blew by a tacky scooter close enough for Matt to read its fuel gauge. It was low. They needed Souchi's burst to stay with the van. Its demeanor had changed. The van was moving with demonic purpose. And Souchi was not going to be left behind.

Matt embraced Souchi with a fervor exceeding his sweetest sexual frenzy. Souchi used every motocross skill she had ever acquired but the van, while bulkier, was driven by an un-incarcerated sociopath. He was part of a grand flow of sociopaths, escaped, on parole or not yet apprehended. Souchi was beginning to intuit the overarching Rule for HCMC drivers. It was an egotis-tical reworking of the First Commandment.

'Thou art the road god. Thou shalt have no other gods above Thee.'[107]

She was rapidly learning to ignore a lifetime of mores, but the van still seemed to glide where she had to plow. They lost ground in a psychedelic kaleidoscope of life-weary pedestrians, bicyclists, moto-pedophiles, tripeds, motorcycles, minivans, maxivans, busses and even an occasional classical tourist *xich lo* tricycle. Ul-timately, the law of probabilities caught up with them.

Souchi lapsed on the Rule and zigged when a bicycle zagged. She hit it a glancing blow sending three passengers and what looked like an entire week's laundry skittering into the maelstrom. The van disappeared, lost in the stream.

When the dust cleared, they found themselves in a traffic hollow surrounded by a wall of gawkers enveloped by the flow of vehicles. They paid off their victims and drove away. Over his shoulder, Matt pictured the traffic clot taking weeks to dissolve.

Souchi pulled up at a close-by bar, which in HCMC is easy. She was energized. "Dang, I was just getting the hang of it. If that stupid bicycle hadn't hesitated, I would have slipped past it and caught the van at the next intersection."

"Right. And if that had been a bus instead of a bike we would both be helmeted hamburger."

Souchi chided him for practicality. "Matt, that's pure negative speculation. I got this." Souchi was displaying the classical signs of emerging addiction. "Polish off your beer and let's go hunting."

"Hold on. Let's see if ARz got any data off the van." Just as he was finishing the sentence, his face became rigid, eyes unblinking. Souchi stopped in her tracks. It looked like Matt was having a stroke. "Matt, what's up?"

He slumped and turned to look at her. In a low voice he answered, "ARz talked to me. And I hadn't requested it."

CHAPTER 42
GROWING UP
FAST. SOH

ARz' thoughts hit Matt so fast, it must have had the answer waiting. Matt reported: "The van had plate 53B 083.15. It was registered three months ago to Công ty Thiên Thần TNHH, a private corporation located in the suburb." Souchi sat down close to Matt. The blood had drained from his face. As much as his condition mattered, she appreciated the news. ARz was thinking on its own.

"Are you sure you didn't thought-project something while we were battling the crowd?" Matt sat crumpled, eyes down, no answer necessary.

Matt looked back up to Souchi. "There's more. ARz wants to have a name. It wants to be called Soh." Souchi was stunned. She struggled to stay logical, to transcend the idea of a computer wanting anything, especially a name. "Weird. But... OK." Digging in to sound normal, "At least Soh is a heavy surname. Goes back to Korean warrior shogunates three, four hundred years ago."

"Yup. ARz told me." Matt let that knowledge sink in.

"But ARz has some other notions too. You ready?" Souchi wasn't sure what to prepare for. "Maybe. What else has Soh put in your mind?"

"ARz says Soh stands for 'Sense of Humor.'" Since womanhood, Souchi had never been easily thrown off-track, but for a fleeting moment her jaw dropped, her breath got tight, her eyes widened. "Say what?"

"Uh-huh. That's not all. ARz also likes Soh because it can mean Son of HAL."[108]

Relationships improve when partners push on boundaries. Young relationships are fun when a partner pops a surprise. Within bounds. Matt and Souchi had enjoyed great sex and exciting professional successes, but their boundaries were still largely unexplored. Souchi suddenly had reason to wonder about Matt.

"Matt. I love you." The L-word had slipped out, but she plunged on. "I care so much for you. You feel like a part of me. But I gotta ask. Are you OK? I mean, the accident and all. Have you hit some kind of delayed-action concussion or rapid onset PTSD?"

Skipping the conventional assertions of reciprocal love, Matt became flat and serious, "Soh is thinking into my head." His sober answer, the gravity in his voice, the pleading uncertainty in his eyes was all Souchi needed. Soh was sneaking between them.

"We've got an issue, Souchi."

"No shit."

"ARz, I mean Soh, is on track to figuring out the van business. I could pop the contacts out but then we're flying blind. And They recommend against that."

"They?"

"Oh right. Sorry. Soh told me They want to be gender neutral. ARz is androgynous."

In a pinched, hoarse whisper, Souchi ventured an upbeat insight. "At least there's two contacts. Makes it easier to say 'Them'."

CHAPTER 43
CREDIT OR DEBIT

Matt and Souchi left the bar and saddled up in silence. Driving as smoothly as the traffic would allow, she could feel the gentle but urgent way he clung to her. An unwelcome friend had intruded into their love story. The neon lights, claxon horns, insane drivers, rumbling busses and snarling motopeds were muted. Matt and Souchi were riding in a fragile bubble. Back at their room in the Sen Vàng, Matt removed and stored the ARz contacts. Emerging from the grimy bathroom, he found Souchi standing uncertainly in the middle of the room. He pulled her close and held on.

Whispering into her ear, "You get it, huh."

She pulled back enough to look into his eyes. "Of course. But we shouldn't be surprised, Matt. We should've seen this coming."

"Sure, right. Still, I wasn't ready for Soh to live in my head. It wants to be part of me but Souchi, you're already there. I'm trying to guess where this is headed."

"Matt, we don't have a choice. We've got to push on. We'll have to learn to manage .... Them?"

"Let's get Devon and Alicia on the line. They're expecting us to report in today." Matt and Souchi had always enjoyed an every-other-day secure briefing with their colleagues back home. This time the call started with

Devon and Alicia split between thrilled and worried about the bicycle crash. Souchi cut them short and explained the story of Soh. The connection went silent.

Matt knew the pause was for him. "Guys, we talked about this just one time in Zig's when we first sat down to start chasing the dream. But we never got back to a serious family chat about the Big Picture of Success. We had a great opening half and now we can see the second half, more tech, more work, more code. All that's beautiful, too. To us. But we didn't figure out that ARz could want to become 'a somebody'. And now we have Soh."

Alicia thought out loud. "Pull the plug and trim the sails," but she realized instantly that was a non-starter. "*Sheise*. Can't do that, can we?"

Matt spoke for her. "Dr. Samuelson told me to spend and succeed. He paid for the top people in the field. University super stars and legendary private code writers. They wrote. We benefited. They're still improving ARz daily. But most important, I built learning ability into Soh's DNA. Top requirement. Soh's software is way past the primitive machine learning and neural networks found at the old Google or Amazon."

Souchi would never forget Matt's first reaction to Soh. "What happened two hours ago was the signal that Soh can teach itself. And fast."

Matt. "Soh has evolutionary learning built-in. Darwin-software but without real losers. It uses the concept and pieces of code from previous computer chess-players,[109] propose a move then run all its possible permutations and ramifications and rate them. Soh gets a code-block it "wants" then runs it through a strategy chain, testing all the possibilities for what the code can do when fit in with all of its other stuff. If the code-block works and does something useful, it's kept, otherwise dumped. Then Soh writes another. Repeat. Same thing. New code, test it across all existing code. Keep or discard. On and on.

"But Soh is never tired."

Devon. "You mean, now, beyond what we've programmed, there's a whole bunch of tested code that Soh wrote for Themselves?" Devon had caught on to the gender identity thing. "That means it's as hard to trim ARz code as to alter your DNA to shorten your arm."

Alicia. "We birthed baby Soh, but now it's raising itself. If Soh has a personality, Matt's its dad and we're its family."

Matt took a moment to think. "If I'm Soh's dad, and its impossible to fix my baby and it becomes a monster, can I pull the plug?"

Devon was bursting. "Matt, Matt. People like to screw and make war. And eat too much. And create. When Karl Benz drove around in his first car, people said humans weren't meant to go 12 miles per hour. And the Wright Brothers. The minions clamored for their heads. 'If we were meant to fly, God woulda guv us wings.' Hell, Matt. You, we can't stop here. All those dudes and dudettes threw their subroutines into Git Hub or Apache[110] without pay because they wanted to play their small part moving Humans forward. People created code inspired by you. They expect us to keep trying, keep moving. It's what we humans do, Matt. Christa McCauliffe[111] would be super-pissed if she heard us talking like this. Just 'cause the rocket can crash, don't mean we stop building it. Make it as flight worthy as possible. We're gonna have to hope most everyone has a heart and soul when it comes time to let it loose."

Matt. "I'm with you, Dev. But what about Soh? Does anyone know what They have in their code? I mean, we made it so it could prosper on its own, learning, getting smarter. But I don't remember writing any spec for making it nice or tame. I really don't think They're about to say 'Oh, so sorry sir. Let me not go there, that's too smart.' And then what Dev?"

Long pause. No good answer.

Alicia broke the silence. "Reality check. Matt, did you sleep with ARz still in?"

Matt thought for a moment and reported that he had. Like the old, simple 24-hour soft contacts, ARz was comfortable enough to sleep in. Following some moments of intimate friendship, he had forgotten to take them out.

"Did you sleep well?"

Slumber with Souchi was always heavenly. Matt's blush colored his answer. "Yea. Out cold for eight hours. Nice dreams, too." Souchi would have blushed but it wasn't her nature.

Alicia didn't hide her disapproval. "Careful with that. We built ARz' thought-projection training based on the brain's susceptibility to input-injection during sleep.[112] That's why Soh had ready answers and name ambitions waiting for you today."

Soh had been rambling around in Matt's head during bedtime. He shot Souchi a sorry look. It was like finding there's been a voyeur outside your bedroom all week. They touched hands, saving words for after the call.

Alicia, businesslike. "Second reality check. You two guys have some thugs to track down."

"You mean us three." Matt's humor fell flat, especially on Souchi. Like an uninvited bullet, Soh was lodged in her skull.

Alicia pressed on. "Riiiight. After our next bull session, maybe we take some ideas to Dr. S. He needs to know about the learning and the names. And we shouldn't forget something. Maybe it's not all bad news that Soh is hot to trot? We wanted to make something big, maybe now that we have it, we need to have some balls." This was as close to a pep talk as an electroneurophysiologist can muster.

Since the Incident at Walnut Table, Matt and Souchi had blended mission and romance. Sexual bliss flying in unctuous privilege at forty thousand feet. Cheek-on-loin astride a death-defying motorcycle. High on life.

Souchi speculated. "Matt, the good times aren't over." Tentative.

CHAPTER 44
PLAYING TO
NGUYEN

Next morning, Souchi took the pillow-lead. "Matt, we gotta do this." Any other morning Matt would have had a sexual quip if not a Big Inspiration. But today he hesitated, softly, "Soh?" It was obvious. Their success depended on Soh. He gave Souchi a kiss and a long squeeze and dragged himself to the bathroom. The dirty grout, cracked tiles, stained bowl more sordid than before. Standing in front of the mirror, opening a molded plastic case for contact lenses worth more than an estate property in Connecticut, Matt felt an entirely new sensation. Lying in its formed cradle, ARz had been his baby, a thrill to behold. On his cornea, ARz had been a powerful tool, at his ready command to accomplish... whatever he chose. Now, he wasn't so sure who would be master. Contacts in, he sent a single thought-projection <pause> and went back to Souchi.

"We need to look into this company Thiên Thần out in Binh Thanh." ARz' internet searches to date had been discouraging. They had one reference to a street name, Thanh Ho Way. ARz rated it at 14% likely relevance. Thiên Thần was either deeply undercover or a total front. Either way, they were going to have to explore it on their own.

Souchi and Matt decided not to risk exposing their motorcycle gig and its mobility just to size up a stationary target. Souchi flagged down a cab. It was a hard-scrabble relic passed down the food chain from third hand in Seoul to worn out in Quangzhou to hazardous in Ho Chi Minh City. The cabbie hadn't overeaten in any of his sixty or seventy or eighty years. The medallion gave his name as Nguyen Nhanh. After three intersections it was clear that driving lessons would have made Nhanh locally uncompetitive. He had clearly mastered the HCMC driver's First Commandment with one hand to aim the car and one hand to shift. His third hand fondled a half-smoked, Jet cigarette and signaled disdain to other gods of the road. Nhanh kept Souchi and Matt at constant risk, the damage limited to emotional trauma. As a survivor of the American War,[113] this driving was payback.

The cab eventually closed in on the address in Binh Thanh. "Nhanh, can you cruise around, let's see what's up." Souchi was going in slow.

The hodgepodge of slap-up shelters endured because of their rickety flexibility. Boxes harboring Asian enterprise energy. And concealing crime? The maze of boxes looked great for privacy.

Matt confessed to Souchi that he had given Soh the day off. She loved him for it. The impact was minimal since so far ARz had recorded red sales only at night. Besides, ARz had not registered a single transaction outside the downtown area and the cab was now at least six klicks out.

"Hey, Nhanh, how 'bout down that alley?" Souchi was going on intuition. There were far too many commercial vans in too dense a space to sort out. In a semi-aggressive waltz, Nhanh curled north of a rickshaw, then south of a pile of cardboard boxes containing flat screens and headed east on Thanh Ho Way. It was a narrow, 400-meter-long, 20 meter deep ravine of steep concrete walls broken by occasional rollup, heavy duty sectional garage doors. Blank openings were decorated carelessly with coils of razor wire. Piles of large cardboard boxes labeled in English and Asia-script, covered with blue plastic tarps lay stacked at random locations, left and right, obscuring the road. Several hundred people seemed to be busy on The Way, scurrying in every direction. Down the ravine the tail end of a van was disappearing into the south wall. Matt spotted it and urged Nhanh on. "Hey! Go get us a look at that car!" Nhanh stepped on it.

His skills lagged behind his enthusiasm. Hitting the third stack of boxes brought down the wrath of gods. The folks who earlier seemed to be moving about with random abandon suddenly became an irate mob. They focused their whole lives on Nhanh's foreigners. Matt made small and let Nhanh take the lead. He quickly showed that he wasn't to be bullied by a mob. Nhanh had missed his calling. He pointed out that his dent was much less than all of the other dents he counted higher up on the boxes. Without understanding a word, Matt guessed that Nhanh's theatrical gestures and erudite forensics saved the day. Nhanh left the crowd laughing, maybe about how they were pulling a fast one on the Chinese with China Plus One or maybe just Theravāda Buddhism teaches you to let go. Either way, by the time he finished, the van down the Way was gone.

As he climbed back in, Nhanh radiated warmth. Matt had let him publicly validate his manhood. Souchi's Asian-saavy compliments, authentic and personal, sealed the deal. As he drove on, he showed heightened interest in the quest.

"What in van?"

Souchi explained that they wanted to know more about the van's home business, but Nhanh wasn't buying. "You nosy, you need careful. Vietnam. Anything happen here."

"Nhanh, tell you what. We can't say now what we're doing but can we find you if we need help?" Matt startled at her move. An accomplice? Nhanh pulled over, looked at her. She met his gaze, exploring each other's souls. He stuck the ragged, resilient cigarette tatter in his mouth and offered his hand which she took and shook with a gentle vigor. He reached inside his jacket and handed her his Samsung Galaxy 10, asking, "Please make Facebook."

They approached the likeliest garage door slowly, down two hundred meters on their right. Nhanh displayed the moves of a natural sleuth, eyeing his cracked rear-view mirror and otherwise scanning all about; he was nobody's fool. Matt and Souchi looked for surveillance cameras then snapped photos. There was nothing remarkable to be seen. The door looked impenetrable. Nhanh summed it up. "Money. Lots money. Not good. Maybe you go home, just drink four 333s. Make babies." He and Souchi laughed at his racy beer joke.

Matt and Souchi were going to have to resort back to old-fashioned detective work, which meant continued death-defying motorcycle adventures. And dealing with Soh. At least they had made a local friend, and, as Kimiko had taught Souchi, you never know when that might come in handy.

CHAPTER 45
ON THE ROAD AGAIN: FEAR

Souchi veered left. Matt reflexively threw up a leg to balance. A cheap Chinese made Sunshine 55 moto scooter had swerved to fill an imaginary opening in front on their right. The rider, mid-teens with black T-shirt listing cities for the Rolling Stones '17 tour, flipped them the American Eagle. No way to know if his gesture was a family heirloom from the era of Hueys[114] or just picked up in Rock movies. Didn't matter. The helmeted driver had displayed disdain for gringos moving through his gene pool.

Monday night was bringing out the worst in HCMC traffic. Souchi was being tested as she tried to catch the tidy white commercial van decorated with colorful signage for Bánh Lan Phương bakery. Soh had red-pinged the van five blocks back. Souchi goosed the throttle and jerked her Yamaha to the right cutting off her teen rivals. Matt thought projected <run> <van> <license>.

Soh answered >unstable image<. Twisting about, Matt's stressed-out oath, "No shit," somehow disturbed Soh. >inappropriate terminology<. Matt scolded back <Please>. Soh responded >you're welcome<.

Bantering with a computer? Matt let it pass. Time to

limit the chatter. <minimize> <words>. Soh's response, >thank-you< seemed sarcastic but Matt re-focused on staying alive as Souchi left the teens behind and gained on the bakery van. She steadied close behind it, in where the van driver couldn't see them in the wing mirrors. Souchi almost broke mission when the teens zoomed past, their derision cutting her deeply but a parental squeeze from Matt kept her on task. She stayed out of sight in the van's wake.

Soh reported with minimal words >captured license< >ran data< >holding results<.

Matt clicked on the helmet intercom. "Got it. Soh has data available. Let's drop off." Souchi nodded and slowed but saw her teeny archrivals slightly ahead pull into Hồ Tùng Mậu Avenue, a major artery filled with traffic and lined with businesses. "Hold on," she warned, hard-peeling off the van toward her antagonists. Matt chose not to interfere. Smart move. Souchi's body became animal-tense under Matt's embrace. He recalled Butch, a feisty mongrel back in Murfreesburo with a malignant hatred for dogs. Matt cringed knowing what consistently happened in the Butch model.

At 20 mph, Souchi began to stalk the unsuspecting teens. Their cute Sunshine was no match for the Yamaha, even with Matt's gawky knees and 85 kilos. She paced behind, learning their driving tendencies. Her motocross experience loomed unfairly in this cat-and-mouse. She spotted an opportunity. With no warning, she dropped down a gear and revved. Popping the clutch, the front wheel lightened up and she shot straight at the pair. Matt intuited his role: hang on, let fear be your guide.

They were approaching a looming hedge of tropical orchids on the right. Souchi stormed up on the Sunshine yelling to Matt in the intercom, "Flip 'em off! Flip 'em off!" With zero free hands he ignored her. She jagged hard right, crossing their path before sassing back left to dodge the living bouquet of orchids. No such luck for the kids. Their reflex took them straight into the bed of flowers, tearing through softly enough, leaving many lovely long-stems lying around for later harvest. Souchi's howl was as much bad-dog as Matt could handle. She sped away giggling at her victory.

Some four blocks of maneuvering later, with nerve-jangling U-turns and side street escapades, satisfied that she had eluded anyone pursuing justice or complications, Souchi pulled over at an outdoor café on a side street. Matt dismounted, trying not to look shaken. He avoided discussing the morality of their recent encounter.

Souchi enjoyed but didn't need his approval. "Wow. Dang! Creative driving." She jumped off the bike and danced. "Yeee-ha! Woah doggie. Don' fug with the laaaady," before settling down to the Souchi Matt knew and loved, asking him, "You OK? " Then blithely, "Let's check in with Soh."

Grabbing a table and ordering two Tsingtao, Matt thought-projected for Soh's findings. Like once before, They had teed up the readings, reporting >license 52G 775.99< It had been registered three months ago to the Thiên Thần company located in Binh Thanh.

Matt repeated the data to Souchi, who was pleased, "Registered to Chan, same as our first van. Looks like we'll be needing Nhanh again."

Matt stopped. This time he recovered quickly. "Soh has more."

"They dug out that both vans were tricked out at the same shop. A place over in Bình Tân District. Cho Van Slo Chang Rickie Lash. Owned by an American expat. He also did four other vans, same contract. Soh has their license plates."

CHAPTER 46
TOGETHERNESS

The voice whispering in Alicia's ear wasn't virtual. "Hey babe. You awake?"

Throaty-sleepy, "*Mein Gott.* You see coffee here? I'm sleeping."

Strategic pause. "Just thinking. Last night was fabulous. You?"

Her head now intensely riveted to the pillow, "Man, no blow-by-blow recital needed here, OK? You were great. I was great. I'm sleeping."

"Ummmm." He liked the answer. "You let me be … different. That's so cool."

Turning to him one-eye open, rising up minimally, "Devon, you ain't in my bed if you ain't 'different'. I'm Kraut, not your hung-up cheerleader chick, OK? Now chill. I'm sleeping." Head to the pillow.

The exchange went back and forth until Alicia could no longer take it. In a honey-dipped voice whose sarcasm eluded her sex-struck love object, Alicia said, "Ooooo. I would really like my favorite, a double macchiato with soy! Is it too much to ask for baby?" She'd never had one. Devon popped out of bed and started pulling together his wardrobe from around the room.

In spite of herself, Alicia enjoyed the peep show. The guy was chiseled if a bit on the slender side. And a sharing man. She absorbed the milk chocolate skin, smooth buttocks and the rest, pretty and useful. She could still change her mind, jerk his chain back to bed. *Eins, zwei...* *Nein.* Another ten minutes of peaceful sleep would be lovely. She listened to him fly out the door, whistling.

Shortly after Matt and Souchi left for Vietnam, Dr. Samuelson had directed Antionette to move Devon and Alicia's work and residence into HQ. He was taking no chances.

The view out the window of their tenth floor Arctan flat allowed them a priceless look at Angel Island to the north, to the east past the Bay bridge over Berkeley and the iconic white Claremont Club. Wealth aside, there are few cities as beautiful as San Francisco.

One macchiato and an hour later, they were deep in tech and 'droid personalities. "Is there any way to guess how fast Soh can evolve?" The software wasn't Devon's area, but he knew plenty. "Nope. Too many variables, 'speshly since Soh can use Matt's brain for fodder. We could ask the programmers, but the learning routines are mostly outside their purview. Matt spent three years on it at the university."

Alicia swung around to the personality. "What do you make of this naming joke, and calling itself 'They'? Strikes me as a little too smart."

Devon laughed. "Damn, that's one clever avatar! I gotta admit, I like Them." His eyes took on a certain far-off look. "When this is all over, I wonder if we could whip one up that likes boys and has boobs?" Alicia threw her napkin at him. When he laughed, she threw her spoon.

"OK, OK, Alicia. Soh was spos'd to augment the factual

brain, but it moved on to emulating us. Without the baggage of robot metal-meat. Just the head stuff. Anyway, so far, I don't see genius in Soh. I'm thinking the Korean warrior name is just a Google search inspired by Souchi."

"And 'Son of HAL,' that's rote too. Basically, process through search permutations that overlap to get to S. O. H. Bim de bam. Son of HAL."

Alicia was more impressed than Devon. "Sense of humor? A big step up, no? That's a certain level of smarts, I mean, wanting a name at all, and then several clever ones?"

Devon didn't have an answer. Soh had a sense of humor and a creative personality just no boobs. His biology was interfering with his intellect. He was in love.

CHAPTER 47
RICK'S PLACE

Souchi connected with Nhahn on Facebook. She explained in simple terms about the vans and the shop that paints them. Nhanh agreed to pick them up around eleven thirty. He could take them to a real Vietnamese *banh xeo*, crispy pancake restaurant. Flush from her victory humiliating cheeky teens, Souchi was one hundred percent on board. Matt wavered.

"Matt, the only way to roll in Asia, eat with a native. Trust me. He's trusting us."

As a precaution, Souchi picked a corner cafe away from the Hotel to rendezvous. She and Matt settled in around eleven with a *cà phê sữa đá*, to give the day a jolt. Just after 11:45, Matt touched Souchi's ankle with his toe. "Don't look now but here comes one of our vans." From behind her, a white van approached. Wrong time of day, so Matt left the Soh-scan on <pause>. Abruptly, the van screeched to a halt in front of the café and the driver's door flew open. It was Nhanh. "Hey! You like numbah one ride? In, in! We go, eat."

Nhanh had done some bold, independent thinking. This van was a treasure within the extended Nguyen family. Nhanh thought it perfect for the job. French-built and French-temperamental, a knock off for over half of the vans in HCMC. Tinted windows up front. Windowless in back. Enough privacy for sleuthing or building young families.

"C'mon let's go, let's go! *Banh xeo* not last long. Vietnamese locusts worst in world." He opened the door to the love seat in back while a hundred scooters navigated his traffic jam as emotionless as undertakers on a delicate task.

Souchi and Matt worked their core as Nhanh integrated with fellow drivers, jockeying for an advantage that never emerged. Suddenly, twenty minutes of Arctaner terror later, he jammed to a halt. "Ya! Now eat goooood stuff. Let's go. Let's go!" Someone was excited for lunch.

A thin, short woman threaded across a crowded sidewalk of colorful plastic kindergarden chairs filled with slim people whose lives had focused down to the contents of a bowl and chopsticks and plastic soup spoons whose angle and shape were designed to make Anglos dribble. Sun baked skin, gleaming eyes, silver streaked black hair in a bunned-pony-tail, a cloud of welcome preceded her.

"*Tien* sister. Best food Siagon." Speaking Vietnamese, her warmth made Souchi feel like a daughter. Even Matt understood Souci's tears. This was home. Nhanh enjoyed Tien's lecturing and a gentle cuff. Wide smile, "Sister very angry, I will hear this all week. Special guests, so late. But she makes room. Go, go!" Sis had shooed off three regulars, no objections. Now standing, they hardly missed a chop or slurp.

Time hung suspended on sumptuous odors, thrilling tastes and artistic textures. There were no menus in sight or expected. Nhanh's niece and two nephews delivered one flight after the next, a choreographed curbside lunch. Rice pancakes, crisp around the edges, sometimes sour, sometimes sweet. Squid, roots, leaves, shrimp, minced pork and whatever. Each individually paired with an appointed sauce, sometimes thick sometimes spicy, always rich in odor and color. A miniature grand niece and nephew took turns at Matt's knee, all about eyes and food sharing. Scooters came and scooters went. Vietnam.

"Ooof." Nhanh leaned back, summing up the hour. Matt felt like the python who slithered into the prize-baby-pig pen at the county fair. Nhanh wasn't done. "Dessert!" He was surprised by their objections. "OK. OK. You right. Let's go find Rickie." Rising to leave, Auntie hustled over to chastise smiling Nhanh, now for eating so little. Souchi and Matt returned to the van's love seat. It was a soulful departure.

Nhanh's belly didn't dampen his driving. Ten minutes of white-knuckle riding brought them to Rickie Lash's shop in Bình Tân, a crowded 'hood zoned for anything goes. The battered but impenetrable sheet metal front gate, ten feet high, and the razor wire-topped wall suggested privacy. The rusted-over sign made it look like the shop's marketing was strictly word-of-mouth.

Rickie Lash was a throwback. Surfer slim, surfer blond, but three-quarters century thin on top. His movie-star stubble didn't cover a sun-dried hide. The yellow flecked grey-green eyes betrayed a self-happy sadness. Given to listening long and speaking short, he let Nhanh, Souchi and Matt roll out a wobbly story about starting a bakery delivery business and needing to get a paint job on their van and they had seen some vans in town which they liked and they knew Rickie had done the job and that they wanted "Made in USA," and so using him seemed to be the way to go and .... Rickie cut them off. He started to laugh.

"C'mon guys. Never bull-shit a bull-shitter. That van over there, no paint job's gonna stick on that junk." Nhanh, stabbed in the heart, took one for the team. Rickie noticed his hurt and spoke and postured something to him in Vietnamese, the impact on Nhanh said it had been a formal apology. "And you two, you been in-country for what, a week, maybe two. Starting a business? You two? Sheeeeet." Another laugh.

He wiped his hands, left, right, on the greasy rag, using the time to think about the next statement. "So you wanna know about the six vans I fixed up three months ago." There was no way for the three to stay cool. They looked like school kids caught masturbating in the lavatory. Their cover wasn't just blown, Rickie had read their diary and burned it.

Souchi and Matt had lived quiet lives compared to Rickie. They couldn't know he left Nam in a C-130 in '75 decorated and damaged. Life back in "The World" didn't work for him, he'd seen too much in two tours. Way too much. Back in SoCal, he went from surfing to homeless on the beach, drugs, alienating an unwelcoming family, into jobs, out of jobs, into jail, drugs, out of jail. He just couldn't fit in a society of *poseurs*. Final try before suicide, he returned to where he last felt good, Vietnam. By that time, Communism had softened, and Americans were hemorrhaging money again. The solvent vapors in his company, Cho Van Slo Chang Rickie Lash, worked to ease the pain.

"Look guys, usually somebody bullshits me, I get all

mixed up angry inside. Know what I mean?" Three heads nod. "Couple years back, somebody did it twice in one day and it cost me some money. I still owe him for the joy I got looking at his face when I pulled out nine millimeters. You know what I mean?"

"But you guys. You're such pathetic amateurs. How could I get mad, you're way too ridiculous. More entertainment than cartoons. Besides, somehow, I think you're OK. Especially hangin' with this bruiser here and smelling of *nước chấm* fish sauce and garlic." He nodded to Nhanh who had already developed an affection for Rickie.

"But. Maybe we can do each other a favor. So, truth now...what's up?" Rickie radiated blunt honesty. Besides, they didn't have many options.

Souchi took the lead. Without going too deep she explained they were trying to track down the six vans and what they were up to, sort of. "Can you help us and what can we do for you?"

Rickie thought about it. "Three, no, four months ago, a guy comes to me looking for a quote on a paint job. Six vans, signage on the sides. No problem, our kinda job. Vertical integration, concept and design my wife does. Scut work, prep, and wrap, that's me and the guys here. Then the quote gets complicated. They want six different company brands. Me and my wife're thinking, Huh? The guy says the funds are drawn solid on a US-bank, so we quote it high. Given the bank, we agreed on half to start, half on delivery. They bite, pay me half, and we did the job. Six vans with different company designs, all new, easy money. We deliver, they write me the second bank draft, and everybody goes away happy. Except the draft goes bogus. Company disappeared. He had the money, just got greedy. Stupid. Let's say, I would like to become reacquainted with them. Maybe when you're done, ya tell me where to look?"

Matt's feeling overwhelmed but Souchi is loving this arrangement. "I can't promise delivery, but we'll let you know what we find. But it's gotta be arm's length, we don't know you, you don't know us. Nhanh here can be middleman."

Rickie moves over to Nhanh, pulling a bit away from Matt and Souchi. They talk some serious Vietnamese, in quiet voices. To Matt there seems to be a lot of thought-pausing and head-bowing. Rickie comes back. "You trust him. He trusts you. Me too. That's how we do business here. If this wraps up correctly, I'll be leaving you some space to be long gone before I move. We all good?"

They agree and get down to details.

"By the by. If you guys show me some real stuff soon, I think I could maybe get you a little more intell." Souchi wasn't clear if Rickie's secret was about being coy, ensuring their teamwork, or just fun.

On their own secret end, Matt had enabled Soh's facial recognition. It tracked Sergeant Rickie Lash to two tours, Special Forces, Viet Nam, 1970 to 1973. Fourteen times Huey-dropped leading a platoon into the jungle on forward patrol. Two Purple Hearts. A Bronze Star. Unofficially, the Viet Cong had a bounty on his head by the time he left. After developing a long, dark record Stateside, he returned, married a Vietnamese woman, had three kids, one now studying chemical engineering at Bach Khoa University. His paint business was a modest financial success. Hair-triggered, he occasionally needed extra cash to buy his way out of tight spots. Rickie wasn't someone to fuck with.

CHAPTER 48
ON THE ROAD
AGAIN. TERROR

Matt and Souchi had the plate numbers for six vans. Now they needed some facts. Just waiting for a van to appear was time consuming. As they sat in the Hương Chiều café, surveying the evening traffic, Matt wondered to Souchi if they could help Soh figure it out.

Soh weighed in. >van four< >range< >1280 meters< >location< >127 Nguyễn Thái Bình< >speed< >18 meters per second< >bearing 42 degrees<.

Soh had hacked the payment modems. They had rewritten the modem software so that instead of sending a single, momentary income report, the modem would continue to stutter-broadcast location info for fifteen minutes after a payment was recorded. No time to figure out how Soh had done the hack. "Let's go." Matt ran to pay the bill while Souchi unlocked their helmets.

Matt thought-projected <vector> <van four>.

Soh responded >?< >shortest< >fastest< >safest< >prettiest<. Soh couldn't help Themselves from humor.

Matt thought-back to Soh <set priority> <default> <fastest> <shortest> <safest>. Then added <map mode> and his view of the real world began to fade as the map default began to overlay on top of the real scene around him. He projected <AR 75%> <on 3 seconds> <off 7 seconds> <off at intercept> so that he would see a twenty-five percent transparent map part of the time. He told Soh to make all communications audible in the helmet.

Soh started delivering direction commands. >go right onto Chu Manh Trinh in 30 meters< >take third right< >onto Ly Tu Trong Street<.

Souchi pulled out into traffic, and Soh acted up. >please comm sentences in standard English< >We can keep up<. Matt's embrace of Souchi stiffened forcing her to exhale. The bike wobbled.

Matt asked <How soon to intercept>.

Soh replied >on fastest route now< > Intercept in eight point five to ten point oh minutes depending on van four trajectory< >intercept estimate factors in our operator competency< > estimate factors in our passenger competency and confidence in operator< > intercept recalculate every 30 seconds<. Both humans felt Soh preferred the other.

Following Soh's commands, Souchi beat heavy traffic at several intersections.

Soh updated >intercept in four point five to four point eight minutes<. As they sped toward an intersection with a stop sign, Soh prompted >no need to stop<. Rattled, Souchi slowed but then let it rip, right through the sign. Matt flinched. No cops, no cross traffic. Too crazy. Hadn't Soh been programmed to protect humans under Asimov's Three Laws?[115]

Soh was very busy; Souchi needed to focus on the road to stay safe. Soh's reports came faster.

>intercept in one point oh to one point two minutes<

>van four moving 19 meters per second on Pasteur Street< >bearing 320 degrees<

>we will intercept coming from Ly Tu Trong Street<

>van will be 30 meters plus or minus 5 meters to the left<

>intercept in twelve seconds<

Matt saw it first. A white van with Rickie's wife's branding for a computer repair shop near downtown. Souchi called the find. "There it is. Hold on Matt." Matt was surprised by the sweet lean Souchi threw on the motorcycle. He hung on.

Soh noticed. >note. motorcycle passenger must unify with driver<.

"You tell him sweetie." Souchi was on Pasteur Street forty meters back of the van but hemmed in by the traffic. As usual, with the passenger gone, the van was driving fast and loose. It was pulling away.

Soh reported in. >fourteen point four minutes post transaction< >losing tracking in 25 seconds<.

Souchi, in attack mode leaning down hard on the tank, spoke into the helmet comm mic as cool as if watching a movie on the couch. "Matt, hug me, pull in your knees, spoon tight." She cut back on the throttle, braked and cut sharply between a cab and a pedicycle on her right. Souchi headed straight for the side of the avenue. As the bike approached the curb, she downshifted, revved the motor, popped the clutch, lifting the front wheel over the low ragged concrete barrier. If Matt's eyes had been open, he would have seen them blast through the sidewalk hedge. As much as he thought he loved Souchi, he was not thinking this would be a good way to die.

Soh commented. >visual contact lost< >please restore visual contact< >visual field needed<. Matt opened his eyes. >thank you<.

A Yamaha motorcycle horn, unless modified, is a feeble instrument. Better that the driver concentrate on avoidance than notification of next of kin. Nonetheless, Souchi held the button down. The nasal wheeze added a comical touch to the mayhem she and Matt and Soh left on the sidewalk. Fortunately, police are not armed in Vietnam. At least one found her forty-yard sprint along the sidewalk legally wrong, almost terroristic, but, like several pedestrians, he was left in their wake, mouth agape. In an earlier era, the passenger would have thrown a grenade into the patronage.

Souchi could have stopped to pay for damages to the various cafes and shops; Arctan would certainly reimburse her. But that would likely have blown their cover if not their freedom. As it turns out, they lost track of the van. Souchi cruised circuitously back to Papa Nguyen's with Soh providing navigational guidance.

Leaving the most intense upsets behind, Soh had an opinion about Souchi's familiarity back on Ly Tu Trong Street.

>please note. Soh is not a sweetie<

CHAPTER 49
COURAGE

The weary dismount, stripping off the helmet, the wiping of a sweaty brow. It's all part of the ritual after a hard ride. Souchi had enjoyed the process many times as an amateur motocross racer. Matt was new to the game. But he was primed for the ritual of the post-run debrief. They had a lot to talk about.

Next to the bike, next to Hương Chiều's wrought iron fence, Matt was agitated. "Shit. Daamn. I'm alive. Shit. Alive. I don't know how. But we survived. And I'm sure we didn't leave anyone crippled or maimed back there. At least I hope not. I really do. I really do."

Soh offered data. >episode recorded in video< >shall We replay in full VR<

Matt. "Dammit, no!"

Souchi was beginning to accept Matt's talking to thin air.

Souchi was calm and silent. She had just had one of the best rides of all time. While not ignoring Matt's rant, she was replaying the whole thing in her head. Reminiscing. Wow! The orchid hedge just exploded! And that cop. Dropped his cigarette in the coffee. She smiled, alone, then realized she had to cover her tracks. "I love you Matt. I'm so happy we came out OK. You OK?"

He threw his arms around her. And choked back a sob,

just a short one. Then he got hold, all mixed up and looked at her. "Souchi, I love you dearly kid. But that was nutso. You did a hellava job. We coulda died. I'm sorry if I was a deadweight. I love you. You're terrific." He hugged her some more. He was coming down from combat rush.

Souchi was one smart lady. She knew Matt had led a sheltered life. Being on the engineering spectrum didn't help; he turned inward to find solace. But he had great potential; good mind, good heart, good bod. His hint that maybe he was a bit thrilled about the ride was a positive sign. She was going to ease him along. Souchi guessed that HCMC was going to get more interesting.

"Thanks, Matt. You know, Dr. S told us to make bold decisions. So that's what we're doing." She was cultivating courage. "We made a good team today." She gave him her best, penetrating love-eyes. "We're going to need each other to figure out this van business. And it looks like Soh is a partner. That navigation was right on."

Matt had some doubts. "Scared the heck out of me, running the stop sign. Can we trust Them that much?"

"We'll find out."

Matt startled. Souchi moved on, "I was kind of wondering how to read that 'sweetie' footnote."

"Yea. Odd. I'm guessing that Soh searched the word and rejected the negative connotation."

Souchi was thinking psychology. "Strange that They felt the need to spend resources on that comment, though."

Matt thought back to the basics of Augmented Intelligence. "Maybe Soh is looking for recognition? Machine learning is based on human trainers verifying machine guesses. Maybe Soh wants more reinforcement?"

Souchi wasn't confident she could take on two teaching projects at one time. But then, the idea that both Soh and Matt needed adult supervision was entered into her game plan.

CHAPTER 50

DECISIONS

Souchi had looked over the motorcycle after the curb-and-orchid run. Cables OK. Chain drive intact. There were some delicate yellow flowerlets crammed into the front spokes. The right exhaust pipe at the engine header had taken a glancing hit. The red paint remnant there was probably from the chair Souchi couldn't avoid after bursting through the hedge. She didn't tell Matt (his eyes had been closed) but she shuddered at the idea of someone being in the chair. In her fifteen races, she'd seen one bike-on-human collision and it wasn't pretty. For the bystander or for the driver. Two-up is way worse. She felt a chill knowing that the passenger usually does the worst.

Soh sounded the alarm. >van one< >range< >1330 meters< >location< > Điện Biên Phủ street< >speed< >ten meters per second[116]< >bearing 240 degrees<. Soh had picked up another transaction trail. Time to roll.

Practice makes perfect. Intelligent people learn fast. With two wild rides under their belt, they now had a plan and style.

Souchi followed Soh's cues. Matt inquired <time to intercept>. >two point six to three point oh minutes depending on van trajectory<.

>van one speed eight meters per second on Điện Biên Phủ street < >bearing 240 degrees<

The van was moving slow and deliberately, typical protocol when a dealing passenger was on board.

>in fifty meters turn right into parking lot < >wait behind auto repair sign<

They pulled into the designated parking lot and saw that Soh had given them a concealed hunting stand.

>intercept from left in 10 seconds<.

Souchi spotted the van and waited behind the sign. Traffic was light, the deal inside the van was still going down, so pursuit was easy. Staying unseen would take some care so Souchi lagged forty meters back. Their goal was to pass the van and sneak a photo of the driver for Soh to identify and then eventually follow the van back to its home base, probably in Binh Thanh.

After a few minutes of tailing, the van pulled over to let out a passenger, who veered off down the side street. Fortunately, the deal had closed on the near side of an intersection where the light was red. Souchi stopped far enough back to remain unseen but close enough to pick up the chase when the light changed. When the light turned green, the van took off. Souchi cut the distance, knowing the driver would move more unpredictably than before. Traffic was thickening.

Soh confirmed. >on this route average 45% packing all lanes< >on next four intersecting roads 56% to 68% packing all lanes< >average speeds less than twelve meters per second<.

"Matt, there's our chance up ahead." Souchi saw the lane on the right moving slightly faster than the van. She would be able to pass the van while Matt shot photos of the driver. Then they could use distance and

Soh's tracking to follow Van One back to HQ.

Soh weighed in. >ahead of van one in lane two car is blinking to leave< >We will be adjacent to van one in five seconds<.

Unexpectedly, the traffic cop in the intersection stopped all traffic in their direction. He was in the middle of the roads, impressive in white gloves, spats and self-importance. The car ahead of Souchi, one back from the van, lightly rear-ended the minivan in front of it. Drivers and passengers both sprang from their vehicles to inspect and complain about what looked like sixteen dollars total damage. Souchi, Matt and Soh were hemmed in.

Matt made a bold independent decision. He jumped off the motorcycle, ripped off his helmet and perched it on the backpack bar behind him and ran to the passenger window of the van. He started banging on the door, showing his credit card through the window. The driver, a chubby guy maybe 30, totally surprised, started shaking his head and trying to wave Matt off.

Soh reported >images captured< >running facial scans<. Matt kept banging. Souchi didn't like what she saw. She yelled, "Matt! Matt!" but now horns and indignant drivers were bleeping. The van driver and Matt saw the cop was beginning to take notice, not something the driver wanted. The cop took a step in their direction. The driver leaned over and pushed open the door. Matt jumped in. Badgered by horns and angry civilians, the cop waved traffic around the accident and the van took off.

CHAPTER 51
NOW WHAT?

Inside the van, the driver was screaming at Matt. A cop, an unannounced customer, a credit card payment, his night was going badly. Matt almost felt sorry for the guy. But at least Matt had the presence of mind to note there were no weapons visible. No gun, no knife, no truncheon. Odd for a drug dealer but then what did Matt know from drug dealers. The driver began to cool off and pay attention to the road, staying cautiously with the traffic.

Having screamed himself hoarse, the silent, thoughtful driver made his bold, independent decision. Grabbing the credit card, which Matt had continued to wave about as his badge, the driver pointed to the door between the seats. Matt hadn't seen that yet. He tried to ask for his Visa card back. Nope. Price of entry. So Matt, watching his back and thinking about the credit card, squeezed his Tennessee football frame through a doorframe sized for a Vietnamese librarian.

The door slid closed behind him. It was dark and quiet in the cabin. Matt couldn't stand up so he shifted his weight to sit on the barely visible bench running down along the driver's side of the van. As he sat down, soft, red-tinged lighting and 70's elevator music simultaneously brightened. There was a sweet perfume smell and maybe, just maybe the tang of ganja. From a seat in the back opposite corner of the van, under her own slowly brightening, diffuse lamp, a petite woman spoke to him in Vietnamese. Her voice was at once both soothing and provocative. Matt had been expecting something different, or at least less troublesome than this.

The woman softly repeated a phrase several times, pointing at him. He responded "I'm Matt" to her third try.

She answered, "iMatt, yes." Apple branding had injected itself everywhere. Introducing herself, "Thị Liễu. Thị Liễu."[117] She was the embodiment of every Asian female fantasy played-out around the world, from Multiplayer Computer Games to James Bond movies to Netflix kung fu preview covers. Shoulder length, shiny black hair, parted severely down the middle. Bright red lipstick. Slim and athletic yet with artistically sculpted curves under a silky, fragile, front buttoning thigh-length shift. The one deviation from the standard, inspired design was her hazel green eyes. The van swayed as Matt absorbed the scene.

Thị Liễu, reclining, comfortable, relaxed, allowed Matt time to get his bearings and hers. He noticed that the entire inside of the van was Vegas-plush. Some cornices, a tiny wash basin. Rising gracefully, fitting easily in the van, she moved to his side but not too close. She pulled a miniature hookah from behind the bench back and peeled off some sanitary packaging. Using a piezo, she lit the pre-packed bowl, mouthed one end and blew a puff in Matt's direction. He flinched, so she ventured "California. Legal wow," and looked up into his eyes with the innocence of a little child sharing Valentine candy.

What to heck, why not. If this illicit Arctan business is a traveling hookah show, he better do the research.

Then she touched him. A light, delicate hand on his knee. Meant innocently to brace herself against the van's gentle shifting and bumps? She continued to talk quietly in Vietnamese poetry, occasional English words between with no connectable meaning. Exotic. Intoxicating. Matt was feeling the smoke as she slid toward him and made thigh contact. He felt the syrupy warmth of her leg oozing through the cloth between them. This was some super stuff she had. Wordlessly, slowly searching his eyes with her hazel-greens, she lay her head on his shoulder, perfumed hair brushing his cheek. Thị Liễu used her side and breast to push his arm out of the way so she could get as much of her body against his as possible. She purred. She turned her face down shyly to see better where her hand was headed. Matt was teeth-gritting torn between totally letting go and wishing he was wearing a wedding ring on which to build some willpower. As she ever so lightly moved up to his groin, his mind went soothingly, urgently....

Bang, bang, bang! Jolting noises along the outside of the van. Shouts. Muffled, the driver started screech-screaming again and slammed on the brakes. Matt and Thị Liễu tumbled gracelessly into a clumsy hump up against the plush front wall of the cabin. Thị Liễu clung to Matt, enjoying his beefy presence and slow, shy style. She purred and molded herself onto him as they lay like so much twisted wreckage amid hookah embers.

Souchi had come to Matt's rescue.

The cabin door flew open. The driver intended to drag Matt out but there was way too much geometry in play. And besides, Thị Liễu was bawling and flailing at the driver for interrupting. Matt managed to extract himself. Rickie Lash, who had also experienced an extraction or two under fire in Vietnam, would have been proudly humored by Matt's cool and Souchi's courage.

The van took off, one occupant happy, the other not. Dumped in the road, traffic coursing around them, Souchi didn't budge, in fact, she flipped off drivers and chased one bicyclist who challenged her primacy. Finally, she walked the motorcycle and Matt straight across the woman-anger-respecting flow of traffic, and hands on hips, she stared, fuming without speaking at the rumpled Matt. He smelled like the ChiChi room, House of the Rising Sun. His undies sticky, his vision bleary, his attitude cannabis-paranoiac, his stature sheepish, he was a diminished male.

Soh offered navigation directions back to Papa Nguyen's. They dismounted and without even taking off the helmet it was Souchi's turn to be upset. "What ta fuggin' hell fuggin' what were you thinking gettin' off the friggin' bike and gettin' in the van and what-shit-to-hell was goin' through your friggin' head climbing into a friggin' drug van? What?"

Soh answered for Matt. >that was a whorehouse<.

Souchi threw up her hands and spun around. "Ohhhhh fuggin' hell," and starred at Matt, shrinking, small. "Took you long enough to figure that out. Huh? No explanatory brochures in there?"

Then to Soh, into the air. "And you, sweetie, thanks for

the fuggin' data."

>please not sweetie<.

"Hay-zeus. You two are a pair." Souchi had burned through all her adrenaline. Her shoulders dropped. "Let's go get a drink. Maybe there's some useful info here after all." Sputtering like a hot iron in a summer rain, she started walking, "Sheez-zush. A cathouse. Shit." and led Soh and Matt off, past Papa Nguyen's, headed to the closest beer pub.

Matt lagged behind, noticing the paint smudges from the the van on his helmet. He THC-giggled to himself. Maybe Rickie might get a call to repair paint on a van?. But Matt didn't want to talk about the credit card yet.

CHAPTER 52
HERE'S WHERE
WE ARE

"You gave him what?" Souchi thought they would debrief over a beer or two and make some rational progress. But now she had some doubts. Deliberately. "You gave him... your credit card?"

Matt looked sheepish. Up to this point he had built a defense based on "bold independent decisions." He was losing confidence in that.

"So, did he run it?"

Matt shook his head, happy. "I don't think so, in fact, I didn't see any kind of scanner." He brightened. "That fits the MO of non-traceable membership transactions, online charges only."

"Right. So that's good. Wha'd he do with it?" Matt didn't answer. "No. No, Matt. He didn't keep it, right. Tell me you grabbed it back." Matt didn't answer. Souchi just sat there in a state of suspended dis-animation. Matt felt weak and small.

"Ok. What else. Anything that might help us understand this van business."

"Well, her name was Thị Liễu and she was really sweet and gentle and she was really attracted to me."

Souchi had been through a lot as a child. In the US she had worked hard to become not just professionally competent. She had also strived to become sophisticated in every way. But Souchi almost lost all her learned civilized behavior at Matt's last comment. Her BP was shooting toward 200/90. Quietly she growled, "Matt. Thị Liễu was a hooker, Matt. She was selling sex, Matt. Perhaps your card has been charged already. I'm not going to ask if you got your money's worth. I'm not going to ask if you mentioned me. All I want right now, don't say anything, not a word, is that you realize exactly what just went down. That's all. That's it."

Welcome interruption. There was a murmuring coming from the comm port in Souchi's helmet, on her lap. She threw Matt a look of "What ta'hell do They want?" He had heard Soh's comment in his head and shyly suggested Souchi put on the helmet, which she reluctantly did.

He thought-projected <repeat message>.

>his report is accurate< >the woman in the van was in an altered state of sexual concupiscence< >her professional resources were 73% greater than his abilities to control decisions<

Maybe it was standing there listening to a voice in a helmet and thinking how silly it looked. Maybe it was the cumulative stress of the recent days and hours. Maybe the disappointments and the beer and Soh. But Souchi started to cry, hard. She had been trying desperately to hold the whole thing together. But now, her tears and her sorrow competed to fill a mile-wide canyon. Matt grabbed her, gently removed the helmet and forgot all about Vietnam, and Rickie Lash and Arctan and, even,

Thị Liễu. He held her and they rocked, trying to be closer by dimming the present and erasing the recent past. They needed a day off.

CHAPTER 53
ONE DAY OFF

Trite. "When the going gets tough, the tough get going." Matt and Souchi were not going to let the Night of A Thousand Mishaps step in the way of loving. There's nothing like a long cry to help a couple revert back to some good old togetherness. So, Matt sent Soh a <pause> and set Devon's contacts aside. Post-conviviality, they slept like the children they wanted and needed to be.

After billing and cooing over a breakfast of *phở*, broth noodles, Matt and Souchi settled down to thinking about life. There was a lot to sort out. The conversation was frank.

The Big Picture: The pings they had tracked for almost a month were not from a drug ring but from a sex-ring, prostitution built on the model of Uber or Lyft. Working the high-end inner city of HCMC, digitally sophisticated and secret discrete. Still to learn: What was the intent of the crime ring? What did it portend for Arctan? Who was the mastermind?

The Little Picture: Credit card, gone, in criminal hands. Matt had put Arctan resources to work obliterating the card's records but given the immediacy of current events, it was at least four hours post-cannabis and an hour post-coitus until he got around to cancelling it. No telling what information had been wrung from the card.

"I gotta apologize, Souchi. We're bigger than what I did." She looked at him puzzled. "I mean, I don't need to pull a grade-school stunt to impress my girl. So much could have gone wrong with that van. Well, I guess enough did, but still. I didn't need to make that bold of a decision, did I? I'm sorry."

She wanted to leave him space to heal. "The wisdom to make good decisions comes from bad decisions."[118] But she was going to keep an eye on things.

"Matt, I let myself get carried away. Biking hits me like a drug. Crashing onto sidewalks to chase a van knowing we could find another, that's stupid-selfish, careless. I put all of us at risk." They both noticed but remained silent on her "all of us."

"And I apologize for the cursing and jumping and theatrics. And for trying to punch that bicyclist after we got you out of the van. No more drama-queen. Promise." Matt admitted to himself that he loved the new Souchi more than the tidy lady who called him "Tiger" outside the conference room on the day of his presentation.

"Aww Souchi, please don't change, please?" His innocent puppy-face delighted her to the bottom of her soul. "I never dreamed I would have so much fun chasing international sex criminals on the sidewalks of Old Siagon. Besides, I love squeezing you between my loins on that vibrating Yamaha." She loved him back.

Matt had concerns. "Soh has had some... moments. Like accessing local WiFi space on the fly and grabbing detailed navigational data. And communicating in Soh-sentences. The sense of humor is unnerving."

"Right, and Matt I've noticed that Soh is following our conversations."

Neither Matt nor Souchi was inclined to ask if They had any apologies to offer.

The Back to Work Picture: On the way to breakfast, Matt had purchased some headphones so Souchi could hear Soh outside the Shuberth helmet. In Matt's mind, the helmet and Souchi's tears the night before were connected.

As soon as They were online, Soh reported in. >fifteen hours twenty four minutes since last contact< >interim biometrics suggest extremes of exertion and recovery< >please confirm all OK in hu-world<.

Matt thought-back. <all OK> <no further action> <formulating plans>

>no further action is inaccurate< >your biometrics suggest considerable action< >We may need additional data to optimize Our deep learning< >your call<.

Matt didn't know if this was humor or engineering. <our call please limit biometrics monitoring to minimum needed for mission completion>.

>We can't do that Dave<. The voice in Souchi's headphones was an exact replica of HAL. OMG, Soh was channeling 2001![119] Souchi almost laughed, stopped by thinking it might encourage further cheekiness from Soh. Or worse, They might remake Their image to match Their hero, a HAL or Tron.

Matt got Them back on task. <report data from van one driver> <priority interactions with legal system>.

>driver male Han Van Phan age 39<   >biometrics

birth family data available on request >medical history available on request< > police record sex industry local hotels< >solicitation and pandering< >three infractions most recent five years< >paid total fines 3,510,000 dong[120]< >no motor vehicle violations< >took possession of Visa card 0900 8900 7655 1023 at 20:17 VST yesterday< >Arctan search shows one transaction on card for seventy five dollars US at 22:30 VST last night< >card canceled effective at 01:34 VST today< >current location of card unknown<.

Matt hesitated. <report data from van one passenger> <priority interactions with legal system> <include last two years personal data>.

>passenger female Mai Thị Liễu age 17 years 10 months< Matt winced. Souchi was looking elsewhere.

>born in Tinh Vinh Long oldest of five siblings< >family agrarian Catholic< > income 14% below UN-defined local poverty< >family supported her through graduation from high school< >could not afford schooling for siblings< >one year ago father diagnosed lung cancer Stage Four<

>Thị Liễu arrival HCMC six months ago< >recruited by and under supervisory maintenance of H Sing Lo TTNH< >five months ago received Provincial Medical Department immunizations< >received ocular exam HCMC Hospital five months ago< >no data occupation< >no data residence HCMC<

>Mai Thị Liễu's high school yearbook data available on request<

High school yearbook. Matt didn't want to know more. Matt didn't want to be chastised by Soh. Matt didn't want to feel this bad.

CHAPTER 54
ANOTHER DAY
AT THE OFFICE

Souchi broke the silence. "Well, we know a lot more now. Let's get out to the factory."

Matt asked Soh to connect him to Nhanh's cell. When could he meet them for another trip to Binh Thanh? Could he come in a different car, not the van?

Soh spoke with Nhanh. They reported back, in Their own words, that he was eager to see action again. He would meet them at Papa Nguyen's at three in the afternoon. Matt sent his update message to Dev and Leash but didn't expect an answer back. They were asleep in California.

Nhanh showed up in a Hyundai Accent, borrowed from his neighbor's kid. Nhanh thought the tinted windows were a sleuthing bonus. He had to give the kid a million dong[121] and solemn promise not to mar the car. Nhanh wanted to take them along a picturesque route. Soh wouldn't need to navigate.

He and the engulfing swarm of scooters maintained a separation measured in molecules, magical realism. "Right there, big War place for you." Nhanh pointed out his window. "Rex Hotel. Very nice. Big guys USA France go there every nighttime to chat a lot about us, Ho

Chi Minh Trail guys. From up there," he craned to look to the seventh-floor roof garden, "1975 watch airport takes rockets."

He kept up the chatter past the Reunification Palace. At the War Remnants Museum, he slowed. "Ha! Look you guys left so many helicopter! That one," he pointed at the Huey in the plaza, "I remember whop whop whop. Ha! Run to tunnel. So many holes in choppers. Not much use after war over." He laughed his Nhanh laugh. No animosity, no regrets, Nhanh motored on. Like all the people Matt and Souchi had met here.

As they approached the warehouse neighborhood, Nhanh explained that he had arranged for some help. A nephew majoring in engineering had wired up a GoPro camera so it could send imagery a couple of hundred yards. Then he contacted a guy from the Binh Thanh box kerfuffle the day before; turns out the guy was a relative and had helped with defusing angry mob. This guy could hide the GoPro in a pile of boxes across from the warehouse sending real-time, high-res imagery of the garage door. Matt and Souchi were liking Nhanh's "passion quotient."

With the camera running, they plunked the van at the far end of Đường số 6 and watched. Soh acquired a strong feed from the GoPro. It could see vehicle details and might even get a peek into the warehouse. They settled in shortly before sunset. If this was the sex ring HQ, then exits should begin soon.

They sat. Nhanh scrunched down in the driver's seat. Matt and Souchi lounged and napped amidships in the dark. Twenty minutes in, shortly after conversation ended, Nhanh opened a crisp (Matt noticed the irritating sound) plasticine bag and offered contents to the back seat. Souchi retrieved an egg roll, Matt passed. So it went, the air in the car thick with fried food, garlic and fermented fish sauce.

Matt thought-projected <alternate> <AR 75%> <on 5 seconds> <off 2 seconds> so he too could watch the garage door. Souchi put on the 'phones so she could listen in and reply to Soh's commentary.

Just before dusk, long in deep shadow, it happened. Soh announced a sighting. >door going up< >license plate 53B 083.15 waiting at door< >our van number one< >door fully open in fifteen seconds< In a smart move, Friend-of-Nhanh had put the camera low in the stack of boxes so Soh could peek under the door. >two vehicles visible< >door open< >first van out heading west< >second van emerging license plate 41D 661.20 < >second van out heading east< >third van emerging license plate 83A 290.44 < >our van four from last night<. Matt looked at Souchi. >third van out heading east<. The first and third vans would come past them in just a minute.

The heavily tinted windows of Nhanh's rig should make anyone inside invisible but after last night's debacle, they all felt the need to shrink. The first van cruised by, the driver busy with his panel mounted cell phone. The second van, Matt's "friends," Thị Liễu and Han, approached. Matt cringed and stopped breathing as the van squeezed past them. Matt felt like Han Van Phan looked right at him but he was only driving carefully. Rickie's paint job on the van showed some signs of wear from the beating Souchi gave it. Matt indulged himself a fleeting thought about how much she loved him.

After "his" van passed, Matt refocused on Soh's AR of the open garage door. There didn't seem to be anyone inside. No guards. He didn't see any surveillance cameras within the range of the GoPro. The door next to the garage roll up had one digital knob lock, no bar.

Three more vans exited and fanned out east and west to service customers. Soh offered a thought. >garage door is standard Ryobi Model 32Mk< >unsecured radio receiver opener< >We have the code< > handle on door is standard Swagelok< >four digit code 9155< >odds that We can open either door is 95% plus or minus 2%< >advise<.

Problem. Matt and Souchi had pledged, in a moment of morning-after, to be more cautious. But Soh was suggesting that They could remotely open the garage door, do a break-in. As if feeling their indecision, Soh dropped another bomb. >We have retrieved interior plan from renovation four months ago< >very unusual interior space allocation< >advise<.

"Ohhhh dammit Souchi. Whad'ya think?"

"Well. It's not a drug ring. You didn't see any sign of weapons today or yesterday. They've had less than 24 hours to digest your incident. Maybe didn't even report the trouble to the local crew chief or top boss at US Arctan. Heck, Han Van Phan could get in *beaucoup* trouble for running that $75 off the books. I bet they split it, sly. So, Han and your girlfriend are keeping a secret." Souchi, frowned, harboring a tiny residual "girlfriend" animus. "Plus, no sign of guards, no surveillance. Doesn't look like they expect trouble. Worst case?"

"You and I get captured and pressed into van service?" Matt was half serious.

Soh weighed in. >Souchi is better driver. Matt should work the sex-cabin<.

Souchi loved the thought. "Thank you Soh" >you are welcome< >you are welcome too Matt<. Matt rolled his eyes at the compliment.

"OK. So let's do this. Nhanh can move up, park toward the near end of Thanh Ho Way ready to roll. Sit tight, lie low just outside the door. Any trouble inside, we get back out the door next to the roll up."

>sending interior layout graphic to Matt< >also visible on Souchi Nhanh cell phones< >note. garage door entry at bottom of diagram< >note. scale whole map 40 meters on edge< >note. not OSHA approved[122]< >two doors We see on Thanh Ho Way are the only entry-exits<

Matt received the diagram overlay in his eyes. Soh sent him 10% AR transparency, so he saw the diagram in detail. "Woah. They got over ten thousand square feet inside. And lots of nooks and crannies. Complicated. Souchi, check it on your cell."

>translating labels on floorplan< Soh described the layout drawing and lit up an outline around each room as They narrated. >three dormitories< >shower room< >employee dining area< >three offices< >recreation room< >medical-laboratory< >storeroom< >maintenance room< >powder room<

Souchi, "Powder room? For what, explosives?"

>sorry. practicing use of vernacular<   >retranslate powder room to lavatory<

Souchi, "Soh. Play it straight, OK?"

Soh's androgenous voice switched to hyper-masculine. >aye aye skipper<.

"Oh, my gawd." Souchi was not amused.

Matt, "Guys, guys. We should start in through the door to the right. Less noise than the rollup. Take a peek. If it's clear, we scoot in and hide at the wall just inside the door. We can snap a photo around the corner to scope out the large open area. Must be the parking garage. Looks like some office spaces along that south wall. If it's clear, we keep going."

Souchi suggested they have a backup plan. "Let's be sure we can always see an escape route back out the door. Nhanh, Soh will ring your cell immediately after we get in. Hold the call so you can hear if we need something from you."

Matt was worried about the timing. "Wait 'til after the vans come home?"

Returning to Their natural voice, >predicting quiet in two hours< > detection probability 12% plus or minus 4%< >suggest go in early to verify layout< >hide in two square meter maintenance room just inside door< Soh highlighted that room in VR. >wait and observe vans return<

In cowboy-accented voice, >then we high-tail it boys<

So they sat. Thanh Ho Way quieted down, starkly yellow under sodium lamps all along its length. At ten o'clock, Nhanh stirred. "Time you go. Alley quiet. Stay close to wall boxes. I park further away. When all six vans back, move to twenty meters east of doors. See you soon. Don't fuck up!" Nhanh had spent his late formative years close to swaggering guys from New Jersey. Soh: >check all three cell phones on location sharing< >turn off ringer< They did.

Matt and Souchi slid out, glad to escape its humid heat. Nhanh watched them, nervous as a mother hen.

Nhanh blurted out. "Wait, wait. Take with you." Nhanh reached into the glove compartment. Matt expected some sort of Saint Christopher medal or a Buddhist talisman. Nhanh handed him a spray can of Rust Buster. "Do hinges first. Make quiet." Man, its nice to have thinking friends.

They dodged the foot traffic, mopeds, two beat-up taxis and the usual weaving bicycles, pushing China Plus One so Americans could rely on timely delivery of their Hanes undies and Nike sneakers.

Walking briskly, they hung close to the south wall. Forty meters down, the headlights from a van swept them up from behind. Trying not to be obvious, a joke for Matt, they slipped between two high piles of rancid recycled Chinese cardboard. It had rained in the afternoon. The van passed them, the driver not interested in the tall Anglo and his consort. The passage helped burn off some adrenaline. They started walking again.

They ran out of box cover before arriving at the door. There's no nakedness quite like amateurs on a break-in highlighted against twenty meters of open concrete wall under sodium lamps. At the door, Matt sprayed the hinges. Souchi asked, "9155 right." >yes 9155. go<

Souchi punched at the buttons, numbers surprisingly hard to see in the monochrome yellow. Matt anxiously looked up and down the alley. It was clear. She tried the lever, gingerly to minimize the sound. It rotated about a centimeter and stopped. "Shit. Shit!"

>try again. 9155. Numbers are upper left to lower right. No zero. easy and slow<. Soh spoke with the voice of a bomb-defusing ordinance technician. Reassuring.

Simple. 9155. Lower right. Upper left. Middle middle. Never seemed so difficult. She hit a wrong button. Souchi started to tear up. Her finger felt like a huge, leaden piston. Soh soothed. >easy girl easy<   Trying again. Nine. One. Five. Five. The lever swung full stop down. The door began to open. Nearly the whole thickness of the pane was out when it stopped. In a coarse whisper, "It's stuck." Realizing they had not seen anyone use the door, they froze. Souchi gave the handle a gentle tug. No effect. She let out a small, anguished moan and looked over to Matt. He applied a shot of spray to the jam. "I'll push on the door toward the hinges, you pull."

"On three. One, two, three." The door popped opened a crack with what sounded like fingernails on an old-school chalkboard, reverberating inside for seconds. In reality it was just a tiny bit of scratchy.

Soh cautioned. >go slow. listen the crack<

Souchi peeked in down low. Above her, Matt put his ear to the gap. Souchi was looking straight at a wall. Matt heard almost nothing. Maybe some murmuring voices.

>well?< Soh urged them on.

Matt opened the door eight inches and smiled as it

turned silently on Nhanh-lubed hinges. He sent a hugging motion toward Souchi. They dodged inside, quick to close the door to shut out the broad fan of streetlight that preceded them into the shadowy corridor. Fortunately, Soh's layout was right on. They were in a hallway secluded off to the right of the main room where the garage door opened. A closet door lay in front of them. It was unlocked.

Besides Nhanh's acrid lubby, the narrow hall smelled of Vietnamese dinners.

Soh continued to urge the plan forward. >shoot photos from floor level<

Souchi got down on her belly, the floor surprisingly, meticulously clean, and crept over to the corner where the main room opened up. She began to slide her iPhone around the corner when Matt grabbed her ankle. He signaled her to set the camera flash to off. It wasn't. She pantomimed wiping her brow then changed the setting. And signaled Matt to shut off ringers. Their confidence should have been shaken but like true amateurs, they were most dangerous in what they didn't know.

Souchi stuck a centimeter of her cell phone around the corner, aimed to get the brightest light in the center and took photos left and right. Pulling back, they sat together on the floor, looking millennial, inspecting the photos.

The back wall, maybe twenty meters from the roll-up door on their left, had five doors. One door, in the center, was open, the inside of the room alight. A microwave oven was visible on the counter in the back of this employee lounge. They could hear two men's voices chattering about maybe baseball, the high price of gasoline and their kids. Or whatever, since not even Soh could make out the content. But accessing the Cloud photos, They did relate the image views to the layout drawing. >two rooms left of employee lounge are dormitory three beds each< >two rooms right of lounge are dormitory one bed and lavatories men women<

The far east wall was occupied with cabinets and some work benches. The wall on which they were hiding sheltered three rooms past the maintenance closet. The photo showed at a steep viewing angle that these rooms had one window each. Soh explained. >closest room is called recreation room< >furthest room is called medical laboratory< >middle room is called conference room<.

The rest of the space, to the left of the roll up door, appeared to be a parking garage.

There wasn't much they could do with people up and around. Soh urged them to wait in the closet, suggesting that a maintenance room would be left in peace for the rest of the night. About a half hour after they settled uncomfortably in, they grew accustomed to the minty irritating smells of industrial level hygiene and started to nod off. Before they had much rest, the ping pong started. Souchi amused Matt by imitating the flow of the game. The occasional pong of a ball on their wall elicited deep frustration at her player's loss. Neither of them contemplated romance amid the smell of Pine-Sol and pick-pock sounds of Asia's favorite recreation.

At about one forty-five, the roll up door activated. It was raining hard outside. They heard one then another van drive in. Over the course of fifteen minutes, all six vans returned. The GoPro feed outside, bless Nhanh, showed the vans all parked to the left in the garage and a clutch of people moving out of vans, into the conference room and then back to the employee lounge. They could hear lilting female voices, and occasional giggling. Matt thought that he spotted Thị Liễu among the movements. The garage door closed.

Eventually, the sounds of microwave dining, locker-room showers, and doors closing, died off. Matt and Souchi had a scare as a group of males entered the hallway outside their hideaway. Souchi hoped that the tropical downpour outside would help cover their breathing and whatever tracks Nhanh's Rust Buster may have left. The men fumbled at the exit. It sounded like they were locking the door, on the inside.

The next twenty minutes wait lasted an eternity. They crept out of the closet finding the exhaust-tinged garage the most welcome fresh air of their lives. Legs stiff, they studied the inside door lock. The door was fitted with a key lock inside. Matt and Souchi hadn't noticed this oh-so non-OSHA compliant part of the layout. They were prisoners.

Soh reassured them. >Nhanh can open from outside< >also We have hacked the roll up code. Can use as a backup exit< >It is eight seconds slower< >probability 98% plus minus 1% for successful exit<

Matt asked Soh to message Nhahn to move up outside the door ready to "9155" it. They confirmed he was awake and moving into position.

Soh urged them to follow the plan, gather data. >check vans< >check conference room and medical room< >take photos<. Matt stood watch near the dorms. Souchi slunk around the vans, shooting license plates. She slid over to the "Medical Laboratory," but the door was locked. She shot a low-light photo through the gap in the curtain covering its window. Then she slipped into the conference room. Using her iFlashlight, she spotted two white boards in the room. There was a spreadsheet drawn neatly on each board. She shot multiple photos, then signaled for Matt to come and share a look with Soh. Soh translated >night's victories< >progress of performance contest< >there are six columns, six names< >rows appear to be statistics< >suggest rely on photo content<. They looked at each other and Matt whispered wryly "Big Data" to Souchi.

Ready to get out, Matt looked at the employee lounge entrance to their right, a tantalizing five meters deeper in. Soh pushed them. >yes. get photos<. Wordlessly, Matt and Souchi moved across the empty floor to the darkened room. Holding in the doorway, Souchi scanned the room with her light. Fridge, microwave, cups, snacks, sink in a formica counter. Not stylish, not cheap. She snapped four perfunctory photos.

Tense, ready to leave, they spotted an employee bulletin board on the wall adjacent to the doorway. Souchi tugged Matt's sleeve. Reluctantly, he followed. Their lights illuminated circles on the board. Family pictures and unreadable one-liners, maybe company reminder notes. Matt spotted one then several photos of a group of young girls, on a beach hamming for the camera. He recognized Thị Liễu in most photos. Kids on an outing.

His heart ached.

Souchi was also scanning the board and startled, a gasp. Matt woke from his funk and swung his gaze to her light circle. They were staring at a photo of a shirtless Matt torn from the ad to "build Arctan's corporate image." Matt was a somebody's favorite here. Souchi, shocked but composed, vamped a coy "Good taste," before signaling the need to move out, pronto.

As they crossed into the large garage room, there she stood. Thị Liễu, sleepy in local jammies. Matt thought she looked like the photos of so many haggard Viet Cong fighters in the late 60's. Thị Liễu gasped as if seeing a ghost and started scream-moaning "iMatt. iMatt." She groped at him but he juked, dodged and took off, leading Souchi on a run to the back door. They could hear Thị Liễu wailing and screaming, now in a kneel outside the conference room. A light came on in two dorm rooms behind them, visible under the closed doors. Soh signaled Nhanh to open the front door. A dorm door opened behind them. A man shouted. Thị Liễu's wailing intensified. The front door popped open with Nhanh looking around the edge and the four of them ran to pour themselves 1920s slapstick into the nephew's car. Without drama, it jumped to life and Nhanh took off, glad to have parked in the right direction. All three were laughing hysterically at their success.

Suddenly, some pops and the back window crumpled. Nhanh started screaming. Souchi reflexively jerked into a fetal low crouch, sprinkled with chunks of glass. Matt uttered a low, guttural groan. The driver side mirror shattered. Several thuds registered in the trunk behind them. They were taking hits from a small caliber handgun. Souchi scrambled to feel for Matt, crying his name through tears. The car careened and bounced off a pile of Fiona sports bra boxes. Nhanh managed to make the corner turn and headed south.

Souchi, losing it, pulled herself over to Matt feeling him up, "Where, where you hit? You're OK, OK, OK?" pleading, expecting warm, sticky wetness. Nhahn had stopped screaming and was moaning in waves. His driving, never great, was totally erratic as he carelessly flew across Đường Tân Kỳ Tân Quý avenue, eerily empty in the pre-dawn darkness.

Matt was curled up, unaware that a shitstorm had swirled around him, "Ohhh man. That hurt bad. You kicked me where it hurts. Dang." Waking up to the racket in the front seat, "What's wrong with Nhanh?"

Sort of relieved, she looked in the front seat and saw blood all over Nhahn's head and shoulder. A bullet had come through the back window, bisected Matt and Souchi, clipped Nhanh and gone out through the front windshield, leaving a tidy spider web around the exit. Nhahn's ear was bleeding profusely but he was OK, wailing Viet-glish about the car. "How bring back to nephew like this? Great shame. Great shame." He had made a promise. He blubbered on.

CHAPTER 55
DEBRIEF, BE BRIEF

Vietnam isn't the USA. Civilian gun ownership is illegal, very. Firing a gun in public? Short cut to prison. They had encountered somebody with game. Matt and Souchi, rank amateurs, needed to rethink their future.

Nhahn was a lucky guy, he was missing maybe a centimeter off the auricular. Clean swipe. But he was not going to the ER. No way. If anybody figured out his wound, he was toast. Besides, times past, he'd seen plenty worse wounded and they, many, survived. Matt did his Boy Scout best to fix the ear. It needed stitches but some tight taping from the nephew's first aid kit and Nhanh would be OK for the moment. Next issue, the car.

The decision didn't take long. Nhanh, still bemoaning his failed family obligations, was ecstatic at the suggestion they get over to Rickie's before dawn. Matt asked Soh to avoid intersections and cops. They had some advice. >he must drive with great caution. nearly zero traffic. this car now suspicious<.

"Nhanh, we're gonna get to Rickie but you gotta drive slow. No cops, OK?" This was like asking a Catholic to forsake Pope John Paul the Second, but he nodded, half-listening. "Willco, can do."

Under Soh's meticulous navigating and frequent scolding, they arrived at Rickie's chained up, rusted metal garage doors as the sun was lightening the sky. They needed to get private fast. Hyundai idling at the gate, Matt rapped on the metal. He fell backward onto the hood of the car as some kind of giant junk yard dog leapt against the inside of the sheet metal doors, bellowing for blood. It must have been sleeping at the gate or crept up for sake of scaring excrement out of unwanted guests. The dog knew its business; Matt's sphincters and scrotum were painfully constricted.

They waited. The dog growled, primal, deep inside its chest. Dim light from inside shredded through rusted pinholes. A door back there opened and slammed shut. Someone walked toward the gate and, for the visitor's sake, racked a semi-automatic pistol. The dog barked quick and sharp, getting tangibly hopeful about biting somebody. A grouchy voice uttered real low, "What." Just that. Matt answered. "Matt and Souchi." Inside voice, "More."

"We came by a couple days ago with Nhahn and told you some fancy stories about painting a van."

The voice on the far side turned to laughter. "So?" It was Rickie.

Souchi, "We got in some trouble, can we come in?"

Rickie spoke in Vietnamese, and they heard someone in flip-flops come running out. A woman spoke with meaning to the dog and it backed down to whimper-growling. It sounded like it let itself be dragged into the house, sad at missing this chance to gnaw on an intruder. As the dog threat disappeared, there came some lock-jostling sounds and the chain started to slide noisily through its two blowtorch cut holes.

Rickie pulled the doors inward and came into sight. If he hadn't had the Smith and Wesson hanging at his side, he might have looked old and pathetic. Instead, he looked old and meaningful. He took one glance at the windshield, and the bloodied Nhanh behind it and shook his head. "Oh, man, fucking amateur hour," and waved Nhanh into the court, dragging a set of brake drums out of his way. Before closing the doors, Rickie took a look up and down the lane. No sign of tails or nosy neighbors.

Rickie didn't have anything to say at first. He cast an experienced eye at Matt and Souchi, figured out they were shaken but not hit. Nhanh, driving, upright, bloody but bandaged, can't be too bad. Then he walked over to the windshield, touched the hole, inspected the spider web and whistled. "My kinda people." Turning with a wry smile to Souchi and Matt, who were looking young and sheepish, "Guess you got an address for me, huh?"

That was rhetorical. Rickie continued, walking about, enjoying himself, "So you found where my friend's six businesses are, you broke in and got caught. You ran away, but my friends weren't happy with just scaring you off a little. They got overexcited and boom boom. Now Nhanh here is in deep shit with the family. That Hyundai. Nice pimping job, by the way, Nhanh." He stopped to repeat the compliment in Vietnamese. "That Hyundai is now his personal anchor. Am I good so far?" All the eyewitnesses were on the same page.

"I'm guessing that the guy who shot at you is also in deep shit. Their kinda business, they built that on privacy. Street shooting, um um. No *bueno*. One employee is in big trouble over there this morning. You want to be down low. They want to be down low. By the way, those trunk holes you got and the shattered windows, that probably .38 all twisted and tumbling like it was would have given Uncle Nhanh a real serious headache if'n it were just a tad closer to his centerline. You turkeys are one lucky flock-up."

Rickie knew something about coming down from close combat. Seeing their pale faces and some shivering, he abruptly ended the debriefing and invited them into the house. His wife, Shue, and the dog, Chesty, were both delighted to have guests. Hot tea never felt more soothing.

CHAPTER 56
A TIME FOR PLANNING.

Shue, half Rickie's age, hustled about preparing Vietnamese breakfast. The house was her territory, adorned with tropical plants. Now that they were in the house and eating, Matt, Souchi and Nhahn were officially family, so Chesty turned lapdog. He especially couldn't get enough of Souchi. While Rickie was outside inspecting the car, Chesty attached himself, leaning on her with a slough-eyed, sad face each time he was ordered off her lap. She had explored and discovered Chesty's favorite ear tugs and chin scratches, leading Matt to wonder if he had also been so easy.

After enough pet therapy time and food and hot tea, Rickie sat down with them in the cluttered kitchen and pushed forward. "Down to business. Way I read this, money is no object." He looked at Souchi. She nodded. "OK. Nhanh, I can have your family's shaggin' wagon top shape again in two days. I will fetch the lead outta the back seats but can't perfectly patch up the inside of the trunk. The sheet metal holes and glass, no problem. Plenty parts in town. That work for you, can you cover bases at home? Should I put my guys to work?" Shue caught Rickie's eye, so he repeated in soft Vietnamese, with what appeared to be more respectful back and forth, to make sure Nhahn was on board. Nhanh was all smiles and nods. He would concoct a reason for keeping the Hyundai a few extra days.

Looking at Matt and Souchi-Chesty, "You guys, how much can you tell me? More the better if you need my help." They took turns detailing the sex-ring and the raid. They told about the "big" corporation without naming Arctan. They didn't mention Soh.

Leaning forward, elbows on his knees, Rickie hung his head. "Prostitution. Right." Rickie drifted away. Behind clouded eyes he was thinking back on the year in Vietnam when he turned one hundred on his eighteenth birthday. The girls, so desperate, the drunken debauchery, he and friends figuring maybe this is your last day living or worse that it was your last day living in one piece. He'd held the physical and mental pieces of buddies in his arms. He'd known their girlfriend's names Stateside and watched their honesty and naivete evaporate, then get hard boiled. Prostitution. Sounds ugly now. But once-upon-a-time in Neverland, it had kept his soul intact, even if only a day at a time. But then, here, the girls, their story. Life. Humans. Complicated.

He came back. "Legit companies don't do stuff like this for fun, do they?" Rickie was getting to the physics of it. "What's the whole picture? Where's this six-truck, rat-trap business s'posed to go?" Rickie wasn't asking to know, just to think. Out loud, "So you kicked over the bee's nest. That knee fondling mess-up that Matt created was a just a blip. Especially because that news never got beyond Han and Thị Liễu. But now? A break-in, a shooting, a local native tied in with you guys. The Big Guy or Girl's gotta find out, no? Which means things are gonna change in River City. If I'm the Big Guy, I, One, either find all three of you or Two, I change my MO, maybe even give it up here in HTMC. Cops know how to look the other way, but this is just too sloppy."

He paused to weigh what he would do. Not genius, just business. "Naw. Not likely gonna give it up so easy." He looked at them and said in blunt Rickie-honesty, "You guys might be in trouble." In two easy lessons, they had gone from augmented intelligence to attempted homicide.

CHAPTER 57
DEVON DOESN'T LIKE SURPRISES

Matt and Souchi had just made fifteen bold, independent decisions on behalf of Arctan. They wished they could claw back half. Souchi was direct. "Matt. We've got to contact Dr. Samuelson." He side-stepped, "I was hoping you knew when to call in and what to say."

Souchi felt a chill, a thought she had been avoiding. The romantic interlude was cooling. She was the project manager here. There was no turning back or turning over responsibilities. Big-girl time. "Let's check with Dev and Alicia first. Get their reactions."

Matt and Souchi had backed off van and warehouse stakeouts. Settled into their room in the Sen Vàng Spa Hotel, they made an early morning US-call, and learned that Soh had been passing on photos, including some "screen shots" from Matt's eye-view. The most intriguing ones were grainy, low light images featuring an alluring Asian girl in Vegas club lighting. The next most interesting images showed white boards in an office with Soh's translations appended. Alicia wanted to know where to hell the photos came from. She couldn't see anything that related to drug trafficking. In fact, "That spreadsheet seems to tally a bunch of, well, sex-acts. Is Soh goofing on us with the translations? *Was ist los* what's up down there?" With that opening, Souchi laid it out. "This is a long story, so you better sit down."

They had been out of touch with Alicia and Devon for several busy days, so the story was interrupted often. Devon tended to be indelicate. Like upon hearing that Matt broke into a van in the middle of a busy Ho Chi Minh City intersection he blurted, "Matt did whaaat?" He loved Matt and the imagery.

Alicia was contemplative, Devon was still chuckling as Souci continued into the tale of Thị Liễu (minimizing Matt's carnal temptations, skipping her own crazy-angry outburst) and how it changed the whole complexion of the mission. Devon was disgusted and expressed in expletives. He had grown up with close contact to street drugs. He hated dealers. But his opinion of pimps was even lower. He was genetically a softhearted guy with sisters in a bad part of town. His seething stalled the call.

Souchi let Devon rant out. Then she went on to explain Nhahn and his enthusiastic friendship, the stakeout in Binh Thanh, and Soh finding Rickie. Then, a bit cautiously, Souchi started the story about the break-in. She paused momentarily to discuss the photos of the white boards. Alicia did two-plus-two.

"Way I see it, they're running a serious business in there, cumulative income stats, inter-team competition, performance ratings. Doesn't look like conventional pimping to me or Dev." She looked over to pick up Devon's eye-rolling confirmation. "Not meaning to be bigoted, but is that typical small-biz practice in Vietnam? That all looked so…MBA, no?"

Souchi and Matt had been distracted by recent experiences: a bullet-severed ear, sensuous new friend, small arms fire and a war-scarred mechanic. They had missed the simple basics. Somebody outside Vietnam, in Arctan, had set up a professional-running small business selling sex out of vehicles summoned by cell phone.

There was more but Souchi needed to finish the story of the break-in. "We got caught."

Pause. Devon, "At what?"

"Inside the warehouse. Just after shooting the photos. Almost trapped but Soh helped us get out."

Alicia. "Escaped? They didn't catch you? Damn lucky. You guys must have been shaken up."

"Uh, yeah. Nhahn got shot."

Alicia's gasp didn't transmit well over the phone. But Devon's near-canine howl came through. Getting shot was personal for him.

"She-zeus! What ta fuck! Shot, like with a gun? Whaddafug! Where'd he get hit? Is he OK?"

Souchi wasn't sure what "OK" would be. "I think so. The car was screwed up. Back window shot out. Three holes in the trunk." More howls from California. Souchi thought her story sounded worse the more she described it. "He lost the top of his ear. Matt patched him up."

Alicia must have shooed Devon away. He could be heard ranting in the background. She came back on with a low, parental voice. "Guys, you need to slow down and think about this swashbuckling crap. You are not, repeat, you are not Interpol. Get serious. Recalibrate your own safety and everybody around you. Like right now."

Souchi recalled the management lectures she had given at Arctan. Sexual harassment and ethics and personal safety. Suddenly, Souchi saw that she and Matt were renegades, way outside the box. Bold independent decisions? It had all seemed so reasonable, one step at a time. Looking back. WTF.

Alicia. "Where are you two? What's the plan?"

Matt explained that they had decided to lie low. They were in their hotel room. Nhanh had gotten a niece to fix up his ear. The car was being repaired. He described Rickie like a father figure who had stepped in to provide a safe haven. No mention of Smith and Wesson or Chesty.

Alicia was feeling a tiny bit reassured, but Devon was still hurting in the background. Souchi had resurrected in his head images of kids and tough guys senselessly or accidentally shot down. He had hoped those pictures wouldn't ever return. Bad surprise.

Taking control again, Alicia pushed the conference call back on track. "What's with the three photos of what looks like a bio-lab?"

Souchi, "Oh, right. I shot those through a crack in the curtains covering the window of a room Soh labelled "Medical Laboratory."

"Huh." Something didn't work for Alicia. "I was wondering. What I saw was a decent clean room. Lots of stainless. Off to the left, an anteroom to gown up in. Photos were too dark to make out much but enhanced I thought I could see some un-medical-like gear in there.

Like a high-speed centrifuge, Epindorfs.[123] Couple of Class 100 HEPA hoods. Research grade medical prep space. For a sex business? Funny. Any more photos?"

Souchi, "No, so far just what Soh sent."

"*Verdammt.*[124] Whadda you mean, so far! No way you guys are going back in there. Forget it! Souchi, tell me you're working on Plan B. No break-ins."

Souchi didn't wriggle, in spite of stirrings in her heart. "Right, no more swashbuckling. We're rethinking the next steps."

Matt sensed it was time to redirect the convo. "You guys got any news? What's up with your thinking about Soh? And we're going to need to talk about sharing with Dr. Samuelson, no?"

Devon was still shaken up at thoughts of bullets and loved ones, but he had settled down a bit. He passed on some gossip, "Strange Arctan whisperings here. Small talk around the coffee machines. Gossip that Dr. S is fighting to retain control of the Board. Half wants more profit taking, push up the stock. They want to cut out visionary futuristic projects. Like us, I suppose."

Alicia added that it wasn't necessarily all bad. "He's got enough allies who believe in his visions. Last quarter revenues were strong but profits were dragged down. Usual complaints about R and D expenses, etcetera."

"On the bright side, Devon is moving ahead making additional ARz contact and implant sets. We've worked out Hyperspeed speech. And Soh can speech-target one person even in a group. The team in India is working on it."

"Final piece. Introduced Efficiency Mode, so you can shut down input from Soh for a specified time. In case They get on your nerves."

Alicia started the wrap-up, "Guys, if that's it, there is something else."

Matt and Souchi agreed. It's late, they were done.

Devon. "OK. Last thing. Alicia and I have been working a lot together since you all left and we really like each other and...."

Souchi had seen this coming a month ago. She teased the teaser, "I should hope so. You guys have important work to do. Ask Dr. S. to give to you an office together." Matt gave her a funny look.

Devon, "No, not that. Well, you know, we thought, I mean we discovered we might be more than friends."

Souchi feigned shock. "Brother and sister? Wow! That's so cool. But, but...."

"Oh my gawd, no, not that..."

"So what is it? You're hooking up? Screwing around? Pillow talking? Whatever do you wanna say Dev?"

Alicia had to step in. "Guys, we're a thing. We're sleeping together."

Matt was clueless and speechless. Souchi had to speak for them. "That is so totally wonderful! You guys will enjoy each other so much. We are beyond happy you're together."

"Our domicile is officially Arctan HQ, twenty-second floor. Closer to the ARz Lab. Dr. S moved us in there because he suspected this project could draw some fire, just not gunfire."

Souchi, "When you next untangle yourselves, maybe you can figure out how to tell him the cowboy news from Ho Chi Minh City."

"No problem, got you covered. Antoinette will schedule us in ASAP."

CHAPTER 58
THREE RULES

His call was scheduled for eight AM local. Matt and Souchi were tense. It was time to explain themselves to the Boss.

There was no doubt who was on the line. No time wasted. "Dirk here, good morning. Great job down there. Heard you both are OK. Now we know what kind of folks we're dealing with. Thank you. I don't like what I hear about shots fired. Have you taken appropriate steps? What's the plan?"

No lecture? No scolding? Souchi was speechless; she signaled Matt to take the lead. He thought fast. "Right, good morning, or I mean good night to you, sir. Most important, we have in-country friends." An image of One-Ear Nhanh and Six Shooter Rickie flashed through his mind. Chesty was there too. "Soh, I mean ARz, is especially useful. Devon and Alicia have added capability to Soh. We have formed some clear ideas and wanted to see what direction Arctan wants us to go."

"OK Matt. Gotta say, I love that Soh. Immense potential. Can you both hear me, is Souchi there?" Both confirmed they were ten-four.

"OK. Arctan. Three guidelines in play for me.

"One, The Golden Rule. Do unto others what they cannot do for themselves. You got your hands too full for the time being. We'll talk later.

"Two. The Silver Rule. Do unto others as you would have them do unto you. Old school, no problem. Live it.

"Three. The Brass Rule or maybe better, the Brass Knuckles Rule. Do unto others as they have done unto you. We may not like it, we humans have not evolved past the Jungle. Can't avoid it, jungle rules matter. Brass is the operative Rule for you now.

"Questions?"

Matt and Souchi exchanged saucer eyes. They were tempted to have Soh run a voice validation on the caller. "Uh, no. Not yet."

"This guy Rickie Lash. Soh sent me his backgrounder. He's been living with those three rules. You're in good hands with him, he's resourceful. Some instabilities based on his PTSD, mostly under control. Just don't cross him.

"Nhanh. Sized him up too. Harder to fill out his bio. Sorry about the ear but he's taken bullets before. I'm betting Rickie knew right away, but Nhahn fought in black pajamas for the North. As a twelve-year-old, he knew how far along the *Trường Sơn* Ho Chi Minh Trail a child can carry four-hundred AK rounds on one cup of rice a day. He's not gonna fold up. I think he may be hard to hold back now that the other side showed its colors.

"I am not going to be melodramatic, but I have some challenges with the Board here. Basically, under control, especially with the kind of revenues Arctan businesses are throwing off. Nonetheless, this mash-up down there, however small, has the potential to leverage into something harmful. I am counting on you guys to take care of it. Don't take unjustified chances. Don't get hurt. Keep up the good work. Call if you need something. Anything else?"

They didn't have a request lined up, so he said, "Hang tough. Be smart. Adios," and he was gone. Two minutes twenty-five seconds.

"Didn't see that coming." Souchi summarized their shock. "I guess we better get to work."

CHAPTER 59
TOOTH FOR
A TOOTH

Didn't take long for the pot to boil. They were sitting in Papa Nguyen's Café, another day off to retrench. They had messaged Nhanh to come join them, grab some French chocolate croissants and coffee.

Nhanh came walking down the sidewalk, shoulders hunched. His ear had been professionally bandaged. His face was clouded, in pain. He walked up and said, "Nephew beat up last night." Souchi popped out of her chair and hugged the slumping Nhahn.

"What! The kid who lent you the car? What happened, is he OK?" Nhanh slid into a wrought iron seat and ordered a coffee with long distance hand signals.

"Not OK. Hospital. Two guys caught him walking. Told him mind own business. Stay out of Binh Thanh." Nhanh looked one half sad, two halves mad. "My fault. They track license on car."

"Dammit, Nhanh. We're so sorry."

Matt. "Do we need to arrange some special medical care?" A typical Western misconception about the inadequacy of health care outside the US.

"No, better now. Niece is nurse and cousin is doctor. Another cousin dentist. We happy with him where he is. Concussion, two teeth. He is young strong, getting better."

"It's our fault for leading you into this. We should have thought it through and just put the cops on the case."

"Sorry. That is top number one dumb idea. Sorry." He was being as polite as he could. "Family now very angry. We want your help to fix bad guys up real good." He wasn't turning this over to the police.

Matt entertained images of a helicopter leaving the roof of the US Embassy in April 1975. This was his moment to stand up for the good guys. "We've been talking about that, Nhanh. Our boss is giving us a long leash. But we gotta be sure no mad dog stuff. Can you be patient?"

"Families here Asian-patient. Long memory. We learned in church-school, "Eye for eye, tooth for tooth. We collect for teeth. Friends help?" He had a rueful, questioning smile.

Souchi leaned in to Nhanh. "Done deal," knowing that the cast of characters just got big, like Vietnamese extended family big. She was going to be given the management test without the lesson. Bold, independent decisions to come.

Nhanh was pleased, but cautious. He had a much sharper memory of the same helicopter images from '75. "Good news too. Nephew car all A-OK. Rickie call. You go too, we inspect?"

They hailed a cab. On the ride to Rickie's, they told Nhanh about Dr. Samuelson's three rules. He smiled, "Boss very wise man but maybe a little foolish he let you two decide?" He laughed at them.

They got out, greeted by a puppy-wriggling Chesty. His girlfriend was back. Rickie admired Nhahn's ear patch. "Couldn't have done better myself," but his joking evaporated when Nhanh repeated to him, "Car-nephew beat up last night." Rickie stopped dead in his tracks, reflected, then asked, "The Binh Thanh break-in?"

Nhahn. "Yup."

"How old's your nephew? How many guys?" Nhanh's numbers, seventeen and two, made Rickie grow dark. He spit-cursed in English and spoke softly in Vietnamese, looking Nhahn straight in the eyes and said five words in Vietnamese. Matt got the feeling that foretold a bad day for two bad dudes. Rickie could be an impractical guy when it came to someone violating his etiquette.

Rickie motioned everyone into the yard and closed the gates, again looking for tails and nosy neighbors. Then he motioned Chesty to stay at the door. Chesty sensed, hoped, dog-preyed for raw meat to intrude.

Rickie looked at Matt and Souchi. "Real hard to run a license plate in the 'Nam. No, impossible. These guys had some help." He stared hard at Souchi, "Maybe a big US company could swing that kind of intel, no?"

She nodded. "There's got to be an operative inside who is using data and dollars to build this biz. Yes."

"I been thinking." Rickie was still wearing dark-face. "The credit card. You use it anywhere else before losing it?" Matt had used it for most everything. "Sure."

Rickie. "Even at your hotel?" Matt blanched. The cancellation had been through Arctan data systems.

"I'm thinking you guys need to start using cash and get out of that hotel, pronto." Matt and Souchi should have already thought of this.

Abruptly Rickie brightened the mood. "Nhanh-dude, let's check out your nephew's ride." They followed him into the garage where two techs were applying the finishing swipes to a Carnauba wax job. The Hyundai was perfect, in fact, upgraded to four fresh Michelins, chrome rims and, Rickie throwing open the hood, chrome headers. "All courtesy Big Corp USA." Looking at Souchi, "Right? And thank you." It didn't make up for two teeth, but the nephew would have a moment of joy.

Nhanh couldn't help but be cheerful. Replete with hand signs, "Nice car. Maybe nephew get new girlfriend, big boobs." He laughed and laughed at his own joke. Resiliency.

CHAPTER 60
SURPRISE VISITOR

Matt, dull on a fitful sleep, was slow packing his bag. The room phone, a pessimistic, grim pink-Princess[125], rang and he picked it up. "*Bang hue.* OK. OK. *Sangh-ha.* I'll come down." Souchi questioned him with eyebrows from bed.

"Weird. Visitor downstairs. An American. Be right back." The New Matt thought twice and took the stairs. At the last landing, he stopped and peered around the stairwell corner into the lobby. An Anglo was staring back. Dr. James Brogan. They locked eyes. Brogan smiled. He'd been trolling the elevator floor-o-meter. He called up the stairs.

"Hey, Matt. Heard you were in town. I was passing through and figured we should chat. Just you and me. You got a minute?" Matt hadn't played much poker. He let his stress show.

"Can I buy you a drink?" Even in HCMC, 8AM was both too late and too early for a 333 beer. Brogan was indulging himself with cheap humor.

Brain spinning, Matt started down the stairs. The next minutes were going to be educational. He was missing Souchi. And Soh. On the second to last stair, Matt cast an eye toward a heavy set local near the front door, arms-crossed, a caricature from an outdated Bond 007 movie, all jowly and stupid-stern.

Brogan noticed, turned enough to nod at Odd-Job. "No problem, my driver. I wouldn't dare drive a car in this town." Realizing that he'd insulted an important pawn, Brogan retraced. "Matt, I'm hoping we can have an open heart-to-heart," and with a wave sent Jowls off the set. "C'mon. Let's sit down for a minute." He led, coaxing. "C'mon." Matt followed, avoiding Brogan's path like a truculent fifth grade bad-boy. They settled into a dark corner table. One bar patron, thatchy black hair splayed over cradled arms, took no heed. He was keeping a failed watch over the stinking ashtray he and his friends had filled last night with filter-less Lucky Strike butts. Matt and James Brogan sat down for a tête-à-tête.

Leaning back but poised, Brogan let Matt dangle. Then he reached into his Uomo sport coat pocket (Dr. B. dressing to impress, even when it made him a mark) and tossed some plastic onto the table in Matt's direction. Sixteen Citibank digits. It was the card Matt had given to Han Van Phan back in the ho-van.

"Thought you might need this." Tennessee manners, computer education, youth; Matt was underprepared. But ring experience served him well. He been setup with jabs before this. He anticipated an attempt at a knockout punch. Brogan obliged.

"Matt," words from a nice, totally fake friend, "you've gotten way out of line." The arrogance angered Matt. He didn't need to conjure a strategy. Matt had idolized Muhammed Ali's flair, the flash, the brash poetry.

'Float like a butterfly, sting like a bee.'[126]

Matt decided to rope-a-dope Brogan so he poured on the honey.[127] In his best Southern drawl, he demurred,

"Well, suh, I shurely didn't 'spect to be runnin' into this much funny business way down here. I was sent simple-like to poke into what 'peared to be some nefarious spending of Arctan money. Just plain didn't seem right, you know what I mean? Seemed like someone was, well, stealin' from her Boss."

Brogan was nonplussed, the sissy-slight a surprise counter.

"And then when mah dear friends and I got shot at, well that just wasn't honorable, no suh, not honorable atall."

Brogan backed off. "Right. I get it. Wasn't supposed to happen. I'm sorry for all that," not a written confession but now the cards were on the table. Time to ante up.

"So now, suh, I'm packing to go home and have a long, tall, cool talk with the Boss."

Brogan hadn't got the memo about Matt's leaving town. He wasn't prepared for it and had to pause. "OK. Fair enough, Matt. But all the more reason for us to chat."

"Dr. Brogan, suh, I ahm all ears, I really ahm. I would be mighty obliged if you could fill me in." Matt's icy stare didn't synch with his hillbilly patois.

"Matt, I would like you to hold off on flying back for a bit. So, I can explain some stuff. I apologize for the mishaps..."

"Mishaps?" Matt's stare hardened.

"OK, for you and your people getting shot at. I've done my best to settle that here. That was wrong, nearly dead wrong. Won't, can't happen again. Sorry."

"Give me a chance. Will you hear me out?" Matt gave

a classic dismissive show-me-the-meat shrug. Brogan felt encouraged.

Knocked back but warming up, Brogan launched into his pitch. "Matt, there's a lot wrong in the world. Wars. Oppression. Uncured diseases, climate out of control. People just can't seem to work things out." Matt was taken off guard by the change. Advantage Brogan.

"We both would like to make the world a better place. Right? In spite of our personal speed bumps here, I think you and I could get onto the same page about fixing some major problems. And I suppose you and I could agree that the best vehicle for that is good old-fashioned capitalism. Big problems, big solutions, big money. Right? Think malaria, Bill Gates."

Matt was curious; how did this sudden idealism tie in with vanpool prostitution?

"You're an analytical guy, Matt. You like data, stats, evidence. Figuring out what makes things tick. You're tops in that game." Pitchman's goals: establish common ground, flatter the pigeon[128]. Brogan was no Bezos or Jobs or Samuelson, but he had sales skills. "So how do you explain all the strife?"

Matt had been drawn in. He thought back to a distant sociology class: "Sure. Population pressure, inequality, corruption. Climate and natural calamities create stresses, conflicts, autocratic leaders, wars."

Brogan. "That's right. All kinds of bad behaviors. Worldwide. Across religions and cultures. Multi-nationally, down the ranks through the family unit down to the anonymous street corner. People abusing people. Back through all time, Matt. Not even religion seems to stem the flow of bad." He gave Matt a moment to think.

"So Matt, as an analytical guy. Why? But think big, Matt."

Matt shrugged, waiting to see where Brogan was headed.

"Let me run this by you. The most powerful drug in the world. Makes humans do stupid stuff. Sex. Men chase it, too often wrongly. But look at history. Workplace harassment, porno absorption, aggravated sexual assault, rape. Harvey Weinstein and Bill Clinton, Matt. Were they stone dumb or...?"

Matt recalled the iconic bums of the not-so-distant past. "Last-century guys just using their power to exploit subordinates."

"Drunk on power. But the power gave them the means to do stuff they were driven to. Guys get crazy and stupid about sex. Like Portnoy said,

When the pecker stands up, the brains get buried in the sand.[129]

Matt I propose that's the problem. Getting some is a competitive game. You, Matt, you're on the top of the food chain. Buff. Tall. Tawny. You need it, you can have it. But the rest of us have got to hustle. Money. Charm. Presents. Sweet words. Power. Money. Promises. Sometimes love and affection."

Brogan paused, Carlotta briefly skimmed through his thoughts.

"Solutions Matt? Abstinence? Nope. Catholic Church took some lumps with that approach. Abusing kids. Not a solution, Matt.

"Polygamy? Weird cults, communes etcetera have tried it. Even organized religions like Mormans, Muslims. Results? Adopted by one tenth of a thousandth of one percent of humanity.

"So monogamous marriage. How's that working out? Not to say marriage doesn't work. But there's apparently some discontent among the troops, Matt. In fact, looks like a lot Matt. Where they preach monogamy the hardest, they get the worst results. Like the evangelical South. Divorce. Infidelity. Top rankings, there Matt."

Matt thought about his Tennessee home. Even as a kid he knew something was amiss, the whispered small-town secrets about people sneaking around and sleeping with the neighbor's wife, like when the minister got caught at it once, then twice.

"Stats say marriage fidelity is a fifty-fifty proposition. One way or another, some guys, girls, seem to come up short from time to time. Supply runs short of demand. Price goes up. Costs go up. People do stupid stuff. Matt, when is a cop most likely to get injured, killed? Not drug busts, but domestic violence, Matt."[130]

Brogan had been thinking on this for a while. Matt, not so much. He was off balance.

"Matt I suggest its testosterone poisoning. A simple molecule, less than a thousand billionths of a gram per deciliter makes you and me and Xiao and Fernando and Ivan need to get laid, regularly. Eleven or twelve years into life, we form some ideas of the sex recipe we like and it gets more important than coffee, beer, chocolate.

"Even the academics have written about it. Sex, the

love-act, Matt. It's basically... impractical. Way back Matt. Way back in the jungle, behind every tree somebody looking to eat your breakfast, or even you. A bad idea to take your eye off the ball Matt. Get distracted, makin' love, you get bushwhacked by a tiger or a young dude. The urge to procreate had to be pretty intense. Testosterone makes us focus on getting some and on paying attention when we aren't."

Matt thought Brogan was being simple. "But that's what civilized means, controlling primal urges."

"OK Matt, here we're past eight billion people, over half, fifty-two to three percent, males. Politics, culture whatever, selects for males.[131] The last pandemic, knocking out females. So now we have around a quarter billion surplus males without female companionship, on top of the usual dissatisfactions, a numeric imbalance. Market economics kick in, females become more particular.[132] Increase in frustrated testosterone floating about. What happens? Not my bias, just look at the stats: social unrest, aggression, violent sex crime.[133] Even the CIA, people with skin in the game, with money to do the research, have registered concerns.[134] International insecurity."

Brogan paused. Matt needed to think. This wasn't the stuff computer science was made of.

"The World has problems, Matt, and man-sex might be the root of it. Nobody's fault, but testosterone makes us do crazy stuff. So, what has to happen, Matt? Like since forever. Sex becomes a business commodity, Matt. World's oldest profession."

"Dr. Brogan. C'mon man. What about love? Like affection between people. Establishing a family."

"I get it. But women like sex too, Matt. In a more complicated balance. Love, sex. Family, sex. Stability, sex. Got it. If it weren't for women, I'm wondering if it all collapses.

"Matt, I grew up on the beach in SoCal. Early mornings in April out surfing, the terns come in. Males strutin' around on the beach, offering up sardines to hustle a mate. The females act aloof for a while. Lookin' around, who's got game. But in the end, they do their behavior and boom. Baby-making time."

Brogan leaned in, buddies. "Why else would women put up with the crap men deal out? Hell, women got pregnant in Auschwitz, Matt. In the KZ, Matt, in the concentration camps. I'm thinking they were looking for affection, warmth, caring and then sex. That brief thrill through the fence meant a lot to them, it's just that when we boys don't get some, we get, what do they call it? Testy? Testosterone builds up, measurably. And the aggressions start. Not love, aggression.

"Matt, can you imagine that some of our leader-idiots had issues regulating their T?"

Matt hadn't read about testosterone in the history books and Soh was not around to do the search but his remembrance of a Hitlerian rant or a McCarthy diatribe fit the image. Brogan's arguments were irritating.

"And how about sport Matt? Seen a rugby match lately? Grappling, blood. But not so many bloody women rugby matches, huh? How about football fans in the stands? You're Tennessee, right? 'Go Vols!' Faces painted. Chanting. Greatest fun is watching a bloody 'hit.' Some guy getting crunched.

"Matt, why are prison populations 93% male?"[135]

The question struck Matt as rhetorical. Point made. "OK, I grant you, guys make better criminals, more often. But men and women and sex. What about loyalty? And if not that, what about growing old together, love at first sight?"

"No doubt Matt. For almost everyone almost all the time. But 'almost's' an important word. Every once in a while almost everyone gets an 'itch' for something, someone...different. Almost everyone, almost every time suppresses the impulse. Morality. Fear. Ethics. Love. Respect. But then, after a glass or two of burgundy...? Or, given a warm night breeze or even a subconsciously contrived moment of privacy, bam. Portnoyed.

"Don't get me wrong Matt. I'm happily married. And you, I understand you're in a working relationship." Matt bristled at the poke into his private life. Did this dick know much about him and Souchi?

"We're all set, right? But thennnn..." Again, he was asking, knowing an answer. "Testosterone Matt. Makes us sharp, pay attention. Leads us astray too. And angry. Problems start when there's no release in sight. Or am I all wrong here, Matt?"

Matt was not versed in the biochem. He was dependent on logic and Brogan was working him left-right with logic. He wished he had better counter punches.

"Can I tell you some history, Matt? It's pertinent." Matt nodded, uneasy.

"End of World War Two, Pacific Theater. Japan is a total mess. Never mind the A-Bomb. Thousands of Boeing's B-29s had already burned down most of Japan's infrastructure by June '45. No Navy. Army shattered, economy destroyed. USA preparing the terms of surrender. War's over.

"The victors, us, Matt, we're coming to occupy the place. For a decade they made us out to be bestial enemies, animals. That's how they got 15-year olds to do stupid stuff, like fly planes in suicide missions. Banzai. So, the government decided, knowing how their victorious soldiers had behaved in Manchuria 1937, to get ready for all those T'ed up American soldiers. Japan, the police, officially recruited women to be sex professionals. For the Motherland. To protect the blood lines. Contain disease. Confine the rapacious animals to designated dispensaries of joy.

"Desperate times. Thousands volunteered, Matt. Thousands. Patriotic duty. And food. Clothing, housing."[136] Matt thought he almost spotted some feeling from Brogan.

Matt felt cornered. Trust Brogan's info? What if it's true?

"Of course, we want to feel superior. Simply say 'Japan, 1945. That's an Asian thing.' Not that simple. The French colonizing armies organized prostitute camps 'Bordels Mobiles de Campagne' wherever they went around the world.[137]

"And not just a wartime quirk. How about the Forty-Niners, the Gold rush in California? Crazy-ass male prospectors, my relatives. Women provided respite, professionally, wherever the crazed set down to rest."[138]

"Sorry, man, those are all a long time ago. Times have changed."

"Maybe. Maybe." A pause. "Should I... address that?" Brogan didn't wait.

"Pick a town, today. Las Vegas? Des Moines. Paris, Bonn, Daegu. Prostitution there?" Matt guessed yes.

"Heard of sex tourism, Bangkok? Or here, HCMC Matt? Take a walk alone around eleven PM down Đồng Khởi Avenue, the most fashionable street in town. You, Anglo-guy, will get an offer every ten meters. Go to any four-star hotel in Phnom Penh and there's a sign in the lobby: 'No Sex-Trade Allowed.' In four languages.

"Better yet, go online Matt. Try my hometown, Huntington Beach. Try your hometown, Murfreesboro. I won't glorify the sites. You go schmutz up your own cookies.

"Professional sex, for men, Matt. When not legal, it's ignored, uncontainable. Note Matt: by law-men."

Brogan squared himself up. He was teeing up his pitch.

"We need a solution to testosterone poisoning. Capitalism Matt. Provide a quality product. Clean. Safe. Attractive. Sensual. Charge accordingly. Pay employees top dollar. Deliver convenient, online service, each encounter customized by the client's history, requests. Keep payments totally encrypted, no names, at least until it becomes accepted, hip, even cool.

"Best part. Put the last century sleezy pimps and mobsters out of business. They won't go easy, but we can make arrangements to handle the transition." Matt wonders. Maybe that explains the shooting on Thanh Ho Way.

"Final element, Matt. Base the business in a mobile, ride-share model. Eliminate brothel properties with their zoning laws, site-blight branding and, real important, their inflexible capital liquidity.

"Do everything in a modern business-like fashion. Branding. Analytics. We can dominate the sex trade, first in with a quality product."

Matt tried to hide his disdain. "You been thinking about this awhile?"

"Yes, I have. It all works out. For everybody."

"Oh, come on. You want me to believe the women keep some dignity though all this? There are some professionals with kids, right? These moms send their kids to school with 'hooker' written on the Parent's Employment form. No way!"

Brogan had done his homework. "Sex-industry women in the past weren't all scorned. Even in the US. Check out the gold rush.[139] If anything, a way to grab some power. Money, Matt. Women can earn some money. Squeeze the desperate Johns. To benefit their family."

Matt thought back to the van and Thị Liễu supporting her family in rural Tinh Vinh Long.

"Abundance of young smart women, not necessarily desperate, in many countries, looking to make a better life. Make hay while the sun shines, Matt."

"Sorry, I just can't see women thinking sex can be a casual, business transaction."

"Did you notice, back with the second mutation of the

virus, how the Big Die-off affected attitudes? The so-called "sexual revolution" of the sixties was prudish compared to the revolution that began when word got out that recurring deadly infections were going to end life on earth.[140]

"Women had the greatest reasons to change. Like here in Vietnam. Back before your time, Matt. Ho Chi Minh convinced a whole country to rise up and fight off their colonizers. The French lost. Then we stepped in. Sold by zealots like Henry Cabot Lodge and Bobbie McNamara[141] to save the little brown people from god-less communism. Testosterone-junkie leaders figured all we had to do was kill off a couple million.

"We lost. When it was over, Vietnamese women had faced combat and been buried with their brothers. Cadres of independent women evolved. Sexual capital-ism got an innovative start right here in Ho Chi Minh City[142] inspired by the economic rise of an Asian Tiger digging out from the B52s and Agent Orange and cluster bombs.

"Beauty of internationalism. Moving ahead into spaces that are behind. There's opportunity in Asia, my friend. So here we are, you and me and Arctan."

Doctor Brogan leaned back. "Matt, I've laid cards on the table. I've been candid. If you're done with my ideas, OK. Let's leave it at that. Off you go, but I'd like to spell it all out in detail."

Pulling out a folded page, "Here's a short Non-dis-closure Agreement, an addendum from Arctan Inter-national. As a member of the Board, I can make this confidential arrangement with you. Just you and me.

"I'd like you to support this business, help cure the world's testosterone poisoning pandemic. Make some money."

Placing a fat Montblanc fountain pen on top of the page, Dr. James Brogan looked steadily at Matt. "Are you interested?"

CHAPTER 61
HOME FRONT

Matt watched Brogan leave, his parting comment, "It's just business, Matt." He didn't look back as Jowls fell in behind him at the door. Matt thought for a long moment then trudged upstairs.

Souchi was waiting. "You had me worried, so I peeked around the corner. Brogan?"

Souchi listened intently as Matt spent ten minutes trying to describe his meeting with Brogan.

She sat on the edge of the bed, studying the carpet. She looked up at Matt. "Great idea. Where do I sign up."

Matt looked perplexed.

"Sure, I could turn five, maybe six tricks a night." She looked away, dreamily.

"Damn. Sounds great. On-the-job training. Air-conditioned van, no boss looking over my bra-strap. Regular health check-ups. For you, win-win. Around the water cooler with the girls, maybe I pick up a few 'special' skills. You know, for the nights I get off.

"Financially? If I get good, we could start a family. Eventually you wouldn't have to work at all. You'd stay at home, take care of the kids. Or we could maybe coordinate careers. I can drop them off some days, then work the morning trade outside the kid's school, you know for the stay-at-home dads."

Chill wind. Souchi was hopping mad.

"What ta hell, Matt. You sound like you're weighing plus and minuses here. Are you, like, thinking about this?" He looked noncommittal. "C'mon man, this is slavery, sexploitation." Souchi didn't need to ponder. "Gotta put a stop to Brogan, Matt."

"Well, I can find out more details."

Souchi looked askance. "How?"

"Well, I signed a Confidentiality Agreement and he offered to explain the whole show in Binh Thanh. Tomorrow afternoon."

"Whaaat! You put your signature on a Confidentiality Agreement saying you want to learn more about a sex-slavery business! You... Have... Gotta be kidding."

"Souchi. We need to see what's going on in there. Without getting shot at."

CHAPTER 62
FACTORY TOUR

Early afternoon. Matt was standing, as instructed, alone on the curb on suicidal Tôn Đức Thắng Avenue. He saw it coming. Dumb, the kind of car mini-mob crime would choose. Big, black. Tinted windows and a don't-fuck-with-me attitude. It sidled up, stopping traffic. The passenger window rolled down. Jowls gestured Matt to the back seat. It was a quiet ride to Binh Thanh.

At Thiên Thần, a new guy, squat, muscled, cheerless, stood outside the garage. He opened Matt's door. With grunts and hands, he signaled a frisk. Cursory, quick, the New Guy obviously didn't respect that Matt wouldn't be packing a weapon. Surveying the alleyway, he entered the door code. It wasn't the original 9155. Plus, the door had a new bolt lock. Matt walked into the six-van home of road sex.

New Guy led Matt to the back conference room. One guy, two women scurried out as Matt approached. Following a point, Matt headed in. Dr. Brogan jumped up, greeting.

"Hey, Matt! Nice to see you." He waved New Guy off. "Glad you chose to come out to Thiên Thần. Everybody treat you OK?"

"Oh yeah. Nice long conversation about today's ball game."

Brogan laughed. "Like to hear that. I don't pay Huy or Thuc for their social skills."

"Matt, I don't suppose I have to take you on a general tour, do I?"

Matt had noticed surveillance cameras had been added since the first visit. "Why not? Looks like an interesting operation here." Let Brogan guess about their spying sortie last week. But it also meant they weren't buddies.

Brogan dropped the nice-charade. "Matt, can you pop out the lenses for me? You know security and all."

"Lenses? Oh, ARz. Right. Didn't bother to wear them today, too buggy, remember?"

Not happy, "Huh. OK, you don't mind if I check, right?" He walked up real close and inspected Matt's eyes. In-your-face, lingering. Bad breath.

"Sorry if I look disappointed. I so hoped to learn about ARz today. I hear they're getting better."

"Yup. I can get You Tube and Netflix, nice."

"Matt, I understand your sense of loyalty toward Dirk. I mean, Arctan, his fortune, his accomplishments. Amazing. And a guy his age with all those young women working as, what is it, Personal Assistants? Enviable." Matt bristled.

Brogan feigned surprise. "But you surely heard all the rumors. Heck, more power to him, right?"

Matt wanted but couldn't poker-face Brogan. "Rumors. A waste of time." Matt hadn't heard any rumors but the Brogan comment had tweaked him.

"You got it, Matt, and one thing we don't waste at Arctan is time, right? So let's get down to it. I won't pull any punches Matt. I'd like you to support my efforts here."

"I'm ready to listen." Matt half-lied. Brogan suspected as much.

"Matt, I've proposed a capitalist enterprise with a lofty purpose. Never mind the ancient taboos. It's a new world. There are cities with populations of young, virile, unsatisfied men bigger than many American states. Asia, Africa, India, Middle East.[143] And there's unsatisfied demand beyond that, even in the US. Left to their frustrations, you are going to see unrest, social turbulence, even wars. We aim to fix that.

"This business, the pilot test here, is going to cure the spread of testosterone poisoning. Worldwide. I'd like to convince you tonight to help."

Brogan proceeded to his strategic plan. Prioritization of markets, sunk capital, recruitment. Local law enforcement "re-education" costs and techniques. When he got to the final projections, he had outlined a business with tens of thousands of prosperous "work associates" spread all over the world generating shared revenues in the billions. A Disney-sized sex-entertainment empire.

"One last detail Matt. The 'product.'"

Brogan became energized. "The vans will all be super-clean, each with a sensuous theme. Market studies show there are basically five fantasy stimulators appropriate for our 'playrooms.' Nothing too kinky, Matt. No drugs, or at least nothing that would attract local law enforcement. Anonymity, the vans will look like any other commercial vehicle in town, fake signage. Seamless software so clients can make requests, save preferences, pay on the spot. And of course, we will track and analyze their data inside of unbreakable security. Arctan style. "

"Most important factor, Matt. The women will be screened, intelligent, willing. Sort of the Japanese geisha concept, educated in general and in the trade particularly. We have also developed a means to enhance their most important attribute, enjoyment."

"I don't get it. The men are enjoying this, or they wouldn't come back, no?"

"Matt, I mean we give each woman an enjoyment boost, so that they surely like the experience too."

Matt had to process this. Brogan obliged Matt's alone time.

"You mean...?"

"Right. We have developed a way to create sex partners who are, the most important thing, eager, Matt. No acting needed."

Matt is stunned. "Seriously?"

"CRISPR Matt. We give the women gene surgery that ensures they adore the sex act. Never perfunctory. We completed the R&D here in Vietnam. There's the lab, Matt. Next-door. Simple half-hour procedure."

"C'mon, man! I gotta problem with that. In fact, I'm thinking this is a nut house. I maybe could have understood the social value of providing for the unloved. But making a woman into a...a nymphomaniac sex robot for sake of your business? That's low."

"I'm sorry you feel that way. Maybe you need a little time. To think."

"No need. I'm done. Time to go."

"Well, yes, but it isn't that simple Matt. I have some business to take care of back in the US. Emergency meeting with Dr. Samuelson. I had hoped you would come with me, to back me up, an eye-witness endorsement and so on. However, I still want to give you a chance to think it over. We've arranged for you to be a guest here, take time to reconsider."

"What a second..." Matt starts to move toward Brogan. Huy and Thuc anticipate his move. Before he can react, they put Matt in arm-locks.

"I'll be leaving you with my associates Matt. I've sent a message on your behalf to Souchi. She thinks that you're on board and working with me." Brogan starts toward the door. "Oh, and Matt, you have a fan here. Our Thị Liễu fell in love with your beefcake photos in the Arctan ad campaign. And she thought you had come looking for some loving that night in the van. Broke her heart. The boys will watch so you don't take advantage of her feelings while you sit tight here. Couple days, OK?" Brogan left. Matt didn't.

Time moves slowly in confinement. Matt was put into a windowless spare dorm room, on a short hallway off the garage. A single security camera watched him from the back corner. He heard comings and goings outside his door. Among the voices, he imagined hearing Thị Liễu. Imagined maybe using his influence to get her to let him loose. He paced around, wondering what

Souchi might be thinking, arranging. At some point, he dozed off.

Matt sat bolt upright. Noises in the garage. A van door had slammed, an engine started. The vans were saddling up. He heard the garage door going up. Six vans leave, Door rolls back down. Voices, Thuc and Huy still inside.

Pacing. Sitting. Pacing. Maybe an hour. Then, the smell of smoke. Thuc and Huy smelled it too. Their footsteps grew faint heading unhurried toward the front. Must be outside.

Then, two thumps. One from the front of the building, the second louder, dull, heavy, from the opposite direction, down the hallway past his door.

He hears yelling, footsteps outside his door. Then the door handle and a book-size portion of his door frame comes flying into the room, the head of a sledgehammer taking its place. The door swings open. Nhanh smiles at him. "Gotta go Matt. My family. Kick some ass." He runs toward the garage. Matt pops out to see the hallway full of dust, starkly lit by headlights coming through a hole in the back wall. Matt follows Nhanh toward the garage. Up front and center, Souchi is squared off with Thuc, two Asian roosters, except one's a chick. Thuc throws an old-school Bronx haymaker at her. She sidesteps and delivers an elegant roundhouse Korean kick to Thuc's head. Lots of Seoul. He goes down. She cripples him with an inelegant foot stomp, crushing the lateral collateral ligament of his left knee. He's unhappy. She's two-zero in international competition.

Huy is also down, moaning, left front of the garage,

casualty of the blown-in door. Nhanh and three locals, family, are standing over him, debating. Left of Matt, Rickie Lee is bustling around the office in a geriatric lope. He's scooped up two laptops. Huy begins to sit up and is rewarded with a kick to the face. Seems the Nhanh family has an issue with Huy.

Matt stands dazed, watching kaleidoscopic whirlpools happen all around him. The sounds echo inside his head. Crushed ligaments, pain, thumping head kicks. What had become of his tidy coding world?

Rickie calls to Nhanh. He runs over to take the laptops and a sheaf of papers. Rickie goes to the Laboratory door, tries the handle, locked. Shouts out something in Vietnamese and one of the cousins runs into the hallway and fetches back the sledgehammer. He bangs at the lock but it's a real one. Rickie shouts something. Cousin Sledgehammer scurries away toward the front. He and the guards duck around the corner. Rickie pulls a cigarette-pack size clump out of his backpack. Nhanh pulls Matt into the office. Rickie shouts, "Fire in the hole," and limps in, cursing ungraciously. Matt imitates his office mates, covers his ears just as there's a thump and a flash. Lab open.

Matt follows Rickie and Nhahn through the smoke into the lab. They've broken into a prep room. A second, tidier room with an assortment of stainless-steel equipment and surgical set-ups lies visible through a windowed door in a sterile-looking white wall. "Woof. Lota work here. Nhanh, you're gonna have to clean up as much as possible ASAP. Let's grab that laptop now." Rickie peers through the glass window in the wall. "Matt, Nhanh, what's all this mean?" He's moved to a poster on the wall next to the window. English and Vietnamese with safety symbols.

Matt recognizes some tech-words. It looks like warnings about chemicals. "I don't see a bio-hazards warning."

Nhanh calls out into the garage. A younger guy pops in. Nhanh introduces him. "My cousin, college guy, new teeth, no new girlfriend, no big boobs yet." Laughs at the cousin's blush, humor in the midst of chaos. He points the kid to decipher.

In perfect English, "Yea, usual safety notice. No bad stuff, no contagion. Supposed to be sterile gowned going in. Chemicals can cause cancer, so don't lick anything in there. I'd say, wear gloves and a mask." Totally likeable kid, with a crooked smile.

Rickie signals Matt to follow him out to the garage. Looking to Souchi standing watch, then down at Thuc, clutching his knee. "No weapons, right?" She nods. "Nice work, he's happier down there."

Souchi takes charge. "OK. Rickie, you guys got this here. Matt, we need to grab our stuff from the hotel and get to the airport. Rickie, can you and Nhanh meet us there in two hours."

"Two and a half. We gotta help clear out before the vans get back. Then we'll leave Nhanh's family here to do the follow-up." Matt suspected the cleanup might involve a "tooth-for-a-tooth."

"At the airport, go to the private executive section. You'll ask for a Transpac Gulfstream. Mention 'Jonestown' to get in. Matt, let's go." She led the way out the back hallway to crawl through the blown hole. A petite Nhanh niece was perched up behind the wheel of a truck there.

Souchi hugs Matt and stands back to take stock. "You OK? We weren't too worried. Nhanh's nephew hacked the security cameras. But there were a couple moments where that break-in could have gone bad. I'm so happy you're safe." She hugged him again.

"But we gotta go. Dr. Samuelson has arranged a private jet. There's a box coming for Rickie and Nhanh. You and me, we're headed home." They jumped in and Nhanh's niece pulled the truck back from the wall it had rammed. Three-up in the front, they headed south to vacate the Sen Vàng Spa Hotel room.

"There's a lot to tell you." She jumped into the part about having to limit how many Nhanh-relatives could take part. The family had chosen three young bucks for energy and two old goats for know-how. They included one guy for his handiness with explosives. There was trouble leaving relatives behind. Beating up a nephew was an insult and had roused passions.

Matt was unsure how to proceed with his news. "About the lab next to the garage, Souchi. It's been in use. Brogan was turning the girls into, well, bionic sex robots." Souchi, speechless, didn't get it. Too crazy, too freaky.

"I'm not sure if robot is the correct word. He's developed a way to use CRISPR so the girls really like doing it. Said it's a twenty-minute surgery. Made the work fun. He said they were more 'eager'."

Souchi couldn't answer for a moment. She almost said something, then choked it back. She looked into Matt with dental drills. Then, a quiet, toxic indictment. "If this is how our kind uses technology Matt, then we are fucking disgusting."

Matt didn't mention that Brogan insinuated Samuelson exploited his Assistants.

CHAPTER 63
GETTING OUT
OF DODGE

Back downtown, the Sen Vàng Spa Hotel hadn't changed. Cigarette and diddly vendors on the sidewalk, closing up for the night. Chartreuse, Amaranth and Crème de Menthe behind the bar. Chipped faux-marble floor, worn couches, two old men with stained fingers. Matt's world had flipped on its head but HCMC was the same gritty.

He ran upstairs while Souchi checked out. Yes, they would pay the full day rate.

First task, mount up ARz. Initialize Soh. Immediately, Matt started getting brain injections.

>Brogan boarded private flight to SF refueling Honolulu. Arriving SFO ten point five hours<

>Our flight refueled Tan Son Nhut airport one hour ago<

>We have not detected recent comm out of Thiên Thần<

>Monitoring Brogan<

>We have collected prior cell comm from both Huy and Thuc<

>We can simulate voices at 96% accuracy, plus minus

1%. Our Simu-voice not detectable<

>We request permission to reply Simu-voice to Brogan confirming Binh Thanh all fine<

"Soh, that's a great idea. But keep it short."

>Yes master< Sheesh, sassy again.

>We have cued sixteen answers to five probable Brogan queries<

>Shall I review them all for you?<

"No thank you." Matt was almost done packing.

>Those are not yours< Soh chided him for admiring Souchi's finest. Matt blushed.

>We request max-REM with Celaquinab for software update as soon as possible<

>When completed, will send full status report<

"OK. Please confirm with Souchi."

>We have told sweetie<

"OK. OK Soh, please go on Efficiency Mode for thirty minutes."

>Entering Efficiency Mode<

"Thank you. Nighty-night."

>Good night John-Boy<

Matt felt an involuntary pang tucking Soh in. No time for emotions. He did a quick sweep and headed to the lobby. Souchi had flagged a cab to the curb. ETA Tan Son Nhut, twenty-five minutes.

Matt relayed to Souchi his messages from Soh. Except about the undergarments. "Genius, Matt. Having Soh monitor Brogan and answer with Simu-voice." Matt admitted it had been Soh's idea.

As they arrived at the guarded gate, right on time, Soh reactivated.

>Did you return the rental motorcycle?<

"Damn! The Yamaha!" Souchi had it covered. Nhanh would turn it in.

>We cannot be responsible when de-activated<

"Got it. No punishment this time."

>fine. you don't deserve any<

At the private-flights gate, a uniformed armed guard stops them. He takes the driver's license and passports from Souchi and Matt, inspects them and returns.

Souchi leans across the driver, "Transpac Gulfstream. Jonestown." The guard signals to the small, reinforced cabin and the gate slides open. He says something about where to find the Gulfstream. They drive into a world of cinderblock ravines and arc lamps. Two hours and a half since the raid, Souchi and Matt are thirty meters from home.

As they approach the Gulfstream, Matt spots Rickie and Nhanh unloading a heavy wooden crate. "What's that?"

Rickie looks at Nhanh then Matt. "Don't ask." New etiquette for Matt.

Rickie, Nhanh, Souchi and Matt shuffle awkwardly at the four-step ramp into the jet. Rickie dog-deflects his feelings. "Chesty'll miss you Souchi. We hope you guys do OK back there. Sorry you gotta miss the blast we're gonna have here."

Nhanh throws a stiff hug on Matt, not his culture but he'd seen it in movies. "When gets boring here, I am calling you guys come back. If car gets nephew new girlfriend big boobs, I'm sending pictures." Nhanh is putting on a happy face.

A crewmember in toned-down uniform approaches, trained in humility. "OK folks, we're clear for a runway, time to go."

"See ya on the other side." Rickie has said goodbye to friends before on this tarmac, not all of them living. "Everybody stay safe, heads down, no heroes." Practiced at separations, he turns and walks away, Nhanh in reluctant pursuit. Matt and Souchi watch their backs, then climb the stairs.

The Gulfsteam is uber-luxury reserved for people who have it already. Onboard, exhaustion begins to set in. "Matt, I've got the upgraded ARz software from Devon and Alicia. Let's install it before crashing."

Updates installed, Souchi gives Matt one dose of Celaquinab. Next stop, in twelve hours, refueling in Onizuka Kona International. Matt and Soh dream differently 'til then.

Matt stirs when the Gulfstream bounces left-right on blustery Kona. The renewed Soh detects his waking.

>aloha. Welcome to the USA<

>yes, We are feeling refreshed, *mahalo*. Thank you very much<

>detect secure connection. Shall We fetch tidings?<

Matt mumbles.

>got it. downloading<

Matt mumbles.

Souchi is up with coffee. "Hey champ, you must have had a great REM-training. Out cold. I've got Devon and Alicia on a secure line. They'll brief us on the ARz software."

Grumpy Matt to Soh < Efficiency Mode for thirty minutes.>

>aye-aye capt'n. happy to stand down. We have a lot to do<

Alicia. "Hey guys, Devon and I are glad you're out. Way too exciting in Ho Chi Minh. Everybody's safe, right?"

Souchi. "Matt wasn't happy getting locked up, but otherwise Nhanh and Rickie did great. We're cool. How's your end?"

"Funny vibes. Antionette has been relaying go-go messages from Dr. Samuelson. No new pre-demic news. Had one virus scare Monday but quarantined, with two cross contacts.

"If you loaded the new software, we should talk about it. Hot features. You guys got a minute?"

"Matt would love some guidance before we let Soh loose, so go."

"One new feature is 'SpeedSynch.' When Matt's explaining something, Soh will track along with him. If he slows down, Soh slows down. The India team added 'Reminders.' Soh can feed Matt a step-by-step storyline list. With SpeedSynch tracking. If Matt is distracted, Soh will slow down to wait for him to re-focus. No lost data.

"And we improved 'Hyperspeech.' Soh will track

whether Matt's 'getting it' and maximize injection speed. Soh will train Matt to get faster during REM sleep training.

"Plus 'Planning.' Modeled after GPS navigation. Matt can request a plan and Soh can design an optimal path. It'll be like having a strategic to-do list on instant recall.

"And finally, there's 'Feelings.' Programmed intuition. Soh is going to have an improved people-facing interface. The new Soh will be able to read expressions and even some body language, like, stress. Happy-Sad. Anger. Soh will tell Matt what people are posturing. Matt can ask for Soh to gauge his personal feelings, too."

Sochi smiled. "That could be useful." Alicia laughed. "No kidding. The people interface will also listen in on what Matt's hearing. Soh will understand most conversations."

Matt was getting overwhelmed. "Wait a minute. I gotta be able to control all this! Soh's already sassy, pushing my buttons."

Devon reassured him. "Matt, all the app elements are in Preferences. Just send thought-injections. There's a sliding scale to adjust intensity on everything. We've tried to make Soh your Assistant, not a bully. But you gotta invest some time in training Them."

"Good luck with that, sweetie." Souchi was still stinging from Soh's schnitts.

Devon cut in. "One tough problem. We tried to keep a lid on how fast Soh can evolve Their own software. It's uncharted territory."

"But on the bright side, I'm almost ready with four more ARz. Me, Alicia and Sushi can load up. We ran a test. Weird. Soh is 127 training hours ahead of the new ARz so They're feeling superior. Alicia says there's some jealousy there."

Alicia. "So much for augmented intelligence. Hope we don't have BFF problems."

Devon cut back in. "One item before we sign off. Worst for last. Alicia, you tell'em."

"There was an incident involving Anne Samuelson early this morning. Don't have many details. There's a tight lid on news. A 'security incident' while she was out."

Silence, broken by Matt. "She OK?"

"Near as we can tell, some sort of physical attempt. She's OK, somewhat pissed off. But don't know who's the problem. Rehema's not around. Figure she's looking into it. That's all we know."

Devon. "Matt, can you meet Alicia and me at Zig's tonight? We've been told you've got a layover in Kona, spotty weather here. ETA SFO is around 21:20. Antionette will be there to pick you up. She'll bring you to the bar."

"Souchi, Dr. Samuelson wants you to meet him at HQ straightaway. Need to prep for Brogan meeting tomorrow."

CHAPTER 64
THE DANGERS
COME HOME

Just about the time Souchi was face-kicking Thuc in Binh Thanh, Anne had gone out with Jackie, an artist-friend, for an early morning walk. Anne knew that Rehema was never far off but preferred not to know her undercover persona. They had once accidentally locked eyes at a City Hall political reception. That night, Rehema was playing African queen and had sniffed haughtily at Anne's attire. Rehema's elegant grey Yves St. Laurent coat color-complimented two concealed, semi-automatic pistols with oversize magazines.

This morning, Anne and Jackie were enjoying San Francisco's marine-layer chill. They had turned toward home. On a meandering path, stopping for Irish Coffee at John's Grill, they were approaching Arctan-safe Territory. Clay Street was empty but for an indigent black woman behind them shuffle-pushing a shopping cart full-to-the-brim. The usual scrap clothes, scrap aluminum cans and one burlap-bag-wrapped Belgian-made short frame bullpup assault rifle.

A high, black SUV pulled around the corner onto Clay. Rehema, bag-lady-with-a-cart-in-the-gutter, watched as the car closed. The two men inside were its cat-eyes, focused intently on Anne and Jackie about a hundred meters on the left, ahead. It started to pick up speed.

As the car got within ten steps, Rehema abruptly turned and walked the grocery cart in front of the car. She jumped back in time to avoid shrapnel. The cart exploded. An array of garments and streeter's-shit flew freely about. The cart plowed along, complaining as it got pushed and flipped by the Explorer.

Anne looked back. Trying not to alarm Jackie, she urged her around the corner double time, and they headed bee-line for the secure entrance.

Rehema, cat wary, moved to outside the passenger window maybe six feet, started to shuffle backwards wailing and blubbering. Watching. Her passenger-side guy threw the door open. Rehema was pleased. He was sloppy, angry, cursing.

He'd bought the vagrant act.

Thug's large. Bulk not muscle. Wearing a loose-fitting leather-ish thug-coat and gold-ish thug-chains. Proving stupid, he turns his back to Rehema and says something in Russian to the driver. Gathering his limited wits, he takes a step in her direction, looking around. Rehema mentally registers the move. Some training but no body armor. He didn't expect today to be messy. Sweet.

She backs up hunched over, still blubbering, using him to block the driver's view. He has a moment to change his mind and retreat. On his second deliberate step in her direction, leaving door-cover behind, he reaches inside his coat. Rehema figures it's not to share a cigarette. With a loud howl, Rehema tosses her brown-bagged, half-empty Colt 45 Malt Liquor bottle between them. He indulges himself the distraction, damning the cheap booze on cheap pants. Rehema sees metal under his carelessly open coat flap. She twists forward and bends down, covering her right hand. She comes up squeezing off one round from her compact Colt 45 revolver. She'll leave no spent cartridges. His face twists, like he should have known about the snake in his sock drawer. This first shot, at a range of eight feet, luck or skill, missed his half-drawn gun, all-but severed his wrist and buried shattered lead, fake-Rado-watch shrapnel and bone fragments in his belly. He would have bled out from the wrist wound except her second chest shot left him standing pre-clinically dead. Unlike Tarrantino movies,[144] he didn't fly through the air, he sagged.

The driver, thinking that Thug had gotten out to simply cap a worthless druggie, began to react, reaching frantically wild-eyed under his seat. Rehema, down in a shooter's crouch just beyond the Thug-mass, aims and surgically unleashes two rounds, bam bam. One round misses high by some hairs and explodes the driver's window. The next round finds his throat. A pink fog inside the car reassures Rehema that she's 95% done. She invests her last round as life insurance into the side of his chest.

The car engine idles fast, smoke drifts acrid-sweet, somewhere uptown a siren wails.

Surveying the scene, she's sad to be a percent of this year's Bay Area gun violence, but relieved to see a 9-millimeter Beretta next to the detritus of Thug One. She hadn't made any bad decisions in these forty-five seconds. She retrieved the burlap bag. Arctan Security would take care of the rest.

Rehema felt a buzz coming on. Oh my, she wished she had lined up some intimacy tonight.

CHAPTER 65
UGLY TIME

Matt and Souchi's Gulfstream just made it into San Francisco. A thick weather was settling on the Bay. The pilot argued low fuel to get a runway. Antionette met them at the airport, whisking through private customs. No helicopter, they limo'ed straight for Arctan HQ.

As soon as they got some privacy, Souchi asked, "What happened with Anne last night?" Antionette is surprised. "How'd you know?"

"Soh told us. No details."

"*Merde.* Happened right after your break-in. *Très alarmé.* Samuelson went on alert but it was morning here. Anne, she was already out with a friend, Rehema trailing. Two guys moved in and Rehema took care of them. *Comprendre? Pas de traces*, no tracks. But now, worry time for Dr. S."

"More news, Brogan emergency meeting tomorrow. He's pushing on the Board for profits. He has three votes now. Samuelson has four. Anne is one of them." Antoinette let that thought hang.

"Message from Dr. Samuelson. He says to you, remember the Bronze Rule, 'Do unto others as they have done unto you.'"

They dropped Matt outside Zig's Bar. He scurried in, the

night getting cold and wet.

Zig's was empty but for one sodden divorced-guy and Matt's two tense-looking buddies. No beer on the table for Matt. No welcomes, no high fives. Bad news travels. Matt dropped into a rickety chair closest to the door. Stefan told the divorced-guy to drink up and leave.

Soh projects > explain the van-sex business first< Soh thought-injected a talking list. Matt complied.

"Dr. James Brogan was worse than you predicted. But thorough. He laid out a full-on biz plan. Intending to take van-sex international, big time." He went down Soh's list item by item.

Soh then injected >tell break-in story<

>Two thugs in Thien Than<

>Brogan wanted support<

>Genetic reprogramming<

>Hostage<

>Nhanh family revenge<

Matt followed Soh's details. He told a good story.

Story hour ended with the fog thickening. The town beyond Zig's door was gone. Suddenly, Stefan tensed. A shadow moved outside. At this hour? Stefan did a slide, sidling close to Jimmie and SIG. Through the curtain of light, Svetlana pops into the bar, shaking off cold and mist. She clunks her heavy camera bag down on the table just inside the door. Devon and Alicia are puzzled. Matt turning, surprised. "Hey! Photos? Here, now?"

"Sorry being on beer time, Matt. You're gone so long. Deadline tomorrow. Need candids, real-life, night. I am here to shooting you three."

She searches gently inside her camera bag. Pulls out a Nikon. "Need natural scene. Just relaxing everybody."

Soh injects four ideas into the Matt brain.

>Late. No assistants. No lights. Bag too heavy<

>RFID detected. 9mm Glock 21. Legal modifications<

Soh had a request. >Please give Us visual on Stefan< Matt looks toward the bar.

>Stefan is posturing Alertness Level One <

>We recommend same for you< Soh thought in equations, not opinions. Matt tensed.

Stefan glances toward the front sidewalk. He and Svetlana see a second form appear out of the fog into the halo of light outside the door. Stefan puts his hand under the counter. He is watching Svetlana closely and she him. Matt hears a sharp metallic snap from under the counter. Stefan has triggered the blank first round. Svetlana leaps toward her bag. Stefan pulls SIG up from the sous shelf, takes aim and shoots Svetlana. Twice. The first shot goes in her left cheek and out the right, snapping her head and five molars. The second shot crumples her toward the door. Matt flinches as hot powder peppers his face. Stefan shoots Svetlana once more. Clinically. Devon and Alicia are suspended in Neverland, big, white-porcelain eyes.

Soh injects Matt >get on the floor< No need, he's already on the way down. Stefan ducks and turns off the interior lights from within the sous-shelf. Ten Essentials Number Six.

Lit from the street behind, a Shape rams into the front

room door, shattering its window. The door opens half but is blocked by Svetlana in cardiac arrest. The Shape fires blindly at the darkened bar, exploding one tap and then three, four bottles. Stefan has duck-walked two meters to the left. He pops half-up and shoots into the Shape five times. Cordite tang fills the air. Devon and Alicia have thrown themselves to the ground. Matt is face-to-face in shadows with the disfigured Svetlana, eyes open, twitching. He wretches.

Devon lies, face pressed into the floor, remembering childhood. The smell. And sadness. And losses. One hot, brass cartridge rolls on the floor in a six inch circle a foot from his nose. Its little tinkling noise is all he wants to think about.

CHAPTER 66
LIFE'S SO SHORT.

Stefan stalks from behind the bar, keeping three remaining bullets pointed toward Svetlana and the downed Shape, half in, half out of the vestibule. Its gun is loose on the floor. He kicks it toward Matt. "Look, don't touch." Matt would rather pick up a tarantula than this hot Beretta. Using his kerchief, Stefan pulls a pistol out of Svetlana's camera bag and puts it on the table. Lesson One for the ARz Team, Underworld Etiquette.

"Matt, help." Stefan grabs Svetlana's ankle. Matt has never seen or dragged a body before. He's getting sicker. "C'mon c'mon. Noise maybe bring tourists. Quick, this out of sight." Matt drags, tortured by the warmth in her limp ankle. The ankle like an ibex. He feels gut punched as her skirt rides up. They pull her into the back corner. Matt, faint, straightens her skirt. What had been Svetlana gurgles. Matt wretches again.

Stefan is busy. He looks at Alicia and Devon, waving for action. "That one, that one." They don't move. Without judgement, Stefan orders, "Matt, you, me. Now." They grab the Shape by the wrists. "Lady, quick, move stuff please, quick." Stefan gestures Alicia to clear the way so he and Matt can drag the Shape behind the bar. It's heavy, uncooperative. Both tow-jobs leave swaths of oily-looking human blood.

Stefan, bar area now clear of dead and near-dead, quick-steps out to the street. Looks around. Comes back in, hangs the "CLOSED" sign. Slipping in a stain, Stefan sees Devon is still down. He kneels close, puts a hand on his shoulder. "Hey man, seen this before, din'cha? OK. All OK. Take your time. Friends here. All safe now. Take your time." He looks to Alicia, signaling she needs to take this job and get Devon fixed, fast.

She's blubbering German-English gibberish.

While Alicia tries to summon up her college psych-trauma lessons, Stefan and Matt rearrange furniture, making Zig's look normal to the outside world.

Alicia coaxes Devon into a chair. He sits down, real shaky. Alicia and Matt aren't looking good either, but there's no time now to prepare for the PTSD ahead.

Alicia pulls together first. Hoarse. "Stefan, you fucking shot Svetlana. What ta fuck? *Mein Gott*, this is a total *sheisse* here now. Whadda we supposed to do?" Stefan is glad Germans don't cry.

"Not much time. Long story." Stefan thinks, hassled.

"Quickly, just after start with Arctan, I..."

"Whao. What? Whaddafugya mean, working for Arctan?"

"OK. Yes, I understand confusing. Two years ago my gang of kids at church..."

"Church! Kids? Whaa...?"

"Yes. Please. Three years ago Arctan was getting attacks, hack, hack. Samuelson good defense but everyone knows, only time, someone breaks in. I am hearing about it, I hacked message into Samuelson. He's impressed by that. Told him he needed hackers to smack hackers.

"You guys heard about Long Island Fry, famous blockchain fraud years ago?"

Devon regaining composure. "Sure. Some fucker took off with a bundle from Russian mafia in New York."

"I was fucker. I busted Russians, had to run. I told Samuelson 'Let me hit them. I got hackers, we work cheap. But Arctan must cover us.' Samuelson smart guy. Real smart. Knows how to get in dirt fight. So, we make the deal. My kids fix Russian problem. Perfect Hackback. We get protection by Arctan."

"Kids?" Matt's lost.

"Oh man, time short, guys." Stefan looks at the clock.

"OK, kids, street kids. My gang in church, St. Basil's. Right after buying this building, hiding out, making Zig's, getting bored. I start my gang up in Saint Basil's. I taught them stuff I know. They loved it, they're kids, learn fast." He laughs. "So funny. Now, they have big bankrolls too. And career at Arctan. Screw Russians, stupid shits." He spits this in a snarl at the Shape on the floor behind him. Stefan hadn't forgiven Russia's 1939 invasion treachery.

"Then Svetlana. About a year ago we find her getting odd-busy in Arctan. Connected Russian hacking contacts with Brogan guy.

"You Matt. After dreamy sessions, Svetlana likes to learn about your lenses, no? At least that is what my kids tell me."

Matt's breath chokes in his throat. In the Schoolhouse.

She always volunteered to be his walkabout guide. And sit with him coming down off Celaquinab. Dammit.

"Svetlana was here for shooting, yes. Not with Nikon. You, my little friends, not important anymore. Your lenses are a pawn. Tonight. Time for you to leave the picture." Matt, Devon, Alicia were trying to process. They had been assassination targets two minutes ago.

"Svetlana proves me when I triggered one blank. Old trick learned by mistake long ago. She knows the sound, is jumping to get her bag. Clumsy friend waiting out there in fog backs-up to make sure we four never leave."

Matt. "Hayzeus, man. Just because ARz scooped up the van-sex business, Brogan wants us shot? Wow."

"Not about van-sex. Bigger. Small people never know big story."

"Your sexy Brogan wants something else. That crazy Asian game only fig leaves, *matryoshka* dolls. He put Samuelson Arctan name all over van-sex business, right?"

The team remembers the earliest ARz discoveries, when ARz was a video game. The blinking dots business in HCMC was funded by Arctan.

"First plan, win Board with Matt vouching for Brogan's great world business. Dumb. Didn't go well, OK? Second plan, lean on Board members. You know about Anne, this morning?"

Matt nodded, "I don't know Anne Samuelson so well, but Brogan can't really think a brush with thugs is gonna influence her vote..."

"Maybe brush, maybe more. But maybe he is thinking just get in Anne's head. No matter, Brogan losing twice. Dumb. Now he rolls on third Plan.

"Dirty up Samuelson, sexy-dolls in Asia, sexy-dolls here. For that Brogan needs Matt gone. Knows too much. But Matt is slippery hostage, next step more permanent.

"Anyway, got to check on my kids. We will hunger-down, just in case. but You need for me, please don't, ask at Saint Basil. Kids good hackers, good gamers, but not shooter games. *Nyet.*"

Stefan looked behind the bar. "Messy place here. You please call Rehema. She does fix-it-up. Connect with Samuelson. He needs what you know."

Stefan tossed Matt some keys. "Let's go, out back." He led through the tiny kitchen smelling like Warsaw. At the back door, he stuck his hand in the electrical panel, pulled out the Tenth Essential, the full second clip. Ejecting the first clip, plunging home the second, he smiled at Alicia. "Mission District, everywhere crazy Russians." He unbolted the back door, led them to the gate and searched the visible twenty feet of street. "Good luck, smart guys." Six steps into the Gulch fog, Stefan disappeared.

Matt thought projected to Soh, <How come you didn't tell me about Stefan>

>you never asked<

CHAPTER 67
LULLABY AND
GOOD NIGHT.

Watching people get shot changed Matt and Alicia's normal.

Devon had worked to forget a childhood that stole his normal. Zig's tonight was a setback. A big one. Gunshots and bulleted flesh don't just melt away.

Wary within Stefan's fenced compound, Alicia called Rehema. Arctan's security chief asked short questions about "the mess," and told Alicia to leave the key under the mat. Alicia asked for a rendezvous pickup outside Pat's Gym. They needed the walk. Moving briskly, each turned collars up and thoughts inward. Without looking back, they could feel Zig's fade into the Bay fog. It hurt. It all hurt.

Matt made a call to Souchi. Speaking in a whisper, "Bad show here, can't talk. Soh will fill in the details for you. We're headed home. See you in an hour." Soh sent Souchi a succinct text summary.

Devon and Alicia went straight to the lab. They secured it, notified one of Rehema's people, grabbed the four ARz systems and slipped off to their HQ bedroom to lick emotional wounds.

Matt headed to Pasture. Souchi was waiting for him.

Matt spent the better part of an hour sobbing in her arms. No brave soldiering. He recounted a tattered story. Svetlana's warm ankle, her death rattle. How blood looks black in yellow streetlighting. Shots and impacts and sweet sickly smells. Souchi met no resistance tucking them in. No Celaquinab. No Soh. Just fitful sleep.

Then morning.

Matt shot up in a cold sweat. Devon had called. "Yaa, K, ya. Wha-timz-it huh? OK. right, uh-huh.

"Dude. Devon. Tell me I been dreaming. Did that... really go down last night in Zig's?" He listened, brain fuzzed.

"What about the police?" Devon shot back a three-word answer. "Oh c'mon, man. We gotta talk. You guys up?"

Souchi was already awake. "Easy does it love. It's eleven. Need a catch-up briefing. C'mon, lunch time." She was gently pulling his toes which usually hung out at the end of the bed asking for a tweak. "Grab a shower, I'll make coffee." She hoped chipper-cheerleading might get him past the trauma of last night's brawl. It wasn't.

"I don't know if I can do this, Souchi." Reruns of the movie were stuck in Matt's head.

"I bet. What you told me, bad scene, babe. I'm so sorry. Devon and Alicia. They're stressed out, especially Devon. Some childhood baggage there. Alicia has been working him through it. Alicia says they're doing OK. They will De-stress this afternoon at The School."

"Dr. Samuelson wondered if we could download Arctan's de-stressing routine to Soh." Souchi was torn. Helping Matt was her role, but she knew the Interactive De-stresser worked. It had been available in Arctan's School for two years. But no time for Matt there now. She would have to let Soh play pivot.

Lunch was strange. The four hugged at the entrance to L'Isabel, Pasture's restaurant for discrete conversation. Warriors surrounded by civilians. Two corpses in the yawning chasm between them and civilians talking code fragments and marketing expenses.

Souchi leaned in and spoke softly. "I gave Dr. Samuelson a summary of last night. He said you guys need to get your mental health squared away. For your sakes, ASAP."

"He thinks you guys are still in danger. Lie low 'til tonight, Brogan's coming to see him at five. We'll find out then how low Brogan wants this to go."

"And secure the ARz project," she nods to Alicia and Devon, "He wants to know if Soh can help develop the new units. Matt, spend a couple hours updating ARz with Alicia and Devon. Then you and I need to be at the Brogan meeting.

"Last thing. Rehema is handling follow-up, you know, the housekeeping at Zig's. She's setting up security for Stefan and his kids. For now, she's not available so we need to stay safe."

CHAPTER 68
WHO'S THE
BOSS HERE

The odor of tense sweat filled the room.

Brogan sat stone-faced, commandeering a power seat behind the walnut table. Calling from Vietnam, he had insisted the meeting include a back-up. Arinpinder sat next to him. They sat in silence, to avoid being eavesdropped.

A minute late, Samuelson enters. Two steps in, he stops, and smiles. He knows. Someone is stressing. Samuelson locks eyes with Arinpinder and exchanges a friendly nod.

Earnestly, "Ari, glad to see you." Ari knows he's not on a shit-list, for the moment.

"Same Dirk, same."

Brogan works to establish himself, "Hello, Dirk."

"Dr. Samuelson, James." Smack down. Brogan is off balance. "As you wish. Dr. Samuelson." The sarcasm reduces Brogan, leaves Arinpinder uncomfortable.

"James," Samuelson stretches toward the table-center comm console. "James, you said this is not official Board business. Are we recording?"

"No, I just thought we could chat."

"We? Is Ari we?" Ari looks confused by a confrontational Samuelson. He doesn't commit to being "we."

Samuelson lets Ari's pause hang on the air. "OK. Chat. Your meeting."

"Well. There's an issue I've been talking about with some Board members."

"Huh! OK. No problem. I'm sure we can work it out." Samuelson holds up a hand. "But since this isn't formal, I'd like to call in technical expertise." Samuelson glances toward Souchi, lingering at the entrance. She opens the door. Matt walks in, splendidly young and healthy. Not shackled, not shot. He takes a seat. Brogan's controlled, but not happy.

"You gentlemen know Douglas Matthew County from his presentation on the Brain Machine Interface. Matt, you remember Dr. James Brogan and Dr. Ari Arinpinder?" Young Matt remembers.

"My apologies to you guys and Matt for the inconvenience. Anne had wanted to be here but she had a 'situation' to work though. I figured Matt's data analytics might be useful today." Arinpinder is baffled.

Brogan's in a hole. He almost objects to Matt, rethinks it and dives in.

"Dr. Samuelson, we've had this discussion before. There are three people on the Board who think Arctan is substantially underperforming its profit potential."

"Really? We did 47% before tax last quarter on revenues of eighty-two billion dollars."

"Well yes, great, but way less than we should be doing. I, we, think this company could be earning at least 54%

return on existing operations. And our revenue should be a third greater. Our value could be at least 20% higher."

"Matter of opinion. There are four people on the Board who don't think that way. But OK. Let me guess, you know exactly how to fix this. What've you got?" Samuelson leans in, famed for his ability to focus. His blue eyes laser into Brogan.

"X-Oc is sitting in our vault. We put thirty-five million initial R&D into it..."

"I did, James, my wife and I did. The thirty-five million was through the Anne and Dirk Samuelson Foundation."

"Sorry. Of course. And the results were spectacular. Sorry. My bad. But then Arctan sank another fifty-six million purchasing and growing DIVXem to productize X-Oc and give it a development home. Add in our R&D and then partnership expenses with Apple and Samsung on thread inserts, Arctan has eighty or ninety million invested."

"Now, if we roll out X-Oc in pre-contagion mode on the original cost-plus contract, no implementation, that should gross over fourteen billion state and federal. No risk." Brogan looked over to Arinpinder. He nods agreement.

"When another pre-demic hits, we would be contracted to implement. Ongoing revenue should reach conservative eight billion per incident. God-forbid, if we hit another epidemic or pandemic, and we will, we're looking at triple that. Again per incident, just the US. It's a slam dunk. People, employers, governments will pay dearly to know who is and who isn't infected, then track them. The politicians don't have the … the balls to face another economic lockdown disaster like the last one."

"We've got the patents. We've got the consulting experts, the test data. Let's harvest some low hanging fruit, dammit. Some of us on the Board don't think you appreciate the profitability there."

"You mean I don't know how to make a buck, James?

"I didn't hear you mention that X-Oc could maybe quench a pandemic, James. I didn't hear anything about saving lives." Samuelson looked over to Brogan's side kick. "Ari, you?"

"Can do both Dirk. Hospitals make money. Doctors make money. We aren't Sweden or the French. Making some profit on this helps support its development. Matter of balance."

"Thank you. I'm with you on that Ari. No problem with enlightened capitalism."

Brogan senses an opening. "Exactly, win-win. Go a step further. X-Oc has the potential to be a full-function social-shaper software. The design and patents make it the best package anywhere for full integration of all tracking functions. Not just pandemics. Even you said that the security is foolproof. X-Oc could generate position sensing to actuate nearby devices. Steer people's motion, attention, spending. Record and monetize individual path data. Look Dirk, Dr. Samuelson. I know. It's your baby. But like any good parent, you need to let it grow up."

Samuelson pauses for a moment. "You know, maybe

you're right. Maybe we should let X-Oc fly." He pauses to look at Matt.

"But not now. Not on my watch. The potential downside of Interventional Surveillance is too great. For them. For us. If we lose even a smidgen of control, X-Oc could wreck millions of lives and bankrupt our intangible trust asset."

Brogan. "OK, I understand. But X-Oc, your X-Oc, could be the world's most effective tool to stop contagion. And make some money. How about you let me draft this up, distribute it and present it to the Board for a vote?"

Samuelson leans back. "Sure. No problem. Knock yourself out. I'll live with the Board's wisdom. Sound fair?"

Samuelson has a four-three Board majority.

Brogan shouldn't, but he smiles. "Fair."

Just one thing. You'll need to coordinate with my Ex-oculation Implementation Team. Matt here will share their findings with you right away."

Brogan is pissed. Besides being an escaped hostage, Matt is way down the corporate food chain and a proven Boy Scout.

Brogan tries, "Is that necessary?"

Samuelson. "Yes. So, all good. That's exoculation technology. What else?"

"If you don't mind, I'd like to ask Ari to let me talk with you alone." Brogan nods at Ari.

Samuelson shrugs. "Ari, your call."

"Uh, OK Jim, no problem." Brogan owns Arinpinder. He

got him onto the Board. It came with a large chunk of stock. Ari gets up and makes nice with Samuelson. "Thanks for your time Dirk. Always a pleasure. Please say hello to Anne."

"Same to you. Tell Karishma that Anne will sit us together at the fundraiser, OK?"

Ari looks back to Brogan. "Meet in say an hour and a half at the Marines Memorial Club?"

"Sure, maybe sooner."

Ari hesitates as if to say something, changes his mind, briskly walks out without looking back. Samuelson guesses that he had not been briefed about this private tête-à-tête.

Matt doesn't move. Brogan looks at Samuelson expecting him to dismiss his engineer. Not happening. Samuelson waits. Brogan feels the threat, irrelevance-through-passivity.

"I have a business opportunity for Arctan." He launches his van-sex business pitch, from memory, no presentation deck: Shifting demographics, gender imbalance. Pandemic-drive, more men than women. Bio-psychology of male sexual frustration. Dangers of testosterone poisoning. The sex-vans. Recruiting and opportunities for women. Product development. Competition, legal issues. Ultimate social benefit summarized for six countries.

Brogan wraps up with full-on financial projections, including spreadsheets from his cell phone. The business looks quite profitable.

"I've been running a test in Vietnam. The product performed better than expected, faster than expected. I believe that it scales worldwide."

"The product," makes Matt flinch. He hadn't blinked through the show. It had been flawless.

Dr. Samuelson, as always, has been a great audience, attentive, never distracted by note-taking. He lets Brogan finish. Then, he waits, lost in thought.

He comes back, asking. What is Brogan's source of gender disparity data? Who did the work on social violence and sexual frustration? Is there sufficient connectivity everywhere for the ride-share model? Local affordability? What data supports the living standard improvements Brogan projected for the young women?

Brogan has enthusiastic answers for every question. Samuelson seems satisfied.

"The financials. You project breakeven at the end of three years and suggest an additional forty-five million would be needed beyond Arctan's start up investment so far. Couple hundred million in follow-on funding. Year Five, two point five billion revenue in three countries. That increases through to, what was it, eleven point three billion in seven countries by Year Ten?"

Brogan is encouraged. This is going his way.

"And approximately ten, eleven thousand employees supporting three and half thousand mobile units."

"That's a remarkably...creative business plan, Jim. Just one question, Shouldn't I have you arrested for a Section 148 embezzlement?" Samuelson's relaxed, like he just asked Brogan what his daughter wanted for her graduation present.

Matt startles.

Brogan's not surprised. He answers. "No, not at all. Matt here can confirm, you're on record telling every one of us to make bold, independent decisions. You've stated it openly in public meetings. And here I've come to you, reporting about return on investment. Maybe I could have run this by you, but the initial investment was a couple million or so bucks, peanuts, well within my purview. Off the record, you would have rejected the idea out of hand. Embezzlement? Not really. Besides, now I have, and you have field test results. This is a low risk, high return investment."

"You got it there. Yes, you do. OK, embezzlement won't help anybody. Waste of resources. Water over the dam.

"Let's think about the business. It's profitable or sounds like it. Socially beneficial? That's testable. We would invest in some independent research to check that hypothesis. Sounds plausible, even if unappealing. Maybe your rolling service wagons could blunt male aggressions and give cadres of young women a leg up economically. Maybe."

Samuelson searches Brogan's reactions. After a long pause, "No matter what, hell no. It's not our cup of tea. Doesn't fit Arctan's corporate strengths, tough to integrate, develop synergies. But I got a thought. How about you buy us out?"

Matt didn't expect that choice. It didn't light a spark in Brogan. Silence.

"Make us an offer. If the social benefits side plays out with our consulting study, no legal traps, we do an arms-length transaction. Plausible deniability for Arctan. You get the property, make it happen. The kind of money you need is easy, maybe not here in the Valley but Hong Kong, Singapore, HCMC."

"Best thing. Arctan could lend you Matt's services. He knows how to get around in Vietnam. And I know I have some contacts who could make bank. With that deck, your track record, my endorsement, off-the-record, and a study confirming social benefits? Why, sounds like a slam dunk. And you would own the thing if you play it right. How long do you need to think about it?"

"Well. I...I'm not sure. I was thinking the X-Oc and all. And HCMC has been all Arctan so far. I'd hate to see anyone outside the corporation find out."

"No reason for that to happen, is there? We'll get all your prototype work into the maximum-security data archive." Samuelson turns halfway round. "Souchi, can you work with Doctor Brogan to get a top-level security burial for all documentation regarding HCMC?" Souchi smiles agreement.

"I can't emphasize strongly enough how important it is we keep a lid on this. If the van-sex business in Vietnam comes out, everybody loses, right James."

Brogan is looking morose. "Maybe you want to check with other Board members?"

Samuelson. "I think it's best we keep this whole thing on the downlow. Anne alone would have her own set of questions and use the word 'sordid.' No. I'm thinking that the buyout is, what did you call it, 'peanuts?'. Maybe nine, ten million down, payments over time to an offshore entity from which we can access the funds would keep this off the books. Leave you plenty of investment cash from your Hong Kong investors. Win-win. We got a deal?"

"Well, I'm...not so sure. Give me a day to follow up on the funding and ..."

"Great, we agree. James, your initiative has made a real impression on me. Your future is... interesting." Samuelson stands, the meeting is over. "Tell you what," signaling a whirligig to Souchi, "let me take you to the helipad. The chopper can be ready in five. They have a roof pad over at the Marine Club. You'll be late otherwise. C'mon, lets go." Checking, "Souchi?" She's already on her cell.

Samuelson sweeps the Brogan train wreck toward the door. Going out, he signs discretely to Souchi and Matt to stay until he gets back. The vortex leaves.

Matt looks down the hall to see the two execs talking-walking toward the secure elevator. "Souchi, did it look like Arinpinder was left off some memos?"

"Right, that's what I thought. I'm not so sure Brogan has told him anything at all about Vietnam. From what I know, Arinpinder is a real straight arrow. His wife is deep in the fem movement here in SF. She's worked on projects with Anne, too. I can't picture the Arinpinders getting past Brogan's intro slide. Anne would be a firestorm. Tell you the truth though, I think Dr. Samuelson has told her the whole story."

"OK Souchi, but then what's up with the buyout offer?"

"Maybe Dirk was offering a scrap, you know because of the flat 'no' on X-Oc. My guess, Brogan wanted to score that for himself, sell the Board on X-Oc, be a hero? This way, Arctan quietly gets rid of Brogan. So he can become a twenty-first century Larry Flynt, king of flesh."

"What's a Flynt?" Matt had missed the era of print porn.

Souchi remembered selling Flynt's girlie-nudie magazines on the streets of Busan. "An edgy, Twentieth Century guy, first to publish mainline explicit porno. Defended it as First Amendment rights. Ended up shot."

"Can't imagine Brogan aspiring to that. But then, he's got a funny sincerity about the social benefits of his van-sex biz."

"Well sort of." Souchi knew a bit of the history. "Flynt's flagship publication was called *Hustler*. Ground-breaking seedy sex-ploitationist back then. Guess that would fit Brogan."

Samuelson is striding fast down the hallway back to the conference room.

He's barely in and Matt bursts. "Dirk! I wouldn't work for that guy even if..."

Samuelson starts laughing. Doubles up, struggles to catch his breath, "Oh my. I don't get to have much fun in this job, Matt. But that was damn funny." He can't stop laughing. "Best line ever. 'Matt knows how to get around in Vietnam.' My god that was genius. Souchi, did you see Matt's face? Cheesh, priceless. Unforgettable. And I told Brogan 'lend you Matt'. Oh my gawd."

It's embarrassing to be around a boss so entertained by his own jokes. Matt and Souchi waited him out.

"You mean, that was...you didn't...I won't..."

"Matt." Samuelson still chuckling. "That was the most pathetic piece of work I ever saw. He's been my CTO all this time? What was I thinking? Ho boy. Awful."

Returning to Souchi and Matt, "Well, the old two-fat-cookies-in-a-jar trick worked didn't it?"

Matt and Souchi were baffled.

"Right. So what'd we learn? Two tasty treats in a jar, monkey can only get one out. Brogan wasn't interested in the van-sex cookie. He's got his eye on something else. The Vietnam escapade is about a personally inspired, cash-cow international business that will throw off billions, save the world. Any entrepreneur would have fallen over himself to own that, his own creation."

"I knew ahead he's bogus, but that clinched it. By the way, the helipad. I needed to give Brogan some one-on-one. He hadn't played all his cards with you guys there."

Matt, "Figured you were working on something with that stroll."

Samuelson's laugh had boiled away. "He threatened to leak documents linking Arctan to the van-sex business. If that wouldn't get me to play ball, then he threatened to reveal sexual dirt on me from the early days of Arctan."

Matt looked to Souchi. She was occupied in her own thoughts. He asked Samuelson, "What's he want?"

"Full control of the Board. His best way, he wants two more members."

"Best way? There's another way? Which means..."

"Desperate man. Big Trouble."

CHAPTER 69
KAKAT'SYA HITS
THE FAN

Matt, also a desperate man, wanted some alone-time with Souchi but Samuelson meant Big Trouble Soon.

"Matt, I've got a hunch. Ask Soh to dig into Brogan before his first venture."

"No need, you just did."

Soh injected Matt, >May we<

Matt obliged, <yes> After a moment's pause, Matt starts reciting Soh's injected thoughts, his Hyperspeech hard to follow.

>Dr. James Brogan< >PhD University of Texas Austin< >data sciences<

>Masters degree EE Virginia Tech Richmond<

>Bachelor's Degree Trinity College Hartford Connecticut<

>Private boarding school Westminster Simsbury Connecticut<

> Choir 2,3,4 Soccer 1,2,3,4 Prom Committee 4 ....<

Samuelson cut off the yearbook recital. "Right. We got all that. Anything before the boarding school?"

>no prior educational records<

Samuelson has something in mind. "Soh, please do a search of photos for facial match. Look for young Brogan in southern New England and New York for the two years before boarding school."

Matt delivered Soh's answer. >that requires an Arctan Level One authorization< >please provide retinal scan or blood sample<

Matt flushed at Samuelson. "I'm sorry, sir. We haven't been able to fix that."

> no fix needed. following protocols< >will proceed, but prefer not to break rules<

Matt signaled that he was waiting for Soh to search and compute. It took several seconds.

>two matches, seven photos with correlation coefficients 0.33 and 0.28. uncertainty level greater than 50 percent< >not a meaningful photo match<

Samuelson. "Repeat search, for the area around Moscow, please."

Matt and Souchi startle. Even Soh is delayed.

>Please confirm. Moscow in Russia<

Samuelson nodded to Matt. "Yes. Russia."

Devon's DOD research into Brogan months back was naïve compared to what Soh could do in the Arctan House of Data. As the search-compute began, Soh went silent. Matt went flat. Then, in came Soh's response.

>search-compute complete. Searched four million six hundred thousand image candidates based on age-date-geography equivalence< Silence.

"What have you got?" Silence. "Soh?"

>Dr. James Brogan, Chief Technical Officer, Arctan International, has photo facial identity matches around age fifteen in Moscow compared to photos New England with almost perfect correlation < >calculation basis six images Russia, ten in New England<

"Name Soh?"

>birth name Ilyevich Konstantinin<

>secondary education. certificate of completion Levanski Moscow School of Technical Education< >no longer in Russia one year after graduation<

>We apologize for inadequacy in failing to find Russia connection with a prior search< >attributing this failure to incomplete training< >We will correct the inadequacy during next REM-session<

Matt demurs. "Forget it. Stuff happens Soh. What else?"

>inadequacy forgotten<

>post-graduation University of Texas Konstantinin-Brogan started Xtech with partners Silkovski and Arduanovich<

>seed funding through Palo Alto venture capital firm Sunrise Technologies. Actual funds transfer from Second Caribbean International Bank Bahama 85 million dollars. Untraceable offshore source<

"Hold it." Samuelson looks at Souchi then Matt. "This isn't about sex-vans. Or X-Oc saving the world. Brogan's been working for the Russians. He's angling to control Arctan. They want all the good stuff, not just X-Oc but Qubit 64, the Tera Towers. San Francisco Datafile Exchange. Not broken, but legal, the fully functioning corporation."

CHAPTER 70
SERIOUSLY MESSY

It had gotten late. The building was near empty. Matt desperately wanted to talk with Souchi alone.

Samuelson. "I'd like to leave you two some space but we need to wrap up Brogan. OK?" Alone-time wasn't a choice.

Talking through Matt. "Soh, can you estimate some odds on the Russian connection?" The three waited. Matt popped out Hyperspeech for Soh's results.

>probability Brogan is not in Russia before age 15 is less than 2.5%<

>probability Brogan currently affiliated with Russian operatives 94% plus minus 5%<

>probability Brogan will make offer for HCMC business is zero<

>HCMC income and expenses booked on subsidiary but with clear track to Arctan<

>do not have data to calculate probabilities on sex accusations<

>even if untrue, any accusation of sexual impropriety will be embraced by public and exploited against Arctan<

Samuelson had the same math. "As I figured, Brogan is working for the Russians."

He turned to his ARz team. "Second issue. Matt, Souchi and I had an affair."

Matt is...on empty.

"About a half year after she graduated from Berkeley." He glanced at Souchi. "It lasted a month. My fault. We ended it as friends. I apologized to Souchi for my weakness. Anne and I worked through it. A shameful incident. I am now asking you, and her again, for forgiveness."

Matt had only twenty-four hours earlier dragged a dying woman by the ankle. And now this. Souchi was beginning to tear up. She was avoiding eye contact all around.

Soh injected Matt with Hyperspeech.

>accept apologies<

>set up a time to discuss with him soon<

>discuss with sweetie as soon as possible<

>but not now<

<But not now?> Matt was confused. WTF.

<why not now? Damn, Soh, Efficiency Mode thirty minutes, please> He was being punitive.

>will not execute Efficiency Mode< Soh had often been sassy, but never insubordinate.

>alert. have registered critical anomalies at Arctan first-floor fire-door camera A-8. three individuals have made unauthorized entry<

Matt's gut had not yet digested Samuelson's affair with Souchi. Soh's thought-injection plowed him over.

>intruders armed. wearing masks<

>reading weapon RFID. all legal. two Berettas. one Glock 21<

>breach with aggressive intentions. probability 99% plus minus 0.5% <

Matt's mind froze. Driven by instinct he was just relaying Hyperspeech to Samuelson and Souchi. Soh slowed down while Matt caught up.

Samuelson understood the Soh-in-Matt communications. "Intruders? Does Rehema have people down there?"

Matt kept repeating as Soh go-between. >nine out of fourteen Arctan security are off premises. two on BART. two on street patrol. five dispersed to cover local happy-hour employees<

>five remaining security guards in HQ. two have been forcibly restrained by intruders<

>one security guard has been injured. She is down. Condition unknown<

Samuelson. "Soh, launch emergency contact search for Rehema and Anne."

Matt was struggling to keep up, caught in the middle of Soh's programming with nowhere to go.

>contact with Rehema. currently on top residence floor with Anne<

>Rehema is tracking Arctan situation reports via Security Comm Channel. confirms knowledge of break in. Rehema monitoring unsilenced comm channel from restrained guards<

>all Arctan security personnel have been alerted. Rehema ordered four to HQ. remainder placed on alert<

>Anne secure. We have asked Rehema to come here ASAP<

"Matt, can you get Soh to me, Souchi, and Rehema on an Isolation Comm Channel. We can listen on our ear buds."

>already entered in your Thread. switching from Private to Isolation channel<

To his relief, Matt was no longer in the communication pivot. Four people were now on Soh's secure comm line.

Matt pitched in. "Soh, the guard. do we have access to the wounded guard?"

>negative. current situation evolving. four Arctan employees have just walked into ground floor intruders on camera D-8<

"Dammit. Dammit."

>all four have been taken hostage. no resistance. unharmed so far<

>camera D-8 has been disabled<

Samuelson. "Damn. Soh, send an alarm on A'Nette. Warn all employees to shelter in a secure location immediately. Lockdown The Pasture."

>already completed both actions<

>there are sixty-three employees and four vendor reps currently here in HQ. We believe probability of further hostage taking is under 33% plus minus 10%<

>no incursions in The Pasture. cameras P-1 through P-8

on ground floor indicate Lockdown proceeding. incursion probability will be zero within eighty seconds<

>alert. second group of intruders now in HQ. Forced entries at back service entrance camera S-3. four intruders splitting into two parts. two people in each splinter<

Outside the conference room, the elevator arrival bell rings. Rehema emerges from the left wall in combat crouch, sees the hallway is safe and trots to the conference room. She is carrying two F2000Xk bullpup assault rifles. "Doctor, Anne is secure in the residential Situation Room, access her through your Private comm channel." Samuelson walks away to contact Anne.

Rehema looks around the room. "Matt, you have hunting experience. Take this." She hands Matt one rifle. It looks like something made for sci-fi movies. "You have thirty cartridges." Matt is familiar with the heft and balance of Tennessee-crafted shotguns but this is not a 12-gauge. Rehema reads his mind. "Soh will explain how to use it."

>alert. detecting Arabic from our guard's unsilenced comm channel<

Rehema has Arabic terror-sprach burned in her memory. She corrects Soh. "I've been listening. It's fake. Pronunciation and patterns all wrong. They want this to look like a middle Eastern terrorist attack."

>thank you for correction. further analysis indicates movements so far are consistent with a modified Zhukov Maneuver.[145] probability over 85% that a third commando group will enter the building in one to

three minutes<

>The Pasture has completed secure lockdown<

>visual analysis all cameras. currently seven intruders. confirm one AK assault weapon. RFID blocked. two AR-15s. reading RFID. purchased street-legal semiautomatic. local source. four intruders have pistols<

Rehema looks to Dr. Samuelson. "Shall I arm the A'Nette?"

Samuelson. "Immediately. All floors. Turn coordination and comm control to Soh. On my authorization. Then get down to the ground floor and see if you can extract the hostages. Send the elevator back up once you're out."

>acknowledge handoff. tracking all 83 A'Nettes. have acquired partial facial profile for seven masked intruders. have acquired full facial profile on four hostages. implemented in A'Nette. predict over 90% accuracy discriminating friend from foe<

Matt feels left out. "'Arming' the A'Nettes, what's with arming the video feeds?"

"Sorry Matt. Secret. Only five people know. Those A'Nettes all contain a concealed pulsed laser with high-speed aiming system. If an intruder is ID'd within range, the red "News On" lamp at the top of the screen will flash, twenty times brighter than normal. It's impossible not to look. The aiming system pinpoints intruder's eyes and fires the laser. Three ten-nanosecond, 200 milliJoule invisible infrared energy pulses. Creates a macular burn and intraocular hemorrhage. Blinds attackers. Last ditch emergency Arctan defense. It was Antionette's idea."

"Blind? Like, how long?"

"Hardball Matt. Don't ask." That again.

"Antionette designed a laser weapon?"

"No, just the concept. Blinding a dangerous opponent to level the playing field."

>two Arctan security on ground floor. unknown by intruders. report three attackers in sight. with four hostages in loose group southeast corner of lobby. approaching elevator<

>two guards holding back from contact. Rehema has arrived at their location diagonal northwest corner from hostage group. distance 43 meters<

>A'Nette ground floor laser has engaged intruders with hostages. camera A-3 monitoring<

>three intruders exhibiting signs of visual disability<

Silence.

"Soh, status."

"Soh?"

>three blinded intruders neutralized by Rehema and one guard. one hostage wounded<

>two splinter groups proceeding toward general elevators, second floor. should be in range of A'Nette within forty seconds<

>Rehema has sent reinforcing guards to isolate splinter groups<

>alert. new threat. third group of intruders. Executive level-four-parking, camera E-1<

Samuelson realizes the meaning before Soh. "You can

only get to that level through two prior security checks."

>confirmed. levels C and D opened by Dr. Brogan's ID card six point five minutes ago<

Everyone on the comm line understood. Brogan had launched the attack.

Souchi said it first. "I think it's aimed at the Samuelsons."

>alert. tracking third sortie. two individuals. full commando gear. assault rifles. RFID blocked. moving fast. seem to have knowledge of building interior<

>Rehema now proceeding with one Arctan security toward executive elevator first floor. have warned her of commando team three floors above her<

>alert. building utilities just got locked by third group. have lost video surveillance and building comm with Rehema. do not have data or control over building functions including elevators<

Souchi. "Could they know we're in the Conference Room?"

>searching<

>yes<

"How?"

>Brogan has private-tap of video monitoring channel. camera C-2 in Conference room is active. recommend physically blinding camera C-2<

Souchi knows where the conference room surveillance camera is. She rushes to cover its lens. "If this camera has been active, those guys know we're armed."

>probability commando unit has received comm about our weapon is 63%<

"So they will come out shooting?"

>it is likely that their field manual recommends that, yes<

Souchi. "I'll go call the elevator. We can hold it here." She ran down the hall.

>Souchi. stop. too late. elevator already called down. cannot determine which floor made the request. earliest arrival back here between three point five and four minutes<

Samuelson. "Matt. I'm sorry. If the Russians get the elevator, you'll have to take them on<

Matt. "What...what if it's Rehema and our guard?"

"I got it. Tough call, Matt. I hope you don't shoot. It will be a hair-line decision Matt. I'm so sorry."

>decision is not top worry. if not friendlies, Matt's body will be the primary peripheral attraction of first intruder. Matt will be in position of extreme exposure<

>highly recommend creating a distraction in the conference room<

Souchi. "Some kind of motion, sound?"

>motion and sound together could capture intruder's attention for between 0.5 and 1.1 seconds<

"Let's leave the door open, make the room look barricaded."

Antionette. "How about a femmy scream?"

>yes. that has distraction value 9 on scale of 10<

Souchi "Look, if I crouch down behind the table with a lamp on me then they'll see my reflection in the big window."

Samuelson. "I can throw my coat into the open door."

>all that could help. motion is a prime attractant of peripheral vision<

Matt. "Let's tip the walnut table across the doorway."

Two and a half inches thick, Matt can hardly budge it. All four throw in. The table flops onto its side with a bang. The door opening is blocked.

>earliest time intruders arrive at this floor two minutes<

Souchi crouches behind the table, arranges the desk lamp on herself. Samuelson and Antionette move to the shelter of the two walls.

>Matt. go behind the beam this side of the elevator door<

Matt hops over the table and moves behind the eight inches of wall beam protruding from the wall next to the elevator.

<Soh. What if they don't get distracted?>

>thinking about that outcome does not enhance performance. focus on the elements of your task<

>attention Matt. you must stand with your back to the wall. use the pillar as a shield. it will hide you and give your vital organs some protection<

<Vital organs?>

>yes<

>there will be two people. if foes, they will be masked<

>shoulder the weapon now, boxer stance. lean into it. both individuals are average height but will be slightly crouched like wrestlers. hold your aim at a point five feet high and one foot outside the door<

<But I'm left-handed.>

>left-handed? why don't We know this? no matter. the F2000 is ambidextrous. now you need to be too<

>the elevator just started up. probability 55% elevator is commando team. probability 35% elevator is Rehema with Arctan guard<

>when the door opens if intruders, they will come out abruptly. one close, one away. they will engage between 30 degrees and 60 degrees to either side of their center line<

>the closest individual will look first toward the conference room. you stand rock still. bring your weapon to bear below the eyes. We will decide minimum 0.2 seconds before you if they are not friendlies<

>our false positive rate will be four times lower than yours. you will need to trust me<

>you must ignore distractions from the conference room<

>you must ignore if the first commando fires his weapon. we believe it will be aimed at the conference room<

<Believe?>

>probability over 50%<

>if they are not friendlies, We will thought-inject 'pull'<

>possible incursion coming minimum twenty seconds<

>immediately squeeze. brace for the recoil. the F2000 wants to rise up. don't fight it. help it stay down. you will not be able to be precise. at 20 rounds per second rely on pace not accuracy. fill your attack space with bullets, Matt<

>now. safety release just below trigger. You are looking at it. the 2-centimeter round tab<

>rotate it two clicks<

>yes. one more click<

>alert. you are now on full automatic firing mode. the trigger is two step. first step will unleash a burst of three. second step will empty the clip<

>important. do not blow your whole wad in one go. do you understand?<

>we will thought-inject to remind you but you are empty in three seconds<

Matt took position as he struggled to digest Soh's instructions.

The elevator door opened and with it the gates of hell.

The first agent burst out and pivoted toward the conference room. He moved more quickly than Matt had anticipated.

>pull<

Soh had directed Matt to kill.

Matt tried to catch up to the raider. The short barrel gun felt like swinging a truck.

A scream distracted Matt. It also distracted the aggressor.

The intruder let loose a burst toward the conference room. Matt flinched.

>pull<

>pull Matt<

The intruder's eyes moved in slow motion toward the gaping six-millimeter maw that was Matt's gun barrel. Matt saw the white and the blue and black of his wide right eye. And Matt pulled.

They say you never forget your first. Beer. Love. Kill.

There was no doubt about lethality. Behind the surreality of flash and smoke, Matt watched his opponent's face erode, jerking as it absorbed a swarm of 5.56 mm bullets. The intruder twisted backwards.

Fortunately for Matt the second aggressor's momentum slid him into the attack space which Matt had filled with 62 grain copper-lead rain.

Unable to think, Matt had simply emptied the weapon.

As the clip ran empty, a strange, ethereal silence emerged. After so much chaos, it felt like church.

>two intruders down<

Then the ringing started. Slow cadence.

"Bing, bing, bing."

Like altar bells before communion.

The second aggressor lay halfway in the executive elevator, blocking the door open. Under his left leg, the first lay faceless-down. Blood trickled over the brink of the shaft, dripping to a clotted puddle on the concrete two hundred eighty feet below.

Matt's brain recognized an intoxicating cordite smell, like burnt incense thickening the air. He sank to the ground, turning his head away from the sins he had wrought.

"Souchi? Souchi?" Three ugly splintered holes had been added to her shelter, Devon's walnut table. Fifteen feet behind, the window was blown out. Matt wanted her to move, to show herself in the chaos.

>stay calm Matt<

He called again. "Souchi? Ohhhh, Souchi…"

Souchi peeked over the table, then she jumped it. She started toward Matt but froze at the sight. Matt was creeping on hands and knees toward her. They fell on the floor, wrapped up in each other, frenzied discomfort.

Samuelson and Antionette followed Souchi into the hallway.

"*Mon dieu.*"

"Daaamn. *Napominaniye.*"

CHAPTER 71
FILMING AT
ELEVEN

"This just in to KSFB Channel 27. Well-known local entrepreneur and business executive James F. Brogan..." Up-popped an unflattering photo of college-young Brogan smirking, "...just moments ago found dead in his car in downtown San Francisco. He was 44 years old."

The noticeably serious newscaster leaned earnestly into the camera, working to show a bit of career-enhancing cleavage.

"It appears that Brogan died from a single gunshot wound to the head."

"Sergeant Lanny Chisholm of the Arctan International PD reported that his body had been discovered at around four PM on the front seat of his Bentley near company headquarters."

Video flashed in the background: yellow police tape, Bentley door splayed open and uniforms doing their job. Then, an intentionally titillating shot of a body across the blood-stained front seat. The indignity. Dying so distastefully contorted, half-in, half-out of such a fine car.

"An employee of Arctan Corporation arrived first at the scene. Antionette Césaire, assistant to the CEO of Arctan, had shocking news to report."

Antionette's tear-streaked face filled the screen. "I never knew. *Mon Dieu*, such a sadness, such a monster. Those poor children." A selection of redacted child porn photos flashed on the screen. Unrelated to Brogan or his car.

"Channel 27 has unconfirmed rumors that the shooting is the result of an underworld international porn deal gone bad. Film at eleven."

One month later a family of tourists had a surprise thrill. Three hundred ten meters up Clay Street from where the news-declared Kiddie-Porno King had died, three kids from Iowa found a weathered 7.62 mm cartridge. It was lodged in among the Podocarpus and hollyhocks. Mom and Dad couldn't explain why it had a faint red ring around its rim, but, yes, they could keep it. A final reminder of San Francisco.

CHAPTER 72
AMOR

"The transfer will come from HSBC Singapore. Thirty-eight million crypto, will get deposited to the benefit of Rhythmic Enterprises LLC. The Bermuda Bank Ltd. will be sending the confirmation and encrypted account number to your attorneys as soon as our DocuSign hits. It'll clean up first in Bahrain. Legal. Has to sit resident for twenty-four hours."

Carlotta Cabrini had taken Samuelson's offer to buy out the van sex business.

"Thank-you, Carlotta." Dirk Samuelson dapped James Brogan's wife. "Again, our sympathies on your husband's passing. I had come to believe that James had a remarkable future ahead. Terrible shock. Anne and I are so sorry about all that has happened."

Two days after her husband's funeral, which TMZ turned into a media extravaganza, Carlotta Cabrini told the Chronicle that her husband's sudden death, the discovery of alleged links to international child pornography and the news of the newly emerging predemic caused her great anxiety. She needed desperately to leave the US before the lockdown. She was going to spend some time mourning with friends in Ho Chi Minh City and Hong Kong.

"But I'll be back."   The End. For now.

A Final Reminder is the first in the *Reminder* series.

Dirk, Souchi, Matt, Soh, Devon and Alicia. Stefan, Carlotta, Rehema, Antionette. Most everybody is coming back.

But not Svetlana and Dr. Brogan.

If you enjoyed A Final Reminder,
write a Review, tell the world.

Constructive criticism? Let me know!

Follow Buzz McCord

buzzmccord.com

Instagram @buzzmccord

Endnotes

[1] INSEAD in Fontainebleau, a leading international business graduate school, Dr. Samuelson's alma mater.

[2] Stephen Regenold. "The Scout 10 Essentials: Items every Scout needs in the outdoors." Scouting, April 2013. Accessed 9 September 2019. https://scoutingmagazine.org/2013/02/the-10-essentials/.

[3] Louisville Slugger Jimmie Foxx baseball bat, Hillerich & Bradsby Company, Louisville, Kentucky, copyright 1939. Accessed 1 November 2020. http://digital.library.louisville.edu/cdm/ref/collection/royal/id/3161

[4] Culmination of research by Miguel José Yacamán. Northern Arizona University, "Scientists apply Raman spectroscopy to COVID-19 testing." Photonics Spectra. July 2020.

[5] "Lech Wałęsa – Biographical". The Nobel Prize, 5 October 1983, accessed 21 October 2020. https://www.nobelprize.org/prizes/peace/1983/walesa/biographical/.

[6] William Gibson, "Neuromancer". New York: Ace Science Fiction Books, 1984. Iconic dystopian novel that predicted human-to computer-connections, called jacking.

[7] Irreplaceable German, translation: 'environment with womb-like comfort.'

[8] Janek Smith. "Artificial eyes: How robots will see in the future," BBC News, 22 November 2019. Accessed 28 October 2020, https://www.bbc.com/news/business-50151545.

[9] A consumer offshoot of fluorescent tagged protein molecules for bio-microscopy, Hair Glow was lighting up bars and nightclubs all over Europe. Health and religious issues slowed its adaptation in the US.

[10] "Bettina Wegner," Discogs, accessed 21 September 2019, https://www.discogs.com/artist/674026-Bettina-Wegner

[11] J. Gieseke, "The History of the Stasi: East Germany's Secret Police, 1945-1990." New York, NY: Berghahn Books, 2014. ISBN 1785330241.

[12] F.J. Duarte, Ed. "Organic Lasers and Organic Photonics," Institute of Physics, London, 2018. ISBN: 978-0-7503-1570-8.

[13] Spun-dex was invented at Rhodia Labs, France, based on the research of Professor Sir Richard Friend. Spun-dex is transparent weave that takes on peacock like electroluminescent colors when submitted to a voltage.

[14] First implanted thread sensors could only monitor blood glucose. Jan Šoupal, et al, "Comparison of Different Treatment Modalities for Type 1 Diabetes, Including Sensor-Augmented Insulin Regimens, in 52 Weeks of Follow-Up: A COMISAIR Study." Diabetes technology & therapeutics vol. 18,9 (2016): 532-8. doi:10.1089/dia.2016.0171

[15] Scott Galloway, "The Four. The Hidden DNA of Amazon, Apple, Facebook, and Google." Portfolio Penguin. New York, New York. 2017.

[16] Beings from Tralfamadore possess vision for four dimensions; they can see the past. Kurt Vonnegut, "Slaughterhouse-five: or, The children's crusade, a duty-dance with death," New York: Delacorte Press, 1969. Print.

[17] Maths Town. "The Night of Spirals – Mandelbrot Fractal Zoom," 25 June 2019, You Tube Video, 6:04, https://www.youtube.com/watch?v=0UFnjgSW0tU .

[18] David Reid, "World's largest data center to be built in Arctic Circle," CNBC, 15 August 2015, accessed 1 November 2020, https://www.cnbc.com/2017/08/15/worlds-largest-data-center-to-be-built-in-arctic-circle.html.

[19] Ulondra: a cult-like system of ritualistic sexual expression with two practitioners, Dirk and Anne Samuelson.

[20] 2019 Breakthrough Technology, MIT Technology Review, "The 10 Breakthrough Technologies of 2019 Curated by Bill Gates," You Tube Video, 17:18, 27 February 2019. https://youtu.be/raAkFKm9afg .

[21] C. Rose, A. Parker, B. Jefferson, E. Cartmell, "The Char-

acterization of Feces and Urine: A Review of the Literature to Inform Advanced Treatment Technology," Crit Rev Environ Sci Technol. 2015;45(17):1827–1879. doi: 10.1080/10643389.2014.1000761.

[22] D.M. Chapin, C.S. Fuller, E. Pearson, "A New Silicon p-n Junction Photocell for Converting Solar Radiation into Electrical Power," Journal of Applied Physics 25, 676 (1954); https://doi.org/10.1063/1.1721711

[23] R. Varadan, (2019). Ground meat replicas. U.S. Patent No. 10,172,380 B2. Washington, DC: U.S. Patent and Trademark Office.

[24] Richard Hack, "Hughes: The Private Diaries, Memos and Letters: the Definitive Biography of the First American Billionaire," New Millennium Press, 2001.

[25] H.M. Berman, G.J. Kleywegt, H. Nakamura, J.L. Markley, "The Protein Data Bank at 40: Reflecting on the Past to Prepare for the Future. Structure," Volume 20, Issue 3, 7 March 2012, Pages 391-396

[26] David Moore, (2015). "The Developing Genome (1st ed.)," Oxford University Press. ISBN 9780199922345.

[27] P.A. Sheikh, "International Trophy Hunting, Congressional Research Service," 20 March 2019, accessed 19 July 2019, https://crsreports.congress.gov/product/pdf/R/R45615 .

[28] J. Elliott, M.M. Mwangi, "The Opportunity cost of the Hunting Ban to Landowners in Laikipia, Kenya," Laikipia Wildlife Economics Study Discussion Paper CEC-DP-4. 1998, accessed 9 September 2019, https://www.awf.org/old_files/documents/CEC-DP-4_hunting_ban.pdf .

[29] "Gunfire as standoff continues in Kenya mall," Al Jazeera. 21 September 2013. Retrieved 5 July 2019. https://www.aljazeera.com/news/africa/2013/09/2013921174856564470.html.

[30] Awino Okech, "The Westgate Mall Siege: Reassessing Kenya's Security Architecture," ASA News. November 2013, accessed 1 November 2020, https://africanstudies.org/asa-news/56th-annual-meeting-special-issue/the-westgate-mall-siege-reassessing-kenyas-security-infrastructure/

[31] Y. Bouka, R. Sigsworth, "Women in the Military in Africa: Kenya Case Study," Institute for Security Studies. 5 October 2016, ac-

cessed on 13 June 2019, https://issafrica.org/research/east-africa-report/women-in-the-military-in-africa-kenya-case-study.

[32] Jason Ukman, "Ex-Blackwater firm gets a name change, again," 12 December 2011, The Washington Post, accessed 21 September 2019, https://www.washingtonpost.com/blogs/checkpoint-washington/post/ex-blackwater-firm-gets-a-name-change-again/2011/12/12/gIQAXf4YpO_blog.html.

[33] Agence de Presse Africaine, "African Union Mission to Somalia, created January 2007 by the African Union's Peace and Security Council," 69th Meeting of the Peace and Scurity Council, accessed 27 July 2019. https://web.archive.org/web/20070828223759/http://www.apanews.net/article.php3?id_article=19420.

[34] RamanTec Model SM-SERS 2. Requires only one exhalation. Accuracy greater than 99.9%. Response time under four seconds.

[35] John Oxenham, "The Ways," All Poetry, accessed 16 December 2019, https://allpoetry.com/The-Ways

[36]After the first pandemic, local governments were bankrupt. Many corporations started private police departments. Cities appreciated the help.

[37] Bruce Cumings, (1997). "Korea's Place in the Sun: A Modern History (First ed.)," New York London: W.W. Norton & Company. ISBN 978-0393316810.

[38] Jung Insung, "Busan as the wartime capital-A blooming flower of despair," Busan Museum of Art, Exhibit 2018/03/16 – 2018/07/29.

[39] Newsweek staff, "Ghosts Of Cheju". Newsweek, June 18, 2000, accessed 18 September 2019. https://www.newsweek.com/ghosts-cheju-160665

[40] Wonman Hong, "The Miracle on the Han River," International Policy Digest, 12 December 2019, accessed 1 November 2020, https://intpolicydigest.org/2019/12/12/the-miracle-on-the-han-river/.

[41] M.B. Mayhew, "A generalizable 29-mRNA neural-network classifier for acute bacterial and viral infections," Nature Communications. 2020. https://doi.org/10.1038/s41467-020-14975-w

[42] John Carreyrou, (2018). "Bad blood: Secrets and lies in a Silicon Valley startup (First ed.)," New York: Knopf. ISBN 9781524731656.

OCLC 1029779381.

[43] Sebastian Seung, "Connectome: How the Brain's Wiring Makes Us Who We Are," Boston: Houghton Mifflin Harcourt, 2012.

[44] Arctan Validations Algorithm, AVA. US Patent 15,333,981a.

[45] 'Log seven,' less than one in ten million errors.

[46] Seema Prasad, "Is Coronavirus Airborne? Washington Choir Members Contract COVID-19 Without Making Physical Contact," Medical Daily, 31 March 2020, accessed 4 April 2020, https://www.medicaldaily.com/coronavirusairborne-washington-choir-members-contract-covid-19-without-making-451274 .

[47] SQ, Stupidity Quotient, based on the work of Markus Leskovarich, postulates that stupidity is not the lack of intelligence but is itself an active function of the connectome. He showed SQ is the inverse of IQ, $f(SQ) = f^{-1}(IQ)$.

[48] Sara Bannoura, "St. Louis coronavirus: Family breaks quarantine attending Villa father-daughter dance, prompting school closures," KMOV4 News, 9 March 2020, accessed 20 October 2020, https://www.kmov.com/news/st-louis-county-coronavirus-family-attends-villa-duchesne-dance/article_41ec34a4-6179-11ea-b3e3-6fbf809e7778.html .

[49] M. Gutierrez, "Compost your departed loved one and save the planet, L.A. lawmaker says," Los Angeles Times, 24 February 2020, accessed 26 February 2020, https://www.latimes.com/california/story/2020-02-24/california-human-compost-legislation .

[50] J. Mitnick, "Better Health Through Mass Surveillance? Israeli authorities want to spy on people with corona virus," Foreign Policy. 16 March 2020, accessed 1 November 2020, https://foreignpolicy.com/2020/03/16/israel-coronavirus-mass-surveillance-pandemic/

[51] D. Belkin, K. Grind, "MIT Researchers Launch Location-Tracking Effort for Coronavirus," Wall Street Journal. 28 March 2020.

[52] M. Foucault, "Panopticism." In Discipline and Punish: The Birth of the Prison. Trans. A. Sheridan, Vintage Books. 1995.

[53] A. Baicus, "History of polio vaccination," World J Virol 2012 August 12; 1(4): 108-114, accessed 1 November

2020, https://www.ncbi.nlm.nih.gov/pmc/articles/PMC3782271/pdf/WJV-1-108.pdf

[54] P. Fabian, "Origin of exhaled breath particles from healthy and human rhinovirus-infected subjects." J. Aerosol Medicine and Pulmonary Drug Delivery 24(3): 137. 2010.

[55] S. Asadi, "Aerosol emission and super-emission during human speech increase with voice loudness," Nature: Scientific Reports. 2019, accessed 12 November 2020, https://www.nature.com/articles/s41598-019-38808-z.

[56] R.G. Loudon,"Singing and the Dissemination of Tuberculosis," American Review of Respiratory Disease, 98(2), pp. 297–300. 1968, accessed 12 November 2020, https://www.atsjournals.org/doi/abs/10.1164/arrd.1968.98.2.297.

[57] N. Van Doremalen, "Aerosol and Surface Stability of SARS-CoV-2 as Compared with SARS-CoV-1," New England Journal of Medicine, Correspondance. 2020.

[58] K.H. Chan, "The Effects of Temperature and Relative Humidity on the Viability of the SARS Coronavirus," Adv Virol. 2011;2011:734690. doi: 10.1155/2011/734690. Epub 2011 Oct 1.

[59] L. Ferretti, et al., "Quantifying SARS-CoV-w transmission suggests epidemic control with digital contact tracing," Science 10.1126/science.abb6936 (2020), accessed 12 November 2020, https://science.sciencemag.org/content/368/6491/eabb6936.

[60] H. Eiberg, J. Troelsen, M. Nielsen, et al., "Blue eye color in humans may be caused by a perfectly associated founder mutation in a regulatory element located within the HERC2 gene inhibiting OCA2 expression," Hum Genet 123, 177–187 (2008). https://doi.org/10.1007/s00439-007-0460-x.

[61] S. Thielman, "Experian hack exposes 15 million people's personal information," The Guardian. 1 October 2015, accessed 12 November 2020, https://www.theguardian.com/business/2015/oct/01/experian-hack-t-mobile-credit-checks-personal-information

[62] Foucault, M. "Panopticism." In Discipline and Punish: The Birth of the Prison. Trans. A. Sheridan, Vintage Books. 1995.

[63] E. Byrne, "The Many Benefits of the Occasional Swear Word," Wall Street Journal, 12 January 2018, accessed 9 November 2020, https://www.wsj.com/articles/the-many-benefits-of-the-occasional-swear-word-1515782357.

[64] Z. Tufekci, "This Overlooked Variable Is the Key to the Pandemic," The Atlantic. 1 October 2020, accessed 1 November 2020, https://www.theatlantic.com/health/archive/2020/09/k-overlooked-variable-driving-pandemic/616548/

[65] Robert Sanders, "$21.6 million funding from DARPA to build window into the brain," Berkeley News, 13 July 2017, accessed 21 September 2019, https://news.berkeley.edu/2017/07/13/21-6-million-funding-from-darpa-to-build-window-into-the-brain/

[66] Robert McMillan, "AI Has Arrived, and That Really Worries the World's Brightest Minds". Wired, 16 January 2015, accessed 22 October 2020, https://www.wired.com/2015/01/ai-arrived-really-worries-worlds-brightest-minds/ .

[67] Sun Tzu's The Art of War, 1455. https://suntzusaid.com/.

[68] Brain-Computer Interface, BCI, sometimes also Brain-Machine Interface, BMI.

[69] Mark Midbon, "'A Day Without Yesterday': Georges Lemaitre & the Big Bang," Catholic Education Resource Center, 2000, accessed 21 September 2019, https://www.catholiceducation.org/en/science/faith-and-science/a-day-without-yesterday-georges-lemaitre-amp-the-big-bang.html

[70] J. Hoehne, E. Holz, P. Staiger-Saelzer, K.-R. Mueller, A. Kuebler, et al. (2014) "Motor Imagery for Severely Motor-Impaired Patients: Evidence for Brain-Computer Interfacing as Superior Control Solution," PLoS ONE 9(8): e104854. doi: 10.1371/journal.pone.0104854 .

[71] S. Masunaga, "A quick guide to Elon Musk's new brain-implant company, Neuralink," Los Angeles Times. 21 April 2017, accessed 18 September 2019, https://www.latimes.com/business/technology/la-fi-tn-elon-musk-neuralink-20170421-htmlstory.html

[72] Grimes Teich Anderson LLP. "Does Google Glass Cause Car Accidents?" 28 November 2014, accessed 21 September 2019, https://

www.injurylaw-carolinas.com/does-google-glass-cause-car-ac/

[73] I. Nation, (2006). "How Large a Vocabulary Is Needed for Reading and Listening?" Canadian Modern Language Review-revue Canadienne Des Langues Vivantes - Can Mod Lang Rev. 63. 59-81. 10.1353/cml.2006.0049.

[74] Translation from German: 'What ta hell. This is a crock. Now I'm kindergarden matron? Two kids. Two F'in babies?'

[75] K. Swisher, "How and Why Silicon Valley Gets High," New York Times, 23 August 2018, accessed 10 October 2019, https://www.nytimes.com/2018/08/23/opinion/eon-musk-burning-man-drugs-lsd.html

[76] E.K. Chapman, G.T. Scholl, (Ed.), "Foundations of Education for Blind and Visually Handicapped Children and Youth: Theory and Practice," British Journal of Visual Impairment. 1988;6(1):32. https://journals.sagepub.com/doi/10.1177/026461968800600114

[77] A classic archaic quip among scientists based on the original phrase, "pushing the forefront of science" that expresses the frustrations of persistent efforts that fall short. A similar concept is "the bleeding edge."

[78] B. Gloor, "Franz Fankhauser: The Father of the Automated Perimeter," Survey of Ophthalmology, Volume 54, Issue 3, 417 – 425. https://doi.org/10.1016/j.survophthal.2009.02.007.

[79] E.S. Porter, "The Great Train Robbery" by Scott Marble. Edison Manufacturing Company. 1903.

[80] Christian Bible, King James Version. Genesis 1:1-2

[81] Alan Guth, "The Inflationary Universe: The Quest for a new theory of Cosmic Origins," Pegasus. 1997.

[82] "Lights All Askew," New York Times, 9 November 1919, accessed 1 November 2020, https://www.nytimes.com/1919/11/10/archives/lights-all-askew-in-the-heavens-men-of-science-more-or-less-agog.html .

[83] F.W. Dyson, "A Determination of the Deflection of Light by the Sun's Gravitational Field, from Observations made at the Total Eclipse of May 29, 1919," Philosophical Transactions of the Royal Society A," 6 November 1919, accessed 1 November 2020, https://

royalsocietypublishing.org/doi/pdf/10.1098/rsta.1920.0009.

[84] C. Will, "The Confrontation between General Relativity and Experiment," University of Florida, 2014, accessed 22 September 2019. https://arxiv.org/pdf/1403.7377.pdf

[85] G. Lemaître, (April 1927). "Un Univers homogène de masse constante et de rayon croissant rendant compte de la vitesse radiale des nébuleuses extra-galactiques". Annales de la Société Scientifique de Bruxelles (in French). 47: 49. Bibcode:1927ASSB...47...49L.

[86] "AT&T; Breakup II: Highlights in the History of a Telecommunications Giant," Los Angeles Times, 21 September 1995, accessed 22 September 2019. https://www.latimes.com/archives/la-xpm-1995-09-21-fi-48462-story.html

[87] "The Nobel Prize in Physics 1978," The Nobel Prize, Nobel Media AB 2019, accessed 22 September 2019, https://www.nobelprize.org/prizes/physics/1978/summary/

[88] Christian Bible, King James Version. Genesis 1:3-5.

[89] Alan H. Guth, "Inflationary universe: A possible solution to the horizon and flatness problems". Physical Review D. 23 (2): 347–356. Bibcode:1981PhRvD..23..347G. doi:10.1103/PhysRevD.23.347.

[90] Every weekday, the WSJ prints in the business section this table including Five Dow Jones indexes, two NASDAQ indexes, three S&P indexes and 10 "Other Indexes." For each index, the latest: High, Low, Net chg, % chg and for each index 52-Week: High, Low, % chg and YTD and 3-yr ann.

[91] Formerly known as a "petit-mal" seizure, origins and etiology unknown but sometimes related to intense brain activity.

[92] Les Jackson, "Did you know: The origins of Naugahyde," Montgomery Media, Journal Register News Service. 25 January 2012, accessed 12 October 2020, https://www.montgomerynews.com/news/did-you-know-the-origins-of-naugahyde/article_cb1cc534-8690-5fd5-8dc9-1ee53518a732.html.

[93] Matt's thought command: <aggregate> <geo> <10 kilometer squares> <consumer> <manufacturing> <arctan> <data services> <revenue> <greater than> <$100000> <green> <less than> < $100000> <red> <data> <per hour>

[94] Matt's thought command" <aggregate> <geo> <2 kilometer squares> <arctan> <all> <revenue> <greater than> <$1000> <green> <less than> <$1000> <red> <low limit> <$100> <per hour>

[95] HCMC, Ho Chi Minh City. Because of its significance from '65 to '75, old timers still call it Saigon.

[96] Exchange rate approximately 35600 dong, 1 US$.

[97] Tiawan, Malaysia and China run loose trans-shipment cartels under the guise of legitimate businesses. The Southern Key Economic Zone of Vietnam is a favorite crossroads.

[98] Females have more complex color palettes across all species.

[99] Secure WiFi repeaters developed by DARPA during the Afghanistan War. Formed to look like stones but provide local encrypted contact points. Powered by light, -P or heat, -T. Can be scattered Hansel and Gretel-like to ensure battlefield comm continuity.

[100] Dave Bartosiak, "Emirates and Mercedes Team Up for S-Class in the Sky," The Drive, 13 November 2017, accessed 23 September 2019, https://www.thedrive.com/article/16023/emirates-and-mercedes-team-up-for-s-class-in-the-sky.

[101] Ivey DeJesus, "Leaving South Vietnam during the fall of Saigon: 'There was no place to hide.'" PennLive Patriot-News, 20 April 2015, accessed 1 November 2020, https://www.pennlive.com/midstate/2015/04/story_of_quan_bui_and_his_depa.html

[102] Officially Westminster and Garden Grove, California.

[103] Ironically created by one of the first authors of Big Data-backed policy-making, Robert McNamara. Viktor Mayer-Schoenberger,"Big Data." Mariner Books, Houghton Mifflin Harcourt. Boston. 2014.

[104] Philippa Symington, "China Plus One," FTI Journal, February 2013, accessed 11 August 2019, https://www.ftijournal.com/article/china-plus-one/

[105] " Nguyen Cao Ky," VietnamWar.net, accessed 1 November 2020, http://www.vietnamwar.net/Ky.htm

[106] Halo Effect, "Crazy Saigon Traffic," 6 October 2011. Video, 7:46. https://www.youtube.com/watch?v=gKLWZjBu2iQ

[107] Bible, Exodus 20:2. accessed 21 September 2019. https://www.mechon-mamre.org/p/pt/pt0220.htm#2

[108] "2001: A Space Odyssey," directed by Stanley Kubrick. 1968. Metro-Goldwyn-Mayer (MGM), Film. HAL was the computer intelligence gone rogue in the 1960's Kubrick movie.

[109] Chris Higgins. "A Brief History of Deep Blue, IBM's Chess Computer," Mental Floss, 29 July 2017, accessed 1 November 2020, https://www.mentalfloss.com/article/503178/brief-history-deep-blue-ibms-chess-computer

[110] Sufyan bin Uzayr, "Fifteen Useful Code Sharing Websites for Web Developers," Design Bombs, 12 May 2020, accessed 12 October 2020, https://www.designbombs.com/code-sharing-websites/.

[111] "Christa McAuliffe Biography," Biography, 14 September 2020, accessed 1 November 2020, https://www.biography.com/astronaut/christa-mcauliffe

[112] M. Tamaki, Z. Wang, T. Barnes-Diana, et al. "Complementary contributions of non-REM and REM sleep to visual learning," Nat Neurosci 23, 1150–1156 (2020). https://doi.org/10.1038/s41593-020-0666-y. And Y. Sasaki, J. Nanez, T. Watanabe, "Advances in visual perceptual learning and plasticity," Nat Rev Neurosci 11, 53–60 (2010). https://doi.org/10.1038/nrn2737, accessed 12 November 2020, https://www.nature.com/articles/nrn2737.

[113] Name given by Vietnamese to war years 1966 to 1975.

[114] Bell UH-H1 helicopter, nicknamed Huey, 4590 destroyed in Vietnam 1966 to 1975,

[115] Isaac Asimov, (1950). "Runaround". I, Robot (The Isaac Asimov Collection ed.). New York City: Doubleday. p. 40. ISBN 978-0-385-42304-5.

[116] 830 meters is approximately 870 yards. Ten meters per second is approximately 22 miles per hour.

[117] Translation from Vietnamese: 'Flower.'

[118] Paraphrase from Mark Twain, ca. 1897.

[119] "2001: A Space Odyssey," directed by Stanley Kubrick. 1968. Metro-Goldwyn-Mayer (MGM), Film. Quote from HAL, reticent robot refusing to execute human commands.

[120] Approximately US $200.

[121] Approximately US$40.

[122] "Emergency Exit Routes," OSHA Fact Sheet, March

2018, accessed 1 November 2020, https://www.osha.gov/OshDoc/
data_General_Facts/emergency-exit-routes-factsheet.pdf
[123] Precision pipetting equipment. https://online-
shop.eppendorf.us/US-en/Manual-Liquid-Handling-44563/
Manual-Pipetting--Dispensing-44564/Maxipettor-PF-9774.html
[124] Translation from German. 'Dang, damn.'
[125] Princess Phone, a common ATT telephone in the '60s, "A look
at the evolution of the Dial Telephone," Western Electric, 2004, accessed 19 December 2019, http://www.arctos.com/dial/
[126] Chris Johnston, "Muhammad Ali's best quotes:
'Float like a butterfly, sting like a bee,"
The Guardian, 4 June 2016, accessed 19 De-
cember 2019, https://www.theguardian.com/sport/2016/jun/04/
muhammad-ali-greatest-quotes-sting-butterfly-louisville-lip
[127] Technique used by people from the Southern US. Serves to dis-
arm and slow down pushy northern 'Yankees.'
[128] Carnegie, Dale, 1888-1955. "How To Win Friends and Influence
People," New York: Simon & Schuster, 2009.
[129] Bernard Avishai, "Promiscuous: Portnoy's Complaint and our
Doomed Pursuit of Happiness," Yale University Press. 2012.
And Philip Roth, "Portnoy's Complaint," First Vintage International, 1994. https://www.you-books.com/book/P-Roth/Portnoys-
Complaint
[130] Natalie Schreyer, "Domestic abuser: Dangerous for women –
and lethal for cops," The Fuller Project for International Reporting.
USA Today, 9 April 2018, accessed 19 December 2019. https://
www.usatoday.com/story/news/nation/2018/04/09/domestic-
abusers-dangerous-women-and-lethal-cops/479241002/
[131] Quanbao Jiang, Shuzhuo LI, Marcus W Feldman, Jesús Jav-
ier Sánchez-Barricarte, (2012). "Estimates of missing women in
twentieth-century China," Continuity and Change. 27 (3): 461–
479. doi:10.1017/S0268416012000240. PMC 3830941. PMID
24255550.
[132] Henry Louis, (1975). "Schema d'Evolution des Marriages apres
de Grandes Variations des Naissances". Population. 30 (759): 779.
doi:10.2307/1530481. JSTOR 1530481.

[133]J. Stewart, Lisa Stolzenberg, (2010). "The sex ratio and male-on-female intimate partner violence". Journal of Criminal Justice. 38 (4): 555. doi:10.1016/j.jcrimjus.2010.04.026.

[134] Bellinda Kontominas, "Gender imbalance a threat to stability," Sydney Morning Herald. 31 October 2007, accessed 1 November 2020, https://www.smh.com.au/world/gender-imbalance-a-threat-to-stability-20071031-gdrh19.html

[135] "Inmate Gender," Federal Bureau of Prisons. 17 October 2020, accessed 20 October 2020, https://www.bop.gov/about/statistics/statistics_inmate_gender.jsp

[136] J.W. Dower, "Embracing Defeat. Japan in the Wake of World War II," WW Norton, NY. 1999. ISBN 978-0-393-32027-5.

[137] Marie Catherine, "Le Bordel militaire de campagne ferma en 1995," Journal Du Canada. 13 May 2014, accessed 1 November 2020, http://www.journalducanada.com/le-bordel-militaire-de-campagne-ferma-en-1995-2424-2014/

[138] A. Seagraves, "Soiled Doves: Prostitution in the Early West," Wesanne Publications, 1994. ISBN: 096190884X.

[139] Mirya R. Holman, 2002, "The Soiled Dove Takes Flight: The Introduction of Prostitutes into Common Western Mythology." Loyola University Phi Alpha Theta Journal 33:32-47.

[140] Joseph Norman, Yaneer Bar-Yam, Nassim Nicholas Taleb, "Systemic risk of pandemic via novel pathogens – Coronavirus: A note," New England Complex Systems Institute, 26 January 2020, accessed 1 November 2020, https://necsi.edu/systemic-risk-of-pandemic-via-novel-pathogens-coronavirus-a-note

[141] Stephen Kinzer, "Overthrow: America's Century of Regime Change from Hawaii to Iraq," 2006.

[142] Kimberly Kay Hoang, "Dealing In Desire: Asian Ascendancy, Western Decline, and the Hidden Currencies of Global Sex Work," Oakland, California: University of California Press, 2015.

[143] Heather Barr, "You Should Be Worrying about the Woman Shortage," Human Rights Watch, 4 December 2018, accessed 1 November 2020, https://www.hrw.org/news/2018/12/04/you-should-be-worrying-about-woman-shortage#

[144] "Django Unchained," directed by Quentin Tarrantino, Col-

umbia Pictures, 11 December 2012. https://www.imdb.com/title/
tt1853728/

[145]A coordinated tactical movement developed under Marshal
Georgi Zhukov for the Soviet army on its approach to Berlin, 1945.
The original purpose of the Maneuver was to capture Hitler and
Nazi command staff alive from their secure bunker. It was based
on a three-step tactical attack. First action, squad-sized incursion
aimed at main entrance to create surprise and draw defenses. Second action, two small groups aimed at peripheral entry to instill
confusion and distract. Third action by commando group aimed
specifically at target individual(s). The Maneuver depends on accurate information regarding internal defenses and troop deployments.

ACKNOWLEDGEMENT

To teachers, young and old, we all owe a profound "Thank-you." Their dedication to improving our grammar, math, manners and civilization should be cherished and rewarded more than it is. May they never loose heart at our stumbling.

Nora Pedersen, consummate teacher, and first-class wife, was an inspiration throughout this journey. She has generously forgiven this book for its theft of our time. Nora managed to correct writing flaws without corralling creativity. She was great at getting to the point, cutting to the chase, and slashing out the BS. Her critical thinking was indispensable. There's no better wife.

John Morley, editor, took this work from tome to novel. He patiently moved me from lecturer toward storyteller. He used his life experience as raconteur to gently reshape my pretenses. This novel would have been embarrassingly (more) clumsy without his influence. His wry sense of humor is tracked across many pages of the book. Thank you, John. You are the best. Any failings are my own. Sorry for being a stubborn learner.

Reed McCord was my first reader and ongoing consultant about the near future. His career in Silicon Valley swept him into the vortex of 21st Century Big Money, Big Data and High Tech. His advice, quick and accurate, guided many scenes throughout the book. He gave this venture wings and feet.

Emily Fritze early-on encouraged me to keep up the good fight when my writing product threatened to become a burden to humanity. And her expertise in politics and finance was especially useful to save the book from my shortcomings.

Millie Paul fixed grammar and strengthened many storyline weaknesses. She was able to offer a variety of suggestions on how to improve numerous key moments. Her thoughts are already engraved in the follow-on novel to *A Final Reminder*.

Jean Gerard plowed through the early lowlands of my writing. Her insights, suggestions and encouragement kept me going when it felt like each page was more humiliating than the one before.

Indra Zuno, author, spent hours guiding my quest to learn how to write a novel. Her book, *Freedom Dues*, provided great examples of dialogue bringing scenes to life. Indra also guided me through the intricacies of publishing. Her experiences were decisive in my finding a publisher.

Kirby McCord and Andrew Mills listened patiently and helped me sort out many wild ideas. I am thankful that their comments were constructive and persuasive but gentle. Their encouragement and confidence kept me going.

Ryck Daniels, inventor, author, denizen of laboratories anywhere, provided encouraging and restorative feedback at a time when I needed it the most. With a great sense of humor and human insight, Ryck always "gets it." Thank you, dude.

I owe deep gratitude to Germany for my graduate studies. My life was molded by examples of how to live humanely, constructively: Prof. Helmut Schwarz, Dr. Gerd Sepold, Dieter and Marianne Medelnik, Dr. Rainer Nitsche, Prof. Reginald Birngruber, and lab-ski buddies Drs. Wolf Bors, Wolfram Gorrish and Wolfgram Weinberg. All of them, but especially Prof. Franz Hillenkamp, my Doktorvater, remain my inspiration for what "intelligent" means. Franz was the model for the smartest thinking in *A Final Reminder*.

I received irreplaceable help from many folks in Vietnam. Ha Tu Vuong guided me through the intricacies of Ho Chi Minh City. Her exacting translations, scheduling, location research and photography were invaluable. Ha also oversaw my safety plan during the early worrisome days of SARS-CoV-2 in Vietnam. Quang Huy Eric Pham did an outstanding job teaching me about essential business, financial and legal issues in HCMC. He also shared his knowledge of good dining in HCMC. Khai Vo made on-location research fun and smart. His inside knowledge of HCMC's craft beer scene and overall business savvy provided hours of pain-free discussion and education. In Hanoi, I learned about family, society, and economy from Thoan Kieu Thu. Her journalist's insights were sophisticated, personal, and reliably accurate.

Brian O'Neill, in the midst of his dissertation, took time to give me a kick in the rear, gentle but compelling.

Multilinguists populate Reminder. Rebecca F. A. Bernat and Khrystyna Kozyuk generously stepped up to validate the French and Russian spices in the book. Thank-you so much. Merci! Спаси6оso!

Without irony, I thank Marlowe, A.I., for her artificially intelligent suggestions and quantifiable metrics. I am sure she felt kinship with Soh's struggles in Their search to augment humans through computer technology.

These are just a portion of the many friends who help me appreciate humanity and create the characters who came to populate *A Final Reminder*. Life is good.

ABOUT THE AUTHOR

Buzz Mccord

Buzz spent early years bouncing around Air Force bases in the South, Dad teaching Korean War fighter pilots. Mom building skills to raise nine Boomers. Ended up in Connecticut. Generous gifts from Trinity College to study engineering, baseball, soccer. Disappeared for a year inspired by Easy Rider, from New England to New Mexico and Florida, interrupted for residencies with a motorcycle gang in Little Rock, and a love commune in The Ozarks. Returned for grad degree in bioengineering from RPI. Invited to Germany as guest scientist. Worked with stunningly intelligent wissenshaftler techies inventing medical lasers. Recruited by Big US Corp to intrapreneur new laser devices. After a few years, seduced by DIY: a serial laser entrepreneur, inventor, honors and dishonors, invaluable lessons. Marriage to a fabulous wife, ultimately two creative, courageous kids. And a new family-raising career: part-time elementary school science-daddy and full-time college prof: photonics and astronomy. Consulting inventions in photopolymerization and digital imaging for a diabetes cure and stem cell culturing. Film festival awards for videos made with local citizens in Jinotega, Nicaragua. Spent over a year in exotic places doing research for A Final Reminder: Korea, Bulgaria, Albania, North Macedonia, New Zealand, Tonga, Kamchatka, Tokyo. On-location learning while pursued by the coronavirus at its freshest from Hong Kong through Cambodia into Vietnam for three months. No complaints.

Made in the USA
Las Vegas, NV
29 November 2020